Shining Blackness

THE NEPHILIM CHRONICLES

KENNETH DAVIDSON

authorHOUSE®

AuthorHouse™
1663 Liberty Drive
Bloomington, IN 47403
www.authorhouse.com
Phone: 1-800-839-8640

First published by AuthorHouse 3/28/2011

ISBN: 978-1-4567-4013-9 (sc)
ISBN: 978-1-4567-4011-5 (dj)
ISBN: 978-1-4567-4014-6 (e)

Library of Congress Control Number: 2011903042

Printed in the United States of America

Chapter I

NEBULA OF ORIGIN

I saw in the night visions, and, behold, one like the Son of man came with the clouds of heaven, and came to the Ancient of days, and they brought him near before him. And there was given him dominion, and glory, and a kingdom, that all people, nations, and languages, should serve him: his dominion is an everlasting dominion, which shall not pass away, and his kingdom that which shall not be destroyed.
DANIEL 7:13–14

Since your very beginning, we have walked among you. At times, we stood guard over your existence. Other times, we observed your self-willed destruction and chose not to interfere; after all, you did insist it was your decision, did you not? Long before your creation, we walked the confines of this planet. There were others prior to our existence, and they celebrated and welcomed us with shouts of joy when we came to be. Their greetings were as loud as thunder combined with the roar of mighty waters falling from gigantic falls. Not only was it an auditory splendor, it was a spectacular visual display witnessed by all creation, and it appeared like stars bursting forth throughout the galaxies. Yes, it was a beautiful display, manifest as bolts of lightning rushing forth from the nebula of our origin.

In return, we sang our song and lifted our voices up mightily in praise and thanksgiving to those who came after us. Your birth we witnessed. We could taste and smell the very essences of the Old One's words as he sang your song. A song that brought you forth on the day you came to be. And from the dust of the earth, you were. The Old One sang into existence each and every thing that was made, you and us alike. We have known you since you were; but you have no idea, to our advantage, we still walk among you.

Disgustingly, we have looked on, living among you and watching as you deny our existence, even when we reveal our nature to you. Fortunate for us, it has allowed our offspring to increase and strengthen to the point that now we rule your countries, cities, and some of your very souls. Our plan is to destroy all of you. Your denial is our primary means in which we will succeed. Yes, we still walk and exist among you. We live and we still are. We are … the Nephilim.

Chapter 2
IN THE BEGINNING...

Fret not thyself because of evildoers, neither be thou envious against the workers of iniquity. For they shall soon be cut down like the grass, and wither as the green herb. Trust in the Lord, and do good: so shalt thou dwell in the land, and verily thou shalt be fed. Delight thyself also in the Lord; and he shall give thee the desires of thine heart.

PSALM 37:1–4

Feverishly, I sat at my kitchen table with pen in hand. What was once a pad of writing paper now lay scattered across the linoleum floor and covered the surface of my table. As a result of my fatigue, they appeared as large snowflakes, each one displaying its own unique pattern of wrinkles. Yet, they unite collectively to remind me of my ineptness to begin the story; a story which will serve as a warning to those who read and believe. If it were a children's book I had been commissioned to write, perhaps a "Once Upon a Time" would be a perfect beginning. Maybe, I thought, it would not be so inappropriate for this writing. But the seriousness of the truth which is going to be revealed within the writing is beyond the animation of a child's story.

Sitting down at the table in the early afternoon of this bright summer day, I closed the curtains tightly to prevent the sunlight's intrusion and to hide me from the eerie darkness that lurks in the light without. Opening the curtains now, I see the darkness of night. At this very moment, its blackness harmonizes with the crumpled paper to remind me that I have

3

written nothing. My thoughts go back to composition classes in college, and I wish I had worked harder on my academic responsibilities at State Tech and less at my psycho-motor social skills at Disco Tech. My philosophy of "getting by" did accomplish an average GPA which earned me a degree in civil engineering, but now I wonder, *what are the exceptions of* i *before* e?

Perhaps the format of a book I read years ago could be beneficial. After all, it was made into a movie with a popular casting. The story was told of a man who periodically had interviews with a vampire. During the course of the interviews, the vampire related his life experiences to the writer. Yet, I cannot follow the development of that saga. For me to relate the facts given me, I must write what I was told. Over a period of only three days, a childhood friend laboriously poured the saga out to me with all its horrific details. As the hours passed by, he refused to stop, except for short periods to sip coffee or nibble at the quick meals I set before him. On he went until all the events of the story were revealed. Oh, if I had only taken a few notes! My old friend is now gone, and I know our paths will never cross again. How could they? Why he chose me to write this story is baffling to say the least. My part-time work of reporting local sporting events in our little community for a weekly paper does not qualify me for such an important task. I must not forget the reason for writing, but still I wonder why I am to reveal to the world the shocking truths of his story.

The secrets my old friend revealed to me have wrought concern deep within the core of my existence. There, deep within my soul, is a fear of the darkness that lies without … and within. A fear that reminds me I must tell his story, and in so doing, I become an informant. I must warn those concerned, and I must write!

Thoughts go back to a typing class my departed friend and I took as seniors in high school. It served as a required elective and assisted my "get by" philosophy. Yes, there was evidence emerging that my attitude was completed prior to my enrollment in college. If I had only worked harder then, perhaps I could have achieved better grades in my computer programming class in college. Writing computer programs was easy, but in the mid-seventies, it was the key punch operation that gave me fits. Today, I wonder why the inventor of the typewriter did not just place the alphabet in order across the keys instead of scattering them out all over the keyboard in what I call a hodgepodge order. It's no wonder I have such a hard time with my index fingers searching from top to bottom and left to right for the keys I need. That's the major reason my efforts have been reduced to pen and paper. I understand it would be harder to find a publisher for this story with handwritten manuscript, but publication is not my objective at this time; thus, I will not endeavor with my "hunt and peck" method of typing.

My thoughts turn to sweet little Rosie. She sat behind me in typing class, and periodically, I would slowly reach back and rub her silky, nylon stocking-clad knees. With the entire classroom of manual typewriters ringing loud in a symphony of rhythmic pecks, her scream or grasp would bring them all to a halt. My hands would be busy at my typewriter as if I had no idea what disturbed Rosie. As the school year went by, most of the class, including our teacher simply ignored her. Some seemed to expect that sudden outburst from Rosie as part of a traumatic event in her childhood.

One should never think badly of me or Rosie. We were only friends. At times we attended movies or ball games together. Nearly every Sunday afternoon you could find the two of us lounging around at my house. Other times, we just drove around the community talking. Some of our most exciting and meaningful conversations took place while we hiked the mountains and river bottoms of the Big South Fork. I remember we once kissed, upon my constant insistence and no desire of hers. It was very awkward for both of us, and we never attempted it again. We both knew it would endanger our friendship, and the kiss served as a lifelong reminder of the barrier that was impassable at that time. The rubbing of Rosie's knee was done in part for fun, and in part as a reminder that I would be there for her any time she needed me. I would not have admitted it then, but her needs went way beyond the counseling abilities of a teenage friend.

Rosie grew up in a small log cabin outside our hometown of Riley, Tennessee. Her grandparents had given the cabin to her mother when she had gotten pregnant with Rosie at the delicate age of sixteen. Her father's family had insisted on a wedding to fulfill their son's responsibility, and the two of them, with baby Rosie, had set out to make a living. Her father built a small room on the back of the cabin where he and Rosie's mother slept. Rosie and her two sisters spent the first twelve years of Rosie's life sleeping on an old sofa that transformed into a bed at night.

Within only a few years of marriage, the young couple began to experience problems. The young husband began to drink and refused to work. It was hard for Rosie's mother to leave the children with him during the day, so she left them with her mother until they were old enough to start school. It was the late fifties and early sixties, and there were no childcare facilities in the remote small-town area. The father's drinking turned to drugs, and he became insane with jealousy compounded by Rosie's mother having to work long hours at the local diner. She worked for a lot less than minimum wage and often spent sixteen to eighteen hours a day, six days a week to provide for her family. When she refused to give her husband money for alcohol and drugs, he became abusive and often beat Rosie's mother. Sometimes, if the children intervened, they also received the beatings. At those times, her mother ushered the young children into the little bedroom while she tried to manage the rage and violence that erupted in the main room of their cabin.

The environment of Rosie's home remained a secret until Rosie and I were in seventh grade. One day, Rosie did not show up for school, and I knew something was wrong. Rosie, unlike me, loved school. She rarely missed; in fact, she dreaded the dismissal of the school day. When the bell rang at 3:00 PM, we would all shout for joy. Not so for Rosie. Each day as our school bus pulled out from her stop, I watched her slowly begin the trek up the heavily wooded hollow toward the family cabin. Later, I often wished my gift of discernment had been sharper then.

To say we really did not know what happened at Rosie's that Monday morning may not be completely true. We overheard some of the whispered comments by our teachers in the cafeteria that day. It was just enough to cause me to strain my eyes, along with all the other children on the bus that afternoon as we passed the stop at Rosie's drive. That day the bus did not stop for Rosie and her sisters to exit, for none of them were riding home.

After I got off the bus at home, my mother sat me down at the kitchen table with freshly baked cookies and milk. They were chocolate chip, my favorite. As we sat, my mother looked deep into my eyes. It was a glare I never forgot. Mother had the ability to look through my eyes and into the depths of my soul. I could never lie to her. If I did, she knew immediately, because my eyes exposed me. But on that Monday afternoon, her eyes penetrated mine with comfort and love. A comfort and love I would need for the next few minutes and one that would sustain me again and again until her death from cancer.

"Did you hear what happened to Rosie's family last night?" she asked.

"I have heard some rumors, but really don't know the entire story or exactly what happened."

It seemed difficult for my mom to find the proper words to use to begin relating the details that followed. I understood the seriousness of her selections of words and knew that once she organized her thoughts, I would no longer be ignorant of what had happened to Rosie. She proceeded with the tragic events of the previous night at Rosie's cabin.

Mom took my hands in hers and said, "Listen, honey, and I will tell you all that I know at this point. I know you and Rosie are the best of friends and have been for some time. There were many things that Rosie or her sisters never told anyone. Maybe it was the wishes of her mother, or maybe it was just from fear or embarrassment, I really don't know, but Rosie's father had beaten her mother for many years. Sometimes Rosie and the other girls was also the object of his anger."

I listened intently to her voice as she began to relate the gruesome details that transpired that Sunday night. Tears streamed down her face and splattered on the cookie plate and the cookies. At that point, it mattered to neither of us, and the plate was not moved.

"Last night," she continued, "Rosie's mother and father argued and fought long after midnight. It was a vicious and very abusive, physical fight. Rosie's mother was beaten beyond recognition. The girls were also beaten and bruised for trying to intervene. In their futile and unsuccessful attempts to bring the fight to end, their mother hid them away in the tiny closet in her bedroom under a pile of blankets. The girls told the sheriff that sometime during the night they fell asleep. Whether the fight had ended or not, they did not know. But sometime early this morning, Rosie heard a loud noise. She first thought she had been awakened by thunder. After a long period of silence, she thought it would be safe to crawl out from the closet and check on her mother."

I watched as Mom took a deep breath as she paused for a second. I felt the pause was more to gain strength as she carefully found the words to continue, choking back tears as she did so.

"When Rosie went into the little room of the cabin, she saw her mother lying on the kitchen floor. When she walked over to examine her, she saw her mother lying in a pool of blood. Her mother's butcher knife was lying nearby. Rosie sank to the floor and took her mother's head into her lap and caressed her face. She explained to the police that she had tried to talk to her mother to make sure she was alright, but could only feel the coldness and stiffness of her skin."

At that point, my mother stopped for what seemed to me an eon. Her sobbing was turning into long gasps for air, and her body shook violently with grief. I squeezed her hands with mine before embracing her in my arms. After what seemed an eternity, she sank back in her chair and continued.

"When Rosie got up to fetch the other two girls to walk down to Herb's Diner, she noticed her father slumped over on the left side of their old sofa. His 38 revolver was lying on the cushion on the other side."

As she continued, Mom's eyes blinked and she raised her eyebrows as if she could not believe her own accounts of the previous night.

"Rosie covered her mother and father with blankets from the bed so her younger siblings would not see the damaged bodies. She got them up and together they walked the mile or so down to Herb's Diner to use the phone."

Herb's Diner was the name of the little café where Rosie's mother had worked for years. After a long day's work, Rosie's mother still had to make the long walk home. Once there, she often found no rest or sleep as she faced the storms that raged within the old log frame of her home.

My mother's story continued. "It was there that she called the sheriff's department and reported the tragedy. It appears that Rosie's mother was beaten and stabbed to death by her father sometime in the night. Afterwards, the evidence suggests he used his pistol to take his own life."

"Where is Rosie now, Mom?"

"She and the other girls are with their grandmother. I suppose that will be their new home. It seems they spent half their life there anyway," she replied.

I remember the exhausted look on my mother's face. Years would go by before I would understand the pain she experienced that day as she gathered information from the phone and on the radio in preparation for that conversation with me. I don't know how she managed the cookies.

I didn't question Mom's information that day, for I knew she had reliable resources. She was known throughout the neighborhood as being a truthful and honest woman. Other kids in the community often commented to me that my mom didn't participate in gossip like theirs did.

Rosie and I grew closer after that day and were practically inseparable. But we never discussed the events of that night, and Rosie never spoke of it again to anyone.

During our senior year in high school, Rosie and I slowly went our separate ways. She began to date a friend of ours, and the two of them fell madly in love. They were married after high school. I attended their wedding but had no special role in the ceremony. After I departed for college, I never heard from them. Mom would, on occasion, relate to me events of their life that had been shared with her. I remember the story of

Rosie working to put her husband through college and then later through seminary school. Another story was told of the two of them spending a couple of years in India doing missionary work; not the lifestyle I would have chosen, but nonetheless, I admired them for their commitment. Once between my junior and senior year at Tech, I remember mom telling me that Rosie and her husband had a baby. It was a boy.

Chapter 3

THE YEAR OF THE HARE

*Should a wise man utter vain knowledge, and fill his belly
with the east wind? Should he reason with unprofitable talk?
Or with speeches wherewith he can do no good?*

JOB 15:2–3

Rockets race through the dark sky and explode into fiery displays of light. The colors look like a painting on the easel of a mad abstract artist who slings buckets of paint onto his canvas. The patterns of the spectacular display are just as diverse and unpredictable as the paint being slung on the canvas. At times, one rocket explodes, sends large streams of light across the sky, and appears like an illuminated spider web. Other times, several explode simultaneously and become intertwined in a beautiful matrix that cannot be described with words. The loud booms of the explosions rush down to the crowded city streets of Beijing and are not selective in their search for bodies to rock violently with their vibrations. Some of those bodies are observed with hands over their ears; the faces of all are covered with smiles and laughter; all eyes are lifted skyward as if in desire to communicate with the thundering skies. The oohs and aahs are audible. The oil lanterns hanging along the streets reveal the colorful display of the parade taking place. Although it is past midnight of a new year, the crowd is adorned in the best of their attire. The brilliance of their clothing spills forth with burning oranges, bright yellows, neon blues, and greens all solidly dyed into the clothing of silk and satin. The parade slowly moving along the crowded street is as spectacular as the rockets bursting in the night's sky.

Smaller rockets can be seen just over the roofs of the cafés and markets along the streets; the small pops of fire crackers and cherry bombs compete with the mighty explosions lighting up the sky. The smaller display is commonly those of children. They light the fuses with candles, or smaller lanterns, carried in their hands. The children's clothing is no different than those of the adults. The celebration reflects a beautiful scene of festivity.

Down the crowded street parades a menagerie of dragons; some small, some large, some short, and some very long. The main attraction is a large paper and cloth dragon which parts the streets with necessity because of its tremendous size. Several men and women are required to carry the large dragon down the street. Hidden beneath the red and yellow dragon they march onward along the predetermined route with only their feet visible. Bamboo poles used to support the massive creature are lifted and lowered to make the dragon appear lifelike with its snakelike motion. The method of moving the poles is not random, but is one well designed and long practiced. The motion of the dragon makes it appear real, as if it is actually crawling down the street. His head turns from side to side to make eye contact with the crowd. Blazing eyes are illuminated by lanterns beneath its head sending chills down the spine of the crowd and causing many of the children to cry out in fear. Comfort offered by their excited and celebrating parents lends little relief. From side to side the dragon meanders, never straying from its course.

It is a New Year's celebration in the city. A celebration that is repeated every year and centered upon the theme of the Chinese zodiac. The only difference in this twelve-year cycle is the festivities focused upon the year it ushers in. It is 1951: the year of the hare.

The Chinese declare children born this year will be blessed with talent and inherit an ambitious personality. They will be well liked, popular with all people they encounter, regardless of social classes. Their gift of entertainment will make them the center of attention. However, those born in the year of the hare will take on characteristics of a pessimist, and they will display signs of insecurity. When it comes to change, the hare displays fear, but will rarely lose its temper since it is commonly known as being good-natured. Those who own businesses will be well advised to look for those born in the year of the hare, for they are smart. Those born this year will also make correct and prosperous decisions based primarily upon instinct rather than logic. Even though they are driven by their instinct, they do not take chances or gamble upon outcomes. The neatness of an individual with artistic talents found in all their work and possessions (especially in the structure and decorations of their homes) is often the sign that reveals the hare to those around him. The hare finds life to be happy and successful when he or she chooses a mate born in the year of the sheep, pig, or dog. Marriage to any of a different sign can result in disaster and tragedy in the future for the hare.

In the United States, similar celebrations take place on their own New Year. Large cities put on competitive displays of fireworks and children in rural areas duplicate the bottle rocket and firecracker drama. The nation enjoyed very little time recovering from World War II before it entered into the Korean War. In 1950, President Truman announced a national emergency to respond to the strain on economic and military recourses. This resulted in a powerful economic position for him. It is a year later, and there is excitement in the air. It is the year that television will showcase color, which will be more memorable than the fireworks in China or the United States. The year of the hare will see CBS introducing the first color television broadcast in five American cities. Later, CBS will extend that color broadcasting to two and half hours a day.

It is 1951, and the United States has developed the H-bomb. The H is for hydrogen, and this bomb is much more powerful than the atomic bomb. The bomb was developed, in part, as an answer to Russia's development of the atomic bomb. The concept of an H-bomb became a reality with detonation on a Pacific Island.

The same year, King Abdullah of Jordan (formerly Transjordan) was assassinated by Palestinian extremists for secretly negotiating with Israel in its early stages of development. Abdullah was praying in Jerusalem at the Al Aksa Mosque when he was killed. Emir Talal, Abdullah's son, succeeded his father to the throne only to be later declared as mentally ill. Emir Talal's son, Crown Prince Ibn Talal Hussein, took over as the king of Jordan and rules until his death in 1999.

It is the year of the hare, and it is 1951. Japan finally signed a peace treaty with the Allies of World War II. As part of the treaty, Japan was forced to give up all its overseas territory. All the Allied nations sign the treaty with Japan, with the exceptions of the USSR, Czechoslovakia, and Poland. In the year of the hare, China joined the USSR in developing a series of economic agreements as a result of the thirty-year Treaty of Friendship signed between them in 1950. It was signed by Mao Tse-tung.

Remington Rand Corporation developed the first electronic computer in 1951; a digital computer called the UNIVAC (Universal Automatic Computer). It follows the ENIAC model developed in 1945, and the company sold the first model to the Census Bureau. The economy was stimulated in production this year when the US Air Force ordered production of the B-52 bomber from Boeing. This bomber replaced the B-36. It has eight engines and is capable of carrying a bomb load of twenty-five tons. The B-52 can fly fifteen thousand miles nonstop.

The same year, New York's beloved Yankees needed only the first four games to defeat the Philadelphia Phillies in the World Series. The University of Tennessee won the NCAA Championship, and a young man named Richard Kazmaler took the Heisman Trophy. The US Open Golf Championship is played at the Merion Golf Club in Ardmore, Pennsylvania, and is won by Ben Hogan with a score of 287.

Among the top ten movies for 1951 are *David and Bathsheba, Showboat, A Streetcar Named Desire,* and *A Place in the Sun.* The Academy Awards declared *An American in Paris* as Best Picture, and the Best Director was awarded to George Stevens for his work on *A Place in the Sun.* Humphrey Bogart won the title of Best Actor for his role in *The African Queen,* and Best Actress went to Vivien Leigh for her role in *A Streetcar Named Desire.* The Emmy awards went to *Studio One* in the Dramatic Show division and the *Red Skeleton Show* in the Comedy Show Award.

It is 1951 in the United States. The nation saw two of their top chemists jointly win the Nobel Prize in chemistry for "their discoveries in the chemistry of Tran uranium elements." Some of the top ten popular books of the year include: *From Here to Eternity, The Canine Mutiny, Moses,* and *A Return to Paradise.* The top five television shows include: *Arthur Godfrey's Talent Scouts, Texaco Star Theater, I Love Lucy, The Red Skelton Show,* and *The Colgate Comedy Hour.*

Among those born that year includes Irish Prime Minister Bertie Ahern, Irish President Mary Maltese, Canadian writer Charles De Lint, business woman Esther Dyson, actor Michael Keeton, musician Phil Collins, and US minister/missionary John Calvin McGarney.

John Calvin McGarney was my best friend. He was born on February 8, 1951. He knew nothing of the Chinese Zodiac until he studied martial arts as an adult. He did, however, know that he was born under the sign of Aquarius. While in middle school, John Calvin was shortened to Calvin.

Calvin became obsessed with anything he attempted. While spending a year looking into astrology in seventh grade, Calvin went to the library every morning to get the daily newspaper. There he would look over the daily horoscope, memorize every sign, and spend the rest of the day giving us our forecast. It was the baby booming ages of the sixties and the student–teacher ratio was extremely large, but Calvin delivered his daily lessons in astronomy to all of us. We grew up in the rural Upper Cumberland Plateau of Tennessee, yet our class was a large one of nearly forty students. Nevertheless, Calvin knew all our signs and managed to cross each one of our paths during the course of the day. As a result, we tried to avoid Calvin, but he never observed our shunning and continued to fill us in with our daily astrological blessings or warnings. The entire class was elated when Calvin dropped the horoscope teachings and became interested in genealogy.

After seventh grade, Calvin and his father made a trip to Byrdstown, Tennessee, to research the McGarney family. His father, Patrick, knew his great-grandfather moved the family of four children to our hometown of Riley before World War I to work in the saw mills. Very little was known of the family prior to that move. It was told that Calvin and his father loaded up one summer day and made the trip. It appeared they had no clue as to whom, or what, they might seek to research the McGarney family. Calvin related the details of that trip to us many times in eighth grade.

He explained that after arriving, they made a stop at the Pickett County Courthouse and were directed by the clerk to try the library. At that point, Calvin felt that it was going to be an unsuccessful trip, but the librarian was fluent in genealogy. She had helped another gentleman in the community gather an extensive amount of data on the ancestors of his family along with many of the local citizens. The librarian made one phone call, and within minutes, a very gentle and polite man appeared at the library and invited them to follow him to his home.

There he wasted no time in asking Calvin and his father, "Are you prepared for anything in your family's past that might be socially or morally embarrassing?"

Patrick asked him, "What do you mean? Do we have criminals in our families?"

The old man smiled and answered, "Your family is my family. We are cousins, and it may seem we are so distant that you would not consider it, but when you begin to look at your family's past, all of our ancestors take on a perspective of family. What I mean is that a lot of people want to develop their family trees and trace their ancestry back as far as they can.

When they begin, many if not most, discover things they do not want to acknowledge and then drop the research in embarrassment and denial."

Calvin's father smiled and shared with the old man and with his son, for the first time, rumors he had heard about his great-great-great-grandmother who lived and died in Byrdstown.

"I heard from my grandmother that my grandfather's dad moved to Riley not only to find work, but because his mother had never been married. Is that true, and is that an example of what you are referencing?"

The old man's eyes locked with Patrick McGarney's, and with a stern look, he simply replied, "Yes, that's one example. Do you want to know about your relatives?"

John Calvin was quicker than his dad with the answer, but they both responded, "Yes!"

Pulling books, notepads, and various printed forms of information from several shelves and drawers, the old man began to fill Calvin and his father in on their ancestry. McGarney was the maiden name of Calvin's great-great-grandmother. She had given birth to four children. All were fathered by the same man and rumors had it that she never knew another man but the father of her children, who she loved dearly. However, the same could not be said for the father of the children. He was a married man and tales handed down over the years suggested his infidelity was not limited to Ms. McGarney. Those that knew him were quoted as saying he probably sired over seventy children throughout Pickett County during his lifetime.

Calvin purchased a book from the gentleman in Byrdstown with hundreds of pages of genealogical charts, which we all found very interesting. Many of our classmates were able to identify some of their own relatives and begin to develop their own family trees. Our history teacher that year allowed us to do reports and projects for grades on our family development. The teacher's integrated process of teaching that year we would not soon forget.

One of the historic lessons Calvin shared with the class in eighth grade involved the Scottish clan of his real great-great-grandfather. It was told that sometime in the Middle Ages, his family clan had a dispute with another one. The procedure for settling disputes was determined by the king; however, it seemed they all followed the same ritual of a battle to settle the dispute. This bout was conducted in a walled and circled pit with spectators sitting along the wall, much like the Roman gladiators in the Coliseum. Each clan provided twenty male combatants, and the fight was to the death. All twenty members of one clan had to be slain before the other could be declared victorious. Calvin's relatives were members of a small clan and had to use young boys, along with members of a related clan, in order to meet the demands set forth by the king. Needless to say, Calvin's family was defeated. As a result, his family was slow to recover from that devastating defeat; thus, they were unable to become a dominant clan throughout Scottish history.

Part of that study by Calvin aided in a nickname we bestowed upon him. It was one that he liked and one that he is still known by to this day. While listening to Calvin recount the development of his family after immigrating to the United States, it pleased him to drop a name on us that we all recognized. He told us that his family clan came to America in the mid eighteen hundreds through the immigration of four brothers from Scotland. One of the brothers had settled down in North Carolina and started manufacturing custom-made shotguns. Another had migrated into the Byrdstown area of Tennessee. A third had moved further west into Kansas, yet the fourth one had moved into the Wisconsin area. It was this brother Calvin knew more about than his own family that had moved into Byrdstown. A son of the brother in Wisconsin had partnered with another man to manufacture an American-made motorized bicycle. Most of us could relate the details of this branch of his family better than we could our own. It was Rosie that first coined the nickname. After telling us the story that day in class, Calvin strutted back to his seat with a big smirk on his face. Rosie had been really quiet and withdrawn that year, and it surprised us when she made a motion with her right hand, as if opening and closing the throttle of a motorcycle, and proclaimed with a loud voice, "Harley!" It caught on.

I think the icing was on the cake, and the name was confirmed after school one day when we were all in high school. By this time, most of us were driving to school; few students rode the buses in high school. Calvin had a love for motorcycles. He zipped around the back roads of the mountains and river gorge as if he were mounted on the wings of an eagle. Often you would see him riding his dirt bike, barefoot and mud-splattered. Again, anything in which he became interested, he pursued with every fiber of his being. It was fun to watch him pop the front wheel of his bike off the ground and ride for what seemed to be miles on the rear wheel. Although Calvin would hit the back roads and sometimes travel where no roads existed, the administration decided Calvin had to wear a helmet if he was going to ride to school and park in the student's parking lot. Calvin was given a helmet by one of the teachers that afternoon to use until he obtained one of his own. There was one problem: the helmet was too large. When Calvin strapped on the helmet and started his little Honda, we all yelled at him and gave him the right hand throttle motion.

Everyone liked Calvin and thoroughly enjoyed his riding exploits. Calvin gave all of us, including Rosie who was riding home with me that afternoon, his usual thumbs up. His big grin spread across his face as he spun the bike around in a circle three or four times and straightened it out for the wooded area through which he would travel home. After a few feet along this course to the woods, Calvin popped the bike to its rear wheel. This was the part we all enjoyed, and we encouraged him on with yells of support.

Separating the parking lot from the adjourning forest area was a drainage ditch. Calvin usually jumped the ditch on his rear wheel and only lowered the front wheel prior to entering into his rutted path through the trees. That day was not the norm. Calvin jumped the ditch on the rear wheel and landed with a thud. The bike bounced as usual, but the oversized helmet slid down Calvin's face leaving a bloody abrasion along the top of his nose and completely covering his eyes. Unable to see, his bike went into a tailspin and slipped in the dirt. Head-over-heels he rolled … with the bike. We watched as a conglomerate of human bones and flesh with cold steel finally tumbled to a stop.

The whole parking lot emptied as we gathered around Calvin to lift the bike from him and assess his condition. He sat up with blood running down his face. Although torn, his clothing probably hid more bruises and scratches than was visible. Calvin shook his head from side to side, grinned, and gave us the thumbs up signal to let us know he was okay. It was Rosie again that slowly gave the throttle sign (I noticed she did not smile and had an unusual look of concern) and said in a soft voice, "Harley, you're crazy!" We all shouted in unison, "Harley! Harley! Harley!" John Calvin was never referred to as Calvin again in high school. He would be known from that day on as Harley.

Chapter 4

THE RIVER RATS

And the streets of the city shall be full of boys and girls playing in the streets thereof.

ZECHARIAH 8:5

Riley, Tennessee, is a beautiful little town located on the Upper Cumberland Plateau in the eastern part of the state. It is located close to the Tennessee and Kentucky border about sixty miles northwest of Knoxville. Historically, it has been a growing little town of agricultural and industrial opportunities. The northern part of the town contains industrial parks, municipal buildings, metropolitan areas, shopping centers, and the majority of the residential areas. In the southern part lie fertile and beautiful farm lands; many of them are cattle farms, others produce crops of corn, soy bean, and tobacco. Separating the north part of the town from the south is the Big South Fork River which flows out of the north and turns westward through the middle of Riley. The river is formed about fifteen miles northeast of town in the rugged mountainous area where the New River and the Clear Fork River merge to form the Big South Fork. From there, the river rushes through a narrow gorge before it slows for its meandering trip through the fertile plateau land. Many of the local farmers jokingly say that it slows to observe the speed limits posted outside the city limits to avoid the "fee grabbing" sheriff's deputies.

The people of this area grew up enjoying the recreational opportunities the wild river gorge offered. Canoeing, swimming, hiking, fishing, and hunting were among some of the pleasures most indulged in. Off-road, four-wheel-drive vehicles and motorcycles were once as common in the gorge as semis were on the freeway. All of that came to an end shortly after Harley's graduation. In the late seventies and early eighties, the National Park and Recreational Department purchased the gorge and turned it into the Big South Fork National Park and Recreational Area. Afterwards, the only way to experience the magnificent scenery of the river gorge was by hiking or horseback. Many that originally objected to the purchase were later elated over the park's existence. At the time of the purchase, the area was experiencing a booming coal mine operation. Several local business men, along with outside companies, became rich overnight with investments into surface mining in the rural areas of East Tennessee. Aerial photos at the time clearly revealed that no mountain escaped the ugly scars of these entrepreneurs, except those located within the park boundaries.

As Route 3 leaves the banks of the Big South Fork, it forms a junction with the River Road. At the junction of River and State Route 3 is a very successful local restaurant called Herb's. Herb's was named after its owner and operator, Herb Walker. River Road follows the river northward for nearly ten miles where its dead end lies in a recreational area below the impassable gorge. During the early sixties, Riley annexed the entire River Road area against the wishes of the farmers living there. The children of the city's new annexation were known as the "River Rats." These children became familiar with the rough terrain of the gorge at an early age and knew it as well as the backs of their hands.

I was part of the River Rats along with our little gang of seven others who graduated together in 1969. Although all economic and social classes were represented in that rural area that spread along the east bank of the Big South Fork River, generally speaking it was a low socioeconomic area. My family was certainly far from being poor. In fact, it seemed my parents' income allowed us to often help other families when financial disaster struck.

Our home, like Harley's family's, was located along the river bottoms. Even though my family owned and operated a large farm, inherited from my mother's family, we still lived in the remodeled and modest old farm home of my grandparents.

Harley's family had recently built a home on the back of his grandparent's farm that was not visible from the road. A decorative mailbox with the "McGarney" name on it, along with several visible rutted motorcycle trails, marked the entry of their graveled driveway. Harley's grandfather, Ed McGarney, was a charter member of the church and helped with its construction in the mid-thirties. Afterwards, he became its first pastor. His tenure spanned over twenty-five years until he retired in the late fifties. His son Patrick was selected to succeed his father as the pastor and was the speaker at our baccalaureate service. Patrick was a second generation minister for the community's Pentecostal church.

It didn't surprise any of us when Harley's interest in genealogy quickly turned to religion during our freshman year in high school. As usual, he went head over heels into this new interest. It fact, it would be the last field of interest we had to endure with him. By the time he was a sophomore, Harley had already preached his first sermon and was teaching the youth class at his church. Even though he hung out occasionally with the River Rats, his devotion to Christianity often prevented him from attending events on our school calendar. He opted not to attend the junior and senior proms. I don't know if it was the wild music of the late sixties and the dancing or the known fact that the punch would get spiked with some locally produced moonshine that kept him away. Nonetheless, we rarely saw Harley outside of school. We certainly could have used him on the football and basketball teams, for he was a superb athlete; undeniably the best in the school. We all respected his devotion and no pressure was ever placed on him to join the teams. It would have been to no avail if we had.

As I reflect on it now, there always seemed to be some distance between Rosie and Harley until we were seniors. They seldom acknowledged one another when we were together. It didn't sit well with me after Christmas of our senior year, when Harley approached me one day after typing class and informed me I was not to rub Rosie's knee anymore.

"It's embarrassing for her and is not funny anymore, Hunter," he had informed me.

"She has never complained, Harley, and she understands I mean no wrong. It's just all in fun!"

"I don't care," he replied. "Don't do it again. It can cause people to think badly of her and you, too. Understand?"

"Sure, Harley, I understand. No problem at all."

It didn't surprise me that Rosie and Harley started dating shortly afterwards. In the months that followed and until graduation, we never saw one without the other. The two of them were inseparable and engaged before our graduation. Sometime at the end of the summer of 1969, they were married. The strain of their social differences probably resulted in the elopement. Rosie worked to help Harley attend Brian Bible College in

Dayton, Tennessee, where she also managed to get a degree of her own. Afterwards, Mom told me she helped him get through seminary school somewhere in Texas. The two of them spent long periods of time in several countries as missionaries. Later, they worked together to plant several churches throughout the southeastern states. I had not seen Harley since graduation until he showed up at my door a week ago. Why he chose to confide in me and ask me to write this story, I'll never know. Could it have been my predetermined destiny to remain here in Riley until his arrival?

"Why me?" I asked him.

"Because you can get 'er done!" was his reply.

That was Harley's way of communication. Not a lot of gray areas existed in his vocabulary. He just dealt with the black and white and spent little time on diplomacy. His yeas were for yeas, and his nays were for nays. In that respect, he had not changed since I left for State Tech in 1969.

I was home occasionally on weekends during my freshman year at Tech. After the first year, I found less time for visits. I was just too exhausted from my *Saturday Night Fever* exploits. After graduation in 1975, I was commissioned in the army as a second lieutenant as a result of successful completion of ROTC. Originally, I enrolled in ROTC only to escape the required PE courses, but I soon discovered that I really enjoyed it. For me, it was a challenge to overcome some difficulties that few of the other cadets faced. I managed to complete the course. No one, including my parents, thought I would ever accept a commission. Certainly, they never imagined I would spend thirty years in the service before retiring to my grandparent's home on the family farm.

My military service was rewarding and enjoyable. I was able to travel the world, although I must admit there were places I would not have chosen. My desire was to retire in twenty years, but I was determined to achieve the rank of full colonel before doing so. At the end of twenty years of the service, I was promoted to lieutenant colonel and decided I would achieve the "Full Bird" one way or another. It took six years to get those eagles pinned on my collar, but it was worth it. New ground was being plowed in the army at that time, and I was a part of it. I re-enlisted to obtain a thirty-year retirement package and then left for home. I never looked back.

I had been home less than three years when Harley came knocking on my door. It was Sunday morning and I admit my mind was not on attending church. The Sunday morning paper was scattered on my sofa displaying the brown stains that I let slip from my large cup of coffee.

After thirty years of "rise and shine," one's body became accustomed to the routine. Disco had gone out years ago, and in its place, I found comfort in a new hobby: reading. Occasionally, a good movie was entertaining and provided an opportunity to get out of the house. But it seems good movies are just hard to come by. In this day, most are science fiction, and to be honest, I just don't particularly enjoy them. Give me a saga of murder in a "who did it" or perhaps a drama with some love and romance, and I can relax with a bag of buttery popcorn and a soda and drift away from the hum-drum bore of everyday life.

Thus, needless to say, it was a surprise to hear Harley's soft tap on my back door; especially, since the only people to ever visit me were Dad and Cousin Jim, and they never came to the back door.

I knew Dad would be at Herb's that morning having his own coffee with some other men that looked to be near his age. I called that group of ancient men the "liar's club." Afterward, he would attend the morning session at church. Hardly a Saturday night went by in which he did not call me and ask me to attend church with him on Sunday morning. I believe Dad's interest in church was no deeper than mine, but for some unseen reason, he rarely missed the Sunday morning service. He seemed genuinely committed to making the church successful. My intentions were good, and I did plan to attend someday, but nearly three years had come and gone, and I had not gotten around to it. Although he could produce credentials to prove he was eighty years old, he looked much younger and was in superb physical condition. After Mom's death from cancer in 1985, he retired. He remained single, yet there seemed to be an interest in women. I felt that someday, when the time was right, he would marry again. That was his business, and he would have no complaints from me when and if he chose to remarry. He continued to work as an administrator with the sheriff's department and kept the books for a large mining company still in operation. The company's main office was located in a western state. Dad and the owner stayed in touch on a regular basis and seemed to be best of friends.

After giving up farming, he signed all the property over to me and built a new home in Riley. I was never interested in farming even though I helped him in high school and during the summer months while in college. If Dad needed me, I was there. I often took military leave during the summer months to fly home and help in the hay fields. I enjoyed driving the John Deere around the fields, and I never complained when I was asked to load the bales on his old ton truck. Particular care had to be taken when I tossed them up to the high school students that were hired to help. Underestimating my strength, I knocked a few of those kids off the truck with the heavy bales. Maybe it was for that reason that I convinced Dad to invest in the round baler. After switching over from square bales to the round ones, Dad and I worked the hay fields alone.

My cousin Jim and his family owned and operated the adjacent farm. They had leased our property in 1999. He made offers to purchase the farm on many occasions, but Dad was determined to give it to me. The offers that had been made repeatedly to my dad were now issued to me on a regular basis. Lately, Dad had expressed an interest in selling his home and moving west. He even hinted that perhaps I should sell the farm to Jim and accompany him. His employer with the mining company had offered him a position and also extended an employment opportunity to me. That job had become more interesting since I talked to Calvin.

When I opened the door and saw Harley, I was surprised, to say the least. And, to say I was startled would be an understatement. Harley stepped in quickly before I could welcome him in and closed the door behind him.

"Can we close the curtains, Hunter?" he said.

I don't know why he asked, for he was already pulling the mini blinds I'd installed over all the windows, but I answered him with, "Yeah, sure. Go ahead, Harley."

"Please call me, Calvin," was his answer. He moved quickly from the living room into the kitchen and dining room areas pulling the blinds closed.

"These too, Har—I mean, Calvin?" I questioned while following him around the rooms.

"Yeah, those too! I don't want anyone to know I'm here, Hunter. In fact I don't want anyone to know I'm even in Riley. Promise you will tell no one. You must promise!"

"Okay, Calvin." I struggled with the Calvin instead of Harley. "But tell me what's going on? What brings you here? What in the world is going on?"

"Don't worry. I'm going to tell you everything, but it will take some time and no one can know I am here."

"How did you get here, Calvin? I did not see or hear you drive up."

He let out a soft sigh and answered, "I hiked up and over the mountain cliff from the gorge. I got in Friday and set up a little camp at the head of Mossy Creek."

I knew the area he was talking about well. It was one of the roughest and least visited areas in the gorge. Negotiating that region was very treacherous. It contained large boulders and thick vegetation covered the creek bed and the surrounding area. Several cliff lines butted out over the banks of Mossy. Other smaller contributory streams dropped their water over the cliffs in times of heavy rains in small but spectacular waterfalls. Some locals referred to the area as the Falls. I knew the hike Calvin had taken. He had climbed up and through a two-hundred-foot rocky ravine to the top of the plateau on the east side of the river. From there he walked along the gorge southward. There were no trails there before the park service took it over, and there were none there now. It was a shortcut known only by the River Rats and used for their swimming and fishing escapades.

"It's been a long time since I took that hike. Has it changed much?" I asked being sincerely interested.

"Not much. The trees are much bigger than I remember, and the undergrowth is not as thick. I suppose the two go hand in hand. I think I like it better now since there are no dead tree tops scattered around all over the place from the logging and cutting of fire wood."

"Is it okay if I still call you Hunter?" he asked.

Hunter was a name he gave me when we were in eighth grade. That year we walked the gorge on Friday afternoon prior to the opening day of deer season. We stayed out of school to do so, but our parents knew what we were doing. We spent the night atop the gorge in our sleeping bags, and the next morning, in the dark, we inched down the cliff into Mossy Creek. We planned to continue the hunt along the river gorge the next day, working our way back home. With luck, our timing would bring us back home late Saturday afternoon before dark. Harley had spotted a large whitetail buck in the Mossy Creek area during the late summer months and was on a quest to harvest him. I later realized he invited me along only to help him clean and drag the buck down to the river bottoms. At the time, I was naive enough to think he desired my companionship. If successful, we would drag the buck close enough for Harley to return home and fetch a pack horse. Immediately upon descending the cliff, we split up and hunted along the thick creek bed. I was given the roughest part along the north. Here the creek had no choice but to follow the base of the shear rocky cliffs. Harley chose the south bank with its oak flats. This is where he had spotted the big buck while on a weekend fishing trip.

I was not as overly enthusiastic about hunting as Calvin was, and I must say that it did not provide me with the excitement and adrenalin rush as it did him. I just enjoyed his company; obviously in ways that were not mutually shared. I had a deer tag, and I loved the outdoors. Shortly after daybreak, I saw the legs of a deer sneaking through the thick laurel. It periodically stopped and turned in the direction of the flats where Harley was hunting. The wind was in my face, and I could literally smell the heavy odor of a rutting buck and hear the soft scuffle of his hair as he brushed against the soft green leaves of the thick mountain laurel branches. When the glistening tips of his dark rack appeared, I slowly raised my rifle and aligned the open sight to a small opening I knew he would pass through in seconds. My finger slowly squeezed the trigger as the buck stepped broad side into the clearing, and the rifle rocked hard against my shoulder. The deer dropped instantly from a well-placed, high-shoulder shot and was motionless. I yelled for Harley to come and assist me in field dressing the first, and last, whitetail I would ever harvest

I heard the grunts of Harley's disapproval long before I could see him. All his planning to harvest the big buck had now come to a rapid end as he helped me drag out some scrub I shot. His frustration succumbed to depression and aggravation, when he looked down at my deer and realized it was the one he was hunting. It was not until later in the school year that he finally forgave me. After all, it was his idea and persistence that persuaded me to accompany him on the hunt. After the apology, he started calling me Hunter, and like Harley, it stuck.

"Yes," was my reply. "You can still call me Hunter. I kind of like the name; although, I must admit, it's been a long time since anyone has called me that. What is the problem with my calling you Harley?"

He grinned and continued. "It's a long story, but I hope I'll be able to explain it all to you before I leave."

I countered with my usually complicated and well thought answer of, "Okay!"

"Now," Calvin began, "I am going to tell you my story. It's very complex, but I need someone to write it down and to get it published. I'm not looking for fame or fortune, and I don't even want my name on it. It's a true story that will scare the dickens out of you. And it's one that must be told. People need to know what I have discovered. Will you promise to write the story? I know it will be a difficult task and may take some time, but it must be written. Will you promise?"

"Calvin, I don't know what you have to tell, but if it's as important as you say, then you really need to get someone who is capable of writing to do it. I only write sporting events for the *County Herald*. My work there is more to help Carol than it is for revenue. I don't know if you heard, but her husband Steve was paralyzed in a boating accident a couple of years ago."

"Yep, I heard," he replied. "It seems he hit a log with his boat while returning from duck hunting on the river, right?"

"That's right, Calvin. She started working at the *County Herald* for her parents after college, and when they retired, she became the editor. She owns it now and has really turned it into an award-winning paper. To tell you the truth, she has my sports articles edited, and often completely rewritten, by one of the employees there. I just bring in the dates, teams, scores, and statistics that seem to be of interest and, *bang*, they make it happen. You need to talk to Carol. Besides, don't you remember how much she liked you?"

"Carol is not the person. She is too busy and will not get it done. I need you to do it. You have the time and you are dependable. If I can get you to say you will do it, you won't rest until it's finished. Am I right?"

I wanted to answer with the "yes, sir" I had been conditioned to for years, but my determination to be a bona fide civilian with no signs of retired military syndrome that many folks despise found me saying, "Yeah, I guess so."

Calvin looked at me cautiously, and I felt his eyes piercing the depths of my soul. It would be one of his few moments of silence during our three day visit.

"Hunter, do you believe in God?"

"Sure I do, Calvin. Why do you ask?"

"No, I mean do you really, really believe in God, the spiritual realm of all that scripture teaches to include demons, a devil, and hell?"

I was a little frustrated that he seemed to be questioning my answer, although I had to admit the fruit of my labors would suggest the life of an unbeliever. My destiny might not be the same as Calvin's, but nonetheless I did believe in God. Did his book of reference not clearly inform him that even demons believed and trembled? It was my turn to glare back into his eyes and reveal that I had knowledge of my eternal destiny, whether it was life or death.

"Yes, I do, Calvin. You cannot believe in one without believing in the other. Why are you asking this?"

"In time," he said.

"Do you believe that demons are still very active in possessing humans?" He continued.

"I don't know. Can one truly present evidence of such an occurrence?"

"Hunter, you don't know what you are looking for. How can they exist and be so active in the days of Christ and just disappear after His ascension?"

At that moment, I knew the conversation was moving into one of a homiletic nature in which I was certainly not theologically able or interested in indulging. It was my goal to distract him, thus, sparing me from the sermon I thought would follow. So, I lied to him in an attempt to change the subject.

"Calvin, I don't know what you are talking about, and I am not familiar enough with your … or, I mean, the Bible to understand it. So, don't preach to me this morning!"

"Hunter," he spoke softly and paused for a second before going on. "Do you believe in vampires?"

I laughed, yet never relinquished the embrace of our eyes and replied, "No, I don't, Calvin."

The change in his expression was comical, but my laughter was short-lived and silenced as his eyes remained glued to mine. He continued his story with a soft, eerie voice. "You will, Hunter. Before we are finished here, I promise. You will!"

Calvin sat down at the dining room table and sipped the hot black coffee I had poured for him. After taking a deep breath, he slowly exhaled, sighed, and began his story.

Chapter 5

HOOK, LINE, AND SINKER

Enter not into the path of the wicked, and go not in the way of evil men. Avoid it, pass not by it, turn from it, and pass away. For they sleep not, except they have done mischief; and their sleep is taken away, unless they cause some to fall.

PROVERBS 4:14–16

John Calvin McGarney began to pour out his life over hot coffee. Keeping his cup filled kept me busy those few days we spent together. I always made a fresh pot on the way back through the kitchen after relieving myself of the cups I had consumed. When he saw me entering in to the adjacent kitchen area to prepare the brew, he would resume his dialogue from the dining room table as if I had been present the whole time. I realized real soon that Calvin needed a response from me or acknowledgement to continue. Therefore, I took a few notes, scribbling more than writing, and listened as he continued hour after hour.

He began that Sunday morning by taking me back to 1969.

"You remembered Rosie and I got married shortly after graduating?"

This was my first opportunity to answer, but he was already moving on with the details, so I let him talk.

"We moved to Dayton where I received my BS in religion and secondary education in language arts. I worked part time, and Rosie worked full time at a department store. She attended college part time and was able to get her associate's degree before we moved to Fort Worth, Texas, where I attended seminary school."

He had started now and was on a roll. This was the Harley I had grown up knowing; motivate him to talk and you couldn't get him to shut up. I addressed him as Calvin while he was here, even though it was difficult; he would always be Harley to me. I could only listen.

"It was really rough on Rosie back then. I guess you knew she became pregnant after a few months of our marriage. We wanted to wait until later to have children, yet it seems we just waited two or three months before taking precautions, and the next thing we knew it was too late. Now, don't get me wrong, we never regretted the pregnancy, for he was the only child we ever had. Rosie chose the name John David McGarney. We tried for years to have another one so John would not grow up alone, but it was obviously not meant to be."

I knew all this, but I also knew I would not be permitted to interrupt.

Calvin continued. "Rosie seemed to have an administrative gift. She could set up schedules for the whole family and manage time like no one I have ever known. Although she was very busy, she never neglected me or little John. In Dallas, she worked as a secretary for the county attorney's office. Still, it took us nearly ten years to pay off our educational loans. After I received my Master of Divinity, Rosie managed to get her BA in elementary education before we left Dallas."

His dialog was punctuated with tiny sips of hot liquid. If he hesitated for any length of time, I took it as an opportunity to interject with a comment or question of my own. Sometimes I find it very difficult to pay attention during a conversation when I have conceptualized a thought or question of my own. And until I am able to share my thought, I lose my ability to concentrate and drift off into a world of my own.

Calvin continued with a question that would never be answered. "You did know that I left the Pentecostal church after I graduated from seminary school?"

He continued on. "Rosie and I joined up with the Sovereign Baptist Council (SBC) afterwards. Now, don't get me wrong, I think there are a lot of real, sincere believers out there in all denominations; but a few things I was taught while I was young were wrong. When I had a chance to study and research Scripture from a non-biased approach using the Greek language, I saw things differently."

I knew that, and I also knew his decision had caused serious problems between him and his father. Calvin and Rosie's visits to Riley became fewer and fewer over the years after his changing denominational affiliations.

When they did visit, religion was not to be discussed. I heard that when Patrick pressured Calvin on Christmas to return to the Pentecostal faith and denounce the Baptist doctrine, Calvin left early the next morning; a few days earlier than planned. Five years passed after that episode before the family saw Calvin again.

Calvin's parents sold their farm during that time and bought a home in a new residential area in Riley. Many felt it was a way of showing Calvin that he would not inherit the family farm he loved so much growing up. I knew that none of that mattered to Harley.

"Besides all that, Hunter," he said, "we were given jobs as missionaries by the SBC. Riley had nothing for us, and to serve God was all Rosie and I wanted from life."

Yep, I thought, after you got on that religion trip of yours, nothing distracted you again. I watched Harley's face and noticed a slight increase of excitement as the words continued to flow from his lips.

"Rosie and I spent nearly twenty years with the SBC as missionaries. We spent time in Southern India before we were forced to leave along with the other missionaries there. That was a story in itself. We barely got out, and for a while, we thought we would be murdered before we made final connections for our flight back to the United States. Afterward, we spent several years in the Congo in Central Africa. There were very little signs of civilization there and even less assistance from the mission board. Rosie and John both contacted malaria and nearly died before we could get medical assistance over a hundred miles away. Perhaps our most enjoyable years of ministry were on the Amazon River. That was the last two years we spent as missionaries. We worked with another family, living, traveling, and ministering from an old houseboat that had been purchased by the SBC for just that cause. We spent as much time in the jungle visiting remote villages and establishing missionaries as we did on the boat. Often, lack of funds for fuel would leave us anchored in a remote area until other missionaries could bring us supplies and funds to carry on."

At this time, I really wanted to interrupt and ask several question about these trips. I have always been intrigued with different cultures. The diversity of agriculture, industry, and the geological scenery I find profusely interesting. I made a mental note that I would ask Calvin for more details on the missionary trips, especially, the Amazon. No chance of distracting him now.

"My only regret was that John did not get to be with us in South America," he whispered.

"Is your coffee cold?" There it was; I managed to have a small part in the conversation, and I capitalized on the chance as I quickly asked another question of paramount importance. "Do you want me to warm it up in the microwave?"

Calvin took another sip as if he had to determine for himself the temperature of the liquid contained in his cup. I wondered if he even knew what he was drinking. He answered neither of my questions and continued as if he heard neither.

"John enlisted in the army when he was eighteen. That was in 1989. He just retired last week like you, Hunter, but not with the officer's pension. He served as a model soldier. His mother and I have been very proud of his achievements. He managed to get his BS in public communications during his enlistment. Did you know he made it through Green Beret training and received the highest marks and awards of his class?"

This was all new to me, but it was certainly no surprise. If John was anything like his dad, all that hard work had been nothing but pleasure for him. I looked at Calvin, nearly fifty-eight years old, and was amazed at the great shape he appeared to be in. How in the world anyone managed to keep a great physique at that age, I'll never know. I thought, Great Scott! You could finish that training yourself right now at your age without any problems!

As Calvin took another sip of coffee, I squeaked in a, "No, I didn't know any of that Har—eh, Calvin."

I needed no confirmation concerning his son's military achievements, but Calvin continued with his own explanation of confirmation when he proclaimed, "It's true!"

"After Rosie and I returned to the states from the Amazon ten years ago, we started helping the DOM (Director of Missions) in southern Georgia to plant churches in some of the rural areas down there. My job was to secure a building and plant a Baptist church in it. We would walk throughout the neighborhoods and invite people to visit. After the membership was adequate and funds sufficient to support the church, we would purchase land and began construction of our own building. Somewhere at this stage, a pastor would be brought in to take over the church. As part of his pastorate, he would continue with the building program, establish offices as necessary for a New Testament church, and put a comprehensive discipleship program into place. It usually took me and Rosie two or three years to accomplish our part, and then we would move to another area and start another church."

Calvin paused long enough to sip the cold java and let out a sigh. It was as if he was bored with this part of the saga and wished to move on to more recent activities. He picked up where he left off.

"A little over a year ago, Rosie and I decided I should take a position of pastor and stay with it until retirement. Some of us have to work much longer before retirement unlike you military folks!" Calvin laughed aloud.

Although I joined him in his laughter, he would never know the blood, sweat, and tears that went into my thirty years of military service. The tone of my laughter, as it lacked sincerity, was perceived by my old friend.

"Our DOM in south Georgia told us that Nevada was a state in need for pastors. They, perhaps, had planted churches faster than they could fill them with pastoral leaders. So after a few phone calls and email correspondence, we decided to accept the pastor's position in Copper Town, Nevada. I spent two weeks on a missionary trip with the Bushmen Tribes in South Africa before taking my new assignment. It was the first time Rosie and I had been separated. Let me tell you just a little about that trip."

Now this was exactly what I wanted to hear. I wanted more details about some of the events which Harley was skipping over like a child skipping smooth stones over the deep still waters of a river. I wanted him to just stop at times and sink into the depths of his story. Now I felt I would get my wish.

"Last spring I joined a missionary team from right here in Riley to travel to South Africa. The team was headed up by Dr. Gordon Black, who is pastor of the First Baptist Church of Riley. We flew into Cape Town and took a nine-hour road trip north through the mountainous area of the Kuru to a village of nearly two thousand. The people lived in everything from mud shacks with curtain windows to modern brick ones, all furnished by the government. The brick homes were not any bigger, but were much nicer with wooden floors and windows. Not one of them had running water. In fact, the water supply to the village was trucked in each day by the government in a large tanker and hooked up to the municipal supply center. The people carried water in large vases or jugs back to their homes. All had little outhouses located at the rear of their homes."

"The Bush tribes of this area had traditionally been sheep herders, but after the white settlers took their land in the mid eighteen hundreds to establish their own ranches, they practically became slaves. Alcohol soon replaced currency as wages. It was not the best of the wineries they became drunk with, but rather the dregs of the barrels. As time went on, many of the inhabitants became alcoholics and others became addicted to drugs. Occasionally, some of the men would get work in nearby towns. This often resulted in broken homes since the fathers were gone for weeks, or even months, from their families. Many had dreams of using their talents in carpentry, furniture making, artistry, or craftsmanship, but none had the financial ability or support to make their dreams come true. Young girls were raped by the men at an early age and AIDS was widespread throughout the village."

"When we were there, it was not uncommon to see men and women walking the streets so drunk they could barely maintain their balance. Rarely was a vehicle seen on the streets, for only a few people were fortunate enough to own a car. Most of the vehicles were owned by two or three white families living in the area. These families inherited the surrounding ranches from their parents who had taken the land from the natives. The town was composed of a small grocery store, an old motel, a building supply, a butchery, and a wine store, all of which were owned by the same white families. The wine was cheap and sold by the gallon for anything that could be bartered for in nearby towns. The gifts by missionaries of shoes, blankets, or other goods to the children were traded off by their parents for wine. The white children did not attend the black public school that ran through ninth grade. They were privately schooled in town by the wife of a white school teacher. No secondary schooling was provided. Any child wanting to attend high school had to leave the town and live in a city nearly one hundred miles away."

"Our ministry there was a great success, for there was a great need and very few evangelical teams had worked in the village. I found our departure to be a sad one. Many of the villagers came out to see us off the last morning we were there."

"While I was gone, Rosie was very busy. She had packed most of our personal household goods and clothing. She had arranged to pick up the rental truck and contacted the parish in Nevada to arrange for people to help us unload upon arrival."

I saw Calvin shifting into high gear now with his story as he brought it stateside. How my heart raced with excitement with the infomercials Calvin intertwined into his commentaries! My curiosity cried out for more, and a thousand questions raced through my mind; so many that I knew there was no need in making notes, for the memo board of my mind was already covered with too many yellow sticky sheets. I resolved to simply listen.

"We only had three days to pick up our rental truck and load it when I returned. It was near the end of April, and I was to assume the pulpit on the first Sunday of May. Rosie and I decided we would drive up I-75 to Riley. Once there, we would stop, rest, and spend a few days with my mom and dad before going west. We thought it would be a long time before we passed that way again."

"It was one of our best visits with the family since high school. I could have stayed a few more days if time had allowed, but it didn't. I think Dad finally realized that it is God who teaches us, not denominational affiliations. I feel it is so important today among the world's religions to understand that if folks are not against us, then they are for us! Yep," he surmised, "it was a good visit!"

It was mid-afternoon by this time and I prepared sandwiches for me and Harley; more out of necessity than habit, for this meal could better be called breakfast for me than lunch. Since neither of us had eaten, I rushed the preparation and practically slammed the plate down in front of Harley. He didn't notice, for the words still flowed from his lips. It was comical to watch his lips alternate continuously from the articulation of a storyteller to the gnawing of a hungry wolf. I discovered it had been days since he'd eaten.

My own thoughts had subsided, as I was content to listen to Harley. I was completely mesmerized. Was it his ability to captivate an audience with his smooth, charismatic style of rhetoric, or was it his hypnotic and motivational methodology? Or did it really matter? I knew he had taken me in—hook, line, and sinker.

Chapter 6

INTO THE CRUCIBLE

Moses fled from the face of Pharaoh, and dwelt in the land of Midian: and he sat down by a well.

EXODUS 2:15

An amber color served as a warning that the light was changing from green to red. The few seconds of indecisiveness that raced through Calvin's mind did not allow his driving skills to synchronize with the programming of the traffic light's perpetual phase. As a result, the yellow rental truck lurched to a stop with a squeal of protest issuing forth from the rubber tires. Calvin managed to stop the truck on Highway 3 where the street sagged down toward the river bridge, but the hood of the truck was resting in the middle of the intersection on the near deserted streets of downtown Riley. People strolling on the sidewalks stopped to observe the truck and its occupants and to contemplate the loud thud they heard in the back of the truck, which was harmoniously vocalized with the screaming tires.

Turning quickly in her seat to face Calvin, Rosie asked, "What was that?"

"Oh, I think it was probably the old butter churn that Mom gave me this morning. I just placed it in the back without tying it down. I thought it would ride just fine, but I guess I was wrong. Don't worry; it'll be okay!"

Rosie smiled at Calvin and suggested, "Let's pull over down here and check it out, okay?"

Calvin released the grip of his right hand from the steering wheel and reached over to take Rosie's in his. He squeezed her softly in an effort to ease her concerns and replied, "It'll be okay. Don't worry."

The red light gave way to green, inviting Calvin and Rosie into a new world of adventure. Ever so slowly, the truck inched forward as if it was less eager to move into the welcoming arms of the voyage than Calvin and Rosie. Gaining momentum from the boot of the driver, the truck moved onward, towing the little Honda Civic down the hill to the river and across the bridge. There they turned north on Highway 3 and passed the River Road Junction and Herb's Restaurant.

Calvin and Rosie commented briefly on the café. Herb was well up in his years but had recently renovated his dining facility. It would probably be the last of any renovation of its kind; nevertheless, it showed Herb Walker's ability to adapt to change and meet the needs of customers. His quaint restaurant was still a favorite on the weekends. Although he still made no reservations, the waiting lines on Friday and Saturday nights indicated they were much in need.

Eastward on Highway 3 they travelled to I-75 near Oak Ridge. There, they turned north on I-75 to Lexington, where the fuel gage indicated a need for diesel. Calvin was known to ride motorcycles like a pro; however, that skill was never transferred to automobiles, and certainly not to big yellow rental trucks. When he turned off to fuel the truck at a very busy intersection south of Lexington, Kentucky, he discovered the merchant retailed gasoline only. Since the tiny area provided no pull through, it took Calvin nearly fifteen minutes to turn the truck. It was comical to watch as Rosie and the store manager moved from front to rear and from side to side to assist him in turning the truck. The manager's assistance was given energetically because no one could enter or exit his pumps until Calvin moved the truck. After that episode, Rosie persuaded Calvin they should only stop at bigger gas stations that had pull-through gas pumps. She laughed, squeezed his hand, and promised to remind him of that resolution.

From Lexington, they turned westward on I-64 traveling though Frankfort and Louisville, Kentucky. Onward they went into Indiana and Illinois. At midafternoon, Calvin and Rosie made their third stop for fuel on the west side of Mount Vernon, Illinois. This exit was in a rural area, and after fueling, they decided to pull the truck over to a picnic table provided by the little convenient store. Here they rested for a moment and ate lunch.

Prior to resuming their trip, Calvin decided to check out the churn that fell earlier that morning. He soon discovered that any sound generated over the loud idle of a diesel engine, and from the rear of the large truck, was not caused by such a small item as an antique butter churn.

Rosie stood on the ground between the truck and their Honda while her husband unlocked the door and sent it soaring upward on its rollers. Afterward, Calvin climbed into the truck and she heard a loud moan of frustration. She knew the sound and wasted no time in climbing up to determine its cause. Lying on its side in the middle of the truck was Calvin's Harley Davidson motorcycle. He had owned Hondas and Yamahas at different times in his life, but he could never afford or justify the expense of a Harley. By the year 2004, Rosie and Calvin had achieved a lifelong goal of being debt free. Not only did they owe no one, but they had managed to place a generous amount into their savings. This account they collectively referred to as their retirement fund. It was referred to individually as emergency cash by Calvin and mad money by Rosie. With a little of Rosie's mad money and a good portion of her son's reenlistment bonus, Calvin's dream of owning a Harley became a reality on his fifty-third birthday.

It was February of 2004 when he got the gift, and it would be a few months before he could use it, but Rosie and John David would never forget the look on Calvin's face when he came home to find the bike in his living room. It was a tight fit for John David, but he finally got it through the door with a little help from his mother.

When Calvin declared he was probably too old for a Harley, John and Rosie both laughed and said, "Don't worry, if you can't ride it, one of us will. Besides, maybe we will let you ride along on back from time to time if you promise to be good!"

Now the bike was lying on the ground for the first time.

"What are we going to do?" asked Calvin as he moved to the door of the truck to look for someone he might ask to help him lift it.

"We'll have to pick it up!" was Rosie's simple and accurate evaluation of the situation.

Calvin looked back at his metallic gray FLSTF Fat Boy, and then looked down at Rosie and answered, "Rosie, this thing weighs nearly seven hundred pounds. You and I cannot lift it!"

Rosie had watched Calvin initially tie the bike down in Georgia with a thin nylon cord. She doubted then that it would hold, but she bit her tongue and didn't question the man of the house. The smooth ride up I-75 to Riley did not tax the strength of the cords; neither did it sooth her doubts. She figured it was only a matter of time and suspected it was the motorcycle and not the churn at the traffic light in Riley. She decided it was not the best time to tell him "I told you so." The abrupt downhill breaking in Riley had snapped one of the cords which allowed the others to release their laborious efforts in supporting the bike in an upright manner.

"I suppose we'll just leave it here and let it bounce all the way to Nevada!" was Calvin's solution.

Rosie quickly scanned the motorcycle and replied, "John Calvin, the bike is not damaged. The right rear turn signal has a small scratch on the bottom of it and will never be noticed. The front mirror is only loose and you can tighten it and the right rear foot peg is scuffed a little, that's all."

She continued. "Now, the leather sofa is a different matter. It is scuffed and torn in a few places, but I never really liked this furniture anyway. So don't worry. We'll use the sofa and recliner to wedge the rubber section of the front tire and tie it down to them. They have both shifted some and are wedged in tight to the other furniture in the front of the truck. Now grab hold and let's lift this thing up. We are not lifting the total weight of the bike in a dead lift; the bike itself will be a lever to offset the force needed to raise it."

Calvin never enjoyed the moments when Rosie's intuitiveness reigned supreme. He knew she was right and grunted as he moved to help her. Rosie stepped across the rear wheel of the bike and grabbed the frame. She planted her foot firmly on the rear tire to prevent it from sliding. Calvin stepped across the front of the bike and grabbed the forks with both hands.

Rosie knew it was moments like these that prevented Calvin from thinking clearly, which left him temporarily aggravated and frustrated. It would take only a few moments for her to distract him from the negative and pessimistic forces that tried to overtake him and steer him astray. In a few moments, she would have him back on track. He would take charge and provide all the answers he and she both needed.

Calvin understood the "John Calvin" title Rosie had just used. Those words also warned Calvin that it was time to settle down and grab control of the situation.

"Okay," he said. "On three!"

He did not doubt they could lift the bike. His major concern was for Rosie. Regardless of the physics involved, she should not have been lifting something so heavy. But there was no time to argue, for Rosie was already prepared for the "three."

"One, two, three," she said, and the Harley was in an upright position.

Calvin quickly straddled the bike to balance it, and his boot pushed the kickstand down on the floor of the truck.

"I packed ratchet straps in the plastic box behind the sofa," said Rosie. She opened the little box and removed four bright red ratchet straps and handed them to Calvin. She seized the moment and would not give in until she was convinced that he was free from the frustration. She knew her preacher man's needs and grinned to herself, for she also knew how to meet those needs.

"John Calvin," she said, "fasten them across the back of the couch to its backside legs. It won't hurt a thing. The sofa is heavy and wedged into the corner and won't move. The little rails on the side of the truck will not hold. We can push the rubber part of the tire deeper between the sofa and recliner and the two of them will keep it upright. We might have to stop occasionally and tighten them, but the straps will hold. We'll make it!"

Calvin surveyed the furniture and realized she was right. Clouds of confusion thawed from his cranial sphere, and he began to move quickly to secure the bike.

Afterward, the yellow truck rolled along I-64 westward to I-70 passing through the congested freeways of St. Louis. At the western side of St. Louis, near the exit of Wentzville, Calvin and Rosie stopped to spend a peaceful night in a motel. The first day had been frustrating and tiring, but it passed.

Early the next day, the two made their way along I-70 crossing the state of Missouri into Kansas City. From there they headed north on I-29 into Iowa and crossed over into Lincoln, Nebraska, on US 2. At Lincoln, they merged onto I-80 and traveled westward to North Platte, Nebraska, where they spent the night in a cozy little inn. The second day of their journey passed with no disastrous events. They both agreed it has been a good one.

Early on the third morning, Calvin and Rosie enjoyed a continental breakfast and were soon on the road again. Onward they travelled on I-80 westward to Evansville, Wyoming, where they stopped a little earlier than usual. That day they get a room with a hot tub, relaxed, watched television, and enjoyed their first full course meal since leaving Riley.

The next morning, they slept in later than usual. With a good night's sleep, they arose to complete the last day of their westward trek. Before noon, they descended from the Rocky Mountains of Wyoming and Utah and worked their way through Salt Lake City. It was the fourth day, and the rental truck moved on, chewing up the remaining leg of their journey.

In the early afternoon, they stopped at a rest area near the Bonneville Salt Flats in Utah. Calvin watched Rosie frolic in the salty plains, barefoot. She discovered the surface of the flats was much rougher than it appeared to be from the interstate. Calvin joined her and helped her dig salt and fill a plastic soda bottle to display with her other souvenirs collected throughout the years of her travels. After another one of their "ice chest" snacks of sandwiches and vegetables, they drove the remaining few miles through Utah on I-80 and entered into Nevada. They turned south on US ALT 93 at West Wendover, and within moments, they discovered there was no cell phone service. A technological instrument they frequently used was now gone. The service was not available again until they entered the city limits of Ely. In Ely, Calvin called the secretary of Copper Town Fellowship Church to let her know they would be arriving much later than originally planned. It appeared it would be near dark before they arrived at the parsonage. Rosie wanted to stop at every scenic and historic marker along the highway, and Calvin tried to oblige her curiosity. The smiles on Calvin's face captured by Rosie's digital camera would serve as evidence that he enjoyed the stops just as much as she did.

The clerk, Beth Rogers, assured Calvin that there would be no problem with their late arrival. Her husband, Philip, would be at the parsonage with keys to help them get settled in for their first night in town. She would get on the phone and reschedule the volunteers to unload their truck tomorrow at 9:00 AM. Beth laughed and told Calvin that it would give Rosie and him a chance to sleep in on the "first day on the job."

"Besides," Beth added, "most Fellowship members are retired and don't stir as early as those who work!"

With that bit of news, Calvin resolved not to worry about the time as he picked up US 50 in Ely and started the long, 150-mile stretch to Copper Town. He was warned by Beth to fuel up before starting their last leg of the journey. From the city limits of Ely to the city limits of Copper Town, one would see only miles of high desert topography and no gas stations.

Far away on the horizon, they saw the beautiful snowcapped tops of the Ruby Mountains. The road wound through canyons to reach the crest of mountain ranges, only to drop once again into the arid desert landscapes that were common to the state of Nevada.

The light faded fast as Calvin drove due west into the setting sun. He ascended a majestic mountain range and started his descent to Copper

Town. He and Rosie pulled the truck off Highway 50 to an overlook above the town and walked to a rocky rim to enjoy the spectacular scenery. The sun was sinking fast into the western horizon with colors much too vivid to be described. The shutter of Rosie's digital camera assured them the sunset will be recorded in more than the couple's memories.

Only a few miles of the lonely highway remained before it entered the little town that would become their new home. The highway as it snaked around the mountainside below them and entered the village was visible. From the overlook, Copper Town was probably only a mile away, but Calvin and Rosie had to travel nearly four miles along the mountainous roadway before reaching the city limits of their new home. Unaware to them at this point, they soon dropped from an elevation of nearly ten thousand feet to seven thousand feet, where the town was located.

Pine trees grew dense on both sides of the road and covered the mountainsides along the western slopes of the town. At the western outskirt of Copper Town, the pines released their grip on the area, surrendering it to the dry arid desert. There the trees were replaced with tumble weeds, goat heads, and cacti.

Returning to the truck, Calvin began the last miles of the drive down the winding road along the southern slope of the mountain with the headlights of his truck at full beam. The sun had disappeared and darkness emerged. As the road took its last sharp turn westward into town, Calvin glanced back in the rearview mirror at the road he had left behind. He had now reached the big canyon running parallel to the highway, before it too faded into town. Looking toward the road in front of him, he saw a homemade plywood sign erected on the side of the road. The words were haphazardly mixed with uppercase and lowercase red letters; it read as: "Speed Trap Ahead." Calvin looked at the speedometer which read forty-five and then back at the speed limit posted just beyond the sign. That read thirty miles per hour. Rosie watched Calvin as he began to place his foot on the brake to gently slow the truck to the speed limit. Her satirical grin and raised eyebrows added little to the warning of the red letters, for both were forgotten as suddenly the brakes screamed and the truck came to jarring halt. Heavy black marks were left on the cooling asphalt.

Calvin had been looking for wildlife all afternoon and had only seen one antelope to this point. When the animal darted from his left and stopped in his lane, he thought it was a mule deer. The bumper of his truck was now only feet from the startled creature. Calvin's eyes were slow to fixate on the furry creature, for he was still somewhat startled by the suddenness of its appearance. Upon closer observation, he discovered the animal was a dog. A big German shepherd stood broadside in the road just a few feet from the truck. It was a beautiful dog with a light brown coat turning to black along the top of its back. His massive front shoulders and front quarters flowed downward to his hind legs and reminded Calvin of a Corvette. He loved this breed of dog. As he looked closer, he noticed that the brown around his neck and front shoulders was streaked with a reddish brown liquid. But before Calvin could determine the source of this coloration, the big dog turned to face him. The sadness in the dog's brown eyes shocked Calvin. However, he had no time for speculation, for the dog turned and disappeared into the thick pines to Calvin's right. Turning to look at Rosie, he noticed her eyes were still fixated on the road.

Calvin started to make a comment, but he was interrupted by Rosie's scream. Her seatbelt was unsnapped with a quick movement, and she was instantly sitting beside Calvin. She wrapped her arms around his neck and squeezed him tightly. He felt the trembling of her body and turned to see what startled his wife. In the place of the German shepherd now stood a man. His face was set on the direction in which the dog disappeared. He was taller than an average man with a slim build and a slightly hunched back. His nose reminded Calvin of a hawk's beak, and his thin frame was eerie looking in the dim light. He was completely engrossed with the dog's trail, making Calvin wonder if he was going to move. With a toot of the horn by Calvin, the man snapped his head around to glare menacingly at Calvin. Unlike the shepherd, his eyes revealed no fear or sadness. Quite the contrary; his glare was one of defiance and anger with Calvin, who dared to interrupt his world with a blast from the truck's horn. A threatening look was given to the driver of the truck as a warning to be silent and not interfere with the man's pursuit. His eyes appeared like burning red ambers of coal found in the bottom of a dying campfire. They glistened with yellow red hues as they reflected the truck's lights.

With no indication of moving, he turned back to face the direction of the departed canine and appeared to ignore Calvin with his defying presence. Calvin wondered if he was going to move from the road. One thing was evident: he would not sound the horn again. With no indication of compliance or hint of ever moving, the man disappeared as suddenly as he appeared. The movement of his departure seemed to be faster than one would have expected from the old gentleman. His motion was fluid and gave the impression that his legs never moved. "He seemed to float," Rosie said in a whisper.

"Truck lights in the darkness can play tricks on your mind," Calvin responded, in an effort to comfort his wife. Nonetheless, she had voiced his own observation.

Chapter 7

COPPER TOWN, NEVADA

A city that is set on a hill cannot be hid.

MATTHEW 5:14

Slowly, Calvin drove forward, making sure the truck did not exceed the twenty-mile-per-hour speed limit. Another sign beyond the speed limit read: "Welcome to Copper Town—Population 428." He entered into the dim city lights of Copper Town, where the loneliest road in the nation merged with the small town's Main Street. Amber lights perched atop low metal posts lining the sidewalks, looking more like jack-o'-lanterns than street lights. Prior to the intersection of Main and First Street and to the north was the town's only mechanic garage. Although it was an old block-and-stone structure, it was very well maintained. A fresh layer of white paint showcased the building and reflected the night lights of the town. A single garage door faced the street from the L-shaped structure with a single door opening on the east wing. The building was lacking a southeastern corner and had a glass-front wall that cut from one wall to the other in a unique forty-five degree angle. No other windows were present, but through these Calvin and Rosie saw the office furniture. The interior decor of the garage looked more like the reception area of a doctor's office than a garage.

Directly across the street to their left was a recently constructed building with a large sign carved in thick bleached timbers that read: "Copper Town Veterinarian Center." An immaculate lawn sprawled beneath water falling from the sprinkling system. Security lights mounted on the four corners of the building caused the water droplets to shimmer in the night air. A parking lot and kennels were located to the east and rear of the building and had their own structure of bright security lights. What the street lights lacked in their ability to brighten up the town streets, the security lights made up for.

After passing these businesses, Calvin and Rosie saw First Street. To the right it was labeled N. First Street, and to the left was posted S. First Street. What the lights did not reveal to Calvin and Rosie was that most of the thin asphalt roads became gravel or sand quickly after leaving Main Street. Two blocks north, First Street became the North Loop Road. This road circled the north side of town at the foothills of the Toiyabe Mountain Range. It intersected Highway 50 again at the west side of town. The only other street running east to west on the north side of town was Pine Street, which ran only from First to Third.

A short distance along North Loop was the entry into the town's small, yet still operating, silver mine. The mine produced enough silver on an annual basis to keep more than thirty men and a woman working in Copper Town. It provided a relatively large margin of profit for its local owners.

S. First Street ran two blocks before turning into South Loop Road. On the south side of town, the road wound through a short and curvy section of the mountainous area before it, too, returned to Highway 50 on the west side of town. This road was paved. A short distance beyond the veterinarian clinic, and on the same side of the road, was a riding stable. The owner lived near the stables and employed a few of the younger folks in town through the summer months. These young folks conducted horseback rides on trails established throughout the mountains. Sage Street was a near mirror image of Pine Street to the north. The south side of town was largely a residential area.

Most of the homes were double-wide trailers which had been assembled there in recent years; however, a few single-wide units were present. Interlaced with these were old wooden frame homes, some of which were nearly a hundred years old. Ruins and remnants of structures and mine shafts could be seen on the western exit of town and the downward descent into the desert area. The city had not allowed these old structures to be demolished, as they contributed to the authenticity of the city; this aided in generating tourist revenue through the summer months.

On the mountainous peaks of the South Loop Road was an expensive and elaborate home constructed near the crest of the mountain where it overlooked the town. It was the only home constructed on the high peaks of the south side of town.

Calvin and Rosie noticed a used car lot on the right after going through the first intersection, followed by a small street cutting north to a parking lot. Beyond the parking lot, a well-lit helipad showcased a shimmering crimson helicopter. The full moon and security lights combined to produce an eerie blood red haze around the vehicle, which appeared to flow out into the area of the helipad. Beyond that small and unnamed street was a long building that ran the entire block from the corner of Second Street. The large structure contained a casino which included a bar and grill. A massive sign along the top of the building flashing and blinking with bright red, yellow, and green neon lights declared it to be such an establishment. The buildings on both sides of the street were constructed side by side, maintaining the appearance of an old Western ghost town. A ghost town it was not. Although small, it was a thriving little community. People traveled for hours to spend time at Gionni's casino building.

On the ground floor of the massive structure at the corner of Main and Second Street was a small hardware store. Above the hardware store in the Gionni complex was a small apartment rented to the Fellowship Church as a parsonage for their minister. It was on Second Street that Calvin and Rosie turned right.

To the back of the casino and hardware store was a large parking area that was accessible from Second Street. Pine Street dead-ended into the large, paved parking area of the casino. Into this parking lot, the big yellow truck turned, finally coming to rest behind the hardware store and at the foot of the long, wide metal steps leading up to the parsonage. A middle-aged man skipped out from behind an antique green '48 Ford truck, clapped his hands twice, and whistled. Two lively and bouncing Jack Russell terriers emerged from the back side of the parking lot and began to jump and dance at his feet. The man looked at Calvin and Rosie, twisted his ragged-looking straw hat sideways, and gave them a big wave of welcome; bigger still was the smile he wore on his face.

Beyond the parking area and at the intersection of Second and the North Loop Road sat the beautiful, old, stone Fellowship Church building. It was constructed in the late eighteen hundreds from rocks hauled in by horse and wagon from the foothills of the mountains. The stones had withstood the dry desert air, yet the interior had been renovated several times since its erection. Calvin's glance at the building reminded him of the historical research on Copper Town that he did on the Internet. It was a beautiful building, and although modernized, it reminded him of the Old West.

It seemed that around 1862, an old trapper was traveling from the Ruby Mountains to the southern part of the Sacramento River in California. His journey brought him down the canyon from the east as he traveled through this area of Nevada. Very close to where the casino sits today, his mule kicked up a large rock and stumbled. When the trapper walked back to check out his mule's hoof, he noticed the rock was a large chunk of gold. In less than a year after staking a claim, over ten thousand people had flocked into this area. It was originally known as Gold Mountain.

Over the course of a few years, millions of dollars of gold was dug. Unfortunately, like so many other areas in the southwest, the gold soon disappeared, along with all the people living there. In less than ten years, the population went from ten thousand to around four hundred. It never became a ghost town because a few people stayed and kept the town alive, eking out a living the best they could. Some were ranchers and found that herds of cattle and sheep could survive on the wild grasses on the desert floor and along the canyons of the mountainous regions. The town again grew to a couple of thousand in the early twenties when silver was discovered. One local family found silver in the very mine that was still in operation today. Others moving in and trying to find the ore were unsuccessful, or they found that their efforts were more costly than their earnings. Soon afterwards, the town population sagged again to four hundred.

The name changed from Golden Mountain to Copper Town in 1951, when copper was discovered to the west of town near the foothills. Again the town grew over night to several thousand as the copper ore was extracted from one of the largest pits in the western states. Over ten years of mining had produced copper ore from the area. Again, the ore disappeared along with the people. During the booming years of the copper flow, the town was incorporated under its new name of Copper Town. After the copper boom, a lonely little group of about four hundred people remained. They were the descendants of the original homesteaders who remained after the first rush of gold miners.

Calvin's thoughts were interrupted by the gentleman, with straw hat and yelping dogs, who was walking across the parking lot to greet him and Rosie. Calvin and Rosie both stretched their arms over their heads, rising on their toes. They took a few steps forward to shake hands with the man. He shifted his hat again to the other side as he grinned even bigger than earlier. He cackled a crazy "hee hee haw" and said, "You must be the pastor! I'm so glad you're here, and welcome to Copper Town!"

Calvin immediately took a liking to this guy and felt his friendliness was sincere. His silly and fun attitude, or goofiness, did not hide what Calvin discerned to be a highly intelligent person. The preacher observed that the man was also sizing him and Rosie up—under the cover of a comedian.

"Thank you!" Calvin said and introduced himself and Rosie to Philip Rogers.

Philip laughed the crazy laugh again and said, "These are our dogs! The black one is Blackjack, which we call Jack, and the spotted one is Daniels. Jack Daniels." He laughed again and said, "I guess you know where we got those names since you're from the South. And especially, since I hear you were born in Tennessee?"

"Yep!" Calvin said. "I get it. Is Beth with you?"

"Nope, she is working late tonight. She's a bookkeeper and a darn good one. She had to complete some work for the Gionni Silver Mine. She does most of her work, as do a lot of us around here, for Alexander Gionni. He's the council chairman and wants to meet with you at the casino Friday morning at nine o'clock. I told him I would give you the message and directions if you need it. And besides all that," Philip continued, "it'll give you a chance to unload tomorrow and get a few things in line on Thursday before your meeting with our council chairman. You should have plenty of time; that is, if you don't plan on starting Wednesday night church back up tomorrow night."

Calvin thought a second and looked at Rosie, who just grinned. "Well, I don't think I would have time to prepare by tomorrow night. Have you not been having midweek services on Wednesday night?"

"The last two preachers conducted only Sunday morning services and we didn't know if you would want to start them again or not," Philip answered.

"Well," Calvin responded, "I think we will wait until I get a chance to discuss all the reasons for only one service with the church council, and then perhaps start them next month. What do you think, Philip?"

The laugh Calvin would hear many times in the days to come rang out again across the parking lot; that laugh alone was enough to make the preacher and his wife feel welcomed.

"Well, preacher, I don't know. You are no longer in the Bible Belt, and things are a lot different out here. Most of our church is retired old timers like me. You won't see them much when the sun goes down. They don't like to drive at night. But Beth and I will be there, preacher, if you want to have it. Talk to the council chairman about it Friday morning."

"Would you like to open the parsonage and show us around, Philip?" Calvin asked. "Rosie and I are tired. We would like to shower and get ready for bed. It's been a long trip, and we are exhausted."

"Sure, preacher. Come on up and let me show you around."

Although Philip looked to be ten years or so older than Calvin and Rosie, he bounced up the stairs in seconds and moved like a wild goat climbing the steep slopes of a mountain to escape the danger from below. Jack and Daniel were under his feet all the way. He unlocked the door and disappeared inside. A flood of light surged from the opened door and security lights illuminated the stairs from the switches Philip flipped on from inside the entry. Calvin and Rosie entered into their new home in Copper Town.

The entry was decorated in large, white marble tiles with golden borders. The walls were white with the same gold pattern duplicated in elaborate molding. Off to the right was another double-door closet. The entry reminded Rosie of a mudroom, but she had never seen one so expensively decorated.

Moving patiently through the entry, the couple saw a large open area with golden oak hardwood flooring. To the right was the living room with large windows facing Main Street and Second Street. Several antiques were included as part of the furnishings in the room. A grandfather clock stared at them from the left of a door that opened out to the porch; the porch spanned the full length of the front of the apartment and was constructed above the sidewalk to the front of the hardware store underneath. It was covered with the same intricate wood carvings used in the interior trimming. Antique chairs, tables, and a swing were dispersed on the porch. The rails and posts were also freshly finished with a glistening coat of shellac.

Inside and to the left of the main entry was a modern kitchen with all the appliances the couple needed. In the far left-hand corner was the dining room. The furniture there took on a deep mahogany look and matched the shining cabinets in the kitchen. The kitchen counters were finished in the native Nevada marble, and the floor was covered with a beige ceramic tile that captured the lighter colors of the countertops. Along the eastern side of the kitchen and the dining room wall were large double doors that opened inward into the second floor of the casino. Calvin gave the doors a visual inspection and noticed there was no means of locking them from the apartment side of the parsonage. The fresh shellac had settled into the crack of the entry and showed no signs of usage.

Philip seemed to be reading his mind and chirped in with, "You don't need to worry about those old doors. They've not been used in years. Besides, I think the backside has shelves along that wall with a ton of junk on them. If it would make you feel better, we could put a decorative dead bolt on it for you."

Calvin did not hesitate with his answer. "It'll be okay for a while, but I would like to get a bolt on it pretty soon. I think Rosie and I would both sleep better just knowing that the doors were locked from within."

Philip, who was moving to the only door in the flat which led into a separate partitioned room answered, "Okay. Heeheehaha, your wish is my command, preacher! But remember this: you're not in Kansas, Dorothy! Out here, preacher, we have very little crime. I cannot even tell you the last time we had something stolen in town. People leave their keys in their cars; windows and doors are rarely locked. We look out for one another here, and I think, or hope, you two are really going to like it here and stay with us for a while!"

Philip opened the door; it led into the bedroom and bathroom. The bedroom was located to the right of the main entry and covered the entire half of the western side of the building. The room also had large windows along the wall. Upon entering the room, a large walk-in closet was constructed along the wall to the left. Off to the right was another set of French doors leading into the bathroom, which was complete with a hot tub. Rosie and Calvin looked at one another and smiled. That night the tub would help soothe their tired and sore muscles.

"Well, what do you think?" asked Philip. "I guess you will have to sleep on the floor tonight unless you want me to help you unload the mattress."

"No," Calvin explained to him, "we have an air mattress with an electric pump, sheets, blankets, and a couple suitcases of clean clothes in the back of the truck. I think we can get it up in two loads, and we'll turn in for the night."

"Heeheehaha!" was Philip's answer as he handed Calvin the keys. "Here you go, preacher. Come on down with me, and we'll get those bags up here. The little lady can stay right here."

Philip was already out the door beckoning Calving to follow. Amazingly, he was standing at the back of the truck with the dogs laughing when

Calvin stepped out on the back balcony landing. I wish I had half that energy, thought Calvin. How in the world does he move so fast?

Calvin and Philip unloaded the few items the couple would need and made only two trips as Philip had promised. The dogs were of little help, but made every step that Philip made. Afterward, Rosie and Calvin spent their first night in Copper Town with a much needed, deep, and restful sleep.

Chapter 8
THE COUNCIL CHAIRMAN

Ye blind guides, which strain at a gnat, and swallow a camel.

MATTHEW 23:24

The sun was beginning to peak over the Toyibee Mountains from the east. Calvin stood upon the balcony overlooking Main Street and watched as the light coming over the mountains from the east pierced the vast desert plains to the west. The blackness he saw in his early morning studies was now fading, and the town was coming to life. He commented aloud to himself how beautiful the high desert area was in the early morning hours.

Rosie was busy singing and cleaning the kitchen. She prepared breakfast for her husband and served him at the small circular table on the balcony. Breakfast was not her meal.

She looked forward to starting her afternoon runs as quickly as she could lay out a course around town. With so much to do upon their arrival, it would probably be a week or two before she could get started. She was excited the night before when she discovered the large storage area and utility room in the back of her kitchen had been stocked with weeks, or perhaps months, of supplies. The little deep freeze beside the washer and dryer was crammed with all types of frozen foods. Shelves in the pantry and kitchen had been stocked with canned foods; the refrigerator was stashed with fresh vegetables, milk, and other diary products. She dragged

Calvin from the bedroom in the midst of his inflating an air mattress to show him. He commented to her that they had never experienced a reception like this one.

The streets were now beginning to showcase a variety of activities. Delivery trucks pulled in and out from the backs of stores, while people parked along the streets. It was not overly busy, but more so than Calvin had expected. A school bus pulled out down the street from Loop Road and headed into the brightening desert. Calvin watched as it made its way down Main Street and out into the desert on Highway 50. A mile or so westward, he observed it turning north and disappearing into the northern mountain range. From the corner of his long porch, he leaned out and looked down Second Street toward the church. He could not see the church, but across the street from it, he observed an old rock building. The structure was unique in design and seemed to be vacant by the nature of its appearance, except for the black smoke that climbed upward from its chimney. Oversized proportionally to the building, the large smokestack protruded skyward from the back of the building. A pungent odor from the escaping smoke filled his nostrils. The diminishing smoke complimented the fading of darkness with a new day spreading light across the village.

Calvin watched an old man emerge from the rock building with an old coal bucket and walk to an adjacent garden. He spread dust and ashes throughout the rolls of growing vegetation and turned on a watering system. His jacket was zipped tight to his chin, and an old, worn Mexican sombrero cast shadows across his dark complexion. A jet black mustache swept down the corners of his mouth, formed small curls at the end of his chin and nearly touched the collar of his jacket.

After he dumped the ashes, he kneaded them into the soil with a hoe and returned to the building. In doing so, he saw Calvin leaning on the rails of the balcony watching him. He waved at Calvin, and the preacher felt as if the little man had been looking for him all morning. They exchanged waves and greetings were shouted from one to the other. Calvin recognized his response to be in Spanish, and he laughed and yelled back with the few Spanish words he knew, "No obalo Española!"

He felt he had pronounced it correctly, but the little man laughed, waved again, and yelled back to Calvin, "No speak English!" They both laughed and waved again as he disappeared into the building with his bucket and hoe.

Rosie joined Calvin on the balcony with fresh coffee, and they spent a couple of hours sitting together and discussing the beautiful contrast of the mountains and desert floor off to the west. At 9:00 AM, they watched as Philip's truck entered Main Street from South Third. From their perch a block away, they could hear the laughter of four teenage boys sitting on the rails in the back of the truck. As the truck turned in below the balcony, Philip looked up at them and waved; he was on time. Although it was not audible, Calvin imagined the laughter rolling from his lips and observed Jack and Daniel lying on the seat next to Philip. The young men looked up, but did not wave. As the truck turned in and disappeared behind the hardware store, Rosie and Calvin walked through the apartment and to the back door. Calvin expected to see Philip and the dogs on the backside balcony after he swung open the door; however, when he stepped outside, he saw that Philip and the boys were standing at the back of his truck, quietly discussing something. The little man walked across the street to join them. To his surprise, Jack and Daniel were still stretched out on the front seat of the truck. They sure look exhausted, he thought. They must have been up all night.

Philip finally noticed the couple on the balcony and gave his usual laugh and managed to turn his hat sideways with his left hand and wave with the right. The boys looked at him and laughed, and then turned to glare at the balcony. They did not wave at Rosie and Calvin. Rosie leaned over the railing to watch as Calvin worked his way down to join the work party that had gathered below. Philip and the boys had already come up with a plan; they would carry everything upstairs and Rosie would direct them where to place it. They declared that the pastor's wife was to lift nothing heavy, and the preacher nodded with his approval.

A brief introduction of first names was made. The Hispanic gentleman was called Antonio. Philip explained to Calvin that Antonio did not speak English. Philip communicated with him in Spanish. Although it was easily observed that Philip's Spanish was not the greatest, he was successful in getting his thoughts across.

The first task at hand was to unhook the family car and move the towing trailer to the back side of the parking lot. Calvin drove the car into the storage garage near the rear of the building, which Philip had told him was furnished by the church. Next, they needed to unload the Harley, which would allow them access to the furniture and large boxes stacked in the front of the truck. Within moments, Calvin had the homemade ramps in place, and with the help of the young men supporting it on both sides, the motorcycle rolled gently to the pavement. Once there, Calvin started it.

If the sound of Philip's laughter echoing down the street failed to awaken those who chose to sleep late, the thunder of the Harley did not.

Calvin rode the soft tail into the metal garage and parked it beside their car. He wished he could spend the day riding rather than working, but he knew there would be time for that in the near future.

Philip and Antonio climbed up into the truck and began to move furniture and boxes to the rear. The two men had no problem moving the boxes around and to the back of the truck for Calvin and the four young men to carry up the stairs. It seemed to Calvin that Philip was not as energetic and enthusiastic as last night, but he managed to keep everyone busy unloading the truck. At times, Philip and Antonio would drop from the back of the truck and help tote furniture into the flat. This provided them with more space in the back of the truck to slide more boxes and furniture to the rear. The process allowed no rest breaks, and the truck was rapidly vacated.

Rosie watched from the top of the stairs and gave directions to where the men would place each load they carried. Her shouts of "to the bedroom," "to the kitchen," and "to the living room" could be heard before the men reached the top of the steps. She was eager to get settled in, and if there was a pause in the assembly line, she opened a box and began putting things away. She managed to completely arrange the kitchen during the two hours it took the men to unload. When Calvin pulled out his wallet to pay the crew for their assistance, the four young men drew near. Philip quickly moved forward and closed Calvin's hand around his wallet and looked at his four assistants.

"This has already been taken care of by the council," he said, as if to remind the boys.

The young men dropped their heads and turned, climbing back into the rear of the truck. When Calvin looked for Antonio, he noticed the little man was already moving across the street toward the rock building, from where the early morning smoke had completely dissipated. He turned back to Philip who laughed and also turned to leave.

"What is the old rock building across the street?" Calvin asked.

"Oh, that?" laughed Philip. "That's the old crematory, spooky looking, eh?"

"Well, I wouldn't say that. It appears to be very well built and still structurally sound." Calvin searched for the words to keep the conversation simple, yet he yearned to gain the information that would abate his curiosity. "You say it's the old one? Where's the new one?" he finally blurted out.

"There is no new one here. In fact, there is no mortuary in Copper Town. You have to go all the way to Round Mountain for embalming or cremation. You won't be doing a lot of funerals here, preacher, but when you do; chances are you'll be driving up there. Some will have the bodies of their family members cremated up there and ask you to do rites after they pick up the ashes. If they want to bury them, it's pretty expensive to bring the bodies back down, but some do. There is a cemetery on the old Foothill Road just off the north Loop, but not a lot of bodies are buried there. Are you making plans for a funeral, preacher?" Philip's laugh was louder and a degree of sarcasm was detected by Calvin.

"No," he answered. "I hope the funerals are few and far between, but I did see smoke coming out of the chimney this morning. Why?"

"Oh, that?" giggled Philip as he continued. "The state closed the old one down a few years ago because it did not meet the new specifications mandated by legislature. It seems the law was sponsored by a state senator who owned a chain of funeral homes and crematories. One might think it was a conflict of interest, but nonetheless, the law was passed. The law does not prevent us from disposing of animals as long as they are not diseased. So we get rid of road kills and other small animals that are found along the road. The state department of transportation even brings dead animals in from as far as sixty or seventy miles away."

Calvin noticed Philip was finished with the line of questioning and was moving toward his truck to leave, but he continued talking. "As for the smoke this morning, we have an old geezer here named Slim who breeds and raises German Shepherds. One of his dogs got loose last night and roamed up the mountain on Highway 50. Someone hit the dog. They never stopped or reported it, but that's where Slim found it this morning. Antonio took care of it. I hope the smoke didn't bother you or the missus this morning."

Philip completed the sentence and the conversation while opening the door of his truck. He was through talking, and Calvin wondered if he had offended him. Before he could dwell much upon the thought, Philip pulled out, circled the parking lot, and drove back near where Calvin was standing. He smiled at the preacher and grinned while twisting his hat sideways. Calvin heard the loud giggle erupting through the open window and noticed the young boys on the back of the truck did not laugh with Philip, nor did they return the preacher's farewell wave. Perhaps it was in protest of the wages they had just lost.

"See you later, preacher," Philip shouted as he waved good-bye through the open window.

Leaning over the rails of the balcony, Rosie cupped her hands to her mouth like a megaphone and yelled, "John Calvin!" When her husband turned to look, she waved, blew her husband a kiss, and motioned him to come up.

"It's time for lunch, and I've made your favorite," she said.

Wow, thought Calvin, with all the work she's been doing, I don't know how she found time to make homemade tuna salad sandwiches with chips and cola. Wow! He skipped a step and jogged to the bottom of the staircase. From there, he quickly covered the distance to the top level, taking two steps at a time. Upon landing with both feet together with a thud, he snapped to attention and teasingly saluted his beautiful little wife. The salute was followed by a tender kiss on the lips of Rosie.

After eating lunch on the front balcony, Calvin and Rosie spent the afternoon emptying boxes and putting the contents away. Calvin carried the boxes to the rear balcony, broke them down with his knife, and dropped them to the parking lot below. He decided this would be the fastest way to get them down. Later, he vowed, he would stack the boxes and ask Philip what he should do with them. By late afternoon, he had nearly emptied them all. The pile on the ground had grown in height and circumference.

From the living room, he smelled smoke; he walked to the front porch and peered over the balcony where he saw white smoke rolling from the chimney of the rock building. He decided he would call the building "the Rock." He wondered what was burning there now.

"Last boxes, Calvin!" Rosie said and dropped them at the door leading out to the front porch. She disappeared back into the flat and Calvin followed her. He broke down the boxes in the living room. Carrying them through the main entry, he dropped them to the ground. As they floated downward in a spiraling motion, laughter rose up to him from the boxes below. He looked down to see Antonio scurry into the parking lot to avoid the new supply of boxes. The little man had gathered a collection under both arms and yelled something at Calvin, which he did not understood.

Perhaps, he mused, I don't want to know what he just said; after all, I nearly hit him with those last two boxes!

Antonio continued to laugh as he made his way across the street and into the old crematory. He emerged only seconds after he entered and started back to the pile of boxes. The smoke became heavier from the fresh supply of boxes that was fueling it. Calvin moved back inside to the living room and wiped the sweat from his forehead with his arm; he sighed with contentment. He realized he would not have to ask Philip what to do with the boxes; he was elated that another animal was not fueling the burners of the Rock.

Calvin and Rosie continued to work laboriously until the early evening. Exhausted, they sat down on the second floor porch to watch their first sunset over the high Sierra Desert. They finished the last of their tuna salad sandwiches, washing them down with bottled water. The humidity was low, and a white salty grit covered their skin in place of the damp sweat of the humid southeast to which they were accustomed. They welcomed the break and continued to gulp down bottled water as they had all day.

Calvin was the first to see the old green truck pull out from the west side of town and make its way up Main Street toward them. The turn signal revealed the driver's plans to stop at the McGarneys. As it turned down Second Street below them, they saw the big smile and wave of Philip. A lady sitting at the passenger window waved up to them with a grin nearly as big as the driver's. Jack and Daniel bounced back and forth from Philip's right arm to the lap of the lady. It seemed as if the cooling air of nightfall had brought the two little dogs back from the land of the dead.

The antique truck was in great shape. Calvin would later be told by Philip that the little '48 Ford had been in his family since it was newly bought.

"Looks like we are going to have visitors," Rosie commented.

"The back parking lot has been filling up for the last hour or so," Calvin replied. "I think most of them are going into the back of the restaurant or walking around front to the casino. Philip told me the casino owned it, so that's where their customers park."

A loud laugh roared down the hall from the back entry followed by a, "Hey! Anybody home?" It was clear now that Rosie's analysis was the correct one. The couple was about to host their first visit from a church member.

"Yeah, Philip. Come on in." Calvin replied as he moved to the back of the apartment to greet the two visitors.

As they entered, Philip made the introductions. "This is my better half, Beth," he said. "Beth, this is our new pastor, Calvin, and his wife, Rosie."

As the group made small talk, Calvin observed the woman he and Rosie had communicated with via telephone and email over the last few months. She looked to be near the age of her husband. She was an attractive lady, very short, and petite. Calvin noticed the distinct difference in their attire; Philip wore casual, but neat, clothing, and Beth was dressed in the attire of a business lady. She smiled and laughed at all of Philip's jokes but had a more serious nature. One thing that was obvious to the preacher is the love they displayed for each other.

"Would you like to join us at Gionni's Restaurant for dinner?" Beth interjected over the constant barrage of jokes from her husband.

It was Rosie who answered. "No, thank you. We are really appreciative of the invitation, however, we just finished off a stack of sandwiches I made for lunch today. Besides that, we have a lot of work to finish tonight before we call it a day. Perhaps a rain check?"

"Yes, that would be wonderful," said Beth. "Is there anything we can do to help you?"

"No, this is the slow part; just picking through the smaller items and deciding where we will put them," Rosie answered.

"We want to get up early tomorrow morning and travel to Carson City to return the rental truck. That's the closest place, and I think it's nearly one hundred and fifty miles one way. And while we are there, Rosie and I want to do a little shopping, so that will take up most of the day tomorrow," said Calvin.

Philip answered Calvin by telling him that in Nevada people referred to travel more in terms of time, specifically hours, than miles. He reaffirmed this lesson by stating, "It'll take you two and a half hours to drive over to the capitol city. A lot of speed traps along the route near Fallon, Silver Springs, and Carson City. So watch your speed."

Calvin wondered if Philip knew he was sometimes guilty of driving just beyond the speed limit. How could he know that? he thought and dismissed the idea. A few more pleasantries were exchanged, in which Philip reminded Calvin of his meeting at the casino with the council chairman on Friday morning and explained he should not be late. Beth told Rosie of the barbeque the fellowship was having on Friday evening at six-thirty in their honor.

"It's going to be at Luther Gionni's ranch at the head of Golden Canyon," she said. "Just head east on Main Street, and when the road curves left to wind up the mountain, you will see a little gravel road straight ahead. You can't miss it; it's the only road that runs up the canyon. The Gionni family owns the whole canyon and the alpine meadows on both sides. Their son took the ranch over a few years ago and raises a variety of livestock: cattle, sheep, horses, and dogs. He also owns two veterinarian clinics, the little one here in Copper Town and a very large one up in Round Mountain."

Rosie listened to Beth's details of the Gionni family as Philip and Calvin chatted to the side.

Beth continued. "You will really like Luther and his wife Sharon. They are young and energetic and have really done a lot for Copper Town and the Fellowship Church. Besides, this barbeque is just for the two of you, sort of a 'Welcome to Copper Town' gathering."

Rosie promised she and Calvin would be there. The conversation faded as Calvin and Rosie escorted Philip and Beth to the rear of the parsonage where they exchange good nights. The preacher and his wife worked until midnight storing their household goods.

Early the next morning, Calvin began his last drive with the big yellow truck. Rosie followed him to Carson City in the little Honda where they returned the truck to a dealer. The couple spent the rest of the day shopping and sightseeing. They stopped in Fallon for Chinese; one of Rosie's favorite foods, but not one that Calvin overly enjoyed. Darkness had swallowed Copper Town by the time they returned to the parsonage. After getting back to their new home, they retired with a cup of tea to the front balcony. The scenery of the night's desert was illuminated from the full moon. It was calming and subdued the lights of the town.

Early the next morning, Calvin finished the preparation for his first sermon to be delivered on Sunday morning while eating breakfast on the balcony with Rosie. Afterward, they took a short walk through the parking lot, past the helipad, down the North Loop Road to Second Street, and back to the apartment, passing the church and the Rock. Calvin promised Rosie that the next day they would lay out a three-mile course around town for her to begin running next Monday. Rosie loved to jog and kissed Calvin on the cheek after his promise. Back at the parsonage, he prepared for his nine o'clock meeting at the casino, which he and Rosie had passed earlier on their stroll. Calvin would need less than five minutes to walk up the street to the casino.

After taking a few notes on his writing pad and tucking it into his shirt pocket, the preacher picked up his Bible and prepared to leave for his first meeting with the council chairman. His wife's kiss on the cheek was well received, and Calvin thought how nice it would be to just spend the morning with her. When she turned to continue her work in the living room, it reminded him of his pressing schedule, yet he could not help but linger a few moments to watch her. She looked objectively at each piece of furniture from different angles to determine where they would finally come to rest. This methodology of observation, combined with the trial-and-error method of constant moving, was Rosie's way of arranging furniture. At times, in the middle of watching TV, talking, or reading, Rosie would jump up and move the couch or drag the recliner to a different section of the living room. Although he repeatedly told her she was driving him nuts, she never ceased.

The walk to the casino was quick, and Calvin found himself looking through a set of double doors which were swung wide open at the entry of the casino. After entering, he noticed another set of double doors opened near the back of the casino lobby. He paused in the entryway for a second to view the interior. His presence drew attention from the people who had already claimed seats at some of the many slot machines positioned down the floor of the entry and along the walls. Once they checked out the new preacher, they wasted little time in returning their attention to their entertainment.

The building looked somewhat like a larger version of a saloon one would see in a top budget Western movie. Expensive and eloquent wood paneling decorated the entry of the casino and continued throughout the large bar and grill area to the right of the entry. Although it was called a bar and grille, this section was labeled a restaurant by the locals. Drinks could be purchased at the bar, and most of the patrons did enjoy a drink, with or without their food. A small glass of wine as a night cap, or an occasional shot of vodka and tonic, was not considered by them as a sin or a vice. Nor did they choose to discuss the morality of drinking in moderation.

The front of the casino was darkened by heavily tinted windows framed by gold and silver trim. The walls between them were painted in blues and reds, which reflected some Egyptian architectural influence from the decorator. From the outside, Calvin could not see through the mirrored glass, but from the inside, he could see the activity on Main Street. The dark tinted windows served a dual purpose; they did not allow the bright sunlight of day to pierce the darkness of the casino. Unknown to Calvin, it was the rule of the trade. Casinos keep the lighting the same twenty-four hours a day so the gamblers never know what time it is. Once the customers become hypnotized by the gambling devices, or games before them, they often stay until their pockets are empty. Rooms and meals were usually less expensive there, which also aided in keeping them within the walls until they were separated from their cash.

Calvin looked through the second set of opened doors and observed a large conference room. It was arranged so that it might easily serve as both a banquet room and/or a conference room. He could see a third set of double doors behind a bar in the back of the room. They matched the main entry doors and the doors leading into the conference room. Calvin was somewhat amazed when he realized the doors in the parsonage with no bolt were identical to them. The doors behind the bar were bolted with a massive brass bolt that reminded the preacher of a bazooka. Unknown to him at that time, the doors leading into the conference room had the same bazooka bolting system on the interior, allowing them to be locked from the inside.

The bar located in the rear of this private section was colossal in size and length. It ran about thirty feet along the rear of the room and was divided into noticeable thirds. The center portion was raised a foot higher than the outer sections and ran the span of the two doors located directly behind it. On each side of the doors and behind the outer thirds of the bar were two massive bookshelves. Both spanned from floor to ceiling and from the doors to the corners of the rear wall. The ceiling in this room was high, yet Calvin estimated each shelf to be perhaps fourteen to sixteen feet tall. There were no ladders to either shelf, and the preacher wondered how the items on the upper shelves could be obtained. The shelves to his right contained impressive collections of various types of bottled liquor. Some were large, some small, some old, and some new. All types of shapes were represented, and each bottle was clean, displaying a small luster of light from the chandeliers hanging from the ceiling. The shelves on the left held an assortment of colorful old books and parchments.

Behind the bar was a bartender busily wiping a countertop that clearly displayed no need for his labors; his suspicious glare was fixed on the preacher. His demeanor reminded Calvin of a large female eagle as she spreads her wings wide and revealed her spearlike beak and razor sharp talons, which she would not hesitate to use in order to protect her nest. The nest, in this case, was a rectangular table directly in front of the bar.

The table was placed with its length perpendicular to the bar. Along each side of the table were three chairs. No chair was on the short side nearest Calvin, but at the head of the table, and facing Calvin, sat the council chairman. Like the bartender, his eyes were fixed on Calvin as he listened to a man sitting to his right. The preacher could not see the man's face, since his back was turned slightly and his gaze was locked on the chairman. Calvin broke the stare of the chairman to view the remainder of the conference room. The wall to Calvin's right contained rolls of windows identical to those in the casino's entry. Those inside the room could easily view all the activities without, but those without only saw reflected images of themselves. A large stone fireplace was centered on the left wall. From his seat, the council chairman could observe all activities at the entry and inside the gaming and restaurant section of his business. No one could view the interior except through the doors. Calvin thought about stepping deeper into the gaming room to escape the gaze of the chairman and the bartender, but he realized he could not escape their scrutiny; his plan was futile.

Looking at his watch, he noticed it was 9:00 AM. The council chairman would be late he assumed, but he was wrong. The right fist of the man sitting at the head of the table crashed hard on the table. The council chairman opened his hand and placed a pointed finger into the face of the man seated to his right. Calvin could not read lips, nor would he have understood the dialogue that took place if he could. Nonetheless, the dialogue was brief and the tall man to his right pushed his chair back in a display of frustration and anger; he rose to leave with no rebuttal. At the head of the table, the pointing hand turned to an open gesture motioning Calvin to enter. Calvin waited as the other gentleman exited and glared into his fiery eyes. He looked at the man's hawk like nose and recognized him. That is the man I saw chasing the German Shepherd Tuesday night, he thought. They locked eyes for a second time. Calvin responded quickly with a greeting.

"Good morning, brother. How are you? I'm sorry I almost hit your dog the other night. He just came out of nowhere and stopped right in front of the truck."

The tall man grabbed Calvin's upper arm and nearly dragged him into the gaming room, possibly in a futile attempt to escape the view of the chairman. His face slowly moved within inches of Calvin's and displayed a sinister growl. He exhaled slowly in Calvin's face, and then inhaled in the same deliberate manner; lifting his head up and backward like a child smelling an opened box of sweet chocolates. His eyes closed as he tilted his head upward to face the ceiling. There was a short pause as if he was cataloging the smell of Calvin's aftershave. Then quickly, as though he remembered where he was, his head snapped back down to Calvin's and their noses touched.

"Listen to me, preacher! I am not your brother and don't dare blame my dog. He didn't suddenly appear in front of you. Now answer this question, preacher, and answer truthfully: how fast were you going when my dog appeared?" Before Calvin could answer, the man dropped his arm and disappeared out the front door.

Calvin straightened himself from the encounter and walked into the inner room. The eagled-eyed bartender seemed to be more relaxed now as he poured liquor from a bottle. A small woman dressed in a black clingy dress appeared with a tray and swept up the glass from the bar. She walked to the head of the table and set it down to the right of the chairman, who slid it to his left. Calvin's eyes ventured briefly to the woman, whose low-cut blouse revealed more than he cared to see. Although her body seemed to be that of very young woman, her face showed signs of aging, and her dark eyes looked to be blank and expressionless. Her clothing matched her long, shiny black hair, a direct contrast to her smooth, milky white skin. His eyes lowered, in observation only, to see dark nylon stockings flowing from beneath her skirt and disappearing into the tops of her black high-heeled stilettos. Calvin's eyes had seen enough, and before lustful thoughts invaded the sincerity of his inspection, he turned his head back to the man at the head of the table. The council chairman's smile suggested to Calvin that he had caught him looking, but Calvin knew it will be a waste of time to explain. His thoughts were pure, and he watched as the chairman motioned for him to sit in the same chair the tall man before him had occupied. The preacher sat.

A deep baritone voice emerged from the throat of the chairman as he spoke with confidence and authority. "Good morning, preacher, and welcome to Copper Town. I am Alexander Gionni, council chairman."

Chapter 9

SONG OF THE NEPHILIM

For thou has trusted in thou wickedness: thou hast said, None
seeth me. Thy wisdom and thy knowledge, it hath perverted
thee; and thou hast said in thine heart, I am, and none else
beside me. Therefore shall evil come upon thee;
thou shalt not know from whence it riseth:

ISAIAH 47:10–11

Nightfall spreads its blanket of darkness over the last blood red light of the setting sun. The stargazers embracing the blackness of the prevailing night outnumber those who stretch forth their arms at dawn to the warmth of the flame. With the fading light, horror will soon fall upon the laborers of day scurrying to their homes. Their feelings of comfort and achievement from labors since youth are warped with desolation. Desolation bred, in part, of sorceries and enchantments. With the coming of night, comes the Nephilim of old.

Upon the rocks they climb from the secluded tombs that hid them from the flame. Up they go! At times they levitate from one high, rocky crag to another. There is no scientific explanation or logic for their motions. They merely do that which they were created to do. Can one say to its maker, "Why hast thou made me so?" With no consumption of human blood, they have the ability to compress their bodies into the forms of men by day to walk among them; but at night, the human forms are shed like dirty clothes prior to the entrance of a hot bath.

Their leader is the first to reach the uppermost pinnacles that jut from the cliff line over the town below like the maiden head of a giant ship. What was once the Song of the Nephilim, long ago was reduced to a mere hum. The hum begins prior to the ascent. It is continuous, for the Nephilim have no need to breathe. Hundreds of them are climbing after the leader, and he hears the distinct sound of each. Some are low, baritone like his; others are higher pitched. From the high, soft drum of the tenors and the altos to the throbbing lows, the chorus of humming echoes throughout the mountains in a beautiful and harmonious a cappella. They all knew the words they sang eons ago, but to voice them now would be sheer hypocrisy. Thus, they hum the song they once sang for the Ancient of Days. Climbing to their perches, they appear as vultures prepared to soar down upon the remaining mutilated corpses of a battlefield in a valley below.

All eyes are upon the leader. He now stands above them with his eyes closed to allow no stray beam of light to pierce his inner being. As with all Nephilim, their eyes need not be open to see. Their leader is now in his created form. The magnitude of his stature is near sixteen feet, and the long nails of his fingers curl like claws extending well beyond the finger tips. The claws on his toes are no less in length and might be considered, in error, as the enabling force that grips and holds him to the pinnacle. He spreads his arms and leans horizontally over the rocky crag. His body is perpendicularly suspended from his perch. It is not the claws that support him; it is simply because he wills it to be so.

The other Nephilim find their own perches and duplicate his actions. Under their arms flow long, web like wings that stretch forth from their wrists to their hips. Each wing is supported with three large ribs jointed uniformly beneath their armpits. A similar web like tissue spans from the top of each arm to the base of each ear; ears are pointed and positioned near the top of the head. They are shaped like wolves, and the ears could be easily confused as horns. The light of the moon reveals dark, beautiful cobalt bodies, smooth and shiny.

If they chose, they could bring to remembrance the brilliance of their first nature. It was a time when their dark blue bodies resembled torches and burned like the golden rays of sunshine. Yet, they choose not to envision such as they were, for they no longer desire to remember. They are that which they have become, shining creatures of blackness.

Arching his spine backward, his nostrils open wide to the direction of the town below. This arching position is beyond human ability, yet it is similar to a diver leaving the high platform. Although their bodies become distorted, the Nephilim remain suspended in midair upon their perches. The wind is on the leaders back, but the odors from the town are easily discerned by his well-developed olfactory senses. His mind quickly diffuses the odoriferous conglomeration and sorts them spontaneously into unique and individual categories. When it comes to men, odors are unique and each one allows him to trace the genealogy of its owner; he needs no DNA samples. He smells a campfire with beef roasting on the pit; in another camp, a whole lamb is roasting. The smell of steaming vegetables and fruits is nearly overwhelming. They prepare their evening feast after the labors of the day.

Soon, the Nephilim will begin their labors of darkness, and before the night is washed away by the dawning of day, they too will feast. The vegetation in the valley has a weak resemblance of its spectacular past. The leader remembers a time when he walked through thick and lush vegetation. It was a day when the earth had no garden of its own; for the earth itself was the garden of the Ancient of Days. Trees grew to the size of skyscrapers, and animals roaming through the garden were larger than boxcars. The numbers of Nephilim were greater in those days, for they had been created and entrusted as caretakers of the garden. Their leader, the Prince of the First Heaven, received the Seal of Perfection from the Ancient of Days. His voice was like the sound of soft tambourines and trumpets. He was filled with wisdom and was flawless in beauty. The Ancient of Days had anointed and established him as the ruler of the garden. He walked back and forth amidst the fiery stones and was permitted to stand upon the Sacred Mountain of the Ancient One. And then, iniquity was found in him. His heart was lifted up and his wisdom fell into corruption due to his created splendor. He rebelled against the Ancient of Days seeking to establish his own throne upon the highest point of the Sacred Mountain. His treason resulted in his being exiled form the Sacred Mountain and stripped of his garden lordship.

The Guardian Nephilim called him the Prince of the Air. He and his kind communicated with each other verbally and nonverbally through telepathy. The Nephilim moved by thought to all parts of the garden to meet its needs. At times they healed the large animals that were injured. Other times, they tilled and planted new species of flora for the pleasure of the Old One. Their purpose was to be guardians and caretakers of the garden which was the delight of the Old One.

After his exile, the Prince of the Air declared war upon the Sacred Mountain. He rallied the allies of many of the Ancient of Days' creations, including the Nephilim. The leader remembers the terrible rebellion. Many of the Nephilim, himself included, chose not to join forces with the Prince, and they remained loyal to the Old One. Although they had lived for millions of years and could have lived forever, rebellion brought an end to it all. Hundreds of thousands of Nephilim were beheaded by the Prince of the Air. Some escaped into the depths of the sea, where the Prince had no power over them. Only when they ventured into the atmosphere from the cold waters could the Prince's telepathic powers be used. The Ancient of Days, with disappointment, cast judgment upon the entire planet, and it fell into a chaotic state, covered with water. Thus, the Prince of Air had no domain to rule.

After eons of darkness and water, the Ancient of Days once again brought the Earth back into order. His garden was reestablished, yet a new creature in the likeness of the Ancient of Days was placed in its midst and given domain over it. This new man-creature was given complete rule with no Nephilim guardian; he answered only to the Ancient One. The Prince was stripped of his power over the Nephilim and they were permitted to walk the dry land once again, but they were denied interaction with the man-creature. The new regime was short-lived, for the newly formed creature fell from favor. The Prince had tricked him into disobeying the orders of the Ancient One. In so doing, the Prince and his followers gained control of the first Heaven again; the heaven where all that is visible can be touched and is located within the atmosphere of the planet.

The human and his mate were cast form the Garden. A new leader of the Nephilim had been called to resume their work; again, becoming the Guardians of the Garden. No one was allowed to enter, and their power was enhanced to prevent any creature from entering this region of the garden.

On the outside, time passed and man began to multiply and cover the face of the earth. The daughters that were born were increasingly bestowed with beauty and splendor. Although not human, the Nephilim were endowed with humanlike characteristics. Men referred to them as "mighty men" and sometimes as "men of renown." The Nephilim lustfully cast their eyes upon the daughters of the men. Succumbing to that lust, they left the Garden to claim wives of their own among the daughters of men. From his perch above the village, their leader remembers well the result of his treason. They, too, had fallen to disobedience and left their first domain: the Garden. He and the other Nephilim lost the appearances of children of light and were cast into darkness. Their lustrous golden sheen was transformed to a dark blue. That which was as visible as light to them became blackness and the blackness became shades of gray. Not only was the vision of light removed, but the imagery of light was taken away from their memory. They had the ability to orate about things of the light, but could never see the brilliance again; nor could he visualize them within his mind. The pain was, at times, unbearable.

Their leader suppressed the pain and focused on the blackness of night. In the darkness, the grays became lighter, and his vision was enhanced, proclaiming him a creature of the night. His head turned slightly to the right, and one eye twitched open. There was a new smell in the air. Over the strong odor of gopher wood and tar, there was a dampness he had never tasted. The arid desert environment was watered daily with heavy dew from the Ancient of Days and irrigated from the rivers through manmade trenches. Although he found it hard to believe, he listened to the proclamation of the prophet. A mad man, he first thought, but now he wondered why he had prophesized a storm. Besides, was it not madness to build such a large wooden structure? If the structure was inhabited, the pitch the prophet used to connect the beams within and without would produce an intolerable stench, especially, to the Nephilim. If that alone was not enough, the prophet was filling it with all kinds of animals. "What were the words he proclaimed so many years ago?" he asked himself. "Oh, yes." He remembered. "It's going to rain!"

Chapter 10
KNOWLEDGE PRECEDES WISDOM

How long will it be ere ye make an end of words? mark, and afterwards we will speak. Wherefore we are counted as beasts, and reputed vile in your sight?

Job 18:2–3

Upon entering the inner room of Alexander's Casino, Calvin observed the layout of the room. Nothing, or no one, it appeared was to block the owner's view through the two sets of double doors leading to the street. His table was much bigger and more elaborate than the other six rectangular tables making up the room's decor. Three tables to each side ran lengthwise in the same north-to-south manner as Alexander's. Each table had an identical, yet smaller, lead chair tucked in at its head. In addition to the head chairs, each table had six other chairs, three on each side. Seven chairs to a table and seven tables to the room. This was the only furniture in the room with the exception of the oversized bookcases and bar.

Calvin was amazed at the enormous size of the bar. Everything in the room was much bigger than he originally thought. The bartender lowered his eyes as if inspecting his own efforts in polishing the large top. The unique design created an image in the preacher's mind that it was more of a large altar instead of a bar. Now that he was closer to the two large mahogany doors behind the bar, he was able to see the handcrafted and decorative carvings. Inlays of sliver and borders of gold were interlaced throughout the wooden structures. Strange lettering was meticulously engraved on each of the doors. The lettering was above Calvin's head. He estimated the inscription to be nearly eight feet above the floor. The doors were identical in design to the ones in the parsonage, but they were much larger in comparison. The silver and gold in these doors was not painted; it was genuine.

Looking through the dark glass windows into the bar and grill, Calvin concluded the inner room did not run as deep as the bar and restaurant located on the other side. This observation made him wonder what was beyond the double doors behind the bar; they certainly were not exit doors. He made a mental note to look for an exit door on his and Rosie's next walk along the backside of the casino. Perhaps if there is a window, he could peek through; after all, there was no harm in looking.

His thoughts were interrupted by Alexander.

"What do you think of our little town, John Calvin?" Alexander asked, never breaking eye contact with Calvin.

Being called John Calvin by his parents, or Rosie, usually was a warning that a stern lecture or rebuke would follow. But Calvin denoted a tone of respect and inquiry by the use of his name. Spoken by Alexander, it offered a feeling of comfort more than anxiety. Subconsciously, and for the first time in his life, Calvin thought, you know, I rather like John Calvin. Maybe I'll start using it, and wouldn't this be a great place to start?

"Well," he began, "I think it's a great place to call home. The rustic and rural architectural structures remind me of the Old West. I think Rosie and I will be here for a long time. There is a lot of potential for our ministry here."

Alexander was slow and deliberate before asking, "What do you mean by potential, preacher?"

"I think, in my role as a pastor, we can expand the church membership, provide more support to the community, and maybe build a fellowship hall to the rear of the church."

Alexander's face grimaced with Calvin's response, as if he was in complete opposition to these potential plans. He managed a smile, which was more of a smirk, and leaned back in his chair.

Calvin realized not only had he misjudged the size of the double doors, but he had underestimated the physical size of the man who sat at the head of the table. This man could very well be as tall as Shaquille O'Neal, but he was not as heavy. A hint of the muscular frame underneath the black polo shirt was evident by the massive forearms which rippled with each movement of his arms. Nonetheless, the overall appearance was of an old warrior who had fought many battles and won them all. A scar streaked down the right side of his face, protruding from his black hair line down into his cheek. A small line barely creasing his eyelid indicated that apparently one blow had made both scars. His deep-set eyes rested below dark, thick eyebrows which served as a helmet of armor and prevented the use of an eye patch. Another scar started along the side of his mouth and moved in a jagged path along the lower side of his jaw, growing wider and deeper as it stretched down below his ear. Scars that would be disfiguring to most men added a certain amount of intrigue to this man sitting at the head of the table. Calvin resolved that Alexander could make it in the movie industry as a mobster.

He wouldn't need much acting lessons with that sinister look, Calvin thought. All he would have to do would be to stand still and simply glare into the camera. That stare alone would send chills along the back of most viewers.

Still, Calvin was intrigued with the man and wanted very much to know more about him.

"So, preacher, you feel that you can come in and convert the whole town to Christianity?" Alexander questioned.

Years of serving as a missionary, minister, and pastor had prepared John Calvin for this question.

"That is the Great Commission that Jesus gave us before he departed," he replied.

Before the preacher could continue with his response, Alexander broke in with another question. "Do you feel we are living in the end of times, preacher?"

"Yes," was the reply. Again Calvin's lips moved to expound upon the answer, but he was silenced by the chairman's continued interruption.

"But Jesus in the book of Luke taught that when he came back, he would find no faith on Earth; and in Matthew, he stated that upon his return, the Earth would be as it were in the days of Noah. A supportive statement was given by the Apostle Paul when he wrote, 'Concerning the end days, that man would not endure sound doctrine.' So, John Calvin, it seems to me one of your goals may need to be reevaluated in order to bring it into line with the Chronicles of Truth you follow?"

Calvin had debated this line of questioning many times and was as quick as the chairman with his answer. "It is written that no man knows the day or hour of Jesus's return, thus we are to labor while there it is still day, for the night cometh when no man can work. We are also told that the fields are ripe for the harvest."

Alexander's smile assured Calvin that he too had debated the same theology, and he shot back with, "Tares and wheat are sown together and are to be left until the harvest to be separated. Those two plants are biologically different. One cannot be changed to the other no more than a goat can be changed to a sheep or a sheep changed to a goat. Tell me now, preacher, what is the theme of your message, or plan, to convert the non-Christians here in Copper Town?"

"My goal is simply for them to believe. I use the format of the Roman Road to lead the lost to Christ and will use it here in Copper Town. Are you familiar with it?"

Now Calvin decided to fire back with questions of his own in seeking to gain control of the conversation.

The council chairman slowly tilted his head back and looked at the ceiling. His nostrils were pointing to Calvin, and the preacher was reminded of the same action performed by Slim only minutes before. Alexander's deep breaths were like tentacles searching to find an entrance into the depths of Calvin's mind and soul. His face, as it lowered, appeared as if he had considered a thousand responses to the preacher's question in only a matter of seconds.

"I am. Yet that approach, to me, appears to teach that for a person to enter into the Kingdom of your God and have eternal life, he is only required to believe. So, is it safe for me to say your ministry here will be faith-based? If one will believe, he will be converted?"

One simple "yes" was all Calvin needed to answer both questions, but he repeated it again to let Alexander know he had perceived both. "And, yes!"

"Will that process of faith and believing serve as redemption for demons, preacher?"

"No, salvation is for man."

"So you say you believe in God. You do well, the demons believe and tremble. Is that not written?"

"Yes, it is, but salvation is for man, not demons."

Calvin wondered where Alexander was going now.

"Oh, I see now. It is determined by works. For a person to enter into the Kingdom of God and have eternal life, he is only required to believe?"

"That's correct!" Calvin answered as he wondered what direction Alexander was going in. Calvin waited for him to continue.

"So, it is a works-related salvation you will preach?"

Calvin was quick to respond. "No, its not works, but faith. Faith is that instrument by which man reaches out to accept God's grace of salvation through the finished work of Jesus."

"But," Alexander continued, "if it is man's ability to reach out, then it is man's works, and he can boast, for he has achieved something the unbeliever does not have. Is it not written that salvation is a gift of God, not of works?"

Calvin interrupted the council chairman. "It says we are saved by grace through faith and not of works lest any man should boast. It is a gift from God."

"But it appears to me, preacher," Alexander continued with a slight hint of boredom in his voice, "that you are putting faith before grace. My question to you would be, why do some exercise this faith and others do not? I would suppose you'd argue it is man's free will?"

Calvin again was quick to answer Alexander and replied," I do believe in free will."

"Hmm" was the only response he received from the council chairman. "We will discuss that later. I have some other questions I would like to ask you concerning a study I have been conducting for years. Do you think you can help me?"

Calvin confessed he does not know everything there was to know about the Bible, but would try to help the chairman if possible.

"Besides, if I don't know, I will try to find out."

Alexander smiled and nodded. "Good answer."

He continued. "I see you use the Old King James version of the Bible. Let me share a passage with you from that version which I find fascinating."

Alexander lowered his eyes and quoted a passage, which Calvin recognized as one from Genesis.

"The sons of God saw the daughters of men that they were fair; and they took wives of all which they chose."

Alexander paused and stared steadfast at the preacher. It was a trancelike glare which Calvin was unable to break, and he watched Alexander's lips form a question. "The sons of god, what does that mean?"

Still eye-to-eye like two giant rams locked in combat high on a mountain slope, Calvin began cautiously to answer with how this was explained to him in seminary school. It was one of many interpretations his father and grandfather had disagreed with. Calvin felt they were both in error.

"This was a polygamous relationship. It was instigated by the sons of Seth and the daughters of Cain. The Bible passage explains the amalgamation between the Godly descendants of Seth and the wicked ones from Cain."

It was Alexander's turn to interrupt, and he fired back. "Surely that cannot be, for the daughters of men would not exclude anyone. It must be inclusive concerning all men and their daughters, including Cain's. Secondly," he said, his voice rising in volume, "the meaning of 'Sons of God' does not have the same meaning in the Old Testament as in the New Testament. There are many references in the New Testament that clearly explain the 'Sons of God' as becoming such through conversion. It is used here and in four other places in the Old Testament with reference to angels. The Rabbinical teachings for the Hebrew language in Genesis and Job defines 'Sons of God' as beings brought into existence by God's creation. This included angels as well as men."

Calvin opened his mouth to object, but the cold palm of Alexander's upraised hand prevented his interruption.

"Preacher, the way I see it is the way it is taught by the Hebrews. And don't forget they wrote it that Adam was created in the likeness of God, but all humanity are his descendants and all were created in the likeness of him. Is it not written that Adam 'begat a son in his own likeness, after his own image?' All men born of Adam are the sons of men. Even Jesus, referred to himself as the Son of Man in the gospel of Luke where his genealogy is traced all the way back to Adam. Is that not so?"

Calvin knew a simple yes or no was all Alexander would accept, and he answered with "Yes."

"It was never taught any differently by the Hebrew people. Your study of church history in seminary school should have revealed to you that your explanation of that passage was never taught or interpreted the way you perceive it, until the third century."

The slight pause in his speech, coupled with the fact that the chairman's hand was now palm down on the table, provided Calvin with an opportunity to respond with his rebuttal.

"When Jesus commented on the meanings concerning the resurrection of the righteous, he explicitly stated that when risen they will neither marry or are given in marriage; for he says, they are equal to the angel. So you can see that angels are sexless and are unable to cohabitate either with themselves or with humans."

It was Alexander's turn, and he did not hesitant with his reply. "Yes, the passage does imply angels do not marry. Jesus's text concerns marriage after the resurrection, but he does not say they are sexless. That would mean all the righteous dead would also be sexless and would result in the Word being in error. For your Bible teaches that husbands and wives will know each other 'as such in the world to come.' That means they may not have intercourse, but there will be a sexual difference."

Calvin could not believe he was about to share his family's theology with a stranger, but he said to Alexander, "My father and grandfather both interpret those passages as you do, but I do not. And I will never be convinced that you, or they, are right."

Alexander's face displayed his boredom; he had grown weary of the subject and Calvin's dogmatic answers.

"You may be amazed at what life can teach you, preacher, if you *will*," he emphasized. "Just let go of traditions and personal biases. It is only the truth that will set you free."

Before Calvin was allowed to respond, Alexander cleverly changed the subject. "What do you think of the parsonage, preacher?"

"My wife and I have both commented on the design and practicality of the apartment. The architect is to be complimented. It is the nicest home we have ever lived in. Do you rent it to the church?"

"It is my contribution to the church. Everyone in Copper Town works, and everyone supports the other organizations and businesses within the town. You might say we support one another."

"So I take it you are an active member of the Fellowship Church? After all, you're the chairman of the church council."

"No, I am not an active member. I'm not even a member. From time to time, I may drop in to check on you." Alexander winked at Calvin. The subject seemed to have invigorated Alexander, and he continued explaining the council to Calvin. "All activities, organizations, businesses, or whatever," he sighed, "are directed by the council. It is for the survival of our community. We are a family here. There is no other leadership group but the council. Philip is very active in the church and will assist you in meeting your needs as long as they are not counterproductive in achieving the short- and long-term goals of the council."

"What are those goals, Alexander? Are they articulated in the individual associations? Does the Church have a copy of them to ensure they are conducive to our Covenant, Articles of Faith, and most importantly the Scriptures?" Alexander leaned back in his chair a second time as the barmaid placed another glass near his right hand. She remained at his side. The glass was opaque, and yet, Calvin was able to discern the liquid in the glass to be a dark red wine. Alexander grasped the glass in his hand without shifting it to his left hand as he did the other drink. A rise of both eyebrows was followed by a smile that flickered across his face.

"All in time, preacher; all in good time. But our time today has come to an end. Once a week, as council chairman, I meet with leaders of our community. I am scheduling you, as the leader of the church, for Friday mornings at ten. Does that meet with your approval?"

"Uh, sure, I'll pencil it in on my calendar."

Alexander managed a laugh and said, "Next week, let's discuss your 'free will,' shall we?"

Calvin nodded, thinking at least he would have the topic and time to prepare. Next time, I'll not be caught off guard, he thought.

"Before you go, let me introduce you to two of my, uh, employees. This"—he raised his hand up toward the barmaid, which she grasped tenderly with both of hers—"is LeBazeja. I know it is hard for Westerners to say, so we just call her Lee. The big ugly guy behind the bar is Dormin, her husband."

They nodded their heads to Calvin as they were introduced. In unison, they said, "Welcome, preacher."

Alexander dismissed Calvin by saying, "I have another appointment waiting so if you will excuse me, I'll talk to you again next week."

"Will I see you in church on Sunday?" Calvin asked. After all, it was his responsibility as pastor to invite everyone to services.

The look on Dormin and Lee's face was a clear indication that the answer would be no, even before they shook their heads no at his request. The same definite negative was echoed by Alexander.

"Should I ask Slim or does he attend?" Calvin asked.

"Listen, preacher, I will give you one piece of advice: stay away from Slim."

Dormin and Lee nod their heads as if to reinforce the warning Alexander delivered.

"Why is that?" asked Calvin.

"John Calvin, you and your wife are to stay clear of Slim. He is important to Copper Town and is a member of our council. But he does not like people, especially … preachers. Do you understand?" Alexander thundered.

"Yes," Calvin answered, as he rose from his chair and turned to walk away. Halfway through the inner room, he turned to give the three of them a final wave. He watched Alexander slowly sip the wine from the small, delicate glass. Lee had moved behind him, placing her hands on the sides of his head and with her index fingers massaging his temples. Her head was tilted backwards, and she appeared to enjoy every swallow of the liquor Alexander was slowly sipping. Dormin looked on with what appeared to be a genuine smile of approval.

A slight squeak escaped the old hardwood flooring as Calvin exited the inner room. As he methodically plodded along, he was unaware of the scene unfolding behind him: Lee had moved from behind the table and was following him to the door. Behind her, Alexander and Dormin both tilted their heads backwards with their upturned nostrils pointing in the direction of the preacher. Both breathed deeply and slowly, their lungs expand like a large beach ball. In the twinkling of an eye, the dimensions of their human bodies changed. If Calvin had seen them, he would have accurately calculated their heights to be over ten feet. Alexander's massive oversized chair now seemed to be more fitted for his body. Dorman's head was near making contact with the ceiling. The quick release of the inhaled air rushed forth as if it were air escaping from a balloon that had been punctured with a pin. Both men assumed their original size. Lee's hair noticeably shifted as a breeze from behind her swept past and touched the back of Calvin neck as he stepped through the doors. Calvin shuddered and turned to find the source of the cold breeze, only to see Alexander and Dormin as he last envisioned them. Grins were uniformly perceived by the preacher.

For the first time, Calvin was aware that Lee followed him and was within arm's reach. He shuttered as he noticed for the first time two large Mastiffs lying under the table at Alexander's feet, one to the left and one to the right. Looking deep within the red glowing eyes of the two large Mastiffs, he saw lips slightly curled to expose razor sharp fangs. The dogs appeared to Calvin as two large lions crouched just before they made a final leap upon their prey. How did I not notice them? He thought to himself. They were within inches of my legs, and I never knew they were there!

"Oh!" Calvin exclaimed as he was yanked by his left arm into the casino's gaming room and out of view of the room's occupants. The exclamation was not from pain; it was caused, rather, by the shock of reentry into reality from the time he had spent in the surreal inner room. While in the room, time seemed to stand still. And now the sudden yank on the preacher's arm had rescued him from the hypnotic spell. But now that he faced reality, he was reminded that the yanking on his arm was similar to Slim's aggressive approach earlier. A sigh of relief whistled through his teeth when he turned expecting to see Slim, but instead he faced a young man who appeared to be in his early twenties.

Accompanied by a charming young lady of the same age, the young lad maintained the deathlike grip on Calvin's arm. They both displayed looks of helplessness and fear.

"I need to talk to you privately, preacher," he whispered. "Real soon."

"Anytime," Calvin exclaimed in a voice loud enough to let others who could be listening see he had a heart to serve and was always available. "Just drop in anytime."

"Sh," he whispered. "Not so loud, preacher. Meet me next Friday morning; eight-thirty at the old copper mine."

He turned and entered through the inner doors with the young lady. As they moved through the doors into the council room, he turned, forcing a smile, and offered a rather loud farewell. "It has been a pleasure meeting you, preacher. Gotta go. Have a good day!"

The young couple disappeared into the inner room as the doors began to close. Calvin watched as the motion of the doors stopped just short of being closed. Through the narrow gap, Calvin saw part of Lee's body and realized it was her that was closing the massive portals. Her head drew slowly to the crevice and paused a second to stare at Calvin. The coldness of her glare sent shivers down his spine. Her eyebrows were pinched together, and the threatening glare of her narrow and shallow eyes portrayed distrust and animosity. With their eyes locked in a dueling contrast, Lee slowly closed the doors. Calvin heard the scraping sound of a large metallic bolt securing the entry.

Chapter II
THE FIRST WEEKEND

And on the seventh day God ended his work which he had made: and he rested on the seventh day from all his work which he had made.

GENESIS 2:2

Calvin pushed down on the large crash bar of the main entry. The door that had been propped open on his entry was now closed. A click told him it was unlocked, and with an effortless shove, he escaped from the dark casino and emerged onto the bright, sunlit sidewalk of Main Street. Behind him, the massive door softly closed with the same clink of metal. A slight breeze swept across his face from the southwest and carried a hint of the dry heat of the desert that would soon follow the coolness he now felt. It was shortly after 11:00 AM, and the temperature was already in the mid seventies. In a few short weeks, summer would arrive, and the temperature would be near ninety by this time of the morning. Accompanying the higher temperatures would be a long awaited influx of tourists. At the peak of summer, the streets would be full. Both sides of Main Street would crowd with parked cars spilling over and filling the large parking lot behind the casino. They would line both sides of all the side streets, making driving tedious for motorists.

One activity staged for the tourists was Old West gun fights on the streets. Other activities would also be available. Bikes, motorized or not, would roll through the streets. Many of them would travel along the well-marked trails through the surrounding mountains and canyons. On foot, tourists would hike into the high mountain areas. While there, some would enjoy fishing in the cold mountain streams, and others would enjoy camping. Many would try their hand at prospecting, but few would find anything of value. Places of solitude would be as difficult to find as the precious stones and ore. Those physically conditioned to endure the long rugged trials into the back country would find less traveled paths and few people on them. The desert would boil dust and sand from dune buggies and motorcycles racing through it. Several national runs of both would be sponsored by the town through the summer months. The fifty-mile course throughout the desert and mountain area for cross-country motorcycles was on the International Circuit. Other dust clouds would form from herds of wild horses and burros fleeing the invasion of their desert homes.

That day the streets were nearly empty. Two cars passed in front of Calvin from different directions reminding him of the snipping action of large shears. The brightness and warmth of the sunlight rejuvenated the preacher and his steps quickened. He, too, with much less effort than the council chairman, breathed in deep. The air was stimulating, and he laughed aloud at the memory of the ugly encounter with Slim. A world that sometimes portrayed a degree of freshness and pureness was now invading Calvin's thoughts; he quickly changed directions and trotted across the street. His quickened steps were not necessary to evade traffic; rather, they served to put distance between him and the casino. He decided to wander along the streets to make a few observations, take some notes, and become familiar with the layout of town.

After crossing the street, the preacher turned left and walked eastward. His Bible and notepad were clutched tightly at his hip with his left hand. He waved to the owners of each shop he passed. It had only been three days since their arrival in town, but obviously everyone knew him, for they greeted him as "preacher." The Bible he toted on his hip was not needed to authenticate his identity.

Upon reaching First Street, Calvin noted the veterinarian clinic to be larger than his initial observation. The parking lot was nearly full and a lot of activity was taking place around the kennels to the east, and as many as were visible to the south. A small group gathered outside the clinic, each accompanied by dogs, saw him standing at the corner. They also waved and shouted, "Good morning, preacher!" Calvin returned their waves and yelled a warm, "Hello!" All ceased their activities in anticipation of a visit from the new preacher. Some held their small dogs under their arms; others grasped the leashes of the breeds sitting obediently at their feet.

They sincerely displayed a deep-rooted care and love for their companions with constant petting. Perhaps a deeper manifestation of their love was displayed by the animals being included with the dialogue. The love was reciprocated by the dogs with wet laps upon the hands and faces of their owners.

Some of the people were disappointed, yet others were relieved when the preacher turned to retrace his steps down Main Street.

"Dogs!" he said aloud in a newfound revelation. "Everyone in this town seems to have dogs as pets."

He stopped and jotted this discovery from his morning reconnaissance on the blank pages of his new notepad. The preacher continued to wave at the owners of the stores, but found himself more observant now of their pets. He noted that not one of local store owners was without a pet, and … they were all dogs.

In one store, he saw a small Pomeranian, in another a Poodle. He saw one owner with a Siberian husky, another one was petting a Chow, which she affectionately called Solomon. The preacher stopped and jotted down a third observation: with all the dogs in town, not a single stray animal could be found roaming the streets or alleys. All the pets stayed close to their masters, and the use of leashes appeared to be more of a custom than of a necessity. The dogs all seemed to be lethargic. Could it be the increasing heat rushing in from the desert floor?

"Must be the heat!' he said aloud. "Even the animals are affected by it."

At the intersection of Main and Second Street, Calvin made a pretense of stopping to rest. He leaned against an old wrought iron lamppost and looked down the street. It was the casino he now wanted to observe more closely. The two-story building occupied the entire block and contained several stores, including the bar and grille, restaurant, casino, a hardware store, and the parsonage. Because of the excessively high ceilings, the building stood over thirty feet from the sidewalk. The parsonage roof was six to eight feet lower than the roof of the casino. That would explain the normal-size walls contained in the apartment reserved for church pastor. A long, wooden porch extended over the sidewalk for nearly forty feet at the entry of the casino. It ran along the front wall of the casino and was separated from the parsonage porch by a large open gap. The roofs of the porches both dropped sharply downward from the top of the building and were supported with large beams embedded into the outer edge of the concrete sidewalk. The porches provided a covering for those walking below on the sidewalks. A door centered between two windows had been constructed on the walls of each porch. The porch above the casino was much taller than the one at the parsonage. From the streets, the doors and windows above the casino appeared to be only decorative, with no signs of use. The Western shutters that had been installed to frame all the windows were covered with bright, fresh paint. They complimented the color scheme of the casino.

Calvin crossed Main Street and walked north along Second Street, opposite the windows of the bar and grille. They were identical to the dark ones installed along the front of the building. From the outside, Calvin saw only his reflection, but knew he was visible to those within. The dark tint prevented the bright sunlight from entering.

Approaching the back parking lot, Calvin detected the slight scent of smoke. He stopped to observe the source and discovered Antonio was busy tending the garden at the Rock. The preacher leaned against a wooden utility pole to watch the little man work.

Antonio removed his large hat, wiped his forehead, and in doing so, noticed Calvin. He acknowledged him with a wave. Calvin returned the gesture and glanced at the rear of the casino to his left. One set of double doors (normal size, he noted) was located at the back of the bar and grille. Another set was located at the back of the hardware store. Both, Calvin concluded, could be used for loading and unloading supplies and goods. The hardware store had two large sets of windows in the rear which matched those along the side and the front of the store. There were no other exit doors on the back of the casino. The preacher now realized that there was one entrance into the council room and wondered where the large doors behind the bar led. He jotted quickly on his notepad: the doors must lead to a storage room or entry to the second floor. Is it possible there could be a lower floor?

He slowly scanned the building and found there were no other windows or doors along the first or second floors along the rear of the casino, except those in the restaurant, hardware store, and parsonage. On the roof, he observed the top of a black dome near the back of the building. The dome had not been visible from the street and sidewalks of Main Street. By its location, he knew it must be situated near the rear of the council chairman's conference room.

Not wanting to draw attention by lingering any length of time at one place, Calvin resumed his walk onward to the North Loop Road. Turning west, he walked to Third Street and took another left, which led him past the church and back to his apartment. Nearing the Rock, he glanced across the street, hoping to see Antonio. The little man was gone. Fresh-worked soil stood as a testimony that ever-intruding weeds had been replaced with fresh soil and fertilizer by the keeper of the Rock.

Calvin completed his morning walk when he reached the foot of the staircase leading up to the parsonage. He rushed with a desire to spend time with Rosie. A few hours with her would erase some of the confusion and frustration that was now seeping inward to his soul and distracting his mental imagery. He needed some encouragement from the lips of someone he had known for more than three days. Only Rosie could speak such words.

Calvin and Rosie ate a light lunch and crashed on their bed for a short nap. The dry heat of the desert established this as a daily custom for Rosie and her husband. The daily nap would come to serve as a restorative of energy zapped by the midday heat and to confirm intimacy.

After their nap, Calvin spent time with Rosie on their daily devotional; then he completed and typed the notes for his first sermon. At 4:00 PM, they dressed and prepared for the drive to Gold Canyon to Luther and Sharon Gionni's ranch for the barbeque. Philip's earlier explanation that it would not be a long and drawn-out event relieved some of their anxiety.

"We'll be out of there before dark!" he had told them with that perpetual smile and laugh of his.

Finally, the time of their departure was at hand, and the McGarneys begin their drive. The little Honda pulled out from Second Street and turned left. As they drove, they discussed a proposed route for Rosie's running, which she planned to begin Monday evening. She had spent her life getting up early in the mornings to exercise and run, but she had now resolved to sleep in a little later and exercise in the evenings. The transition of day to night had become her favorite time. If she could have time stand still, it would have been at dusk. Calvin promised they would lay the course out the next day using the Harley's odometer.

They passed the old speed trap warning sign. Instead of traveling left up the mountain on Highway 50, they left the asphalt surface and headed due east on the dusty dirt road of Gold Canyon. They realized quickly it was not a public road when they approached a beautiful, ornate gate that blocked both the road and their progress. A little Hispanic man pushed a button from inside his booth and the gates, like arms, open seductively, inviting the car and its occupants to enter. From a window in his booth, the little man waved to them. His booth was built into one of two massive rock structures that supported the gates on each side of the driveway. These two colossal rock structures, along with the gates and tall stone walls, portrayed a desire for the owner's privacy and warned trespassers of the security measures he would use to maintain it.

Ahead, Calvin saw a small swirl of dust generated from a vehicle on the road. He drove slower to prevent the blinding dust of his own wheels from crawling into his car. Glancing into his rearview mirror, he discovered his dust served as a beacon to those who journeyed after him.

To their right were cultivated agricultural fields. Some were fenced with lush alfalfa growing thick and tall, ready for the first harvest of the year. Other fields were fenced with grazing cattle. To his left were mountainous meadows containing a large number of sheep. The woven wire fences on both sides of the road were the straightest Calvin had ever seen. The fields ended at the foot of the canyon walls, but grassy alpine meadows covered both sides.

Calvin drove upward along the private drive. He barely noticed that the small grade up of the incline continued six miles up the wide canyon. Near the end of his drive, he saw the canyon walls closing in from the right and left.

The valley grew smaller as both sides of the canyon walls rushed to form a sheer cliff line blocking his progress. Below the cliff wall, but above the canyon floor, sat a large mesa of several acres. A one-way lane driveway spiraled upward around the edge of the mesa to the right, and a mirror image driveway descended from the upper home and ranch on the left. The mesa contained several acres of land upon which sat the estate of Luther Gionni.

Gionni's home had been visible for some time on the drive up the canyon. Anyone watching the road from the house would have known they were coming long before the phone call they received from the gate. That day was no exception. No one traveled into the canyon without permission from Luther Gionni. The land was posted with signs of: Private Property; No Trespassing; and Violators will be Prosecuted. Unknown to Calvin and Rosie, no one dared to violate the wishes of Luther.

The layout of the location reminded Calvin of a fortress. Luther's house had a southwestern design of concrete, disguised to appear as adobe mud, and was topped with red roof tiles. The same tiles adorned all the other buildings and the walls around the estate. All the barns, sheds, and storage buildings reflected the same architectural design. The house was huge. Later Calvin would be given a tour of the gardens that surrounded a large kidney-shaped swimming pool located in the backyard. Beyond the gardens were the barns and corrals which housed several award-winning Paso Fino horses. Luther was a top breeder, and his horses were well known throughout the West. Closer to his home and to the south was another series of buildings housing dog kennels. Calvin and Rosie observed several Mastiff dogs with litters of puppies. Some of the other visitors told the couple that Luther's love of the Mastiff breed had been shared by his father.

The evening passed quickly and was enjoyed by the preacher and his wife. Calvin met more people than he had anticipated. He was thankful that a test to match names with faces was not administered afterwards, for he surely would have failed. Rosie was no help to him on such a test, for her recollection of names was worse than Calvin's!

The Gionni's had spread two long wooden tables with a feast suitable for a king. Meats of lamb, pork, beef, and seafood were side by side with vegetables too numerous to name. Fruits, pies, and cakes along with soft drinks and wine were on the tables. The only memorable event of the evening was when Rosie ordered her steak cooked well done. The cook dropped his utensil and nearly fainted. It seemed he wasn't accustomed to preparing steaks in that manner. Calvin noted that all steaks were served rare, the way he liked his, but Rosie would have no part of rare meat. Luther moved to the large open grill and personally prepared Rosie's steak for her.

In the Western sky, the sun was warning of its departure with fading waves of sunlight. The other guests followed the example set forth by the sun and began their trip back to Copper Town. They all seemed to be determined to arrive home before darkness arrived. Calvin and Rosie were the last to leave, and as they begin their descent from the mesa, they could see the long line of dusty automobiles working their way toward Copper Town. Each vehicle was etched into the valley floor by its own little swirling cloud of dust. Calvin thought, the dust you leave behind for others to eat is often the same dust you'll eat yourself … if you falter behind.

Chapter 12
INTO THE RIVER OF PEACE

He opened the rock, and the waters gushed out; they ran in the dry places like a river.

PSALM 105:41

Like waves of the sea, the darkness ebbed away and light gushed forth upon the sandy beaches of time. Tide and time were both set into perpetual motion at the foundation of the world, and tirelessly they proclaimed their longevity.

Calvin felt molded to his bed, but the cold desert air creeping into his bedroom through the open window caused him to drag the blanket to his chin. Rosie lay sleeping; the blankets surrounding her were cast aside hours ago and Calvin turned to rub the smooth skin of her bare shoulders. Both learned years ago that clothing was not a necessity for sleep. After several nights of sleeping under mosquito netting in the depths of the hot African jungle, they had awakened each morning to find their sheets soaked from perspiration; more from the hot humid nights than from their intimacy. To combat the nightly soakings, they cast aside their pajamas and slept nude. Rosie's naked body was evidence they had never seen the need for pajamas again.

Now, she lay motionless under the gliding hands of Calvin's caressing. That morning there would be no wellspring of responding arousal. She slept on, oblivious to her husband's touch. The preacher laughed quietly, for he knew she was a sound sleeper, and if exhausted, it would take a typhoon to pull her from the river of peace in which she drifted. He softly kissed her bare shoulder before gently covering her with the sheet. Cautiously, he fell back and rose his elbows high enough to allow the fingers of his hands to intertwine beneath the back of his neck. He was reflecting on the events of the past few weeks. Rosie and he had decided the night before that that day would be a day of rest. It would be the first in several weeks. They also vowed that all Mondays, henceforth, would be scheduled as the preacher and his wife's day off.

His thought back to Quitman, Georgia, where he and Rosie had planted a church nearly three years before. Quitman was a small town west of the outskirts of Valdosta. There they worked long and hard to secure a building for the new church. The Mission Board for the Fellowship Assembly had placed them there and was most helpful in providing their financial needs. Perhaps, salary wise, they could have used more, but such was the limitations of most missionaries. Through some advertising and public awareness, most of which was conducted door-to-door, the church began to grow. Within a year, they moved to a larger building, and funds were budgeted to purchase land for a future building program.

An outpouring of credit was given by the congregation to the preacher and his beautiful wife for their charismatic enthusiasm. They loved their work, and it was an apparent fulfillment of their motivating hearts.

The most difficult phase of their work in Quitman was locating a pastor once the church was thriving with prosperity. That endeavor was complicated twofold. First, a preacher would be needed who understood and enjoyed the rural lifestyle of the South. The other reason, not secretly spoken, was the congregation's unanimous declaration of their desire to keep Calvin and Rosie.

Although they had decided to settle down in an established church where Calvin could retire, they understood the church's need for a younger couple who could be with them for many years. Under a long tenure, churches traditionally showed astonishing growth. Calvin's plan to retire within five to ten years would not be beneficial to a new church.

The couple continued their work until a young seminary graduate and his wife agreed to move to Quitman. The Association had high hopes for a long tenure, for the new pastor had been born and raised a few miles away in Thomasville. The couple drove back and forth from their parents' home in Thomasville for two weeks while Calvin was on the mission trip in South Africa. While packing, Rosie had cleaned and painted the parsonage for its new occupants.

During Calvin's two weeks of missionary work, he caught the flu. One of the team members from Cape Town was a nurse and able to help him stay on his feet with prescribed medication. The long sleepless flights from Cape Town to London and then to Atlanta had been exhausting. He was unlike his wife, who could sleep soundly on commercial air flights. At times, he had seen Rosie fold a pillow in London, tuck it under her head, and fall head first into that river of peace where she now floated; and there she would drift until the plane touched down in Atlanta. Not so for the preacher; he could never sleep during flights.

His plane touched down in Atlanta shortly after midnight. His mission trip had been successful, but the happiest moment was when he saw Rosie. She had driven up from Quitman and was waiting at the gate to greet him. The two of them drove until after daylight to Valdosta, where they picked up the big Penske rental truck and drove the short distance to Quitman. The rest of that Tuesday afternoon was spent loading the truck. It was not an overly exerting or time-consuming task since the church turned out in large numbers to assist. Afterward, the congregation took them out for dinner and presented them with a plaque and a generous gift of cash for their travels.

It took them all day Wednesday to make the drive to Riley, Tennessee. There Calvin planned to spend Thursday and Friday visiting with his parents and resting before his trip westward to their new job in Nevada. His mother had other plans. From early morning until after dark, she orchestrated Calvin and Rosie in several laboring jobs she had planned in anticipation of their visit. They cleaned the garage and the basement on Thursday. Friday was spent painting the kitchen and dining room. The two of them were not only relieved, but elated, when the time of their departure for Copper Town arrived Saturday morning.

After four days of driving, they had arrived in their new home the previous Tuesday night. Wednesday and Thursday had been spent unpacking, rearranging furniture, and returning the moving truck. Friday was busy with meetings, sermon outlines, and the preparation of Sunday School lessons. All day Saturday members of the church dropped in unannounced to welcome the couple to Copper Town. Saturday evening Rosie was invited to choir practice and afterwards volunteered to help a group of women clean the church. Then the first Sunday morning rolled around, and the time for the first service was now at hand.

"Boy!" Calvin said aloud, with no fear of awakening his wife. "That was some service!"

Rosie had played the piano and sang a hymn as a special. What a great performance it had been! She had such a beautiful voice and played the piano flawlessly. Many times over the years while she played, Calvin would cease what he was doing to just sit and enjoy her music. It was her gift of ministry, and she exercised it willingly. The preacher found that her music provided an inner peace for his soul. The church had given her a standing ovation. A reaction the two of them were not accustomed to, yet it seemed sincere, and they had embraced it with gratitude.

The sermon on the other hand was a disaster. Try as he might, the people sat like statues. He had started a series in Philippians in which he hoped to demonstrate the joy of the Christian walk. Later, he showed how joy was manifested by rejoicing, especially during worship which would include singing, praying, testimonies, teaching, and preaching. Through this joy, which was shared by the Apostle Paul, he felt the church at Copper Town would be able to sustain all the suffering and assaults that could come their way. They would do it together through spiritual unity. The ultimate goal was to bring them together as a close family-type congregation committed to supporting one another. But with all his efforts, they remained expressionless.

Occasionally, one would take a bite of a doughnut; then one would sip from a cup of coffee cup while another would sip from their bottled water. Someone even left their seat to retrieve another sausage biscuit from the kitchen. Through it all they showed no sign of responding to the preacher, as they looked on with hollow eyes. When he spoke soft, they watched. If his diction became louder or more intense, their gaze did not change. There was not a nod of approval, yet no hint of disapproval. There was no amen, no sigh, no cough, and no sneeze. Like zombies, they sat through his over-prepared sermon. After two men declined to give the benediction, a brief period of silence fell over the church. He was astonished and could not find the words to continue, or to close, the service.

After what seemed like an eternity to the preacher, one of the women announced, "I'll do it, pastor." Before he could voice approval or disapproval, she closed the first Sunday morning service with prayer. Immediately following her closure of "Amen," the nature of the town's people changed. Like buzzing bees, the members prepared the potluck lunch. Excitement broke out in the church as each person began to explain to Rosie and Calvin what they had brought. The preacher and his wife contributed nothing; for they were unaware this meal was being prepared. The preacher and his wife were told they were not expected to bring food the first day on the job; however, the women asked Rosie what she would like to bring next Sunday. Obviously, potluck was a weekly event.

The smell of fresh coffee joined the odor of the food dishes. Some of the men pushed to the front where they were fed by the women. This was something new to Calvin. Normally, he was accustomed to the men allowing the women to take the lead in the lines or, at least, couples eating together. Before the line had dwindled, one man had returned for seconds and pushed his way to the front stating, "I'm going to make sure I get what we paid for."

God! Calvin had prayed under his voice. What have you got us into?

Lying in the bed, he unfolded his arms and rolled over and kissed the bare shoulder he had earlier rubbed.

"Sleep on, my beloved! Sleep on! God knows you deserve the rest!"

He pulled the sheet back and swung his feet to the soft carpet floor. Within seconds he was soaked by the steamy hot waters of the shower. Thick, foamy lather was rubbed over his skin and through his hair. He slowly altered the hot water to cold as he rinsed. He shivered as the hot water faded away and the cold washed away the last suds through the drain. It was his way of taking a shower: quick, methodically, and with no waste of water. He whispered a prayer of gratitude for the hot water for many a day he showered without it. The preacher was wide awake and alert as he leapt from the shower stall to grab a towel. He dried even more quickly than he showered and bounced back into the bedroom, where he refrained from his usual Tarzan version of "Hallelujah." He then dressed quickly and continued with his morning routine.

From the large chest sitting near the bed, he yanked a lower drawer free from the swollen grip of the old wooden unit. This was the drawer that housed their riding clothes. He would surprise Rosie today with a ride on the Harley. He pulled on the old jeans and bright maroon shirt. Her vest and riding chaps he placed gently at the foot of the bed. From the upper closet shelf, Calvin grabbed their helmets, and he collected his own leather from the drawer. He worked his way to the kitchen. There he deposited his gear on the counter in order to prepare breakfast for his sleeping beauty.

"Thank God for microwaves!" was the statement that escaped from his lips as he placed bacon on the rack and set the timer. This was the way Calvin enjoyed working. He developed a plan of action and then set about to fulfill it. Each quick step, or slide in his socks, was prioritized and carried out with precision. He had to hurry. Although Rosie slept sound as a rock, she never slept late. With his left hand, he opened the refrigerator and pulls out a carton of eggs. The right hand moved to an overhead shelf where he grabbed a mixing bowl. Both hands hurriedly work in unison to break eggs in the bowl and dump the shells into the garbage can. A drawer was opened and silverware was removed and placed on the table.

Onward he labored. His head was bent to the task, and his neck as like iron sinew. Blue eyes beneath bronze brows twinkled as his body moved to literally transform his thoughts into a physiological splendor. Soon the table was set. Hot coffee, eggs, bacon, and toast, along with fresh orange juice and strawberry jam, were placed in the center of the table. Between tasks, he managed to dress and apply sunscreen. A few years ago he had developed sun poisoning and had been plagued by it since. The sunscreen and long sleeves were now needed to protect his pale white skin from the heat of hot summer days. Calvin turned to enter the bedroom to awaken Rosie only to find her standing in the dinning area looking over the table. She stood before him dressed only in her black leather chaps and vest.

"Wow!" he said. "You look great!"

"Thanks."

"Hungry?"

"Starved … in more ways than one!" She said and moved back toward the bedroom.

Calvin realized he would have to warm a breakfast that would grow cold; he had to cool the ambers of a burning fire. He followed her to the bedroom.

"Thanks, Calvin. Thanks for letting me sleep in this morning and thanks for breakfast. I can't remember when it tasted so good."

"You are welcome, babe."

He used the nickname he gave her in high school coined from a song by Sonny and Cher they declared to be theirs.

"Where do you plan to take me on the Harley, Harley?"

"I have no place specific in mind. You'll just have to sit back and move out on the highway with me."

"Okay! Again, thanks for being so nice this morning."

Calvin whispered a, "You're welcome, sweetheart," and kissed his wife on the forehead. Rosie leaned back and pulled her long, dark hair back with both hands in anticipation of another kiss. She was not disappointed. She grasped her coffee mug in both hands, savoring the warmth of the heated ceramic and the touch of his lips.

"You sit here and relax, babe, and I'll load these dishes and clean the table."

"I'll help you, Calvin."

"No, you sit. Today is your day, and by this afternoon, you'll be more prepared to get back into your running."

"We have not determined a course yet."

"That's part of my plans for today, Rosie. Not all, but part of it. Now finish your coffee and get your boots on."

There is a surging noise of a pump gushing water through the chamber of the dishwasher as Calvin and Rosie exited the back door and headed down the steps to the garage. Rosie waited outside with helmets and gloves as Calvin raised the door and entered. He unlocked the ignition of the cycle and slipped the keys into the zipper pocket of his jacket. Flipping the ignition on with his right hand, his right leg moved across the seat. This motion was one he perfected long ago to prevent his boots from scuffing the leather seat. His left hand squeezed the clutch lever before his right foot hit the concrete pad. Calvin touched the starter button with his right thumb, and the fuel-injected engine of his Harley fired instantly; it thundered and sounded much like the helicopter that sat on its pad across the large parking lot. The sound of the engine was near deafening as it echoed in the confines of the metal garage.

After up-shifting to neutral, he swung his foot backward, moving the kickstand up with his left foot. Pushing the bike backward, he straightened his wheels, down shifted to first gear, and rolled outside. Rosie closed the garage door and watched her husband put the kickstand down. He put the bike back in neutral and let it idle, still thundering. After pulling on their helmets, she watched Calvin place his right hand near the motor's head. He would not ride until he felt heat from the shrouds. They both knew the foregoing of this warm-up had resulted in expensive repairs for Harley enthusiasts.

The preacher nodded his head and Rosie handed him his gloves as she too climbed on the bike. Calvin was not one for doubling on a motorcycle, but he loved to ride with his wife. She could mount and dismount without moving the bike, and once on the road, she never wiggled around. Such actions by passengers had been the cause of many a motorcycle crash. In fact, there were times he placed his hand on Rosie's knee just to be sure she was still there.

With Rosie mounted up, Calvin flicked the odometer to zero and eased the bike forward to the curb of Second Street. They both waved back at

Antonio, who had stopped his work in the garden of the Rock to watch them ride away. They were so excited about the day off and the road that was set before them that they did not notice or smell the smoke swirling from the chimney.

The Harley's tires rolled forward reaching out like a cat to claw the asphalt. At Main Street, Calvin turned left and thundered eastward along the street. Echoes from the buildings magnified the sound and drew looks from all those along the street. Some moved to the windows and doors to wave at the preacher and his wife.

At Loop Road, Calvin turned south and began to circle the city. He noticed a small dirt road that turned left from the Loop and headed to the top of the southern mountain range. At the highest peak, he could see a network of antennas. The only other road off of South Loop was a paved driveway to the left leading up to a large chateau and estate nestled in the side of the mountain. Although the dark walnut logs were well maintained, they portrayed the large mansion with an accent of darkness and seclusion. He was told Sunday by one of the congregants that the council chairman lived there, and it was the only house on the mountain. From the upper balconies of his home, it was reported there was a spectacular and breathtaking view of the town. A large security fence, cameras, and guard dogs excluded anyone from the Gionni Estate unless invited. A lot can be said about security fences, the preacher thought. They can protect those within while they protect those without.

The Harley rumbled slowly along Loop Road until it circled to the campground. Here the road, although paved, became a little rougher with cracked asphalt and potholes. The Harley rolled downward through a heavily wooded area which was part of the park. This area was reserved for tent campers and secluded from the pull-through areas of the lower camp. Campsites were evident on both sides.

After traveling through the main section of the park, South Loop Road rejoined Main Street. As they rolled past the main office building, they both noticed Slim standing in the door. The cycle wobbled a little as a result of the cold shiver that ran down the spine of Calvin. Both the preacher and his wife waved to the owner, but neither received a response. Slim rudely turned and walked back to his office.

At Main, Calvin turned left and drove to the intersection of Main and the North Loop. There he turned right and rode to Second Street, where he turned right. As he passed the parsonage, he glanced at his odometer.

"Three miles exactly!" he shouted to Rosie.

Her arms slipped beneath his, and her right hand displayed a thumbs up. She understood. Her course has been mapped out.

This time at Main Street, Calvin turned right on Highway 50 and began the run to Fallon. There they spent several hours looking at new bedroom furniture, which Calvin promised Rosie years ago. Before their return, he treated her to her favorite meal: Chinese.

Chapter 13
WHEN THE WATERS ASSUAGED

Every moving thing that liveth shall be meat for you; even as the green herb have I given you all things. But flesh with the life thereof, which is the blood thereof, shall ye not eat. And surely your blood of your lives will I require; at the hand of every beast will I require it, and at the hand of man; at the hand of every man's brother will I require the life of man.
GENESIS 9:3–6

Reddish, sticky, and damp clay oozes over the black talons of the Nephilim as they walk from the depths of the sea and climb to the high mountaintops. The scraping of steel-like claws on the rocky surface sounds like human nails scratching a chalkboard. The sound is nearly as audible as the low hum of the Nephilim. This day a slight hint of pleasure in their voices can be detected. The clan's leader is one of only three that has not lost the gift of the Raphah; a gift of healing conveyed by his will through the laying on of his heavy-clawed hands. It was given to him at his beginning by the Ancient of Days, known now by the man-creatures as Elohiym.

The clan's leader almost breaks out with the words of their old Song, but he does not, for he reminds himself the Nephilim have lost the privilege of singing it. The song of praise offered up to the Ancient of Days can no longer bring pleasure to him because of their thwarted rebellion. But still, secretly in his darkened and doomed soul, he feels gladness on this day. He emerges from the deep chasms and valleys making up the highways beneath the surface of the sea and breathes deep. For him, the breathing is a fulfillment of appetite. It was not necessary for survival; thus they subsisted for eons in the belly of the deep seas. They were created immortals by the Ancient of Days, but the characteristics of their nature were altered at their defeat in the Garden.

He manages a smile and does not attempt to hide his large and massive form, there is no need. Looking down upon the craft of gopher wood and pitch, he knows the only humans existing upon the face of the earth are inside. The duration of the plight was only months, for those in the wooden craft above and those walking the murky bottoms beneath. To the Nephilim it was no new experience, for they had walked the underwater passages for thousands of years prior to Elohiym restoring order on Erets.

After reaching the tops of the rocky and mud-covered mountains, he squats along with the other Nephilim. Like wolves stalking a hare, they stare down at the massive wooden vessel. Through the verbiage of their hum, they communicate a new plan. Only ten clans remain. Each consists of seven Nephilim for a total of seventy. A small number compared to the tens of thousands that once roamed the earth. Not a large group, yet they nearly destroyed the man-creatures, for only eight of them had entered into the wooden barge.

Elohiym had placed his seal of protection upon them, at least those that were his chosen Maseth. To attempt to break the seal upon the chosen and destroy the Maseth would be certain death for the Nephilim. They were given permission to seduce the Maseth, if possible, by the Old One. If the seduction was successful, the Old One often lifted his seal of protection. At times, the lives of the chosen were given to the Nephilim.

All that were not Maseth were given to the seductive will of the Nephilim. The Nephilim knew the seal would not be present upon humans selected as Maseth until the Old One decided to make it known; thus, care had to be taken by them in dealing with the complicated coexistence of the two human species. The seduction had to be fulfilled before they could reveal their true nature to the humans. If humans chose the ways of the Nephilim after revelation, they would become slaves. If not, they could very well be chosen to carry the Seal of the Maseth. The Nephilim would be revealed to the believing Maseth. A more dangerous and threatening factor would be the calling forth from the Maseth of the Bachar, or Torch Bearer.

The Old One had spoken into existence ten swords to be yielded by the Bachar. Together, the Bachar and the sword had the power to destroy any clan that sought the lives of the Maseth. The swords, called Drows, glowed at times with the brightness of the sun. Other times, they appeared as transparent glass, and at times they looked like burning torches. With no explanation of their constant changing, they could assume the appearance of all three. Only the Bachar could discern the mood and the power of the Drows to which he was betrothed. Each was created separately; yet collectively their power became one for the person, or Nephilim, that possessed them.

The different attributes of the swords of Maseth were never revealed to the Nephilim, and the Old One hid the swords within the earth. He warned the Prince of the Air, Prince Qadar, that if any Nephilim clan broke the order of the new covenant, he would call forth a Bachar from the Maseth. The Bachar would be given the knowledge and understanding to yield the sword of the clan. The Bachar would use the sword for complete destruction of the clan.

At the death of a Nephilim, their bodies turned into a black powdery dust and their souls departed into the Prison of the Dead. There they would remain until the Old One chose to create a new form for their departed souls to dwell. At that time, the fallen ones would be cast into the burning orb for a never-ending life of darkness. Faithful Nephilim, which had passed long ago, would enjoy the co-existence with the faithful man-creatures and dwell once again upon the dry land of Erets.

The leader of this clan proclaimed he would strive for their survival by close observance of the new covenant. He had chosen the name Shachar for him and his followers long ago. It explained their metamorphic change after the failure of their treacherous and traitorous rebellion. The Old One had changed their lustrous golden skin to dark cobalt. Yes, he would use the humans for pleasure and for slaves, but he also understood the power of Elohiym. Man had been given their rules of life in the *Book of the Maseth,* and if they disobeyed, the Shachar would be there to gather them in and reap the pleasure of their fall.

The new covenant was contained in an ancient manuscript for the Nephilim. It was known as the *Book of the Kimriyr.* The leader of the Shachar vowed to follow the *Kimriyr* until the Time of the Final Order.

With the passing of time, man began to repopulate the face of the earth. In those days, there existed no languages, for all men spoke the same tongue. Through deception and seduction, the Nephilim assisted Prince Qadar to gather the people together in one city to begin an approach to the Mount of Elohiym. Qadar reasoned within his heart that this approach would span the first heavens to the third, where he could use the man-creatures to battle and defeat the Old One. The Shachar took a passive role in the plan and watched from the high mountain tops. After some time, the Assembly of the Old One descended upon the tall construction. With a song from his lips, the words entered the minds of men, and like a virus, they could no longer communicate. It was the end of one language and the beginning of many. Unable to communicate, the men left the building and begin to migrate to other areas of Erets. The Nephilim clans followed them.

The leader of the Shachar chose to keep his clan close to Edum, the place where man had been created. As a declared enemy of the Old One, he felt this would provide a strategic military advantage; from here he could better observe the Old One's interactions with his man-creature. It would be an objective of his to learn more about the Maseth and the Sword of the Bachar.

It was not necessary for the clan to abide together to maintain its existence, for their telepathic abilities enabled them to communicate with one another throughout Erets. The leader divided his clan, leaving four members of the Shachar in the area of Edum to report the progress of the Maseth. He and two others migrated to the north where they were able to enslave large numbers of the man-creatures. It appeared that the men were spreading about the surface of Erets, but the Ancient of Days was keeping his Maseth close to Edum.

The Nephilim were driven by a lust that had been forbidden to man under the new covenant. In the original days, the Nephilim were rewarded for their diligent care of Erets, and the life thereof, with a warm drink of blood from the animals. Large animals would swing their gigantic bodies down to the Nephilim enabling them to sink their fangs deep within the animal's neck to suck the warm crimson nectar. They drank their fill. The blood they withdrew was only a small amount considering the proportion of blood content of the enormous creatures. Afterwards, with the devotion and love they shared for these beautiful animals, the Nephilim would rub their hands over the wounds left by their fangs and watch as the flesh healed instantly. It was the gift of Raphah. Such gifts of healing had been lost by all but three Nephilim. Needless to say, most of the Nephilim had no desire to heal their donors. Many times now with smaller animals, they drained them completely of their life fluids leaving the carcasses to rot. They had no need of the blood to survive, for they were immortal. They had evolved with an addiction of blood.

Shachar's leader taught his clan to secretly exist among men by taking small doses from several animals instead of mass feedings. With a steady and ample supply of blood, the Nephilim could walk among men without the overwhelming desire to fall upon their neck and drink the life from their bodies. The Shachar had mastered the art of proper dieting by consuming the blood of animals only. They raised dogs, horses, sheep, and cattle to fulfill their need and to live unknown among men. The new covenant had forbidden the blood of men, but the Nephilim knew why. The blood of men quickened and enhanced their own powers.

With human blood flowing through their veins, their strength soared to incredible levels, their mental abilities were heightened, and their telepathic powers soared. Even the ability of flight was enhanced with prolonged time and velocity. On the other hand, it prevented them from taking the form of man until the effect wore off. This could take weeks or months, and as a result, they hid away in the darkness of night to prevent human exposure. The gray and lighter grays of daylight vision became complete dark, and they could not walk in the light of the sun. Only when darkness was upon the face of the earth was their vision restored.

Alexander constantly reminded the Clan to never reveal themselves to a human who might believe in their existence, and yet reject the ways of the Kimriyr. It could be doom for any Nephilim that did so. To drink the blood of the Maseth would bring forth the Bachar. The Clan would never know the time or place of the Bachar and may live in fear for years before he arrived. One thing was sure: the Bachar would come—with sword in hand. Taking the life of a Maseth resulted in immediate death for a Nephilim unless permission was granted from the Ancient of Days. The leader witnessed a Nephilim from another clan drain the blood from a Maseth. Afterwards he severed the head with his long razor sharp talons and defiantly shook his fist upward to the heavens. The Nephilim was disintegrated into a cloud of black dust and quickly carried away by wind.

Days pass! For an immortal who has existed millions of years, one day is as a thousand years and a thousand years is one day. And with the passing of time, the leader of the clan ventures to the land of Macedonia, a non-Maseth country. With his assistance and supernatural powers, he builds an empire of human slaves. His identity, nonetheless, is discussed with his puppet leaders: Philip of Macedon and his wife Olympias, Princess of Epirus. The Shachar leader grew fond of Olympias and watched the hot-tempered queen lash out often at Philip. The two were not as close as historians would later declare them to be. She bore the king a son whom they named Alexander.

Olympias was beautiful to behold, and the leader decided to take her. The seduction was no difficult task, for she was drawn to his charm and power. Their time spent together in the absence of the king found her to be with child. History would call the child's father Philip, but history again would be in error. The young lad was the hybrid son of a Nephilim Clan leader who would come to know his real father and the way of the Kimriyr. Faithfully he would follow his father for over four hundred years, an average life for a hybrid. He would enjoy the company of many human wives over that span; but as with all hybrids, he would never have offspring of his own.

Olympias later introduced her son, Alexander, to the Nephilim and the ways of the Kimriyr. Young Alexander developed a fondness for the leader of the Shachar and sought his assistance to achieve his ambitions of becoming more powerful than his father. The Shachar leader liked young Alexander and was eager to tame the wild steed, Bucephalus, for him. It was reported that no man could ride this wild beautiful horse, and the kingdom would fall into the hands of any man that could. It only took seconds for the Nephilim leader to drain enough blood from Bucephalus to leave him weak enough for young Alexander to ride. Not only did the young new leader ride the wild horse, he led him around the arena like a puppy. In the presences of the Nephilim, the horse fearfully allowed the young boy to ride him. The Nephilim way was to blend pleasure with business, and the leader of the mighty clan set into motions his plans of power, which would include the young boy Alexander.

When the young Alexander was twelve years old, the clan leader was summoned to Edum by the guardians in his clan. He returned a year later to find the young boy threatening to expose him and his mother if the Nephilim did not immediately take the throne from his father and crown him king. Little did he understand the magnitude of his threat. No one knew the Nephilim had returned except young Alexander; yet, it mattered not. Without hesitation, Alexander separated the young man from his life. As much as he wanted to sink his fangs into the jugular vein of his youthful body and drain him of his blood, he yielded to the ways of the Kimriyr. The body was buried in the hills, and Alexander immediately took the form of the young boy. In no time at all, Olympias discovered the fate of her son and that it was her beloved Nephilim who took his appearance and assumed his position. She embraced the arms and bed of Alexander frequently and soon gave birth to a second Banah, a female. She was given a human name but was known among the Nephilim as LeBazeja. She would later be taken as mate by a Nephilim called Dormin.

As young Alexander the human, the Nephilim leader was required to study under the great human teacher Aristotle. At times, the boredom was unbearable for the Nephilim and he expounded into a realm of knowledge beyond that of Aristotle's. To the Nephilim, it was a game, and he loved it. Yet, he had to exercise patience. After all, time was on his side. His plan did come to fruition, and he was able to share some of his wisdom with Aristotle. History would give honor to the wisdom of Aristotle the Greek. Few knew the wisdom of Aristotle was that of a Nephilim clan leader.

Seven years later, young Alexander the Nephilim chose to become the king of Macedonia. Soon afterwards the people of Thebes revolted on reports of Alexander being killed in a war with barbarian tribes. Alexander returned and stormed the city with his human soldiers. He destroyed the city and every building in it, with the exception of the temples, forbidden by the Kimriyr, and the home of Pindar, the poet. Thirty thousand inhabitants were sold into slavery. This action enabled Alexander to break the human spirit of rebellion and unify the other Greek states.

The Nephilim would go on to conquer Persia with a small army and little funds. For the Nephilim, few were needed and money was no obstacle. Shortly after the conquest of Persia, Dormin joined him for his conquest of Egypt. The Egyptians had welcomed them with open arms because of their intense hatred for the harsh Persian rulers. Onward he went from the Zagros Mountains into Media, and then south to the Arachosia and north to Afghanistan. He entered Bactria and Sogdiana and pushed as far as the Jaxartes River. In Sogdiana, one of his human friends discovered who he was and rejected the way of the Kimriyr. Alexander, in one of his rare moments of rage, killed the man. When Dormin saw that Alexander did not vanish in a cloud of black dust, he drained the man's blood. Alexander parted company with Dormin at Sogdiana. Dormin remained in the darkness of a building claimed by Alexander until he was healed from the curse of human blood. Although the human was obviously non-Maseth, Alexander feared the wrath of Elohiym would bring the Bachar upon his clan. It was always better to force the human slaves to take the life of other humans to avoid retribution from the Ancient of Days.

In early 323 BC, Alexander grew tired of the human role he was playing. To prevent exposure of his historical human exploits, he faked his death on June 13, 323. He and Dormin had laughed at the great plan of his assuming the form of a dead man. He was sealed, they thought, in a gold coffin and taken to Memphis, Egypt. Later his coffin would be taken to Alexandria and placed in a beautiful tomb. The rotting corpse inside was not that of Alexander, the Nephilim, but that of a human replacement. His only son by the wife he had taken wanted no part of the human civilization and chose, rather, to join his father as he moved on across the Middle East. No heir was left. History would never know that Alexander arranged for the four members of the Shachar he had left in Edum to divide his kingdom and reign in his stead. They would argue and fight among themselves until the Greek nation fell.

The Nephilim leader would travel throughout the world and his adventures could fill many books. From that day forth, he would be known among the Nephilim and the Clan Shachar as Alexander.

Chapter 14

A MEETING AT THE OLD COPPER MINE

*He hath stripped me of my glory, and taken the crown from
my head. He hath destroyed me on every side, and I am gone:
and mine hope hath he removed like a tree. He hath also
kindled his wrath against me, and he counteth me unto him
as one of his enemies.*

JOB 19: 9–11

Rosie stretched in the living room in preparation for her first run in Copper
Town. A ritual of warm-up exercises was performed, which had been
practiced for years. She briefly reflected on some of the courses she had run;
some through wet jungles and some across sandy beaches. At times, she ran
across rocky hillsides, and other times, hard sidewalks of the city were her
paths. While floating through the jungles on the Amazon River, she and
her husband had constructed a homemade treadmill and placed it on the
rear of the old house boat. Calvin teased her and said it looked as if they
were on a large river boat and Rosie's running was powering the boat.

She glanced from the living room to the balcony where her husband sat
at the small table. She gave him the thumbs up. She was ready for her run;
he was deep into his morning studies. The wooden table on the balcony
supported his collection of books, pens, and a laptop. A ledger sheet had
been prepared to keep up with Rosie's time and was next to his stopwatch.
He grinned back at her and gave his own thumbs up.

Rosie floated down the steps and walked to the corner of Main and

Second to begin her run. Calvin looked down at his wife in her bright tee and shorts.

"Wow!" he said and whistled softly, looking down at his wife. "At fifty-five, Rosie, you look as good as you did when we were in high school, maybe better!"

"Yeah, I hear you, Harley!"

She bent down with both knees locked and placed her hands flat on the sidewalk with her elbows bent. She bounced up and down a few times, never lifting her hands from the concrete walk. Calvin knew this was her last drill, and at any moment, she would spring forth like a gazelle without notice. He gripped the stopwatch with his thumb ready to hit the timer when she started running. After he logged her start time, he would continue studying while waiting for her return. When she returned to the place she originally stood, he would stop the watch and record her time.

Without ceasing from her bouncing stretch, Rosie turned her head from right to left, checking traffic. The street was clear. She sprung forward like a cat, crossed the street, and was off on her run. As she turned and smiled at her husband, she gave him one more motion with her thumb.

Rosie increased her pace, even though she knew it would take a few weeks to get back in shape. She loved to run to the point of pain and exhaustion. At that level, the fatigue became a joy and sent her into a state of euphoria. Only another runner would understand this combination of joy experienced from physical pain. She felt good and vowed to set a first-day record that would be challenging to beat.

She blew a puff of air from her lungs and quickened the pace along Main Street. She waved at several people in the shops. Their returned waves were mingled with the sound of yelping dogs. She turned south on Loop Road and was no longer visible by her husband.

"What do you think about starting Wednesday night Bible Study?" the preacher asked the small group of members gathered in his church study.

"Well, preacher, most of the members feel attendance will be very low and you should wait until fall."

"Why is that, Philip?" the preacher responded.

"Preacher, if you haven't noticed, the tourist season is upon us. Within two or three weeks, most of the townspeople will be working from daylight to dark. Most of the money made at this time of the year has to be budgeted for the winter months."

"That's okay if only a few can come; it will help us establish a schedule."

"But, preacher, wouldn't it be better to start Wednesday night services when we can get people to attend? That's the only way we can expect growth. You must understand that when winter rolls around, it gets dark earlier. Folks still won't come to church, for most of them are older and they won't drive after dark."

"I agree with my husband, preacher. You will not be able to establish any consistency with a study." Beth joined the discussion. "If you get behind or miss something, pretty soon you just lose interest. Let's wait for a few months and put all our efforts into the Sunday morning service."

Calvin looked at each member of the church leaders sitting around his desk. They all nodded their heads in agreement with Beth ... including Rosie.

"Okay, if that's what you think, I'll go along with it. Would anyone be interested in helping me pass out gospel tracks and church information on the streets Friday or Saturday night?"

It was obvious that Philip was the designated spokesman of the group. He asked, "Have you mentioned this to the council chairman?"

"By council chairman, I assume you mean Alexander Gionni?"

"Yeah."

"Tell me, Philip, what does he have to do with church decisions? Is it against the law, or a city ordinance, to pass out literature on the street?"

"Nah, preacher. There are no ordinances against it, as long as you are not instigating a civil riot or imposing on folks. But Alexander should be made aware of our plans since he is the town council chairman. The interest of our town is his responsibility, and our well-being lies on his shoulders. It's not like he's trying to run the church, but he has kept things peaceful and prosperous around here for a long, long time. He is the one we all look to for advice."

"Okay, I'll run it by him tomorrow morning at our meeting. Just to get his opinion, but Rosie and I will pass out literature and witness on the streets this weekend. Believe me, we know how to be discreet, and we will not offend anyone."

"Great! If there's nothing else we need to discuss, preacher, Beth and I need to leave. We have a lot to do before nightfall."

The others assembled around his desk acknowledged they too had to go.

"I guess that's all I have. We'll see all of you Sunday morning?"

All of them assured the preacher of their attendance as they filed out of the church office.

"Boy, that was the quickest church meeting I can remember conducting," Calvin said to Rosie. "If you are ready, we'll lock up and go home. We should have a few minutes to relax before you start your evening run, eh?"

Rosie smiled and winked at her husband. "Yeah, I'm not running until the sun goes down tonight. It'll be cooler then. There should be plenty of time for an afternoon nap before I run."

Rosie's morning run allowed her to become familiar with the terrain of the course, and she had recorded an impressive time. Her intentions were to run again that night and establish a daily routine along the mountains and streets of the town. With a wink and a nod of his head, the preacher displayed his pleasure with her plans and quickly moved to secure the church building.

"Don't forget you have an eight o'clock meeting in the morning with the young man you met last Friday, and then the 10:00 AM meeting with Mr. Gionni."

"I won't, but you know something, babe?"

"What?" she answered.

"I don't think we should tell anyone about my meeting with the young man. I don't know who he is yet, and he seemed to be very secretive about the meeting. Besides that, I detected a little fear concerning our meeting. Yep, I think this needs to be our secret for the time being."

The alarm clock rang loud in Calvin's ear awakening him to the smell of bacon. Rosie had been up for some time and was preparing a big breakfast just for him. She knew his day was going to be a long one and, besides, she owed him one.

Shuffling his feet, Calvin dawdled into the dining room where he devoured his food like a hungry hyena. After he finished, he rose from the table, took the keys to the Civic from Rosie's hand, and kissed her good-bye.

"Bye, babe. I'll come back and walk up to the casino for the meeting with Gionni."

"Okay, Calvin, and please be careful."

"I will," he declared turning to leave.

He decided earlier not to take the Harley. It would be much too loud and draw attention. Pulling out in the little Honda, he turned right onto

Second Street, waving at Antonio busy in his little garden. At the North Loop, he turned left and drove to the dirt road that turned westward along the foothills of the mountains. About a mile into his journey, he arrived at the old copper mine pit. The pit was nearly a mile long and a half a mile wide. The distance from the rim of the large manmade crater to the surface of the water below was over four hundred feet. The depth of the water was another four hundred feet. Large steep embankments encompassed the crater with only one narrow road winding down to the acid waters of the lake. The road displayed little signs of usage and less of maintenance. An eight-foot chain link fence surrounded the pit and was crowned with razor sharp wire. The fence could be perceived as a modest safety feature, yet it seemed threatening with signs posted every thirty or forty feet. The big yellow signs read: "NO TRESPASSING: VIOLATORS WILL BE PROSECUTED TO THE FULL EXTENT OF THE LAW!"

As he approached the old mine site, Calvin saw the young man standing at the locked entry gates beside a black Chevy Silverado. Calvin's wave of greeting was returned with a slight head nod from the young man; he glanced at his watch. Unknown to the preacher, the young man was more concerned about the conversation that would transpire than he was about the new pastor's punctuality.

"Greetings," Calvin said extending his hand. "I'm Calvin McGarney."

"Hello, pastor, I'm Michael Rogers, Philip and Beth's son. I don't want them to know we've met. In fact, I don't want anyone to know we've talked. You must promise me this will be confidential."

"Michael, a preacher is like a lawyer; the things we discuss will be confidential if that's what you want."

"That's the way I want it, preacher, and that's the way it's got to be."

A long and uneasy pause follows. Michael stared at the preacher, a concerned look etched deep into his facial features. He continued slowly and with a great deal of caution.

"Preacher," Michael began, kicking dust with his foot, "do you believe supernatural beings exist among us today?"

"Yes, of course I believe in the supernatural."

"No, preacher, I know what you religious people talk about, but I don't think you really understand the depths of the question I am asking you."

He stuttered softly, and then asked the question that would change Calvin's life forever. "Do you … eh … believe in things like … vampires?"

Calvin searched the eyes of Michael for signs of an unstable young man who might pull a wooden stake out at any moment and drive it through his heart. He could not help but wonder what in the world he was doing there. The young man's eyes were still and calm, indicating to Calvin he was not in the presence of a mad man. Calvin was torn between laughing aloud and getting back into his car and leaving. Yet, he thought, is it not my job to minister to my flock? This poor soul is obviously deranged, probably beyond my help. He obviously needs professional help.

"Michael, I believe in a lot of things. I can also tell you that there is more I don't know about the spiritual realm than I do know. But to answer honestly, no, I don't believe in vampires."

"You will, preacher, in time … you will. I've called you here to let you in on some of the secrets of Copper Town, but I need your help. Many feel you may be Bachar. Are you, preacher? Are you in possession of a Sword of the Maseth?"

Calvin had no idea what the young man was talking about and again wondered if he might be conversing with a lunatic. "What in the world are you talking about, Michael? What kind of sword are you referring to?"

Michael was still untrusting, but the sigh issuing through his lips was one of surrender. He appeared as if all other options had been weighed in the balance of his unstable mind, and he had no recourse but to trust this new pastor.

"Let me tell you the story, preacher, but now you will know that your life and the life of your wife are in great danger. The two of you will be in more trouble if you talk to anyone about this. You must keep quiet and pretend you don't know."

After a brief pause, which Michael seemed to use as a method to let go of his last reservations in confiding with the preacher, he stressed the words, "You are living in a town that is owned and run by a clan of Nephilim, or what some people call vampires. My father is one of them. I'll ask you now to spare him if you are the Bachar. He is not a violent or sadistic being. Will you promise?"

"Sure," was John Calvin's reply, for he knew he was not going to destroy anyone, especially not some fictitious being like a vampire.

"I am known as a Banah, half human and half Nephilim. How old do you think I am, preacher?"

"You look to be about the same age as the young lady you were with last week. Let me see; I'd say the two of you are about twenty-two."

Out of curiosity, or perhaps it was to distract the young man, Calvin was quick to ask, "What's the young girl's name, Michael? Is she your wife?"

"No, we are not married, yet. She is my fiancée, and her name is Kristin. We have a problem, and that is why I am risking our lives and yours in asking for help. Now listen carefully as I tell you all I know about my dad's clan."

Michael began in the beginning with the origin of the Nephilim and explained all to John Calvin. He explained that after the fall of the Greek Empire by the Romans, his father and the clan spent three or four hundred years around Judea. They witnessed the life of the Old One's son, Iesous. The battle between Iesous and Qadar was subtle to the humans, but the viciousness of Qadar resulted in the death of Iesous. The clan Shachar was present on the day Iesous escaped from the Prison of the Dead. Before he ascended back to the Mount of the Assembly, he left his followers to carry on the battle with Qadar. His followers were known as the Sabeth. Iesous promised to return some day and set all in order. It would be known as the Time of the Final Order. Until he did, the Sabeth would have to carry on the battle.

Iesous revealed only to the Sabeth the locations of the Swords of the Bachar to assist them if the Nephilim broke the covenant and joined in the warfare with Qadar, which they did. Michael explained that some of the swords had been used already in the destruction of Nephilim clans. Qadar convinced most of the Nephilim to help him with his plan to defeat Iesous. They forgot the covenant and left their first state again, only to be destroyed by the Bachar.

Michael explained to Calvin that Qadar does not care who is destroyed in his plan, be it Nephilim, man, or beast. He went on to explain that there were only three clans left in existence. They joined forces to seek one remaining sword and to join it with the nine they have. When the ten are united, they will give unyielding power to the owner.

As he continued to explain the plight of the Nephilim, Calvin was amazed at the parallel of his story with the Bible. Michael often quoted from the Scripture, and his knowledge of Biblical accounts was accurate when he alluded to them.

"Preacher," he broke in, "I am Banah. I cannot have children, but I have inherited some of the characteristics of my father. One of those is longevity of life. I have lived here in Copper Town and in Southern California, where I met Kristin, for nearly ninety years. Our life span is four to five times that of humans. There are other advantages, but the biggest disadvantage is that we are not Maseth. At death, we will dwell in the darkness of doom for eternity."

Calvin listened but was filled with unbelief. He looked around to see if the two of them were truly alone, and then checked to see if he could make a getaway. He was too close to Michael to escape, if he should decide not to let the new pastor leave. He remembered his duty as an under shepherd and offered words which could be encouraging to the distraught man before him.

"I believe all men have a choice as to their eternal destiny, Michael. If you chose to do so, you can escape the doom that is to come. You only have to believe."

"I do believe, preacher. Your Bible says demons believe in God, yet they tremble. They, too, know there is no hope for them. No, I have no choice, preacher. But I need help with Kristin. You see, to marry a Banah will increase the lifespan of the non-Maseth also. Oh, they won't live as long, usually 150 to 200 years, but the aging process and deterioration of the body is slowed. If a non-Maseth woman mates with a Nephilim, her lifespan is usually equal to or greater than a Banah. My mother was thirty-five when she mated with my father, Philip."

Calvin did the math quickly in his head: eighty-eight plus thirty-five. "Are you trying to tell me Beth is over 120 years old?" This time he could not suppress his laughter, and it rang through the morning air.

"Not trying to tell you, but I am telling you. It's a fact, preacher! If the Nephilim find out you are not carrying the seal of the Maseth, they will destroy you. If you are Maseth, and especially the Bachar they have dreaded for years, they will make your life miserable. Part of their torment is to destroy all those around you who are not Maseth, and they will use humans and Banah to attack you personally."

"If what you are telling me is true, Michael, why do you seek harm to your own kind?" Good question, Calvin thought. Now let's see what this lunatic has to say to that one.

"You must remember, I am part human, and there is a part of me that clings to the human way. When I brought Kristin here to Copper Town, I explained the way of the Nephilim to her, and for my sake, she readily embraced the way of the Kimriyr. The Nephilim revealed themselves to her, and she desired to become a Shadow Walker, a woman who marries a Banah or Nephilim. Shadow Walkers experience long lives, extraordinary strength, and heightened sensitivity upon their mating. We have one problem: Kristin has always wanted children, and she knows with me it can never be."

Michael glanced at his watch and rushed on. "I understand you met Slim. He is a dangerous Nephilim. It is a daily task for Alexander to control him, and the clan Shachar walks close to destruction due to his recklessness. Slim despises all humans, and at times, it seems his hatred includes the Nephilim. It appears I am the only Banah he has ever taken a liking to, including his own. We spent years rambling in the mountains looking for the Sword of the Bachar which was reported to be here. We were not the ones who found it, but we were on the right track. Alexander beat us to it.

"Slim taught me to never trust the Nephilim. He caught me gone one day, and with no reservations or shame, he burst into my home and placed the Mark of the Yada on Kristin. That did not please me at all, but we cannot refuse the request of the Nephilim for any possession. That includes our mates. Besides, to object would result in death, but you know something, preacher? Nephilim are not eternal. They can die, and I am ready to fight for the woman I love, no matter the cost."

"How does Kristin feel about this?"

"She has come under the seductive power of Slim and does not think it such a bad offer. She has accepted the Mark of the Yada and is waiting for the Yiqqaha to consummate the pact. She keeps telling me we can raise the Banah as our own."

Calvin was intrigued with Michael's story. Although he was not ready to believe it, he stood in awe with a chain of questions he had to have answered.

"Michael, what is the Yiqqaha?"

"The Yiqqaha is a great feast the Nephilim celebrate every fifty years. It is the time they normally take mates. At that time, most of the Nephilim will consume human blood. The blood is taken through a sacrificial ritual, either from a volunteer or a non-volunteer. The Yiqqaha will go on for ten days. During that time, all women bearing a sign of the Yada will remain with the Nephilim who made the mark to produce a hybrid child. Sometimes the Nephilim will have several women baring his mark that he will use to breed offspring. If he falls in love with a human, he will rarely mark another female and usually lives faithfully with his mate until her death."

"Tell me what is meant by the Mark the Yada."

"Preacher, the Yada is a scar left upon the stomach or breast of a woman that is formed from the spittle of the Nephilim. The scar is small, about a half of a centimeter in diameter. The Nephilim knows those who carry his mark, and he is never far from them until the time of consummation. At the time of the Yiqqaha, all the human servants and wives swear allegiance to the Kimriyr."

Calvin interjected. "They tell me the council chairman makes a lot of decisions here for the betterment of the community. If he is the lead vampire, or Nephilim [skepticism was noted in Calvin's voice], why do you not ask him for help?"

"That's what we were doing last week. But since Kristin accepted the Yada, he says the Kimriyr does not allow for it to be broken unless the Nephilim agrees to the annulment. Slim will not discuss it and threatens to remove my head if I interfere."

"When is the next Yiqqaha?"

"This fall after the Yiqqaha, I can marry Kristin or mate with her, but she is not to be touched until she consummates the pledge with Slim. The thought of that disgusts me; not to mention that Kristin too is having second thoughts. At this point, I am ready to turn against my own kind. Will you help us, preacher?"

"If what you say is true, yes, I will. But tell me Michael, how do you propose we battle these, eh, vampires?"

"I was honestly hoping you were the Bachar and you would tell me. Do you have possession of the sword? Please say yes!"

"I have no idea where such a sword would be located, nor do I have one. So now, young man, or should I say old man, what will we do to prepare for this battle?"

Michael looked at his watch, kicked the dust, and began to walk around the vehicles, examining the sandy desert floor. The action reminded Calvin of his own youthful days in Riley, where he spent hours searching the river banks for deer tracks. Impulsively, he looked down at his own watch and knew the meeting would have to be wrapped up if he was to make his meeting with Gionni.

After a few minutes of a search that seems to reveal nothing, Michael returned to Calvin.

"Preacher, we will have to plan slowly and wisely. I only have time for a few more small details before you must leave to meet with Alexander. To be late or not show up would bring the whole clan down on you with constant surveillance. It is too early in your move here, so they won't suspect you of learning much about their existence; they certainly will be careful about telling you what I have. Preacher, have you ever felt like your brain actually just swirled within your skull? Or, perhaps you had the old feeling of déjà vu? And without a doubt, you've had a dream and it was so lifelike that you were saddened, or relieved, when you woke up. And in that dream, all your senses were alert and active; you felt, you smelled, you saw, you heard, and you spoke. I would guess, preacher, you have experienced them all. Am I right?"

Without a thought Calvin replied, "Yes! What does that have to do with any of this?"

"I'll tell you what it has to do with it. That's the way in which the Nephilim, or fallen ones, seek to seduce you. The senses, preacher, are a part of your soul and remain even when you depart from the body at death. Consider the story in your Bible that involved the rich man in Hell who spoke to Abraham while his body was in the grave. His soul, in Hell, had all senses in tact. The Nephilim are able to read your thoughts, or bring the essences of reality into your soul to tempt you. You must not give in. They know you have the aura, or seal, of the Maseth, and they cannot indwell your soul, but they will try to get you to voluntarily part from the way of the Maseth. You must stay firm through this fight if we are to win."

Michael looked again at his watch, but never stopped his explanation. "Next, the Nephilim can be defeated by mortal man, or another Nephilim, in three ways. If one is strong enough, he can separate his head from his body turning it into dust. The only human that can achieve that is a Bachar; he must do so with one of the ten Swords of Maseth. If a Nephilim drinks human blood, he loses his power to transform to human shape and cannot walk in the sunlight. He is limited to the night and must hide away through the day. This is not permanent, but requires several days or weeks without human blood to recover. It's like a drug addiction to them. The taste of human blood drives them to partake of it, and villages have been destroyed in the past by one Nephilim alone who cannot, or will not, suffer through the withdrawal period. Alexander forbids human blood except during the Yiqqaha. Even then it is well planned in advance and not all Nephilim will partake.

"If you can find the place an infected Nephilim hides away during the day, a green sapling can be driven through the heart. This can be done at night as well, but the Nephilim acquires all his created power at night while in his natural form. To take on human form limits his power. His strength is further weakened if he assumes his natural form in sunlight; thus, he will avoid sunlight."

Calvin looked at his watch and knew he only had moments left. He thought, Wow! I almost believe this young man.

"Yeah, I know time is up, but one more thing, preacher."

Michael handed Calvin three transparent vials filled with green liquid and began his closure.

"Keep these in a safe place. Don't take them in today when you visit Alexander. He will smell them a mile away."

"What is it?"

"It is fresh sap from a young sapling. I withdrew it early this morning before coming to work. Fresh sap is poison to the circulatory system of the Nephilim. It must be injected. You could never get them to drink it; they would smell it mixed with any liquid. But if swallowed, their bodies would simply digest it. You must bypass the digestive system. That's why you will never find one of them working with wood or timbers, especially in the spring when the sap flows. Even when assuming their human form, they have tremendous powers. If fresh sap gets into their blood stream while they are in the human form, they cannot change back until nightfall. They will also have only a portion of their physical strength until they can change back. If you can drive a fresh tapered green spike into the Nephilim's heart, he will die regardless of his form. Then, the head must be severed to prevent the healing by a Raphah. When the head leaves the body, it turns to dust. Does not all this show you that man has crossed the paths of Nephilim and tried to warn others by the stories you have heard concerning vampires? Many of the myths of vampires are true concerning the Nephilim, and many are useless."

"Okay, Michael. I'll take all this you have shared with me into consideration. You can rest assured it will be our secret. I'll not even share it with my wife. But for now, I gotta run."

"Alright, preacher. Be careful and I'll meet you here next week, same time. Slim and Dad always meet with Alexander early on Friday mornings, so we should be undetected. One other thing, preacher: get on the Internet and see what you can find about real giant bodies discovered over the years. You'll be amazed at some of the hybrid skeletons dug up, and yet man denies our existence. Will you do that, preacher?"

Calvin jumped into his Honda. Reaching for the ignition, he responded to Michael through the open window. "Yes, indeed, I will do that, Michael."

As Calvin put the car in reverse, he heard Michael's last words: "Preacher, be careful. Your life and the life of your wife are in danger!"

Chapter 15
KEEP YOUR MOTOR RUNNING

... and the people sat down to eat and to drink, and rose up to play.

EXODUS 32:6

Dust boiled and swirled from beneath the rear bumper of the Honda. It could be traced back to the gate of the mining pit where Calvin left Michael. At times, it swirled in little twisters reminding Calvin of miniature tornadoes. Known as dust devils, they were a common sight in the deserts of Nevada. Calvin sped out onto Loop Road headed east to Second Street. Before turning off, he noticed heavy black smoke swirling from the chimney of the Rock.

"Must have been a large animal killed on the road last night for there to be that much smoke," he said aloud.

Turning down Second he looks for Antonio but saw no sign of the little man. His Honda swerved across the street and came to a skidding stop in the parking area below the parsonage. Calvin was out of the car in a flash and took the steps to the parsonage in sets of threes. Rushing into the apartment, he found his little wife sitting on the sofa watching TV shows she recorded the previous night. Good, clean shows but shows she knew her husband would not like. Calvin rarely watched television; thus, Rosie would tape her favorites and watch them when she was alone. She started to get up to greet the man of the house.

"That's okay, babe!" he said. "You sit still and relax. I have to grab some notes I took for my meeting with Gionni today. I'm prepared for him today."

Calvin moved madly through the kitchen to the storage room and pulled out a large plastic container in which he kept some of his old motorcycle paraphernalia. Yanking out the old wraparound helmet he was given by a teacher in high school, he tucked the vials of sap beneath the Helmet's inner padding. After dropping it back into the bottom of the container, he piled in the other items and shoved the container back to its storage place. Closing the door behind him, he moved back to the kitchen counter and grabbed his notepad, some printed note cards, and his Bible.

"I'm off to see the wizard, babe!" he sang to Rosie. She waved, never breaking her gaze from the new, wall-mounted flat screen plasma television set. Calvin had bought it for her on their first shopping trip to Carson City.

Down the steps he went and began to jog around the corner of the hardware store and up the street to the casino. The outer doors were open today as they were last Friday, and he saw Slim sitting at the table with Alexander. Calvin glanced at his watch. Good, he thought, I have three minutes to spare. He had planned to get there before Slim made his exit and to appear busy looking at the slot machines to avoid a conversation with him. As he focused his vision on one of the machines, his thoughts drifted away. He could have been watching TV with Rosie and noticed no more. From the corner of his eye, he watched as Slim slunk out from the inner room.

"Careful, preacher, the next thing you know, you'll be putting your money in one of those things with the hopes of getting rich!"

There was no time to answer, even though Calvin had no intention of doing so, for Lee was standing at the door motioning him to enter. Calvin watched her hips sway in hypnotic rhythms from left to right. She walked only a few feet in front of him. Her gait seemed to be a little more exaggerated that day than it was the week before. His gaze was more on her clothing than the motion of her hips, and he wondered if this was the everyday work suit she wore or if it was just the Friday attire. He would later learn that it was one of her many working uniforms.

Casting a glance at Dormin, who was still in the never-ending process of polishing the bar, he wished he had not looked as closely at the muscles which motorized Lee's strut. Dormin's look was in part to say, "Caught you looking. Didn't I, preacher?" And in part to say, "Keep your eyes off my woman."

Calvin pulled the chair out and exchanged greetings with Alexander. The glass of bourbon was consumed in one gulp today, and he returned the shot glass to Lee.

"Well, John Calvin, it looks like you have notes, so let's begin, shall we?"

The conversation between the preacher and the council chairman lasted for forty-five minutes. Calvin's plan to smoke the chairman with the topic of the day faded to a debate of survival, and then passed into silence as he listened. The chairman rarely ceased and quoted scripture as if he had the whole book memorized. Calvin had never seen anyone with that much knowledge of the Bible.

Knowing it could appear rude, but unable to help himself, the preacher glanced at this watch. He had become frustrated and somewhat angered at his inability to take part in the one-sided conversation. He was eager for the meeting to end. The digital watch read: 10:45; another fifteen minutes to go! Calvin had no idea he would be rescued by the thunder of Harley Davidson motorcycles riding up Main Street. That sound was not confused with any other and Alexander stopped his lecturing to listen too. They both turned and watched as three Harley Davidson motorcycles circled in a U-turn outside the double doors.

The riders rolled their chopped-out bikes backward to the curb; an area that was plainly marked "No Parking." Before shutting down the engines, all three worked the throttles of their bikes several times, sending the loud sound of gutted-out mufflers into the casino and into Alexander's inner room. After a quick exchange of words, the three dismounted and entered the casino.

With their backs turned, Calvin noticed the patches on the back of their leather jackets. From one of his many studies of Harley Davidson motorcycles, he remembered these men were known as one percenters; or more commonly, they were members of an outlaw motorcycle gang. The first and second riders were full-patched members. The upper rockers above their patches revealed the name of their gang: Red Devils. The lower rockers displayed the location of the gang: California. The last rider, who had to bring up the rear, was known as a prospect. He wore only the lower rocker. He was a slave to the gang and would have to run after them until he was patched in. With what he knew about this particular gang, trouble was brewing.

Alexander watched as they entered the main doors of the casino. Lee was halfway to the meeting room doors to close them as the gang members settled their stares on Alexander and what appeared to them as a bar room. Again, a few words were exchanged by the full patches as they moved to the doors leading into the inner room. They arrived a second after Lee, who was now beginning to close the heavy doors. The leader of the pack pushed hard against the doors Lee was grasping with her hands. Calvin expected to see the doors fly backward and topple Lee, but to his surprise the gang member was rocked backward by Lee's countering shove. Then the first member pushed his shoulder against the left door, another one pushed the right one, and the doors slowly began to open. Calvin did not remember seeing Dormin move to his wife's side. It was as if one second Lee was alone, and then out of nowhere her husband appeared. Dormin's broad shoulders and back were hunched forward, and his elbows flared out like wings. Two massive fists were clinched in front of his body, ready to explode into action as the leader of the gang stepped into the inner room, stopped, and laughed aloud.

"That's some welcome!" satirically squeaked the first rider. "All we want is a little drink of Jack!"

"The bar and grill are outside and around the corner." Dormin motioned with his fist. "This is a private room."

"Well, we like private, and we like this room. We'll just sit over there"—he motioned with his right hand—"at one of those big empty tables, while the chick here gets us a bottle."

"It's okay!" thundered Alexander. "Remember the door, Dormin."

Dormin took Lee by the hand and slowly walked back to the counter. The bikers headed for the front table near Alexander's, and all three took seats at the rear where they could watch the room. The leader was a big burly man, with more muscle than fat; yet his long, dirty, and greasy hair fell about his face and covered much of his eyes. He pulled a large ten-inch bowie knife from the chain around his waist that was acting as a belt and pretended to clean his finger nails, never dropping his stare at Alexander. Without any indication, he suddenly slammed the knife point first into the tabletop and released it. The thrust was so forceful that the knife quivered back and forth for a few moments as if it is trying to free itself. Calvin noticed the nine millimeter Glock pistols tucked into the back of the pants of the leader and the prospect. The other full patch carried a revolver openly and defiantly on his hip. The preacher remembered the gang's rule for guns. They would never pull them out unless they planned to use them. Once they were pulled from the belts, one of three things would happen. First, if you had your own gun and were fast enough, you could take out one or two before they took you out. Secondly, you could beg for mercy. If it was granted, it would probably cost you all your earthy possessions and you would practically be a slave from that point forth. The last option was to prepare to meet your maker. Calvin glanced at Alexander and wondered if he knew any of this.

To his surprise, Alexander was glaring back at the leader with a look that sent shivers down Calvin's spine. The council chairman patted his hands softly and whispered, "Be still and be quiet, preacher. Let me do the talking."

"Philip," he continued, "go next door and bring these men a bottle of JD."

Philip? Calvin wondered. Phillip's not here!

He turned from Alexander to determine the soft rush of movement he heard and found Philip standing beside him with arms folded. Calvin had never seen Philip like this. He seemed to be much taller than the preacher remembered, and his eyes were narrowed like an eagle ready to swoop down on a helpless rabbit. His face was motionless, solid as granite and no signs of laughter.

"Philip!" Alexander repeated which was the last prompt Philip needed. He turned to exit. On his departure, he passed Slim, who was standing at the end of the table, only inches from the gang leader. From his posture, Calvin expected him to launch forward at the gang member at any time. Alexander broke his stare with the biker, leaned backward, and let out an eerie laugh of his own. It was a laugh that wiped the smiles from the faces of the bikers. Looking at Slim, he laughed again. "Stand down, Slim. I'll handle this!"

Slim spit in the direction of Alexander and roared, "I know the patches and what they mean, Alexander! One wears the skull and cross bones, which means he's taken human life. They all have the markings of rape, robbery, and felonies. None of these dogs are Maseth. You know they're free game and permissible by the Kimriyr. I'll tear their throats from their bodies right here in the council room."

Alexander quickly interjected, "Look around, Slim, and be careful what you say. There is one here with the aura of the Maseth. Remember where you are, all things at the proper time and in the proper place. Now, stand down!"

Slim hissed in chorus with Dormin as he moved to the end of the bar closer to the bikers. Philip reentered the inner room pausing only to close the doors behind him. He slid the large brass bolt the size of an automobile drive shaft through brass rings and dropped the massive locking lever downward. Everyone was now locked outside. The gang was locked within. Calvin's hour was up, yet the doors of his departure were no longer open.

Philip walked to the table; slowly and purposefully he sets the fifth of Jack Daniel's down on the table within inches of the big knife. He paused for a minute, as if he was holding the bottle down to prevent it from leaping off the table when he released his grip.

Oh no! Calvin thought again. He's going to reach for the knife!

Calvin wondered if Alexander had thought the same thing, for he boomed, "Philip, stand down!"

Unlike the argumentative nature of Slim, Philip concurred and moved back to Calvin's right shoulder. Glancing to his left, the preacher noticed Lee. Like a guardian, she stood next to his left shoulder, between him and the chairman. Calvin perceived no fear in the eyes of the four men, nor the woman. There was no sign of fear or indecisiveness on their faces, even with the events unfolding before them.

"Barmaid, bring us some glasses!" belched out the man with greasy hair. "It's uncivilized to drink out of the bottle. Besides," he said, turning to look at the other full patch, "no one wants to drink after old sewer-mouthed Springer!"

Springer rocked back and laughed. At this point, the prospect understood he had permission to laugh and joined them. Springer was a shorter version of the leader but still stocky looking. He appeared to be Hispanic with a large black mustache drooping down past the corners of his mouth in long braided strands below his chin. He removed his jacket and laid it gingerly on the table. He revealed a dirty, sleeveless undershirt. This action also allowed him to display the artwork that decorated every visible inch of his flesh. As bikers call it, he was sleeved out—no more room for tattoos.

Alexander was now in charge and carried on with the dialogue. "You have your prospect; let him come and get the glasses."

He motioned to Dormin with his right hand. Dormin walked to the shelf with bottles and glasses and retrieved three shot glasses identical to Alexander's.

"Okay, dude, since the drinks are free, I guess we can do that."

Calvin did not remember any part of the prior conversation in which free drinks had been discussed. He realized this was the way the gang members declared they had no intentions of paying for the bottle that sat before them.

"Prospect!" the leader yelled, even though the biker sat next to him. "Bring us glasses!" They all roared with laughter, and the other full patch planted his large Bowie on the table in front of him.

The prospect slid his chair back laughing and squeaked out, "Right on, Raunchy! Anything you say, man!"

Calvin almost laughed at the name pinned to the leader. Raunchy! How fitting, Springer and Raunchy. They would probably not be able to pick up on the third biker's name since they were normally just called prospect, until they patched in.

Prospect retrieved the glasses, poured them full of JD for Raunchy and Springer and a little for himself. He sat down and joined in with his friends.

"What brings you to Copper Town?" asked Alexander. His tone was not cordial. He was not seeking to make conversation and sounded like a CIA officer who was gathering information that will later be used in a top-secret cohort mission.

While Alexander was now in charge of those standing behind him, Raunchy emerged as the dominant member of the bikers. "We just keep our motors running, man. Pull out on the highway looking for adventure in whatever comes our way!" The gang laughed and slammed down empty glasses. Prospect moved quickly to refill them.

"We just point our bikes into the wind, dude, and let them go. It's really no one's business why we're here and what we're doing." He downed the second shot of whiskey and succumbed to the power of the black label. "Pretty soon, this whole town will rock with the thunder of bikes rolling up and down the streets. We like your little town so well that we have come up to stake out a place for about two or three hundred of our brothers and their friends down in Southern Cal. We're going to party hearty here. Today you get off easy, but in a couple of weeks, you'll have to supply booze for a lot of us. You know, man, I think this room right here might just serve well as our meeting room. What do you think, man?"

"That's certainly in the realm of possibility. Sure, I think we could do that. Are you planning on spending the night in town?"

"Yeah, old man, we are. It's a long hard drive back to Pasadena. We'll hang around town tonight and ride back tomorrow."

"Well then, let me make you a deal. I've got some business going on in here right now, so why don't you move over to the grille and let me treat you to lunch. All you can eat. I'll join you when I'm finished here, and we'll make the arrangements for your group. You know something? We might even make this an annual run. Who knows, in time it could be bigger than Sturgis. And after lunch, I'll just treat each one of you to your own bottle of liquor to spend the afternoon hours with. What do you say to that?"

Raunchy looked at Alexander and then toward Slim. Afterward he scanned the faces of Philip and Lee. When his eyes finally rested on Dormin, Raunchy stuck his tongue out, wobbled it up and down against his upper lip, and let out at yell. "Sure, man! That's cool. We'll meet you over there."

"Prospect," he yelled again as they all get up from the table, "fill 'er up!"

Prospect emptied the bottle by refilling the glasses of Raunchy and Springer. There was none left for him. The knives were freed from the grip of the table and shoved into the sheaths on their hips. It was Slim who walked to the door and opened it wide as they made their departure. His actions were reluctantly performed. It appeared Slim would rather keep them in the council room for some counseling.

Alexander turned to the preacher and said, "I'm sorry you had to witness this, John Calvin."

Calvin's head spun, and he nearly fainted from Alexander's next comment.

"Good day, preacher. Time is up. We have a little work to do here. Next week, just for the fun of it, let's talk about vampires!"

As John Calvin departs the council room, he heard the doors close behind him and the clicking noise of the heavy bolt. The preacher froze in his tracks and listened; the council room filled with laughter from those left behind.

Chapter 16
ROSIE'S RUN

But they that wait upon the Lord shall renew their strength;
they shall mount up with wings as eagles; they shall run, and
not be weary; and they shall walk, and not faint.

ISAIAH 40:31

"Ready, babe?"

Rosie looked up at Calvin on the balcony and gave him the thumbs up.

"Okay, set … GO!"

Rosie heard the click of the stop watch from across the street and saw her husband jot the time on his ledger. She departed with a wave of her hand and rushed eastward on Main Street. Here she could run along the edge of the street watching the oncoming traffic. The sidewalks were beginning to fill up, and she would not be stopped to engage in conversation with those walking up and down the concrete path. Today had been tiring and confusing; her husband had shared with her the encounter with the bikers at Gionni's.

Tonight, she vowed, I'll set a record that will take me some time to break. They had spent so much time together today talking on the balcony that daylight had slipped away. Now, being freed from the captivity of light, the night fearlessly hastened in from its exile. Although she had not planned to run in the dark, Rosie liked the feel of the cool desert air now sweeping into the city. The street lights would illuminate her path sufficiently, with the exception of a short wooded area north of the campgrounds. The desert air was dry with little humidity; here her running clothes would never be soaked with sweat upon her return.

She looked down at her bare arms and legs that she knew would soon be covered with a white, salty grit. Her bright white nylon running shorts and tee barely covered her athletic panties and bra, perfectly acceptable in Quitman. Regardless, Calvin persuaded her to come up with an outfit a little less exposing. She liked the light weight of her clothing. After all, she was not out to draw attention to herself but to enjoy the run. The soft breeze continued oozing in from the southwest, across the desert, and softly caressing her body. Yet, it offered very little relief and failed in its attempts to abolish the heat.

Showing no signs of slowing her pace or stopping, Rosie waved at the people along the streets and in the shops. She noticed for the first time the unusual number of dogs the town people kept as pets. She breathed in deep and released her breath and her thoughts. Come to think of it, I can't remember seeing any cats around here. Maybe I'll be the first to have a kitten, she thought. She resolved to discuss it with John Calvin as soon as she returned.

Rosie crossed the street and increased her pace upon entering the South Loop. As she passed Slim's home, she noticed the tall chain link fence around his small wood-frame home. On the inside of the fence, a couple of German shepherds wagged their tails and effortlessly ran with her to the corner of their enclosure. Being forced to stop, they yelped with voices of displeasure as they could not continue with their new friend. She heard a chorus of dogs throughout the town joining in with the shepherds. The yelping spread along the back alleys and streets. The sounds sprinkled her subconscious mind, but she could not find root with any substances. She was more determined now than before to push her body to the limit. She rushed up the small incline toward the foot of the mountains, remembering the days she, Calvin, and her son ran together. Their son loved to run as much as his mother. John Calvin, on the other hand, did not enjoy it; he preferred to lift weights, box, or spar in the gym. Now none of that was possible, and he promised he would soon join her again on her runs.

Onward she ran, shadowed by the hand of darkness. The dim streetlights of the city faded behind her, and the new moon offered no comfort due to its light being blocked by the thick trees overhanging the road. She passed the entryway of Gionni's home and looked for the ever present Mastiffs. They never barked at her. Sometimes they ran to the security gate and watched; other times they were already there, as if waiting for her. Gionni's large estate was surrounded by a very tall fence on the sides and the rear. The front fence was made of stone standing nearly four feet high and two feet thick. Every thirty or forty feet, the stone ran upward in tall pillars nearly eight feet high, crowned with all four sides angling in and upward to a point. Between the stone pillars were beautiful wrought iron bars spaced close enough to keep intruders out and the Mastiffs in. The bars curved outward at the top just below the pointed pillars and displayed sharp barbed-like ornaments at the tips. It would be a tough task to climb the fence. Security cameras were located along the entire fence, and a monitoring two-way camera was located at the gate for communication with those desiring to enter.

Rosie could see the red eyes of the dogs glaring in the dim lights of the entry. They sat waiting for her. She always greeted the dogs, but they just sat and stared at her with no response. Tonight was no exception when she greeted them.

Although this was the beginning of the darkest section of her run, the road was level and smooth with crushed gravel. At this point she could feel the change in the air lifting from the desert. The wind, softly touching her bare skin, was now cool and especially refreshing as it brushed her lips and spread across her face. Her hair floated backward and shimmered when it met the random piercing of moonlight. Her pace increased again. She ran smoothly, and her breathing was not impaired. There was no bouncing in her stride, and her body moved as a swift streak to the road cutting into the RV park. Her white clothing also reflected the rare infiltration of moonlight like an apparition floating in the air.

She turned down into the wooded area of the campgrounds, a section reserved only for tents. Several little access roads cut to her right and left. Each contained campsites on both sides with picnic tables and water taps. The bathhouses were located at the foot of the small incline that spanned the main campgrounds with the South Loop. Rosie decided she would quicken her pace again and waste no time there, where the overhanging branches grew thicker, and combined with the absence of lighting, it made her footing somewhat treacherous.

She saw the light of a campfire up ahead and off to her right. As she drew near, she turned her head in the direction of the light to catch a quick glimpse of the campsite. There she made out the dark shapes of three motorcycles parked close together. Two men stood near a fire holding cans she could not identify but believed to be alcohol. They laughed as if they knew something she did not. Raising their cans in a toast, they made obscene gestures and let out several loud hoots. She thought it best not to stare and stretched her right leg a little farther than she had at any time that night in an effort to make a quick departure. Her plan to do the same with the left was never fulfilled. Rosie smacked into something solid and wobbled backward; her head swirled, and her vision was blurred.

A tree! she thought. I'm in the middle of the road. How could I have run into a tree?

Grasping for air that didn't come, her head spun and she could not focus on any of the visions that floated before her blurry eyes like a kaleidoscope. Yet, she did not fall. She tried to raise her hands to examine any damage to her face, but they remained at her sides refusing to respond. They seemed pinned to her body. Rosie shook her head several times, and her senses began to return. The fire spinning to her right was gone. She had the sensation of floating backward toward the fire and heard laughter rushing upon her from behind. With the laughter she heard heavy breathing coming closer to her face and felt the breath of someone falling on her lips.

Rosie's vision slowly returned permitting her to see the source of the stench filling her nose. It was a stench mixed with liquor, tobacco, soured food, and vomit. It rushed through her nostrils and flooded her senses. There was another odor she did not recognize, but if she understood the effects of methamphetamine on human teeth, she could have classified it as the rotting teeth of the third biker. Rosie began to understand that she had not run into a tree, but into the fist of Raunchy. His heavy punch into her solar plexus knocked the breath from her. Before she could collapse to the ground, he grabbed her from the front in a bear hug and carried her to the campsite. His tongue was licking her lips, and his nose was rubbing hers roughly.

Rosie's struggles to be free of him were futile. Raunchy licked her throat and chin and planted his open mouth upon her mouth and nose. She gagged. Raising both of her shoes as high as she could, she kicked his shins. Each kick fell hard below his knees and scraped the length of his lower legs. The other two bikers joined Raunchy and grabbed Rosie's upper arms, yet her feet kept up the wild kicking. She looked like a small child in their clutches. Raunchy alternated between laughing with his friends and uttering a variety of profane statements. The wild and drunk gang leader forced another wet and sloppy kiss on Rosie's mouth and pulled back to join his friends in a frenzy of laughter. The slobbery kiss made Rosie sick, for the biker's breath alone was worse than a city dump. She vomited. Afterwards, she decided to change the directions of her kicks.

Raunchy's nose moved close to Rosie's face again as he laughed. Looking deep into her frightened eyes, he seemed astonished that she was not pleased with his romantic advances. Rosie let her head fall slowly back as if inviting his lips to her exposed neck. She heard his never-ending laughter but felt his grip ease while he moved close for another kiss. The preacher's wife snapped her head forcibly downward, and her forehead struck Raunchy's nose. Blood squirted from both of his nostrils as the cartilage separated from the bone beneath. Such damage usually resulted in watered eyes, and this blow was no exception.

"Hold her for me!" Raunchy directed his pals while he wiped his eyes with greasy, dirty hands. His laughter had ceased. The two men tightened their grip. Rosie tried to plan her next move. Her lack of spontaneous reaction would cost her. Raunchy stepped forward with his large right hand squeezed tight into a fist and delivered a second upper cut to Rosie's solar plexus. It was a blow that would have dropped a horse. Rosie slumped forward with every inch of her body throbbing with pain. Her stomach convulsed, and she vomited again. Air had escaped her lungs, and she could not replace it. She heard the men laughing louder than ever and felt Raunchy grabbing her legs with his hands and straightening them out. The pain of the movement was unbearable.

"Hold her arms and legs!" growled Raunchy.

At this time, no one needed to hold her; she could not move. Following the directions of their leader, the two men stepped to the sides of Rosie and grabbed her. With one hand, they grasped her upper thighs and with the other they secured her arms. They lifted her spread eagle from the ground in a near horizontal position.

"Oh, you want to play rough do you?" said Raunchy, coming slowly at Rosie. His big knife was released from the sheath and bouncing teasingly from one hand to other. "Rough, eh? I like rough! Let's just see how rough you like it."

Rosie's breath began to painfully return. At first it was a little gasp of hurting relief. Her lungs could not completely inflate before Raunchy exhaled his foul breath in her face again. Then her gasps were a little slower, and her breathing became a little deeper.

It was Springer's turn to get into the action as he commanded, "Prospect, move up to her head and grab her arms under her armpits."

The prospect did as he was told and locked his hands under Rosie's armpits. Her arms dangled freely, for the men had practiced this ritual to perfection and they knew she would soon struggle no more until they were finished with her. Springer moved close to her right side and let her legs and torso lower to the ground. Now he could assist his friend and watch as Raunchy worked with his knife. He knew he had to follow his leader in this action and patiently would wait his turn.

Raunchy grabbed the bottom of Rosie's tee-shirt with his left thumb, and in one slow and continuous motion, he slid it up to her neck, grabbing the top with his fingers. His actions had captured her bra with the shirt and exposed her breasts. As the other two bikers let out yells of approval, the large Bowie sliced upward through both garments and opened her clothing. With rough hands, Springer and Raunchy pulled the sides apart and aggressively took liberty of fondling her breasts. Her enraged anger suppressed the pain she should have felt from the slit below her chin caused by the mad upward slash of the knife. The blood that issued forth and flowed across her breasts and through the fingers of the bikers did not discourage or distract them. Raunchy stepped back, and with his free hand, he explored other parts of her body; blood flowed downward and across her stomach. Springer moved closer and began wiping the blood from her breast with her slit shirt and bra.

Raunchy knelt down on the ground and pushed Rosie's legs wide apart. He kissed the inner thigh of her right leg and grabbed the crotch of her shorts and panties with his left hand. His right hand followed the big knife. He yanked the garments together away from her body and the big knife sliced upward. In one quick move, he had slit the crotch and the front of her running shorts and panties beneath. Springer yanked them free from her and tossed them on the fire. As before, the blade brought blood. It now flowed from a gash in Rosie's lower stomach, where it mingled with that flowing from her chin. She felt no pain for she was focused completely on the handles of a pistol tucked in the back of Springer's pants. The pistol resembled one that her father owned when she was a child. He taught her to use it once when he was sober. For a split second, her thoughts went back to her childhood.

She had tried to get her mother to leave her dad many times in order to avoid the beatings she received. Her mother truly loved the man and could never do it. Rosie swore never to tell her mother that her own father had touched her several times in places no man should touch a twelve year old. One night the touching went way too far and little Rosie found herself in a position very much like this one tonight. She had, however, grabbed a chunk of wood from the stack near the couch and pounded her dad unconscious with it. Afterwards, she managed to push him off of her and onto the floor. The floor and unconsciousness did not prevent Rosie from delivering several more blows to her father's face and head. She had planned to explain to her mother that her dad had fallen in his usually inebriated condition into the stack of wood. However, it was her father that told the same tale when his wife arrived home from work that night. Disappointment filled Rosie that night as he crawled to an upright position upon his wife's arrival; Rosie had thought him dead. One good thing resulted from it: he walked carefully around Rosie after that day and never touched her or her sisters again.

A year later, Rosie's father had beaten his mother nearly to death one night. Rosie attempted to hit him with another piece of firewood, but that time it did not work. Her father knocked her unconscious with his fist. When she awakened some time later, she found her mother dead on the floor. She had been repeatedly stabbed by her father. After the last stab, he left the long butcher knife in her chest. Rosie had cradled her mother's head in her lap while sitting in a pool of her blood. As she did so, her father just sat on the right side of their old sofa; rocking back and forth with his elbows on his knees and his head in his hands. As she watched him, the same hatred she was feeling now, swelled deep within her soul. She eased her mother's head back onto the floor and softly moved around the sofa to a little table where the family kept their few valuables. A little cigar box on the back of the table held the belongings of her father. One of those was a .38 revolver, which he had used to teach Rosie to shoot.

Rosie looked cautiously back at her father who was still rocking in his drunken stupor. Rosie pulled the revolver out and quietly released the cylinder. She carefully picked up the cartridges one by one and softly dropped them into the openings of the cylinder and eased it closed. There was never a second of hesitancy in her plans. She simply and deliberately walked to the couch, pulled the hammer back on the revolver, and placed it to her father's right temple from behind. The instant the muzzle made contact with his head, she pulled the trigger and the hammer fell with a blast. The sound was a sickening thud, almost identical to someone thumping a large watermelon to see if it was ripe. She tossed the gun on the other side of the sofa and woke her younger sisters, who had slept though the whole ordeal. Rosie walked with them in the early morning hours to Herb's Café where she used a public phone to call the police. Rosie was in shock and the police put the pieces together with their investigation:

Rosie's father had killed his wife with a butcher knife and then committed suicide while his young daughters lay sleeping. Rosie was never asked many questions, nor had she volunteered any. To this day, she never regretted what she did, nor had she any feelings of sorrow or regret.

Looking now at the revolver in the back of Springer's pants, Rosie formulated a plan. The prospect's grip loosened due in part to his inexperience and in part to his heightened arousal. Rosie thought she could make one quick lunge forward and grab the revolver. She would have only inches to spare, and she had to move quickly. If she was successful, she knew there would be no time and no use threatening them with the pistol. They would not be scared and would counter immediately. She would have to use the gun.

Now's the time Rosie, she thought, encouraging herself to move. She knew that there was little time remaining as she watched Raunchy unzip his pants and let them fall to the ground.

She made her move. Swinging her upper body forward and upward, her body was nearly side-by-side with Springer. He smiled in her face at her closeness and grabbed her breast with his right hand. The action turned him slightly toward her. His back was now close to her right hand. She wiggled closer, managed a smile, and pushed her face close to his. He responded and moved closer. It was all Rosie needed to grasp the pistol by the handle and yank it free from his pants. Springer was so wrapped up in the excitement of the moment and the effects of the alcohol and drugs, he did not notice that this woman had his pistol. She began to squeeze the trigger aimed at the left side of Springer's face as the hammer fell with a loud blast and it hit his temple. His blood splattered all over Rosie and the prospect. Springer spun counterclockwise between Rosie and Raunchy and fell to his face. The injury that sent forth blood from his splattered face would never be felt. The biker was dead.

Raunchy saw the woman grab the pistol from Springer's pants and started forward to grab it from her hands, but the pants around his ankles served as leg irons and prevented him from helping his pal. Now he was hopping over his fallen comrade's body like a rabbit and headed for Rosie.

Unlike her father's .38, this revolver was a much bigger caliber. The large magnum kicked so hard that it bounced out of Rosie's hand preventing her from placing the second and third rounds she had planned for the other two men. Raunchy took the last bounce required to bring him within sticking distance of Rosie, and his large fist smashed into her face, knocking her and the prospect to the ground. The prospect fell to the ground in a sitting position and held the unconscious body of Rosie in his lap. He was still stunned by the turn of events and sat there motionless holding the woman.

"Get up and get away from her," Raunchy said to him. "I'm going to kill this crazy, stupid chick, and then I'll have my way with her dead stinking body!"

The prospect wiggled free and let Rosie's body drop to the ground. The back of her head plopped with a thud on the hard ground. Raunchy pulled up his pants and took the large knife out of its sheath. He looked down at a body whose bruised face was now bleeding profusely from the nose and mouth. Raunchy's punch had been so forceful that it split her upper lip to her nose. Blood was still seeping from the cuts produced by his large knife. Her right hand was swelling, and the thumb seemed to be broken from the sharp recoil of the pistol. It didn't matter if she was dead; Raunchy raised the large knife above his head and grasped it with both hands. He would drive it to the hilt into her heart. If she was already dead, he did not care; he would kill her again!

Calvin clicked his stopwatch and returned his wife's wave. His heart soared with love and compassion at the sight of his wife running down the street. Troubling thoughts of the day's events caused his emotions to rage, and he strived to replace his mind's affections with conscious awareness; soon they won out, and the preacher reflected upon them. The episode at Gionni's casino was worrisome, but the meeting with Michael left him exhausted and puzzled. This was all compounded by their late return from a visit with an elderly couple in the church who were both suffering from illnesses which prevented them from attending church. He and Rosie enjoyed the fellowship and found it hard to leave. Their late return had put Rosie running in the dark, but she assured him she would be okay. Yet, he worried!

Sitting down at the table on the balcony, Calvin sipped on a glass of iced tea. His sermon was prepared for Sunday morning, and he vowed that tomorrow he would begin a thorough study of the Nephilim on the Internet. Casting a glance southward over the buildings, he looked for the area he normally saw Rosie cross Main Street.

"No interval times recorded tonight," he mumbles aloud. "It's so dark I can't even see the mountainside."

Only two small orbs of dark amber glowed through the darkness. It was the lights of Gionni's chateau. Calvin looked down at his stopwatch and the ledger and chuckled. She's running a few minutes behind to night, he thought. I'll give her a rough time when she gets back for being so slow.

The preacher stared at the dim street lamp and felt as if his mind was twisting to pull his soul from his body. He wanted to utter something about the ridiculous warning Michael had issued earlier, but any attempt to do so was quickly erased by two large shadows that appeared and vanished in less than a second. They became visible only in the muted light of the street lamp where they seemed transparent as they moved along the side walk toward the RV park. No one else on the sidewalk seemed to notice they passed by. Calvin wished to write it off to imagination, but there was an inward urge to follow; a feeling he often experienced and came to know as a spiritual drawing. When he followed the impulse of this discernment, he had always been prosperous, yet disobedience had led often to disaster. He thought of Rosie, whose path would soon intersect that of his aberration, and his body shook violently and visibly.

With no further hesitation, Calvin decided he would follow his transparent apparitions. He swung over the wooden rail of his veranda by grabbing the corner post. He descended to the ground on the wooden beam like a fireman sliding down a metal pole, rushing to a call. His left foot touched first and anchored the descent, but the right one was already stepping forward to cross the street. Although Calvin did not enjoy running as his wife did, it made him no less capable. He could not cover the distance in the time the two figures he saw did, or thought he saw, but he would be at the RV Park before Rosie would cross the street. Down the sidewalk he raced, stepping left to avoid some and right to avoid others. At one time he split a young couple, and at another time he nearly knocked an old man down. Yet, he did not stop or slow. He looked to the right and left along the streets and down the alleys for the images but did not see them.

Soon he neared the entry to the park and took a shortcut across the watered lawn near the entry. His pace had not slowed as he entered deep into the area along the road. Two large motor homes were parked to his right and a tent trailer to his left. A little man and woman sat at a campfire in front of the tent trailer eating from plates delicately balanced on their laps. The main office was near the center of the park, and the lights were on. Calvin stopped outside, and with a quick glance, he noticed the door was open. Inside three men were gathered in a tight circle engrossed in a heavy discussion. The men did not notice him, and he turned to look up the lane. Rosie would be approaching any minute.

Faintly at the top of the small incline where the lane ended on the loop, Calvin imagined he saw a ghost. It was a tiny white flash; he smiled and relaxed knowing it to be the bright white clothing in which she was running. She would cover the distance in a couple of minutes or so, and he will join her in the run.

There was another campfire burning to his left near the back of the campground. He smiled knowing that even in this awful heat, it seemed no one could camp without igniting a fire. Calvin understood the comfort of an open fire and appreciated it, even on the hottest of nights.

"Come on, babe," he uttered softly and tried to locate his ghost in the dark night. He could not. Loud laughter eerily alerted him to something amiss in the wooded area. Again he strained to see his little wife. The preacher was unaware that now he had been discovered by the three men standing in the office building. Alexander, Philip, and Slim silently wondered at the preacher's presence. The eerie laughter sounded again, and Calvin could see shadows bouncing erratically around the fire. His shoulders shuddered, and his thoughts once more seemed to wrestle in an effort to flee to the campfire and leave his body standing where he is. Calvin ran. He ran faster than ever before and his teeth were gritted in anger and fear. He thought he heard, "Alexander! Help!" but did he? Who would have yelled? Was it him?

It took nearly a minute to reach the campsite. His heart skipped a beat, and he nearly fainted. He saw the bleeding body of Springer lying on the ground, and beyond he could make out the bleeding body of his wife. Her clothes were torn and scarlet, and he knew he could not cover the distance to help her. Raunchy dropped to his knees between Rosie's legs. His large knife was grasped in the palms of both hands as he plunged the knife downward toward Rosie's chest.

"Alexander, help!" He would have no time to wonder the source or reality of what he perceived to be sound. A flash of light pierced his brain like lightening as he fell forward to his face. He was as oblivious of his surrounding as his unconscious wife.

Slim walked down the dark lane from the tent sites headed for the Park Office. His blood boiled with anger, and his form shifted from that of his original creation to that of the human form he had chosen. Try as he might, he could not control it. The three bikers arrived last night and refused to pay for their site. This morning they had desecrated the council chamber, and now intoxicated by liquor Alexander had given them, they refused to quiet their bikes claiming they had to work on them before departing the next morning. The Nephilim wondered how the junked-out cycles even made it to Copper Town and doubted they would ever make the trip back to California. The other campers had complained to him, but they were afraid and did not want the bikers to know they filed such objections.

Walking back into the dimly lit office building, he left the door open, tilted his head slowly backward, and hummed. It is finished, he declared to himself. And before the night is over they will sprawl in their own blood. Alexander wanted to wait, but he disagreed. Sometimes he wondered if the Ancient of Days still had any interest in these dogs called men. Lately, he had encountered very few with the sign of Maseth. With these three, he was willing to take a chance of his own existence by taking their lives and tasting their blood. There was no changing his mind now; he would do so before dawn.

Within seconds of his telepathic message, Alexander and Philip materialized in his office.

"Getting slow in your old age, Alexander?" he growled, moving within inches of his face.

"Age has nothing to do with it, Pavel. I thought we would play this safe and let them leave tomorrow. Was that not the decision of the council?"

"It was not unanimous, Alexander."

"It never is with you, Slim. With all that you have experienced in millions of years, what could possibly happen tonight that would be new to you?"

"He's always been like that." Philip joined in. "Has he ever been any different? Should we expect him to change now?"

It was almost a statement in defense of Slim's decision, but to no avail. Alexander had insisted they abide by the council decision, but Slim could not be persuaded to comply. In the heat of their continuing debate, Slim thrust forward between Alexander and Philip, pointing to something outside. They were both cautious in turning their backs on Slim, but in so doing they observed John Calvin standing outside glaring up into the tent area. He did not know they were aware of his presences. Almost immediately, he took off running into the dark woods and disappeared. The Nephilim listened to the man's thoughts as he yelled to Alexander for help. All three stepped outside to watch him run up the lane. His form in the night air reflected a black shimmer they knew to be of the Maseth. As he veered off the lane and toward the biker's camp, the Nephilim focused on the bright grayness of the flickering fire. They saw the third biker sneak up behind the preacher and smash the back of his head with a large crescent wrench. One biker's blackened form was on the ground and the Nephilim glared at the crimson flow. It was the only remaining color they could discern in their eternal world of black and grays. As the blood flowed from his head, the Nephilim observed the same color flowing from the dark body of Rosie lying on the ground. The third biker had already started downward with his knife to stab the preacher's wife. The tip of his blade was only inches from her body.

Before the knife could descend further, the Nephilim were there. Alexander struck the biker from behind with the tips of his fingers. The large hand of the Nephilim, now completely in his massive original form, stabbed with a spear-handed thrust that entered the center of Raunchy's back and exited above the sternum. His rib cage was ripped in half. Alexander lifted him from the ground and turned him slowly to permit him to view the massive form of a Nephilim. The knife was deliberately and slowly removed from the biker's hands as the Nephilim forced Raunchy to look deep into his glowing eyes.

Raunchy's eyes dropped to the Nephilim's large fangs; his body would have wiggled if not paralyzed by the impaling hand. Raunchy looks down at the long black talons at the end of Alexander's hand and understood what had happened to him. For a second, he knew that this was the man he threatened yesterday in the bar. Perhaps he would have apologized if there had been time. His life faded from him through clouding eyes, and he was no more. The hand of judgment from the Nephilim was his last sight.

Alexander shook Raunchy from his hand, plunged his massive arm into the open fire, and rotated it like a skewer. The human blood bubbled and hissed upon his arm as it burned. The Nephilim had sterilized his arm from the putrid blood of a defiled human. Alexander did not look long at the blood, nor did he let the odor drift into his lungs.

The third biker stared in unbelief. His death would not be as quick or painless. Slim picked him up over his head and threw him like a bag of clothes into a nearby tree. His back struck first, and his body nearly wrapped around the tree. The snapping sound of several bones breaking within his torso was audible. Before his body could slump to the ground, Slim snatched him up by the back of his neck and turned his face to him. The Nephilim's enormous head was nearly three times that of the prospect, but the Nephilim drew his face next to Slim's in such a manner that they were eye to eye. A few seconds passed before Slim slammed the man's back downward over his thigh. The other two Nephilim watched as the man was folded backward. Again, Slim let him dangle across his thigh for a few seconds before grabbing him by the nape of his neck and drawing him up to his face. He appeared as a cat playing with a little mouse.

The prospect was unable to move from paralysis, but his eyes were wide open. The fear in his face was futile as he glared at the large, three-inch incisors protruding from the corners of Slim's mouth. The warning from Alexander was too late; Slim sank his fangs into the neck of the prospect which nearly sliced his head from his body. The Nephilim leaned backward with the biker's body clutched in his hands and his fangs still planted in his neck. A hum burbled within his throat as he fulfilled the vow he uttered only minutes before. He drank deep the blood of this human.

Chapter 17

ENTER THE TEMPLE OF THE NEPHILIM

Yea, they have chosen their own ways, and their soul delighteth in their abominations. I also will choose their delusions, and will bring their fears upon them;

ISAIAH 66:3–4

He struggled to free himself, but discovered he was unable; the yell for his mother to come to his aid was no more effective than his struggles. The blob that held the young lad appeared as a large orb of chewing gum. Any effort to make his body free resulted with long ropy strings of gum yanking him back and burying his body again. It reminded him of the chewing gum that stuck to his shoe last week in the church parking lot; the type which welcomed visitors with open arms into its place of rest, and then readily embraced their soul. The grip of its old nature was most aggressive, and scraping can never rid one completely of the filth it leaves behind.

Like a child helplessly buried in an avalanche, Calvin yelled once more for his mother. Something in his subconscious mind told him this was a dream, but the realness of the blob had awakened fears in the core of his existence. He continued to struggle, more in an effort to awaken than to escape the trap of his dream.

A throbbing pain in his head beat like a drum; the rhythm rippled from the back of his head to his eye sockets. His swollen temples throbbed in perfect harmony with the drums and climaxed with a loud clash of cymbals. The pain was excruciating; nevertheless, it freed him from the grips of the blob. He was unable to move his body or open his eyes. He felt the touch of someone's hand lifting his head slowly off the hard surface he was lying on, and the drums ceased to beat. The hand moved gently to his forehead, gingerly massaging his face and cheeks in soft, circular motions. The cymbals joined in the quietness. Calvin's pain was gone, and there was a new calm in his soul that allowed him to relax as the hand lowered. He struggled to move and open his eye; both were in vain.

There were sounds about the preacher to which he now gave heed. By concentrating on a single sound, regardless of its intensity, Calvin was able to visualize the source and its surrounding. He heard the sound of a fire crackling somewhere in the darkness. Listening intently, each pop and snap brought a spectacular panoramic view into the sky above his face. There, the stars shined with a splendor he had never seen; each star sparkled and glistened uniquely. The display reminded him of a Bible verse: "There is one glory of the sun and one glory of the moon and another glory of the stars, for each star differs from another in glory."

The spectacular and glorious light of each star seemed to rush forward in a presentation to Calvin when he marked it. When he did not focus upon the sounds, he ventured back into the river of peace, and his visions faded. Large transparent beams appeared above him allowing the light of the night to pierce his mind. Calvin realized he was lying in the interior of a glass building rather than on the dirt of the campgrounds.

The preacher heard voices in a language he did not know, a language that had long been dead to the human race. He lent his ear to each sound being uttered and new visions began to appear. By simply listening, he could see what was transpiring on the other side of his closed eyelids. A tall humanlike form draped with a long black satin robe floated from his head to his feet. The robe contained what Calvin thought to be a large, erect collar that extended upward from the creature's shoulders to the top of his head. His long, flowing cape brushed the floor. Baggy sleeves were held together at his waist, extending beyond the interlaced fingers hidden beneath. The robed one moved to join another creature in identical clothing standing near a large altar-like fixture in front of the fireplace. These visions were being superimposed into the starry sky above him. At times, the stars twinkled through his vision as if to remind the preacher they were still there. Calvin surmised the night scenery over his head to be either a spiritual or a four-dimensional hologram. By listening intently, he was able to visualize more details on his two-dimensional screen.

The fire blazed in the night sky, and he recognized the fireplace which sent forth light and warmth. It was the fireplace in the council room. Calvin attempted to recall a word, or a group of words, that could explain his vision, but he found none and simply thought, Wow! He saw that the middle section of the long bar in the back of the inner room was missing. Looking once again at the fireplace, he made the realization that the altar-like platform was the center of the bar. On top, he saw a motionless body wrapped in a crimson satin robe. He watched closely as the robed creature worked intently around the body. The procedure reminded Calvin of a surgeon performing his duties in an operating room. The figure opened the crimson robe of the one on the altar and revealed the naked form of a human. The preacher glared up, or is it down, at the man and was alarmed; it was his face he saw, the face of John Calvin McGarney.

He turned, yet he did not move. He opened his eyes, yet his eyes remained closed. His attempts were accomplished from his ability to focus on sounds. An odor of burning wood penetrated his nostrils. For some reason, he knew the wood to be well dried and seasoned maple. The longer he listened to the burning fire and smelled the odor of the wood, the more clearly he could see. He discovered the altar to be the upper section of the center long bar. It was the same bar top which he saw Dormin polishing. Now, for the first time, he could see the surface. It was solid silver and adorned with golden inlays of intricate carvings. He originally thought the elevated portion of the middle section of the bar was connected to the outer sections. He was mistaken. The upper section of silver and gold, on which he was now lying, was only resting on one long bar.

The two robed figures appeared to lift Calvin's body, yet they never touched it. They floated to the long bar and Calvin's body drifted in midair with them until he was softly placed atop the bar. From the bar, he had a better view of the center altar from which he left. It was resting on a brass stand. Four brass horns extend up and outward beyond the top of the altar. As the robed creatures conversed, three other figures appeared around the altar. Their transparent appearance reminded Calvin of the two ghostlike figures he saw earlier traveling down the street toward the RV camp. One on each end of the rectangular altar kneeled and faced the other; one to the north and one to the south, and on the long side between the altar and the fire was the third. The one behind the altar kneeled and stretched forth his arms to the horns on the rear corners. There his hands were coupled with those of the other two on the brass horns. Along the top of the arms of the glasslike creatures, and running from their wrists to their heads, were thin, fin-fashioned membranes. The fins were erected and flared upward, reminding Calvin of the fins of a large fish. Below the arms were longer and more complex, but similar fins. They appeared as wings, especially those of bats.

Another robed figure moved to the altar and the preacher observed a fourth being standing between him and the massive double doors to the rear. The two kneeling glass figures on each end rose and moved backwards. As their upper bodies appeared to float, their legs extended to the floor. The one in the middle folded his winged arms and moved away from the altar. All three of the crystal creatures moved in unison as one. On Calvin's screen, the flickering red, yellow, and orange colors of the fire shined through them. The fire, as it passed through the creatures, reminded him of light passing through prisms. To the preacher, all the colors of the rainbows circled on the ceiling of the room in multiple sizes of crescent-shaped light.

The crystal figures moved to the side of the fireplace next to the main entry and stood side by side. The preacher miscalculated their size. If not for their hunched backs, they could not have stood erect in the room. Calvin lay as a corpse on the bar. Without moving, he tilted his head back and drank the odors of the room. He smelled damp earth.

The three robed creatures around the altar remained stationary until the crystal figures were at rest along the west wall. There they replaced the positions vacated by the glass figures. Calvin observed a similarity in the nature and size of the robed ones to the crystal ones. The robed ones also spanned the distance from the floor to the ceiling with their stature.

Calvin breathed deep once again and the odor of damp earth faded to that of perfume. It was a familiar one that was mixed with the flesh of a woman he recognized with his intensified senses. It belonged to Rosie. Drinking deeper, he saw the entire council room displayed on the screen in the night's sky. On the opposite side of the long bar lay another figure wrapped in a scarlet robe. The robe was tied together with a red satin sash, exposing nothing but the face of the human inside. Without seeing, Calvin knew it belonged to Rosie. With every ounce of strength he had, he attempted to rise from the counter and go to his beloved wife; still, he was unable to move or to open his eyes. He had to focus on the odors and the sounds to see the face of his dear wife.

The robed creature between him and the double doors moved to Rosie and picked her up. She seemed suspended as he moved toward the altar. It was now that Calvin remembered the tragic events of the campgrounds.

Oh God, he thought. She's dead! Tears of sorrow and pain flowed from his dry eyes.

Approaching the altar opposite the blazing fire, the creature softly and gently laid Rosie's body on the altar with her head to the south. With his senses spinning in a conglomeration of confusion, Calvin concentrated on Rosie's breathing and was gladdened when he heard the sound of her shallow and faint breath. Looking closer, he saw the slight rise and fall of the scarlet robe that embraced his wife. He whispered a prayer of thanksgiving that was not heard within the council room, a room in which his sensory perception had been replaced by any logical explanation.

The black figure behind the altar pushed back the hood covering his face. Like a figure of stone, he stared down at the covered body stretched out before him. Although the creature was in his original created form of Nephilim, Calvin discerned the characteristics of a man he knew as Alexander. Unable to voice any objections or concerns about what was transpiring; he remembered his plea to Alexander for help.

Alexander was Raphah Nephilim. He was a healing guardian; a human had requested his help, and he would comply. He was one of only three remaining Nephilim who had retained the gift of the Raphah. Although an enemy of the Ancient of Days, he had vowed to keep the way of the Kimriyr and not to violate the way of the Maseth. He knew eventually the Ancient of Days would be victorious. But he would lead his clan of Nephilim in such a manner that their destruction would not be made premature by the hands of a Bachar. He had the gift of healing, but that night he had to act quickly, for he could not restore life. Only the son of the Ancient of Days could do that. He could heal, and that night he would heal in the Temple of the Nephilim Clan Shachar according to the Book of Kimriyr.

Alexander's hands moved downward and carefully untied the scarlet rope holding Rosie's gown. He slid his left hand underneath her slender waist, lifting it gently and pulling the rope from under her. He held the rope high in one hand dangling it to the floor. With his left hand, he grasped it in the middle while dropping it with his right. Alternately, he raised one hand and grabbed the doubled rope in the middle then dropped it with the other until he had a small bundle. This coil of crimson cord he handed to the figure on his left. The Nephilim tucked the cord beneath the heavy black rope that secured his own robe. Alexander pushed back the hood from Rosie's face and opened the front of her robe. She wore no clothing. Slowly and cautiously, he lifted her arms and slid the robe from beneath her body. Nothing now separated her body from the silver surface of the altar. This was the altar of the Nephilim which was used only for healing and human sacrifice.

A hum softly generated from the Nephilim throughout the room and was visible on Calvin's screen spreading across the ceiling. Rosie's body was totally exposed, and her robe was folded neatly and placed at her feet. As the Raphah moved to her head, the preacher noticed a large cut that separated her upper lip into two swollen and bloody pieces. The tops of her teeth and gum were visible between the cut. Sadness stabbed at the heart of her husband. Her eyes were closed and swollen with dry blood that also covered her neck and breasts.

Calvin saw the deep cut below her chin and a longer one that crossed her lower stomach. What was once a river of flowing blood was now nearly clotted to her inner thigh. In its place a small trickle of scarlet seeped from the wounds. Calvin thought, If only I had been a few minutes earlier. I should have insisted that you not run tonight! A thousand other "ifs" were proposed by the preacher, but none comforted his aching soul.

Rosie's head was engulfed by the large hands of the Raphah. Alexander was careful that his long, razor-sharp claws never come in contact with her body. Slowly, he rubbed the sides and top of her head. The process would penetrate her skull and heal any damage that might be internal. The palms of his hands made circular motions around her cheeks, forehead and temples. The swollen eyes and bruises along this section of her face disappeared within seconds. His right hand covered her upper lip and nose while maintaining the ceaseless circular patterns. His work was not slowed by the blood as it stained the palms of his hands. Alexander's left hand rubbed Rosie's throat and chin as the chanting of the hum increased in tempo.

When his hands move upon her breasts, Calvin's first thought was to yell his displeasure and to object vehemently, but he saw Rosie's face. It was flawlessly healed. Nor, was there a single scar on her beautiful ebony body. Then he remembered all the pain and suffering he and his wife had gone through since their wedding. Interracial marriage was rarely heard of during the late sixties, especially in the rural settings of upper Cumberland areas in Tennessee. Yet, the trials and tribulations they had endured only strengthened their love for one another. Tears streaked his face as he looked upon the beauty of her shining blackness. He understood that now his love for her was greater than ever before.

Alexander continued the circular rubbing of his healing hands over the smooth scar less body of Calvin's love. The cut along her stomach was healed. Unknown to the preacher, beneath the skin, bruised and broken bones were also mended. Any unseen infections, diseases, or old injuries she may have had were also healed by the hands of the Raphah. Rosie would discover the full extent of the rejuvenation of her body in the days to come.

The circular motions came to a halt, and Alexander pulled his hood over his head, hiding his face as he returned to the right of the altar. The Nephilim to his right replaced Alexander at the back of the altar and removed his hood. Unknown to Calvin, the man referred to as Slim was known among the Nephilim as Pavel Swarkovie. The sight of Slim in his human form was frightening to say the least, but his Nephilim form sent cold chills down the spine of the motionless preacher. His sinister eyes had taken in every inch of Rosie's body during the healing, and now he seemed more obsessed with the beauty of her blackness. The blood covering a good portion of her skin had aided to heighten his obsession.

His index finger swooped down to her left thigh before Alexander could intervene and slid roughly upward across her left breast before resting with her chin in his hand. His finger was covered with her damp blood; he raised it to show the others gathered in the chamber.

"Seems to be a waste of blood," he said stuffing the finger, claw, and all deep into his mouth. "Uhmmmm."

"Remember where you are, Pavel? You are in the Temple of the Shachar, and what you are doing is forbidden until the Yiqqaha. Carry on with your duties as part of the Raphah."

"I've already tasted real blood tonight and a little more won't hurt," Pavel hissed at Alexander and displayed his long incisors. He continued the ritual by tilting his gigantic head backward and intensifying the hum vibrating from his vocal chords. The fireplace began to move outward with the same floating motion Calvin witnessed from the movement of the Nephilim. There was no observed means of its support, and every stick of wood remained in position. The fire continued to burn. No ashes were present. Pavel straightened himself, and his head penetrated the glass roof and pierced the stars above the preacher's face. He spread his legs wide from one corner of the altar to the other. The fire moved between them, passing through his robe and coming to rest underneath the altar. Flames from the fire changed in hue: yellow became purple, orange became blue, and the red turned to green. The cool flames rushed up and over the altar in all directions as the dried blood on Rosie's body began to sizzle.

My God, Calvin thought as he again struggled to move, they are going to burn her alive.

The flames consumed nothing, and the heat Calvin felt earlier turned into a frigid breeze. Rosie's blood hissed and turned into red dust that covered her body. Calvin's light display seemed to pass through glass prisms of the room's ceiling in an effort to conform to the new colors of the fire. Slowly, the fire returned to the fireplace, and its colors changed back. The room was again filled with warmth. Like a puff of gun powder, the red dust popped on Rosie's body and soared into the night sky. It divided again into thousands of small red particles among the stars. There each one exploded again into smaller particles. The smaller particles exploded and those after them. The chain reaction went on until the light of the stars were veiled by the red dust. Calvin's screen faded for a few seconds, or a few hours; or was it days? Regardless of the time, the light of the stars prevailed and pushed forward the glory of their existence allowing Calvin to gaze upon his beautiful Rosie. Her skin was no longer covered with blood. She was naked, but she was black and beautiful, and she has been through the fire of purification.

Without warning, Pavel lowered his head and spit upon Rosie's stomach. He declared with a loud voice, "I declare the Sign of the Yada upon this woman!" Gasps of astonishment mingled with anger issued from the other Nephilim. Calvin sensed something was wrong and futilely tried to move. He could not. Like the splattering pattern of lead beads from a shotgun, her stomach was covered with the spittle of Pavel the Nephilim. The liquid almost immediately began to form into what reminded Calvin of tiny mercury balls. Each small bead began to roll toward the center of her body above her naval, until they all merge into one sphere the size of an apple.

The sphere looked like a molten silver ball and immediately shrank to the size of an aspirin. Like the dried blood, the spittle exploded like thunder and disappeared leaving only a gray silvery cloud. That too faded into the darkness. In its place on Rosie's stomach was a tiny white circular scar.

"What have you done, Pavel?" screamed a Nephilim with the voice of Philip.

Alexander immediately charged in to stand before Slim. "Do you know what you've done? You did not reveal yourself to this human; she has not consented, and her husband has the aura of the Maseth. You could very well have opened the door to our destruction if he is the Bachar."

Slim bared his fangs, and his talons flashed on the tips of his outstretched arms. "Since you have discovered the Sword of the Maseth for our clan, I suggest you protect it. Besides, who cares? I'm tired of living like rats hidden away here in this forsaken desert rathole, and I am sick of the blood of dogs and horses. I detest them. This human may be Maseth, but he has chosen to walk with a human woman who does not have the aura. He will suffer the consequences. Don't worry, I will reveal myself to her before the time of the Yiqqaha."

"And if she rejects you and the way of the Kimriyr?"

"Then I'll take her anyway, and if she resists, I'll drain her of her blood right here on this altar."

"What if she is Maseth and not received the sign yet?"

Slim spit into the fire, and its flames blasted out into all parts of the room. "I'll die, but I'll die happy. I am tired of this cat-and-mouse game. Maybe the Ancient of Days has just given up and doesn't really care about these humans anymore, for none of them seem to seek him or his way of life. Few have even heard of the Maseth or his Book of Light."

Alexander stared at Slim for what seemed an eternity. His mind gathered the information he needed from the lessons and experiences of a lifetime that spanned millions of years, and he came to a decisive conclusion. It was one he has never made, but for the survival of the clan, he would initiate it. He spit upon Rosie's naked body and shouted, "I declare the sign of the Yada upon this human!" His spittle splattered on Rosie's upper body, and the salvia formed identical silver beads, as Pavel's had. They flowed from all directions upward and over her stomach before forming into a large sphere between her breasts. It's diminishing composition was followed again by a thunderous explosion, and flames from the fire engulfed the inner room. Rosie had two scars on her body. She had been branded by two Nephilim with the Mark of the Yada.

Slim moved first and attempted to grab Alexander by his throat. The Clan leader brushed his arms aside as if they were the appendages of a child. He followed with a lightening quick thrust of his hand. It was a move that claimed the life of a biker earlier. Before the strike could pierce the body of the Nephilim, Alexander's hand was caught in midair by one of the crystal beings. With movements as blinding fast as the first, the other two grabbed Slim and Alexander; they are not able to break free, nor could they struggle. The one holding Alexander's arm threw back his head and let out a deafening shrill. He revealed his displeasure by displaying his own glasslike fangs. Alexander and Slim were still.

"Alexander, you have openly declared a feud between us," said Slim.

"I have as much right to claim this woman as any other Nephilim who has not revealed himself to her. Both of us now stand in violation of the Kimriyr. We can both move to seduce this woman before the Yiqqaha. Let me remind you, if she rejects both, we will be enslaved to her. Neither of us can take her life."

"What about her husband?" Slim said, pointing a large talon toward John Calvin.

Alexander looked at the preacher, whom he was beginning to like, and replied, "We must honor their mating. If either of us brings her willing into the ways of the Kimriyr, it will void their union."

Pavel glared at Alexander for a second and growled. "You need to remember the scar on your neck. I almost took your head off once. The next time you won't be so lucky."

Alexander glared back at the crazed Nephilim, and his own eyes flared with enraged flames of anger.

"Slim, remember when your own head was torn nearly in half from my hand, yet I was the only Raphah willing to heal you. The next time, I will not."

Alexander regained his composure and motioned to be released by the crystal creature.

"Philip," he said, as he covered, Rosie's body, "return Rosie to her home. Call Beth and have her assist you. The two of you will stay with her until her husband returns. With this deep healing, she will sleep late. When she awakens, she will remember nothing that has happened tonight. I'll take the preacher to my home until he awakens from the sleep of healing, then I'll lay all my cards on the table. I don't know how much he has heard or what he knows, but I'll find out. I cannot erase his memories for he carries the seal of the Maseth, but there are other ways to deal with him.

He looked at Pavel and asked, "What path do you choose as a result of tasting human blood? Choose now and choose quickly. If you chose to live in darkness and continue to take human blood, depart from the clan now and leave Copper Town."

Slim hesitated before giving his answer to the clan. "I'll stay in the Garden until the curse of human blood passes. When I heal, I will assume my position in the clan."

Chapter 18

TIME WALKER

A man's belly shall be satisfied with the fruit of his mouth; and with the increase of his lips shall he be filled. Death and life are in the power of the tongue: and they that love it shall eat the fruit thereof.

PROVERBS 18:20–21

Onward as a shepherd before his flock, Alexander led the Shachar; across rocky, dangerous mountain passes and downward through gorges laden with wild animals and thieves. Both heeded this caravan traveling along their Middle East road, for it was led by a mighty Nephilim warrior. Those brave enough to mount an attack were destroyed with little effort. Alexander led the clan with their human flocks away from Edum, where they had dwelt for hundreds of years. The clans gathered there to witness a Maseth woman give birth to the Son of the Ancient of Days. The rebels in the land and in the supernatural realm thought this son would be part Maseth and part of the Ancient of Days. They knew not the greatness of their error. This child was not as the Banah. He was complete in both: the Ancient of Days and Maseth.

Prince Qadar had immediately set out to destroy the baby. Although he was unsuccessful, he and his followers tormented the Son of Maseth all his life. Through lies and deceitful testimonies of their human servants, they finally succeeded in slaying the Ancient's son. Little did they know that the Old One had empowered his son with eternal life, and within three days, he would restore that life to his son's body. The Ancient One

155

proclaimed his Son would live forever and never again suffer from human or supernatural hands. Soon after the restoration of life, he called his son back to the city of the High Mountain, promising to send him again at the Time of the Final Order. Then he would reign over Erets and all supernatural dominions.

Alexander kept his clan in and near Edum for years where they tormented the Maseth followers of the Son; but when he saw their numbers growing to such proportions it endangered the existence of Shachar, he moved the clan into the mountainous countries to the north.

Alexander's clan moved through time, managing to stay ahead of the Maseth priests being called out as the chosen of the Ancient of Days. In the north, the clan enslaved large numbers of humans together like sheep. In the twelfth century, Alexander aided a young boy and his mother who were nearly starved to death, and in no time, the clan empowered him as ruler of the Mongolian nations. With the Nephilim support, he became a fearful force to deal with. Some human tales still acknowledge the Nephilim as giving birth to large numbers of Banah in that particular time. A large portion of the human race has genes that can be traced to that nation. Slim placed the Sign of the Yada on thousands. Over time, the aura of the Seal of the Maseth was discovered on foreigners moving into the area. Alexander moved the clan again into the kingdoms of Moldavia, Wallachia, and Transylvania, which would eventually be known as Romania.

From Romania, Pavel and Alexander begin to travel separate paths for hundreds of years. In his uncontrolled thirst for human blood, Pavel empowered a young leader known by Vlad Dracul, III. Under the directions of Pavel, Vlad provided the Nephilim with a constant supply of human blood with no direct violation of the Yiqqaha. Pavel's reign through Vlad was disastrous and challenged by Alexander to prevent historical records revealing the existence of the clan. Alexander called Pavel's hand at a council meeting and a vicious fight broke out. The sharp talons of Pavel barely missed an attempt to decapitate Alexander. The ugly scar was still evident in his Nephilim form, and in any human form he assumed. The clan leader made a counterattack that left Pavel lying on the floor of their temple in a pool of Nephilim blood, his head half severed. With only minutes to live, Alexander chose not to let the ancient Nephilim die. Without hesitation he called for the overseers of Qadar to assist with the healing ritual of the Raphah.

Alexander was unable to rid himself of the scar resulting from their dispute. As a result, he left Pavel with a scar of his own; it would serve as a constant reminder that Alexander defeated him. The clan lost strength after that night, for they chose to divide. Alexander moved his flocks and the other Nephilim, except Dormin and Pavel, eastward across Russia to the Barren Straight. He crossed the frozen seas and slowly worked his way down the Pacific Coast settling in the area now called Copper Town, long before European explorers were seen in the area.

Slim remained in Transylvania, while Dorman and LeBazeja moved into the western Pyrenees country that straddled the border between France and Spain. This was a small territory about one hundred miles long. There they dwelt with another Nephilim clan who had empowered the country's first leader, Banu Quasi around 824 AD. It was known as the Basque kingdom of Navarre. When all other groups on the Iberian Peninsula fell to the Moors, the Basque did not. They lived there with the Nephilim clan before the Indo-European tribes arrived in the second millennium BC. They were never conquered until the Nephilim clan departed eastward to Russia. Dorman and LeBazeja remained obscure in the country, never interfering with politics. He had learned that from Alexander.

After 1,200 years of independence and the departure of the Nephilim, Spanish forces conquered the Basque country. The northern region was ceded to the French, and the Spaniards incorporated the southern portions. After their summons by Alexander in the mid eighteen hundreds, Dormin and LeBazeja migrated to the United States with many of the Basque people following them. Upon their arrival, they immediately set out on foot to cross the country to Copper Town. Upon their arrival, they found that Pavel had arrived a few years earlier via the Barren Straight.

High above Copper Town stood the Nephilim leader of the Clan Shachar. He was erect on the uppermost balcony of his mountain chalet. He leaned out over the rails to breathe in the odors of the campgrounds below him. Although all signs of anyone having camped there had been completely removed, along with the fire, he smelled the former existence of the bikers. The odor was subdued by another that overpowered it and stabbed into his ancient mind. It rushed forth like a smoke signal waving farewell; Antonio had started his work. For the little gardener, the night would be long, but tomorrow his garden would flourish with a new supply of nourishment.

Drifting on the currents of the night were the smells of the arsenic and acid waters of the old copper mine intermingling with a fresh supply of paint, oil, gasoline, and battery acid. Michael would also spend long hours working tonight. It would be only days before the acid pool of the mining crater would destroy any remains of the motorcycles.

Many years had passed since the council chairman enjoyed the company of a human woman; he longed for that companionship. Not the company of a slave or one who desired the benefits of mating with him, but one who simply enjoyed his company and the pleasure they both gave to each other. There was a sweet essence of shining blackness drifting among the others tonight; be she Maseth or non-Maseth, he could not determine. But he had placed the mark of the Yada upon her and knew he would be hard-pressed to seduce her. His mark had rekindled the fire between him and his Nephilim nemesis Slim. He would walk from this day with all his Nephilim senses alerted, for Slim was dangerous.

The husband of the woman he desired lay sleeping on a sofa deep within the interior of his home. Upon his awakening, his original form and the way of the Nephilim would be revealed. This one bore the seal of the Maseth. Thus, he had to continue with caution as he proceeded along the path he had chosen to follow.

Alexander tilted his head backward to the overcast sky and sung the words to the evening song; words he had not sung in thousands of year. His heart was heavy, and he let the words slip into the darkness. He cried Nephilim tears into the blackness of the night. His voice rose above the clouds and reached into the starry night.

"Oh, Ancient of Days, will you hear my plea tonight? How long has it been since I have heard your voice and gazed upon the splendor of your beauty? Will I ever see your face again? I know that I have chosen to follow the ways of your enemies and rebelled against you, and I await my eternal judgment with no complaint; for can the created vessel cry out against its maker, why hast thou made me so? In my eternal state of judgment, pain, and sorrow, will you visit and allow me to look upon your magnificent being? Can it be that the song written in your Book of the Maseth concerning the living beasts be a sign of hope for me, a fallen Nephilim?"

In his mind, Alexander recited the words of old: And when he had taken the book, the four beasts and four and twenty elders fell down before the Lamb, having every one of them harps, and golden vials full of odors, which are the prayers of the saints. And they sung a new song, saying, "Thou art worthy to take the book, and to open the seals thereof: for thou wast slain, and hast redeemed us to God by thou blood out of every kindred, and tongue, and people, and nation: And hast made us unto our God kings and priests: and we shall reign on the earth."

"Is it only the faithful living beasts that will declare with the Maseth that you have redeemed us?" he asked. "Or can there be forgiveness for Nephilim that have sinned also? Redeemed, oh Ancient of Days! What magnificent beauty is to be found in the meaning of those words? To receive a new body to dwell in at the Time of the Final Order that will never be subject to failure again is beyond my comprehension. Although it sounds impossible with Man and Nephilim, I know with you, oh Ancient One, all things are possible."

Alexander looked down at the little town and knew it was symbolic of the world about him. Men were following the wisdom and intellect of this world. They had no inclination of the existence of a living God; most did not care. They were only humans following the whims of their fleshly desires, full of deceit and lies. They chose to be brave and strong, making themselves fictitious human champions of their games and charades. They knew not the supernatural forces working in the atmosphere to bring them to their utter defeat.

The council chairman sighed, knowing that a day was coming in which all men, Nephilim, and spiritual beings would bow before the Ancient of Days and proclaim his existence. He considered thoughts he had mused thousands of times: *If only I had chosen to follow the Old One rather than Qadar.*

The Nephilim heard the soft breathing of the Maseth priest in his home. He sensed the priest's efforts to escape the River of Peace and rejoin the land of the living. Spreading his wings wide, the council chairman stepped from his high perch and soared softly through the air. On his descent to the entry level of his three-floored home, he spun slowly in small circles. His actions were similar to a small child spinning in circles until he became so dizzy that he could not stand; yet Alexander's mind was clear. Upon his landing, his dogs rushed in and covered his outstretched hands with wet licks. The priest had awakened and the leader of the Shachar entered his own home to entertain him, face to face.

Chapter 19

INTO THE LAIR OF THE NEPHILIM

The wicked have drawn out the sword, and have bent their bow, to cast down the poor and needy, and to slay such as be of upright conversation. Their sword shall enter into their own heart, and their bows shall be broken.

PSALM 37:14–15

Wrestling on the ladder of his dreams, Calvin found his efforts to rise from the river of peace futile. He could only watch as Philip the Nephilim reached down and swooped up the robe-covered body of his wife. There was no laughter that night in the Nephilim's voice; instead, it was his silence that contributed to the power enveloped by his robe. His silence rung with the quietness of supernatural power; it was the silence of thunder. Philip moved to the back of the inner room carrying Rosie, as if she was a bag of feathers, with Slim trailing on his heels. As they approached the rear of the room, the massive doors were swung open, and they were the first to enter.

Alexander moved to the counter to look down at the eyes of the preacher. Calvin was startled but still unable to move or open his eyes, a state of existence he had maintained throughout the healing ceremony. Through closed eyes, Calvin looked into the dark orbs of the ancient being. The Nephilim was unable to see his eyes, yet he stared intently. The gaze was more of curiosity and inquisitiveness than one of determining Calvin's observation. His attempt to read the preacher's mind was to no avail. It had been sealed by the sign of the Maseth. Nonetheless, he was seeking a faint crevice into the thoughts of the preacher.

With a movement identical to Philip's, Alexander's long arms hoisted the covered body of the preacher and turned to follow the Nephilim trail through the open doors. There was no physical effort displayed by his actions, and the doors closed behind them after their entry. The preacher heard the thud of the heavy doors close behind him, and his eyes focused again upon the ceiling. The crystal figures rushed past, an action he did not see but comprehended by the flickering of light. As they passed from one chamber to another, Calvin noticed the sky above him did not change. To most humans, the living creatures would have passed undetected. Their bodies bent the light from the stars and magnified it into a multicolored display of splendor exploding on Calvin's screen. When he focused upon the sound of the light, he could see them. They were large and took on more of a two-dimensional form than a three-dimensional one. He knew them to be cloaked from human eyes, but he was able to see them. At times they seemed to have no depth, yet they turned and moved in all direction. The various angles of their movements were different; they seemed to turn within the confines of their crystal shape. Any light in their presence was quickly converted into sparkling geometric patterns. The colors became alive with sounds of wind chimes, and its splendor was one in which no man could replicate. With the bending of light and the cloaking of their bodies, their forms moved as heat waves from the desert. Calvin knew it was these creatures he had followed to the campground last evening.

Up a long, curving staircase the entourage moved. Looking forward, Calvin saw the massive steps before him. Looking back, he saw a stony path with short walls on both sides. All was being made known to him through his visionary senses, as they were displayed on the night's sky. The stony path ended at a giant entry constructed from the same quarry as the rocks lining the steps and the walled railings. High above the path it rose and peaked in an arch. A long, slender pinnacle stood atop the arch and spiraled like a spear into the stars. As the Nephilim swept through the entry, Calvin chose to look behind instead of ahead to determine their destination. It occurred to him that for men the visions that lay ahead were the same as those that passed behind. One looking back at his origin saw that which was not seen by the other who chose to look ahead; and the one looking ahead saw that which the other did not when they both came to the end of their journey. For the view of each was no longer significant at death, since from that day forward they would see with eyes of another existence. Thus, he chose to look backward for by looking ahead, he saw the physiological perception of that which was not. Looking back, he saw that which was hidden from human eyes and in its true form: reality. Hanging limply over the outstretched arms of Alexander, Calvin saw what he recognized as beautiful soft ferns growing along the path. Recognizable, he questioned himself. Yes, he thought, but it grows above the heads of the Nephilim.

Other soft and lush vegetation grew densely, intermingled among the ferns. None of which Calvin could identify, for he had never seen their likeness. It became apparent to the preacher that the floral environment he was moving into was not natural. It was a garden in which each plant had been intricately placed among the hand-selected stone structures. It was a Nephilim garden that rendered the memories of a time which had long ago passed away. Rich, fertile soil stimulated Calvin's olfactory nerves, sending pulsating waves of pleasure into the domains of his other senses.

In the center of the garden, the stones were formed into a large dais. In the center, a tall arboretum had been constructed with the same stones. Six tall, slender columns of mortar-free, stacked stones rose up well beyond the giants that had entered within. The same pattern of stones spanned around the hexagon from one pillar to the other, and then rushed forward to support another smaller hexagon over the middle of the garden terrace. Calvin could see no mortar and sensed the rocks clung one to another in order to maintain their existence. On the inside and at the foot of each pillar, a large golden box sat elevated off the ground on four stones, one at each corner. Along each stone pillar and beam grew ivy-like plants. To Calvin, the branches seemed to move with growth and appeared like vipers crawling along the branches of a tree. The vines supported leaves the size of shovels that waved like fans when the Nephilim neared them. The height and forms of each pillar with their large golden boxes were symmetrical. No difference could be determined upon inspection. Although each golden box was covered with a golden lid, Calvin could smell their contents and recognized their source to be that of the soil. No logical observation could be noted, but the preacher also knew the soil was the life blood of each plant growing inside the garden. From that soil, they drew the never-ending supply of nutrients they needed for survival. Calvin knew, but could not explain, that the green sap flowing within the plants had the ability to heal and nurture the Nephilim. Yet, that same life flow in some way had the power to take the life of the Nephilim.

The Nephilim made short the time of their journey into the garden. They did not slow until they stood in the center of the stone structure.

Alexander leaped atop the center dais with the bundle he carried and spoke to the others.

"Slim, you must once again stay in the garden until the soil of Edum heals you from the curse of human blood. You have no power within the garden until it cleanses you. We will visit with you during your time of isolation and take care of your responsibilities in Copper Town. If you chose to leave, you must do so by the western gate and you cannot return to the clan. You will live in darkness in your natural form and cannot return to walk among the human race or to visit this garden again. Do you understand?"

Slim hissed something and spit toward the ground. The spittle disappeared in midair, for the garden itself would not allow desecration. "I've been in the garden many times, Alexander. I know the ways of the Kimriyr and the Seraph. The three assigned to the Clan by Qadar are present and bear witness to my choice of exile into the soil of Edum."

Alexander did not answer. He leaned his head backward and breathed in the essence of the garden which reminded him of that other time and other place. A soft hum issued forth from his throat. He gravitated slowly upward through the center of the bower in a spiraling motion.

Calvin was reminded of his first ride at a carnival for his head spun, and he became dizzy. The garden disappeared as he was carried in the arms of the Nephilim leader. He was suspended in the night air as the spiral ascent came to a halt. The dim city lights were painted on the glass screen that still lay above him. Alexander had stopped with his eyes set to the south; he remain motionless in his suspension. Calvin saw the beckoning lights of the Nephilim's chalet above the city on the distant mountain. Although it was nearly a mile away, he saw the huge doors open, and in the twinkling of an eye, they were there. Alexander walked through the doors and placed Calvin on a large leather sofa in the great room. There was no time involved in our travel, Calvin observed. One moment I was looking and then I was there, or should I say … here?

Two large Mastiffs followed Gionni into the great room and sat one at each end of the sofa where Calvin lay. They would spend the night by his side. A young woman closed the door behind Alexander and moved to the sofa. There she gently raised the preacher's head with one hand, and with the other, she softly placed a pillow underneath Calvin's head. It was her personal pillow. An enticing smell of perfume flooded the preacher's nostrils and penetrated into the very depths of his soul. Something in him longed to touch the odor and taste the beauty of its owner.

"Thank you, Kara," said Alexander as Calvin slipped into the river of peace.

Unknown and unseen by Calvin, Philip followed through the portal of the garden with Rosie wrapped in her robe. Following his exit from the garden, two shimmering, glasslike Seraph followed. Their exit was not as pronounced as the Nephilim's and could be defined as apparitions. Philip made his short flight and descent to the back staircase of the pastor's apartment, where Beth had arrived and was waiting. She opened the door with a key and watched as her husband transformed from her beloved Nephilim to her beloved husband. The two of them worked gently with the sleeping body of Rosie tucking her into the sheets and blankets of her bed. Beth sat down in a chair, which she had placed beside the bed. She looked up in awe and admiration as her husband bent down and passionately kissed her lips. The kiss stimulated every nerve in her body in ways known only among the Nephilim, and one with whom they chose to love. She knew that time would pass before the coals of passion that swelled within her would be smothered by the embrace of her beloved Philip.

Beth had never received the Mark of the Yada, nor had Philip needed to seduce her. She had fallen in love with him long before he revealed his original form. At that time, she was so deeply in love with this laughing Nephilim that it did not matter to her. She had readily accepted his way and the way of the Kimriyr as her own.

They did not communicate in an audible manner as he turned to leave. Her husband had already interwoven his thoughts into hers, and she knew what had transpired and what was about to transpire. Philip was leaving to take care of cleaning up the campground along with their son Michael. By daylight, there would be no signs or evidence of the gruesome campground attack on one of Copper Town's citizens. In this town, Maseth, non-Maseth, and Nephilim all lived under the guardianship of the council. She would wait here until the council chairman orientated the new pastor in the ways of the town and explained what would be expected from him from this day forward. After all, he had called upon the Nephilim in his hour of need and had been delivered. He was now indebted to Alexander.

The smell of fresh coffee penetrated the den like the tentacles of an octopus. They snared the dreamless sleep of Calvin's unconsciousness dragging him back to a state of awareness. He opened his eyes expecting to see the glasslike supporting beams of his 3-D screen of perception only to find massive wooden beams that supported the roof of Alexander's home. He remembered the room well and sniffed for the perfume. A large walnut grandfather clock displayed five o'clock, and the lack of light shining through the glass windows of the entry united to tell him it was the early morning hours. As he sat up, he was greeted by Alexander who seemed to pass through the walls facing the sofa. The wall reached upward beyond the balcony that overlooked the entry. Two large staircases with massive steps rose to the balcony from the left and the right. The wall passed the balcony until it reached the large beams above the narthex and was made up of large panes of tinted glass, identical to those in the casino. Their smoky tints allowed views from the inside, but those seated on the sofa or standing in the entry could not see what was transpiring within. The glass covered wall was nearly three stories high and fifty feet wide. Alexander was in his human form and, without speaking, sat down in a large recliner near the sofa on which Calvin was now sitting.

The source of the aroma of coffee was revealed as Kara entered with a silver tray. The tray supported matching silver cups, an urn with hot vapor escaping the spout, silver cream, sugar containers, and silverware. Kara wore clothing that Calvin felt could be that of a maid. Any impressions of her servitude or slavery were eradicated by a genuine smile that covered her face. She placed the tray on the coffee table in front of Calvin and turned to take Alexander's hand.

"Thank you, daughter," he said and kissed her hand gently. The tender loving kiss of her father assured the young woman of his pleasure, and she disappeared deep within the walls of their home.

Gionni poured the hot liquid into the cups and peered into the eyes of the preacher.

"It seems that fate has brought us together quicker than I had planned, preacher man. I don't know exactly what you have seen and heard tonight, but I think it's a lot more than you want to admit to. Regardless, I am not going to hold anything back this morning in telling you about us and our little town."

Calvin was careful to hold the silver handle of his coffee cup, for he felt the metal cup heating from the boiling liquid inside. He looked at Alexander, whose hand was wrapped around his hot cup, oblivious of the heat generated by the silver cup. He acknowledged Alexander with a nod of understanding and as an indication he was ready to hear his story.

The Nephilim began, as he should, with the original creation. The early morning hours were consumed with coffee and fresh fruit as Alexander related the history of his clan and their interaction with the Ancient of Days. Calvin sat quietly. Occasionally, an "okay, yeah, I see," or a "really" would be interjected into the conversation. Interjections were not needed to keep him awake, but only to confirm to the Nephilim that he understood … and believed!

"More coffee?" asked Kara, entering the room still wearing her smile.

"No more for me, thank you," was Calvin's reply. He had already interrupted the council chairman twice to use the toilet and felt an irresistible urge for a third one. "I'm wide awake and feel as if I have coffee spewing from my eyes."

Alexander waved to Kara, who picked up all the silver utensils and placed them on the silver tray. Again, as the times before, she slipped away into the depths of the home from which she materialized.

"That brings us up to date. Now, come. Let me show you my sword collection as we discuss where we are to go from here."

Calvin followed Alexander into a large office located behind the glass wall. This office, the preacher thought, is larger than a lot of homes. The ceiling was nearly as high as the main foyer. Although the door they entered was an average size, in the rear was a large set of double doors identical to those in the back of the council room. It was an office decorated in golden oak from top to bottom. Large shelves on one side housed a variety of books, old and new, from the floor to the ceiling. Calvin saw no ladder along the shelves and wondered how one accessed the upper shelves. Oh, his newly awakened conscious realized, the Nephilim need no ladder.

At the back of the office sat a very large, tall workbench of sorts that would require a stool to work on. As Calvin rested his gaze on the bench, he noticed the beautiful scrolled work on the bench and the embossed side paneling. The top was highly polished with a lacquer finish and covered with computers, monitors, and other electronic equipment. A large pad of drafting paper was neatly placed on the table. As the preacher and the Nephilim neared the table, Calvin realized it was actually a large conference table.

On the large oak-paneled wall behind the desk was a large collection of swords. All were mounted with hilts down and blades upward. Some were mounted too high for Calvin to reach. Other old weapons were also mounted, including muskets, crossbows, spears, knives, and shields. Two old, yet well-polished, suits of armor stood on each side of the desk as if they were guardians of the wall. Alexander pointed to some of the weapons explaining the different nomenclature and historical contributions.

"I've been collecting swords, preacher, for thousands of years. Most of these were brought to this country, along with the golden boxes, on horse drawn carts. Sometimes they were moved from one location to another on the backs of our slaves. Sometimes we used the local natives to assist our needs. Moving down along the west coast ..." Alexander paused for a second and looked off into a past that was not so distant for him and laughs aloud. "The Indians that came to know us called us Sasquatch! Can you believe that people are still wandering around these areas looking for us?" He laughed loudly again.

"Preacher, now that you know who we are, you may never leave." Alexander was no longer laughing, and his physical form slipped alternately from human to Nephilim and back again like the shifting tides of the sea.

The shape shifting was not meant to intimidate the preacher; it served as communication and a witness to the belief and unbelief that coursed through Calvin's thoughts like blood being pumped through veins. Calvin resented the statement but appreciated Alexander's straightforwardness. He, too, preferred to get to the point and, as his grandfather would say, "Get to the nitty-gritty."

"I serve a higher being than you, Alexander!"

Alexander's shifting was in the form of the Nephilim, and he removed one of the large swords high on the wall and shifted back to his human form. Placing the point on the floor, he clasped the hilt of the two-handed sword and leaned forward toward Calvin. The double-edged sword stood taller than Alexander, and Calvin estimated its weight to be at least forty-five pounds.

"Amen to that, preacher, but let me assure you that it will be him that will lead you out of this town."

Gripping the sword with both hands, it was now the Nephilim that towered over Calvin. The sword was swung high above the head of the Nephilim and nearly scraped the paneled wood ceiling. Calvin wondered if his race was run and the time of his departure was at hand.

Alexander was aware that Calvin was observing the Nephilim's eyes and let his gaze rest on the preacher's neck as if he had identified the location he would place his sword next. He completed his thought. "If the Ancient of Days does not open a door of escape to you, you will never leave. Believe me; I will do whatever it takes to protect the clan."

The preacher countered with newfound strength. "And I will carry on with the work that God has brought me here to do. This very day I will begin preaching in the streets and passing out gospel tracts to any who might believe."

"Goliath found this sword in Erets and claimed it as his own. He never knew it was one of the ten formed for use by a Bachar. In the hands of a shepherd boy, Goliath, the son of a Nephilim, was beheaded by his own sword. The sword emerged later in the hands of a Bachar, where it was used to completely destroy one of the ten clans of Guardians."

The Nephilim replaced the sword on the wall and took another one down. This one was much smaller, better suited for human hands than those of a Nephilim or Banah.

The sword glistened in the hands of Alexander and appeared as burning liquid metal, a firelike metal that was not consumed. He raised the sword, placing the sharp point to Calvin's throat.

"Remember Rosie, preacher! You called on me to help you last night. Remember your wife, preacher?"

Calvin swallowed the lump in his throat at the mention of his wife's name and nodded that he did recall the events of the last evening.

"You would never have made it in time to help her last night. If not for me, preacher, your wife would be dead. You owe me. Remember??"

A small drip of blood oozed down the preacher's throat and into his shirt. The wound was only superficial; Calvin wondered if Alexander would thrust it through him. In less than a minute, the Nephilim had threatened him twice with two different swords. Alexander stepped back from Calvin, staring down at the sword. Its vibration in his hand was noticeable by the preacher, yet the sound it emitted was heard only by the Nephilim. The firelike blade turned to crystal. Calvin mentally likened it to the composition of the crystal Seraph he saw in the inner room. To his surprise, Alexander dropped the sword on the floor and recoiled like a person just bitten by a viper.

Slowly and cautiously, he lifted the sword up by its blade and extended the handle to Calvin. Not knowing exactly what the chairman wanted from him, he grasped the sword with his left hand and watched as Alexander placed the point at the base of his own throat. Their eyes were locked in a stare, and Alexander spoke to Calvin with a subdued manner. "Your turn, preacher. Can you draw blood? Or perhaps you wish to take my life. Now your time has come. Go ahead, preacher; thrust the blade."

Calvin stood firm and did not allow the tip of the sword to move when Alexander slowly released the blade and opened his arms in an arrogant gesture that welcomed the preacher to pierce him. The blade glowed fiery red with Calvin's desire to end the life of the Nephilim, and then changed to an icy crystal when he realized that this was not the way of a Christian.

Alexander continued. "Listen carefully, preacher. You cannot leave here. You have more to lose than you think. Look around you and appreciate that which you have, for tomorrow it may be lost. Preach the gospel if that is what you want to do. Pass out tracts; get any to help you that you can. But be resolved; you will not leave Copper Town alive."

Calvin dropped the sword to a vertical position. Stepping forward within reach of the chairman, he handed the sword back to Alexander who changed to Nephilim form to overshadow the human with intimidation. Calvin stood his ground as his head tilted backward. This allowed him to maintain his eye contact with the Nephilim, who turned away and replaced the sword on the uppermost part of the wall. It was this sword that stood above all the other weapons, demanding the center of attention. Eight others identical to it were displayed below in a semicircle arching downward, four to a side. Yet, directly below the sword was a vacant spot that would allow a tenth sword to complete a symmetrical display of ten. None of the nine were within reach of human hands.

"Day is breaking, and it's time for you to go home to your wife. She will be awakening any time, and it will be better that you are there instead of Beth. Be nice to Beth; she's just helping out, and besides, she likes you, preacher. Rosie will not remember the events of last night beyond the point of coming home exhausted from her run. It is best you do not discuss any of this with her, for she will not believe you, and it will only confuse her. Protect your beloved wife, preacher. Do you understand?"

Calvin answered, "I understand, but remember, 'Yeah though I walk through the valley of the shadow of death, I will fear no evil.'"

"Well put, preacher. I hope those words are comfort to you when the time comes. Come, Kara is ready to drive you home."

Chapter 20
WALKING IN THE VALLEY OF SHADOWS

Yea, though I walk through the valley of the shadow of death,
I will fear no evil.

PSALM 23

The revving roar of a high performance engine belched somewhere to the rear of Alexander's home. Its roar sent vibrations throughout the mountainside and echoed back to Calvin who stood outside the main entry waiting for his chauffeur. He glanced eastward as the first signs of sunlight glistened on the horizon, and he listened intently as the engine's rumble moved from the rear to his right. He looked in anticipation to see what type of vehicle would soon move into view.

Calvin stood alone, for Alexander had not accompanied him outside the walls of his home. The preacher turned to view the town below him to the north and watched rays of light rush through the streets of Copper Town. They brought with them the warmth of another day. The pain and sorrow of darkness were shoveled up and pushed to the west. It was only on the skirt tails of another day that the darkness would again prevail. Calvin looked at the beautiful stone driveway leading to the main entrance from the road. It circled in front of the main entry; and to his right, it branched off into a smaller drive which disappeared around the corner of the house. He leaned on one of the large beams that were part of the support system for a covering that extended outward from the house. This part of the structure allowed visitors to park underneath for protection from the elements. The stones reminded Calvin of the walkway he traveled last night above the council room in the casino.

Calvin reached down to pet one of the mastiffs Gionni had left with him at the main entry, but the growl rumbling from the throats of both, coupled with their lips pulled back to display their teeth, served as a warning against such action. Calvin pulled his hand back and shoved it deep into his pants pocket.

A squeaky sound caused from neglect of scheduled lubrication rather than the deteriorating rust of age drew Calvin's attention. A decorative iron gate swung open as a result of some unseen electronic device, followed immediately by the source of the sound as it rounded the corner and passed through the gate. It careened rapidly toward the preacher. Black marks appeared on the cobbled stones. They were created along with a symphony of disc breaks as a bright red Ferrari slid to a stop inches from Calvin. The engine revved again, and the exhaust spilling from the headers underneath the car bounced from the stones. The sound was deafening to the preacher. The driver's tinted window zipped down well-fitted, felt line tracks and revealed the blonde hair and blue eyes of Alexander's daughter, Kara.

"Need a ride?" She laughed. The night had been long, but she seemed to be as alert as she was in the early morning hours in which Calvin had met her. Her smile was genuine, and the preacher felt his first impressions of her were correct. He liked this, eh, young, eh, lady.

"Yep, I sure do. I'm not in the mood for walking right now, and I can't say I'd rather fly!"

Kara laughed and flung her head to the right, motioning for Calvin to walk around and get in. Her long blonde hair followed the movement of her head like streamers blowing in the wind.

Calvin walked around and got inside. Before he could close the door, the car extended the black markings on the cobbled stones from the original point of termination. She buzzed around the drive and headed for the larger gates of the main entry.

"Dad hates it when I do that, but he never complains."

"Then why do it?" asked the preacher.

"Because I can, or maybe it's just showing off!"

Calvin laughed. He liked both her honesty and her good humor. He expected the car to accelerate once it was through the gates, so he grabbed the bar over his head with his right hand to prepare himself to hang on. To his surprise, the car slowed as it turned right onto the North Loop. Ever so slowly it eased along.

"I don't want to get my car dusty or scratch it with gravels." She laughed again.

"Don't blame you there; I have a Harley motorcycle that I baby the same way."

"Yeah, I know. I saw you and your wife ride by a few days ago."

"Yes, we did. We were laying out a course for her to run. She loves to run."

"Yep, I guessed that. You should have stayed away from that dark area through the park."

Although Calvin had found himself in a talkative mood with this woman, that particular comment pounded his soul like a jackhammer slamming into a sidewalk marked for demolition. His recoil was not necessary to illustrate his displeasure; the frown on his face remained long after his shoulders relaxed.

"I'm sorry!" she said. "Dad always tells me I should learn to be more diplomatic. I don't mean to be harmful at all. Really, I don't. Things are just black or white with me; no gray areas."

The car made very little noise as it rolled silently along the road, yet the soft crunch of stray gravels could be heard above the softened purr of the engine. As quick as the road widened to clean asphalt, the engine roared once again, and the tires screamed with delight. At the corner of Main, Kara stopped and looked both ways. A couple of cars were traveling eastward through town and joined with the stop sign to hold the Ferrari at bay. When all was clear, Kara pulled out and headed south down Main Street. Her car fishtailed to the right, to the left, and then back to the right again. She sat near motionless except for the finger tips of her right hand, which easily guided the steering wheel in counter movements to correct the spinning. Without a word, she raced down Main. She slowed as she approached the opened doors of the casino, revved the engine, and waved at what Calvin saw as nothing. At Second Street, she turned right and pulled into the parking lot behind the hardware store. None of this was achieved without a flurry of gear shifting and squealing tires. She slid to a stop with the passenger's door near the bottom of the steps to the parsonage, and the engine revved several times in quick repetition. Calvin knew it was a command to exit and opened the door to do so.

"Bye, preacher," she said with a big grin. "I'm truly sorry!"

"Apology accepted. Kara, do you go to church anywhere?"

"You know who I am, preacher; do you think there's much need?"

"Sure, there's always a need … for all of us. Why don't you come and visit with us tomorrow morning?"

Kara laughs. "I may do that, preacher. I don't think it will help, but I don't think it will hurt. I'd really like to have you and your wife up for dinner one night. And maybe you could show me your Harley. I like to ride cycles, too!"

"Well, we can certainly arrange that. Talk to your dad, and I'll talk to Rosie. See you tomorrow morning?"

Kara laughed and the Ferrari squealed backward into Second Street and pulled out for Main with the same sound of hot rubber. Calvin laughed and shook his head as Kara repeated the ritual of squealing tires each time she stopped and pulled out. He laughed out loud and wondered what it would be like to ride with her on Highway 50 once she was outside of the city limits.

A few minutes of pleasurable conversation faded away as he remembered the events of last night. He turned and ascended the steps in leaps of three. He landed on the top deck with a thud and found himself nose to nose with Beth. She knew he was on his way back to the parsonage, and by some method, she had timed her departure perfectly to coincide with him outside the door.

"Rosie is stirring a little and about to wake up. I heard Kara pull out from the Loop and figured she was bringing you home. What do you think of Alexander's daughter, pastor?"

"She sounds like she enjoys life and is very pleasant to be around."

Beth chuckled. "Better be careful, preacher. I think she's got eyes for you."

Calvin found the comment somewhat offensive but had learned to be careful in expressing his displeasure with members of his flock. He watched as Beth waved and skipped down the steps nearly as fast as he had ascended. Before entering his apartment, Calvin saw Philip driving down Second Street from the direction of the church. Throwing his arm through the window of his truck, he waved a greeting to his wife. A loud "hee hee ha ha" could be heard; Philip had completely resumed his human characteristics.

"Gotta go, preacher; see you tomorrow. If you or Rosie need us, just call."

Calvin shouted, "Thanks," and turned and rushed into the parsonage to his wife. Entering the bedroom, he saw his precious companion pushing her arms over her head. Her toes were pointed beneath the sheets as she stretched, and a loud sigh escaped from her lips. Sitting down on the side of their bed, he grasped the sheet with both hands and slipped them down, exposing the naked body of his wife. She did not know the action of her husband was not amorous but an act that allowed him to scrutinize her body.

"What's on your mind, Harley?"

She had mistaken Calvin's observation. The memories of the previous night had been erased, and she did not know her husband was looking for two tiny white scars on her dark skin. His scrutiny revealed that they were still there. The trancelike gaze was perceived by his wife, and she stared down at her bare breast. Although tiny, she saw both. Her right hand moved down across her breasts and her stomach as if to brush away cracker crumbs she gathered from the bed, but her effort was pointless. She brushed them again, while sitting up in the bed to examine them closer. Again, her brushing was in vain; she inquisitively looked at Calvin.

"What in the world are these?" she asked. "They were not there last night."

"No, they weren't, but it's probably nothing to worry about. If they begin to spread or become larger in size, we'll travel over to Carson City to see a doctor."

She affectionately looked at her husband. His words comforted her and rendered the feeling that they were not symptoms of a disease.

"You know what concerns me most, John Calvin?"

"What, babe?" he answered.

"I'm afraid this might really spread, and I'll end up looking like you. Yuck!" she said.

Calvin straddled her on the bed and pinned her arms down. "Now that was uncalled for, babe! Say you're sorry!"

"Never!"

"You stubborn woman! How do you feel today?"

"What do you have in mind, Harley?"

"I'm just concerned, that's all. I don't have anything in mind this morning, maybe later. I'd like to take a walk around town this morning, if you think you'll be okay alone."

"Wow! Turning me down, eh? That's a first for you. Yeah, I'll be okay. I feel like I have been hit by a semi, yet I feel like I have the energy of a sixteen year old. Does that make sense to you, Calvin?"

"It makes a lot of sense to me. I'll tell you what; I'll be gone about an hour or so. You take a shower while I'm gone, and I'll clean up when I get back. We'll have a late breakfast and take a ride on the Harley. How's that?"

"Sounds good to me. Give me a kiss before you go."

The excitement or fear of the ride in Kara's car completely distracted Calvin from noticing the thick gray smoke issuing from the core of the Rock. As he planted one foot down in front of the other on his descent from the parsonage, he wondered how in the world he did not notice it. He patted the pocket on his shirt twice to confirm the contents: one small notepad, a couple of pens, and gospel tracts in both English and Spanish. John Calvin McGarney crossed the street and walked to the old crematory. Today, he vowed, I will insist that Antonio take me on a tour of the old building while it's in operation. Someway, somehow, I'll break the communication barrier.

Antonio was not to be seen outside the building, which Calvin found to be most conducive to his plans. He knew the little Mexican was probably inside, and that's where he wanted him to be when he talked to him.

Walking up to the stone building, Calvin grabbed the large brass handle of the door and twisted it while pulling outward to open it. From counterclockwise to clockwise, the preacher twisted the knob several times while maintaining an outward pull. The knob gave way to his constant turning, and he slipped backward with it in his hand, but the door stood defiant, locked in its secure position. He slipped the knob back on the extruding lever; it would not open. Frustrated, he let go of the handle and rapped loudly on the thick wooden door. No one answered his knock. Again he rapped, much louder and longer in duration. Still no one answered.

The preacher was sure he heard something, or someone, inside and waited for an anticipated reply. There was no answer. He knocked again until his knuckles turned red and were almost bleeding. His loud and aggressive knocking was accompanied by several loud calls.

"Antonio! Hey, Señor Antonio! Are you in there?" There was still no answer, and the preacher had no choice but to leave.

He walked around the building toward the garden and observed the flowers and other plants that had sprouted in the lush soil. The garden reflected Antonio's talents as a gardener. Thick smoke still boiled from the chimney making the preacher wonder if it was safe to have such a raging fire with no one around, especially in this arid, fire-prone desert ecosystem. Shrugging his shoulders, he pulled out his notepad and jotted down some notes. His handwriting was gibberish to anyone but himself; even Rosie could not read his writing.

Giving up on getting a tour of the Rock, he walked along Second Street, past the church, and headed to the North Loop. Once there, he turned left, stopping frequently to look around at the mountains, buildings, tracks leading off the road, and anything else that might appear as out of place. He did not know what he was actually looking for, but he felt he would recognize what he needed to discover when he saw it. Gradually, the clean pages of his notepad were filled with more gibberish. He looked to the south and saw the large mansion that Gionni and Kara called home. A vision of her standing on her balcony with a telescope watching his every move perforated his mind. Would she also record her findings and report them to her father, or did she watch in secret, fueled by the lust and desire of her heart?

As he continued walking along the foothills of the long valley spilling out onto the desert floor, his attention was drawn to shifting shadows of sage brush. The motion of the shadows was generated by the ever-increasing altitude of the sun. The flickering silhouettes on the sandy terrain gave him the feeling that death himself was his companion. If not death, then surely his specter was present watching his every move.

Calvin veered off to his right on the old Foothill Road to follow fresh tire tracks. All imprints in the old dusty road had been swept clean the night before. Not cleaned by human hands, but by the shifting sands of the desert perpetually moved by the winds of the night. Calvin continued to walk, stop, and make notes to his paper until his path was blocked by the chained gate of the old copper mine pit, the place of Michael's employment. Finding the gate locked, Calvin continued walking northward along the high fence. After several minutes of walking along the fence, he found himself on the opposite side of the barred entry. Near him was the butte of rock that stood high above the fence. Upon scaling the rocky sides, he found that from this observation point he was able to see the entire open pit below him. Along the acid-filled lake, he saw a couple of vehicles. Calvin cleared the ground of thorns and stones with the edge of his boot. Crossing his legs, he sat down on the sandy rocks and removed a pair of binoculars from the case on his belt.

By placing his elbows on his knees for support, Calvin was able to form a stable mount for the large binoculars, which he carefully lifted to his eyes. Turning the center knob with his index finger, the activity on the lake came slowly into focus. Michael and Philip were parked in a parking area along a well-maintained road near the bottom of the pit, along with a large loader. The area looked like a small parking lot etched into the side of the pit walls. Separating the parking area from the water below was a ninety-foot-high wall. Calvin watched Michael and Philip as they sat on the bench deep in conversation. Zooming in on full power, Calvin wished he could read lips. Since he could not, he looked about the parking area and found fresh tracks leading from the loader to the edge of the pit. At that position, the hefty bucket of the front loader extended well beyond the edge of the parking area. It was empty, and any load it might have held must have been released into the murky, acidic waters below.

Shifting the glasses back to Philip and Michael, the preacher watched them stand and shake hands. Afterwards, they embraced. Their hugs were accompanied with sharp slaps on the back. Calvin imagined he heard the thud of the pats as he watched them release each other and depart toward their trucks.

"Whoa!" said Calvin out loud. "I've got to get down off of here and hide. They'll see me up here for sure."

He slipped over the back side of the butte and ran to the head of the canyon, where he hid behind a large boulder. The sounds of the trucks speeding up the switchbacks on the pit wall reached Calvin. After they passed, he heard them stop to unlock the entry gate. He listened to the rattling chains of the gate and was buried by a cloud of dust that followed the trucks to the top of the crater walls. The sounds revealed to him that one truck pulled through and stopped; the other raced through and continued along the foothill drive toward the Loop. There was an unusual pause between the rattling of chains to secure the gate and the second truck's departure. Eventually, there was silence in the desert, and the dust settled once again. Calvin felt it was now safe to move, so he scurried to get away from the copper pit.

Halfway up the old road, Calvin recognized Michael's truck parked along the road. He froze in his tracks, for he wanted to go unnoticed in his surveillance. The tall muscular frame of Michael could be seen leaning over the front of his truck's hood with a pair of binoculars squeezed to his eyes. A rifle lay on the hood within arm's reach, and he waved a friendly gesture to Calvin. Returning the wave, he watched Michael turn his glasses toward Copper Town. He then lowered them, turning back to the preacher and motioning him forward.

Calvin's apprehension was put to ease when he heard the friendly tone of Michael's greeting. "Gooood morning, preacher! How are you?"

Calvin watched Michael slip the rifle back into the rack in the rear of the cab.

"I'm okay, Michael. I've been better, that's for sure. What's up with you?"

"Well, preacher, I heard about last night. It's kept me pretty busy, but it looks like we are about to get it all cleaned up. How's Rosie?"

"Rosie's fine, I think. I am just not sure what's going on."

"You know what's going on, preacher, and you know that I was telling you the truth now. Rosie will be okay, but we've got bigger fish to fry now, and not as much time as I thought. Listen, you have to be careful walking along these roads. I'm really surprised Dad did not notice your footprints in the sand. I did, and I was waiting to see who it was that left them. You must travel away from the edge of the road if you don't want anyone to notice you. I don't think you meant to be detected today. Am I right?"

"Yes, you are. I came out here today to talk to you and see if you would shed more light on what's going on."

Michael laughed and slapped Calvin on the back. He underestimated his strength as Banah, for the slap that normally found its target to be the back of a Nephilim nearly knocked Calvin down.

"I'll tell you what, preacher; I cannot tell you anymore today for the time is not right, but I do have a plan. The less you know now, the harder it will be for them to get it out of you if they discover what we are up to. They cannot read my mind unless they force me to surrender my will, which they can. They cannot read yours, for you are Maseth. But be warned, preacher; if they catch you slipping in a moment of sinfulness, they will milk your thoughts dry in a heartbeat. So, you met Kara today, eh?"

"Yeah," Calvin answered simply, not knowing what else to say.

"She's been assigned to work you, preacher. It won't be a hard task for her since she likes you. Kara's been single for sometime now. She lures and romances a human until she zaps the life force from him, or he grows old and she casts him aside and moves on. She doesn't seem to have the commitment and loyalty that her father has. Be careful, preacher, and don't underestimate her."

"I know what you're saying. I'll be careful. Now what's your plan?"

"Not now. You meet me here a week from Monday morning at the break of day. There will be a battle. Be prepared to fight the fight of your life if you want to save yourself and your wife. They will never let either of you leave here alive. You know that don't you?"

Calvin made no answer and gave no acknowledgement; his blank stare indicated he understood more than he would presently admit.

"Just meet me here at the pit one week from Monday at daybreak. Bring the vials I gave you, got it?"

"Yeah, I'll be here"

"I would offer you a ride, but its best we are not seen together until the time has come."

"That's alright, Michael. I'm actually exercising some this morning and want to visit a couple more places before I leave."

Michael climbed into his truck and left Calvin standing and coughing in a sea of dust. It's the way everyone drives out here, thought the preacher as he begins his return to Copper Town.

The walk to the Loop was made in short time, for Calvin was driven more now to complete the items on his agenda than to stop and take more notes. His feet moved steadily along the North Loop traveling westward. He turned south toward the RV park and crossed Main Street. Once there, he walked east to the entry of the park and entered, retracing his steps from the night before.

Unlike his previous trek, today his path was well lit, and his pace was slower. As he made his way through the park, he barely noticed the visitors who were still camping in the lower section. The doors of the office were closed and the shades pulled. Calvin wondered who would run the park in the absence of Slim. Nevertheless, onward he went until he reached the road to his left where the previous night's gruesome ordeal took place. He strolled to the center of the site, hoping that he would soon awake to find everything to be just another bad dream.

He found no sign of the fire that blazed bright the night before. No coals, no wood, no oil, and … no blood. What in the world is going on? How can this area be clean to the point that it looks like it's not been used this season? he thought.

"Maybe I have the wrong campsite." He uttered to the trees and looked around to make sure he was in the right place. His visual acuity of the surroundings confirmed that he had not miscalculated his destination. Shuffling his feet in the dirt, he confessed that if he were not a preacher, some offhanded and thoughtless oath into the air would serve best to express his thoughts. Calvin took no notes at the campsite; he simply stuffed his hands into his pockets and began his walk back to the parsonage.

The walk up Main Street found him alone. Calvin's head was down and his feet moved in a short and rhythmic scuffle. Confusion flooded his heart, and he was unable to think clearly.

He was snapped back to reality as he lifted his head and saw his wife leaning over the balcony rail of the parsonage. Rosie was waving methodically to her husband. His steps quickened, and he returned the smile. Her long, white robe was in strong contrast to her beautiful skin, and Calvin knew there was nothing under the robe. He laughed when he noticed his steps had quickened to a run; nothing could slow him now.

Approaching Second Street, the preacher stopped. A roar of an engine sounded as fair warning that a car was fast approaching the intersection with no apparent intentions of stopping. The squeal of breaks shattered Calvin's hypnotic trance. Simultaneously, he and his wife turned to watch the red sports car slide to a stop in front of the preacher.

"Need a ride, preacher?" quipped Kara.

"Eh, no thanks. I live just across the street."

"I know where you live, preacher!" Kara laughed. "Take the long way home?"

It was all Calvin could do to turn away from the bright blue eyes of the Banah, and he prayed silently to himself, Satan, get ye behind me. The war of his two natures battled deep within his soul and his subconscious screamed again, Stronger is he that is in me than he that is in the world.

"Cat got your tongue, preacher? Or are you thinking about it?"

Calvin finally fought through the battlefield where many had fallen and looked up at his wife standing on the balcony; he waved to her again. She hesitated for a second with a confused frown on her face, and then slowly she returned his wave. For the first time in her life, her smile was accompanied by a look of distrust. Confusion had staked a claim on her features.

Kara followed Calvin's eyes to the balcony and she laughed. When Rosie glared down at her, she waved. Rosie returned a half-hearted wave of her own.

"Whoops! Wrong timing, right, preacher?" She winked at Calvin and turned right onto Main. Her little car moved purposefully slow to expose her long blonde hair to Rosie. It reflected the golden rays of the morning sun and waved slightly from the breeze of the open window. She smiled up at Rosie, raised her eyebrows, and waved a slow good-bye. Rosie did not return a wave.

"I've got breakfast ready for you, Harley. Come and get it!"

Calvin grinned at her and skipped across the street. "I'll be right there, babe."

He took the steps in fours and landed flat-footed with a thud on the metal platform. The door was open at the top of the steps, allowing him to look through them. He saw Rosie standing in front of the balcony door which she had closed behind her.

"I guess breakfast will have to wait." He laughed watching her as she slowly allowed her robe to slip to the floor. He entered, closing the door behind him and knowing that the rest of his plans would not be accomplished until the afternoon.

"The Internet, how in the world did we ever live without it?" John Calvin laughed as he flipped up the monitor of his laptop and pushed the power button. He pulled up the little table on the balcony which served as a desk for his study. Curled up in a rocking chair next to him, Rosie pretended not to hear. A barrier existed between them in the form of a book which she had spread open to hide her face. Rosie enjoyed reading as much as watching television, but the barrier today was in protest of her husband's unwillingness to spend the afternoon lounging around the house. It was 1:00 PM, and she still wore nothing but her oversized robe. It served as a reminder to him of what he declined; and a reminder of what was now too late to accept.

The sounds of a pecking keyboard could be heard as it typed *N-E-P-H-I-L-I-M*. The websites flash before him as he read and took notes. He found everything from alien beings landing on earth, to demons, to Biblical explanations, to denial of any existence of Nephilim. This was what Calvin called the "method of madness." He would search and study until a specific item of interest caught his attention, and then he would pursue it. From today's surfing, he became fixated with giants and formed a hypothesis based upon his recently acquired knowledge. "I think giants of old were not Nephilim, but rather hybrid offspring of Nephilim and women." He commented to a wife who had decided that nothing the preacher had to say that morning would pull her from the pages of her novel.

On a blue legal pad he writes "Facts," and proceeded with illegible writings identical to those on his pocket notepad.

FACT 1: A large human femur was found in the Euphrates Valley during the late 1950s. This section of southeast Turkey also contained the tombs of many giant skeletons, two of which contained femurs over forty-seven inches long. The director of Mt. Blanco Fossil Museum in Crosbyton, Texas, had been commissioned to sculpt or construct an anatomical chart to compare the skeleton with modern day man. The director, Joe Taylor, placed the actual femur on a drawing of the lower section of a skeleton. The results illustrated the original man stood fourteen to sixteen feet tall.

Calvin flipped his Bible open to Deuteronomy 3:11 and read: "For only Og king of Bashan remained of the remnant of giants; behold, his bedstead was a bedstead of iron; is it not in Rabbath of the children of Ammon? Nine cubits was the length thereof, and four cubits the breadth of it, after the cubit of a man."

He replaced 1.5 feet for a cubit, mentally factored it with nine and wrote the product: 14.5 feet.

"Wow!" he exclaimed not noticing the rolling of his wife's eyes. "A bed that is fourteen feet long by six feet wide."

Calvin meditated upon the text. Is this the end of giants reported in Scripture? No, he thought, it cannot be. It's only the end of them in the days of Moses, for hundreds of years later they are found again during the days of David. He returned to his research.

FACT 2: In AD 135 after the Romans put down the Jewish rebellion in the Bar Kochba war, a conversation between Rabbi Johnanan ben Zakkai and the Roman Emperor Hadrian was recorded in the Jewish text of Buber's Tanhuma, Devarim 7. After the Emperor had boasted of defeating the Jews, Johnanan took him to a cave which was used by the Amorites for a burial chamber. One of the bodies measured 18 cubits. Johnanan explained that when the Jews were in the grace of God, He provided victory. Only the fallen nature of the nation had resulted in the defeat at the hands of the Roman Emperor.

Calvin wrote on his pad: "18 x 1.5 = 27 feet." Another, "wow!" escaped from his lips and was still ignored by Rosie.

FACT 3: Canton of Lucerne, 1577 AD. A human skeleton

was discovered beneath an uprooted oak tree. It was nineteen foot and five inches in length.

FACT 4: Valence, France; 1577 AD. A twenty-three-foot skeleton was found on the banks of a river.

FACT 5: Italy, 1856. A miner falls through a mine to a burial chamber below. An eleven-foot, six-inch skeleton was found.

FACT 6: Chaumont, France, 1613 AD. A human skeleton found nearly twenty-three feet tall. Most all bones were discovered to this skeleton.

FACT 7: Roman soldier-emperor Caius Julius Verus Maximinus reported to be eight foot, six inches tall and very strong.

FACT 8: Between 200–600 BC. Carthaginian history reported finding two different human remains. Both, unbelievable, reported to be thirty-six feet in length.

Reclining in his chair for a short break and a moment of reflection, the preacher looked out over the buildings of the town to view the gigantic residential home sitting high on the mountain to the south. It was the home of Alexander Gionni. His mind was barbed with thoughts like a single, bull-eyed target shared by several archers.

"All foreign countries," he mused looking at the monitor. "What about the United States?" Again his fingers press on the keyboard of his computer. Madly he typed, stopping only to jot down more notes under the new title: "USA."

FACT 1: November 10, 1975: Brewersville, Indiana. Excavation near town uncovers nine-foot, eight-inch human skeleton.

FACT 2: October 24, 1895: Toledo, Ohio. Excavation of a mound uncovers twenty skeletons. All seated and facing east. Each skeleton was twice as large as present day man.

FACT 3: 1833: Lompock Rancho, California. While digging a pit to store powder, a twelve-foot skeleton is found with double rows of upper and lower teeth. The legends of Si-Te-Cah (giant) by local Piute Indians substantiated.

John Calvin McGarney reclined again in his chair. Notebook in hand, he began to summarize all that he had learned in the last twelve hours. He was careful to document it with the historical events on his notepads and, most importantly, verify them with Scripture. He grinned while thinking: If someone digs up my notepad a one hundred years from now, will they declare it to be unintelligent hieroglyphic figures? Carefully he wrote under another title:

Summary

Nephilim have been around since the original creation. Those still existing are obviously millions of years old. Biblical references to Nephilim are correctly assigned to them and their hybrid offspring. If their bodies disintegrate at death, then the skeletal giants found in the earth must be the hybrid offspring of the Nephilim and humans. According to Alexander's explanation, Nephilim can determine some physical attributes of their offspring. If mating is done in the created form, giants would still be a possibility. If they chose to breed while in their human form, their offspring would be more human and less conspicuous known as Banah.

John Calvin folded his legal pad and turned off his computer.

"Rosie, I'm going to work the streets passing out gospel tracts and witness some for the remainder of the afternoon. You want to join me?"

For nearly forty years Rosie has ministered along side her husband willingly, for she also enjoyed her ministerial work. Her answer needed no contemplation, and she confirmed what her husband expected to hear.

"Sure, Harley. That's part of my ministry as well as yours; just give me a minute to get dressed."

Chapter 21

MINISTERS OF THE STREET

And he said unto them, Go ye into all the world, and preach the gospel to every creature.

MARK 16:15

Rosie and Calvin moved along the streets greeting the residents of Copper Town, as well as the tourists. They recognized several of the people they had met in the last few days, but they found that they were known by all the locals. The pleasant disposition of the two drew others to them like iron to a magnet, thus making their task of passing out Christian literature and church information delightful. The majority of their life had been spent ministering on the streets and byways. Working together, their presentation was well planned and practiced. Few refused their literature, and the couple was not discouraged when they watched some slip it into trashcans located along the busy streets. Calvin had come well prepared with Spanish tracts for the large number of Hispanic people he had observed in the streets since his arrival. Most did not speak English, or choose not to do so. He simply grinned and passed out the literature, greeting them with an "hola," a "gracias" when they accepted, and an "hasta luego" at their departure. It was near the extent of his Spanish vocabulary.

Nearly every encounter with the locals involved a dialogue concerning their dogs. During the duration of their work, the couple passed out nearly one hundred tracts, and they petted as many dogs: small dogs, large dogs, pedigreed, half-breeds, short-haired dogs, and long-haired dogs.

"Rosie, have you ever seen so many dogs in your life?"

"I don't think so. How about the Bushman tribes in Africa? It seemed every family there had five or six dogs. Did they not?"

"Yeah, that's right. But most of those were working dogs, not pets. Some of these folks treat their dogs like kinfolk. Some I noticed treat them better than relatives."

Rosie laughed at Calvin for she knew to whom he is referring. A particular couple attended their church, and the conversation with them on the street had been long and intense. When the talk centered on the pack of dogs and their elaborate leashing harness, the wife placed a finger in her husband's face and proclaimed, "If he doesn't like my dogs, he can leave. And another thing, I better never catch him being abusive to them." It was shocking to Rosie when she continued that she loved her dogs more than her husband.

"You're right, John Calvin. Some of these folks act like their very lives are dependent on the welfare of their dogs. While I've been running, I have noticed you never see them without the dogs, especially after dark."

It was Calvin who changed the subject and nearly toppled Rosie when he looked across the street and yelled, "Hey, Antonio! *Hola, Señor!*"

He grabbed Rosie's hand, looked both ways, and crossed the street dragging his wife behind him. In front of Gionni's casino, Antonio was engaged in a conversation in Spanish with a Hispanic couple. Handshakes and a variety of greetings were exchanged, neither of which Rosie nor Calvin understand. The young lady finally explained in broken English that she was Antonio's daughter and the young man was her husband. The three of them humbly accepted the literature, and the young girl, Palmera, explained that she and her husband were Catholic. Calvin and Rosie listened as she explained that their priest drove down on Sunday mornings from Battle Mountain to meet with a group of Hispanic Catholics in her home. She explained that her dad, Antonio, was a Protestant who attended the Primera Iglesia Bautista in Fallon before moving to Copper Town. Antonio did not attend church in Copper Town since there was not a Hispanic church. Neither he nor any members of his family owned a vehicle in which they could travel. Calvin suggested she ask Antonio if he would be willing to help him distribute gospel tracts on Saturday night to Hispanic people at the Conoco gas station and convenient store.

"It will only be for a couple of hours or so," explained the preacher. His mind was churning like a high-speed motorboat, and he thought, With a little help from the Director of Missions at Fallon, perhaps we can start a Hispanic church here in Copper Town. They could possible use the Assembly Church Building to meet earlier or later in the day on Sunday.

Palmera exchanged several words with her father and turned to Calvin. "He says he will be most happy to help you, preacher, and that he will meet you tonight at 7:00 PM, unless he is called in by Senior Gionni to work. Dad is on call, twenty-four seven."

Wow, he thought. This is better than I thought. I was not going to start working on Saturday nights until next Saturday. His pleasure in Antonio's willingness to serve twenty-four seven was perceived by all of them, including his wife.

"Tell him I'll be there, and that I am most appreciative. If he does not show, I'll understand he is working."

After exchanging the pleasantries of farewell, both families went their separate ways. Calvin spent the rest of the afternoon in high anticipation of his opportunity to work with Antonio. The afternoon faded rapidly into early evening, and Rosie's preacher man practically ran to the Conoco gas station across the street from the RV grounds. His glance at the Rock found no smoke issuing forth from the chimney. This served as a good indication to the preacher that Antonio would be there. Rosie remained at home to allow her husband to minister with another male.

"There's a good murder mystery on television tonight," she informed her husband.

Calvin was pleased to find Antonio already there waiting on the sidewalk for his arrival. Handing two neatly bundled stacks of tracts to Antonio, he rendered his best attempt with broken Spanish and English to explain the differences between them.

"This bundle is written in English," he said. "This one is in Española."

The little man acknowledged his newfound friend, nodded, and replied, "*Sí, señor.*"

As they turned to approach the pumps and parking lot area of the already busy store, the manager rushed out to meet Calvin. His face displayed no satisfaction in that they had singled out his place of business to distribute the Christian material in their hands. He walked briskly and determinedly to the preacher. His hand was not extended to exchange greetings with the one protruding forth from Calvin. He wasted no time in initiating a conversation, and he insisted on being brief and to the point.

"Gionni has instructed me to allow you to pass out your material here at my business, as long as there are no complaints. I don't like it, but it will be so."

Calvin expressed his gratitude and assured him that they would be discrete and inoffensive to any of his customers.

The church music that Sunday was conducted in its customary form, slow and methodical. Afterward, the choir funneled to the left and right from their loft to their seats in the pews. For a brief second, the preacher felt the singing was a prelude to a funeral message he would be delivering. He shook the apathy off quickly and focused on the message he had prepared for the day, one he knew would edify the flock that sat before him.

Stepping into the pulpit he claimed to be his own, he began with a joke he had rehearsed several times. Today he was determined to hear some response from his congregation. However, his own laughter was all that was heard as he completed his introduction. Looking at Rosie, he saw her offer a smile along with a nod of encouragement. He began with his explanation of the Doctrine of Justification, from Romans chapter six.

He reads verse one. "Therefore being justified by faith, we have peace with God through our Lord Jesus Christ." From this verse, the pastor explained that the Christian belief of regeneration, or rebirth, as described in the third chapter of John, must precede the act of justification. He used Biblical references to further his expository sermon.

"Hearing or enlightenment," he continued, "is a prerequisite to justification and the word *calling* is the term used for the quickening of a dead and lost soul by the Holy Spirit of God."

Calvin believed in what he preached and practiced the same. His enthusiasm for biblical knowledge was evident in the methodology of his presentation. Yet, he felt as though he was a wild animal who had been hit by a car and was struggling with its last breath of existence. The congregation watched him like vultures on a utility line, waiting to swoop down on the carcass at death. His body remained motionless in the pulpit; his diction was his only tool.

He showed synonyms used in the Scripture and how a comparison of them could bring deeper understanding. "In verse nine in the same passage," he preached. "The Bible reads: 'Much more then, being now justified by his blood, we shall be saved from wrath through him.' Now," he continued, "it should be clearly seen that justification is by faith and justification is by the blood of Christ Jesus. Thus, we see that there is Scriptural correlation between faith and the blood of Christ. Although the quickening is by a work of the Holy Spirit and is separate from justification which is by a faith which is a result of the blood of Christ, the two cannot be separated. This is only part of the steps of eternal salvation, for in the same book of Romans in chapter eight, verses twenty-nine to thirty, it clearly defines them to be inseparable, yet different, steps of God's plan for salvation of the human soul."

Calvin read the passage to his congregation in the hopes that they would see the different steps: "For whom he did foreknow, he also did predestinate to be conformed to the image of his Son, that he might be the first-born among many brethren. Moreover whom he did predestinate, them he also called: and whom he called, them he also justified: and whom he justified, them he also glorified."

The pastor poured his heart out in a deep, theological explanation of the doctrine of justification, yet the faces of the congregation were expressionless. The organ player marched to the organ with the same march of death in which she left it; prior to the sermon she played the dirge of death during the benediction. The pastor closed the service with prayer, and the entire congregation agreed with a wholehearted "Amen." Food was set forth for the much anticipated, weekly potluck dinner, and the people were filled with enthusiasm. Calvin wondered if they would have noticed if he had used the quotes of Robert Burns for the biblical readings. Feelings of deep depression and frustration invaded his thoughts and refused to depart with the members of his congregation at the end of potluck.

For the rest of the afternoon, Calvin tried in vain to share some of the things he was feeling with Rosie. He confided in her that he felt it was a mistake to come to this area and that maybe they should make plans to leave. Rosie stood firm on the fact that God brought them there, and she was not leaving. Try as he might, he could not get her to see some of the things he had discovered in the town. With her agonistic approach, he realized he would never be able to share the events of Friday night with her. Their discussion turned into something they had rarely experienced during forty years of marriage: an argument. The preacher vowed within his soul he would find a way to leave and soon. When the time was right, he knew Rosie will accompany him. For now, he would keep his peace and extend words of comfort to his wife.

At the close of the day, he offered his apology to Rosie and suggested that she travel to Carson City the next morning to shop for new summer clothes. His apology was accepted along with his suggestion for her to shop.

"Wake up, Calvin!" Rosie urged while gently shaking her husband's shoulders.

"Hey, what's going on, babe? I thought you would get an early start and let me sleep in?"

"John Calvin, the Honda won't start. Come and see what you can do."

"Okay," was his halfhearted and simple reply. He pulled on the jeans he left crumpled on the floor the night before. "What's it doing?"

"I don't know; it just clicks when I turn the key on. The starter won't turn over at all. Do you think it's the battery?"

"Sounds like it to me, but it's not an old battery, and it started the other day. You didn't leave the key on did you?"

"You drove it last, John Calvin. Remember?"

"Yeah, I guess you are right. Let's go take a look. I'll grab my toolbox out of the storage room."

Calvin retrieved his small toolbox and a set of jumper cables from the storage room at the rear of the kitchen and joined Rosie on the way to the garage. He placed the key into the ignition first and turned it to the start position. The only clicking sound he heard was from the key in the ignition; there was literally no other sound.

"Hey, Rosie, see if the lights are working," he said, turning on the light switch with his left hand. His right hand had already moved to the radio, and instantly he heard the sound of southern gospel music roaring from the speakers.

"Lights are as bright as day!" Rosie declared from the front of the vehicle. She walked back to the open door and looked down at her husband with a puzzled look.

"I don't know what's going on. It may be a bad starter, not the battery. It's not making a connection somewhere between the ignition and the starter. I can try to jump it off with the Harley, but I don't think it's going to work. I tell you what; let me crawl underneath and peck on the starter. Sometimes they get frozen up and a good old bang from a hammer jars them to life."

Calvin managed a laugh and told himself there was no need to panic. When he dropped down on his knees in preparation to slide underneath, he realized the low clearance of the Honda would not allow him to do so.

"Pop the hood, Rosie, and let's take a look." He got up and walked to the front of the car and raised the hood. After fastening it open with the prop support, he looked down at the engine, about which he knew nothing. Glaring down at what he did know to be the starter, he saw a jagged edge and broken ends of a cable. Broken, he thought. How can a cable get broken in that location? Sticking his head closer into the small gap, he shined his miniature flashlight into the dark crevice. He jumped from shock, bumping his head on the hood, and nearly fell forward on the engine. The hair on the back of his head stiffened as adrenalin coursed his body.

"The cable has been cut!" he yelled. Immediately, he wished he had kept that exclamation and discovery to himself. He gathered his emotions and attempted to explain, so as not to upset his wife.

"Or it appears to be. I'll have to get in touch with Philip to see if he can fix it. If we can get it off, maybe we can get another one in town and get you out of here pretty soon."

"I'll just wait until tomorrow. That way I'll have the whole day to shop. You don't get to use this as an excuse to get off cheap, John Calvin!"

"Okay, we'll see what Philip has to say."

Within minutes of calling Philip, the preacher watched him drive up Main Street headed for the parsonage. Calvin met him in the garage and shared with him his discovery. Although Philip had regained his old laughing and happy nature, he and Calvin rarely made eye contact. There was something the two of them now shared that would never allow the laughter to appear as genuine again.

"Yep, you're right, preacher. It looks like you have probably run into something along the road that has snipped the starter cable. I'll call Michael and get him to get the tow truck, and we'll take it down to our garage. I think we can get it off today and see if that's the problem. It will take a couple of days to get one shipped down from Battle Mountain. I hope you don't need it before then. We are a little slow, but we'll get it done for you free of labor. All you'll have to do is pay for the parts."

"We can do without it for a day or two, I suppose. It's not like we have a choice. Rosie will be disappointed. She was going to drive to Carson City to shop for summer clothes today."

"I'm sorry. Tell her we'll put a rush on it, just for her."

With that, Philip was whistling for Jack and Daniel who were busy licking the hands of Antonio, preventing him from the morning work of his garden. For the first time in days, Calvin noticed the Rock was not belching a dark spiral of smoke from its chimney.

Within the hour, Philip returned to the parsonage with Michael who was driving their company towing truck. A truck large enough to tow semis appeared to swallow the McGarney's Honda. Calvin was aware of Michael's intentional avoidance of him. Beyond the traditional handshake and greeting, he steered clear of the pastor and allowed his dad to carry on the business end of the conversation.

A ritualistic shaking of hands followed the meeting. Calvin stood in the parking lot and watched the little car disappear up Second Street. The Civic was the McGarney's only four-wheeled vehicle. There was a deep feeling of fear that reigned in the depth of the preacher's soul, and as he turned to make his way back to the parsonage, he noticed the same look on the face of his wife. She stood leaning on the rail of the porch and stared down at nothing.

"Hey, babe, get your leather on and let's ride over the mountain to Ely. What do you say?"

His wife did not grin. She did, however, give him the thumbs up signal. Turning, she disappeared into the apartment. Calvin ascended the steps leading into his home in a halfhearted, one-by-one stride. His mood was not for motorcycle riding, but he would hide that from his wife. Once on the road, he would enjoy himself.

Calvin entered the parsonage with a laugh and kicked his slippers off. He stopped for a second to watch his beautiful wife zip the legs of her leather chaps. She grabbed her vest and boots, retreating to the couch to finish dressing. After sitting on the cushions, she paused and stared again at the walls; her mind was jumbled with a thousand thoughts. She could not seem to bring a single one to the forefront for conversation with her husband. She just sat. Calvin was saddened by the look of desperation on her face. He did not see the smile he had grown accustomed to prior to their motorcycle adventures.

Although the preacher started getting dressed after his wife, he found himself standing beside his motorcycle waiting for her arrival in the garage. She moved slow in gathering her purse and other items customary for her ride, but methodically made the efforts to join her husband. As she approached, Calvin unlocked the ignition, stuffed the keys into a jacket pocket that he zipped immediately, and turned on the ignition. Without stopping, he kicked the engine into neutral with his left foot and hit the fuel-injected engine's starter button with his right thumb. The starter grinded immediately, as it turned an engine that did not fire. Calvin stopped and looked at Rosie; she too had ceased opening the garage doors to look at her husband. The bike had always fired spontaneously at the touch of the starter button. That day it made a futile sound of metal on metal with no hints of exploding into the thundering nature of the beast it usually did.

Grabbing the throttle with his right hand, he twisted it quickly several times to prime a fuel-injected engine that should not need priming. Again he pushed the button and listened to the starter grind vigorously for several seconds before he released it. The sickening sound of a failing battery indicated there would be no usual thunder of a Harley idling in his garage.

"What in the world is going on?" he asked Rosie. Her look was one of total confusion. She had no way of knowing what was wrong.

Calvin repeated the starting procedure again; it was pointless. The bike was not going to start. In desperation, Calvin grinded on the starter until it sagged under the strain of its own fruitless labor.

These were the times in her husband's life that Rosie was able to lend encouragement and support. Today she could not find the words of support, and she knew anything she said would be wasted. She succumbed to her extreme anxiety and spoke words that were wasted.

"I guess when it rains out here, it pours, huh?"

Calvin was filled with anger. Not at his wife, or the words she had spoken, but at the remembering of Gionni's warnings, "You have more to lose than you think. You will never leave Copper Town!"

Yanking his cell phone free from his belt, Calvin delivered his fury to the tiny keys of the phone with a series of hard punches.

Rosie's voice had a touch of sadness, and she barely hides tears, yet she managed to ask, "What are you doing, Calvin?"

"I'm calling the only one I know to call, Philip. Maybe he's still there at the garage and will come and get the bike, too."

He was right. Philip was at the garage. He told Calvin he knew very little about motorcycles, and there was no one in town that could work on them. He informed him that he and Beth would be going to Reno on Thursday, and they would be back on Friday. He volunteered to drop the bike off at the Harley Davidson dealer in Reno for Calvin.

"Don't worry, preacher. I think we'll have the car running by the end of the week. If you or Rosie need to go anywhere, let us know. Beth or I will give you a ride."

"Thanks", was all Calvin could muster before he folded his phone and returned it to the pouch on his belt. His helmet was not as fortunate as the keys of the phone; it sailed through the air, struck the sides of the metal walls with a loud bang, and bounced across the concrete floor. Finally, it came to rest near the same boot that sent it wrathfully on its journey. It spun slowly in erratic circles until it came to a rest. Rosie's helmet followed the same trail blazed by Calvin when she heard the events from his call.

Chapter 22

A MILLSTONE NECKLACE

*And Jesus called a little child unto him, and set him in the
midst of them ... whoso shall offend one of these little ones
which believe in me, it were better for him that a millstone
were hanged about his neck, and that he were drowned in
the depth of the sea.*

MATTHEW 18:2–6

John Calvin shuffled his feet and leaned against one of the white metallic
posts that supported the large canopy covering the gas pumps. He watched
as Antonio laughed and talked with a Hispanic family who had parked
to the side of the station. The mother prepared sandwiches on the hood of
the old car, while her children stood around her eager for the meal they
would soon eat. The preacher kicked a small pebble at his feet and sent it
flying across the empty lanes of the pumps. His kick was a result of his
lingering frustration. A frustration caused by his failed efforts to get Rosie's
car repaired, compounded by his Harley being left in Reno.

First, a battery cable had been sent down from Battle Mountain on
Wednesday. When it was replaced, the car still would not start. Philip told
him it was probably the starter and he ordered one from Reno. Parts for
this particular model were not in stock. According to Philip, the Honda
dealer ordered the starter, and it would be delivered the next Wednesday.
"Don't worry, preacher," he had told Calvin. "We should have you up and
going by next Wednesday evening. I hope there are no other electrical
shortages. Sometimes things like that can damage the car's computer. If

197

the starter doesn't work, we'll tow it up to the dealer and they can put it on one of their diagnostic machines."

For some reason, he felt Philip was keeping something from him, but he had to be patient, not allowing them see his frustration. At least Philip and Beth had delivered his bike to Reno last Thursday. According to Philip, the Harley Davidson shop was really booked for the next couple of weeks, and it could be two to three weeks before they could get to his cycle. The events of the last few days gave him reason to trust Philip less; although his calls to the dealer confirmed Philip's report. At least Rosie would be able to get out of town on Monday. She had explained to Calvin that Philip and Alexander were flying out of Reno to New York tomorrow afternoon. Beth had explained to her that since her husband was going to be out of town, she would pick Rosie up bright and early on Monday, and the two of them would spend the day shopping in Carson City.

"At least something is going right," he uttered, while looking around the asphalt drive for another rock to send after the first one. It was nearly nine o'clock, and his search was not shortened by time but by a frightened scream that perforated the silence of his solitude. Shocked, Calvin turned to find the source of the scream and saw Antonio still standing with the mother at the parked car. The back door was opened and both stood looking down into the backseat. The woman continued to take short breaths. She gasped and her body convulsed. Upon every exhale, she wailed the same bloodcurdling scream. The scenario was repeated several times before Calvin and the lady's husband joined them to look down on an empty backseat. Antonio spoke words the preacher could not understand, yet Calvin empathized with the calming tone of his friend's soft voice.

Immediately, the father turned and ran inside the convenience store. Calvin watched him as he rushed up and down the aisles and into the restrooms. First, the men's room, and after he emerged from there, he madly pushed the women's door open and went inside. He was gone only seconds before he exited again with a look of desperation and fear spreading across his face. Calvin could not hear the words being screamed inside the store, but he could see the lips of the father as he yelled making his way up and down the aisles and then back outside. He threw his arms upward to display his futile attempts and started toward them.

Calvin had no time to wonder or ask questions which he knew could not be understood, for Antonio grabbed his upper arm with a vice-like grip and dragged him to the back of the family's car. The Mexican's finger was shoved into his face and his lips quivered for only a fraction of a second before he uttered.

"Listen, preacher, I don't want anyone to know I speak English. My life and the lives of my family are dependent upon that. Promise me now and promise me quickly you will tell no one. Please!"

"Okay, Antonio. Believe me, I understand more than you realize. What's going on?"

"After this family bought gas, the father parked the car over to the side of the store so it would not block the pumps. He went in to use the restroom and join his wife and children to buy sandwich meat and bread. They left their five-year-old daughter asleep in the backseat. The father thought she was with the others, and the mother did not notice until now. She is no where in the store. Help us scatter out and look around. You take the front area along Main Street, and I'll look behind the building."

Calvin did not linger. He rushed to the street and ran west. He checked the ditch lines and nearby sage brush areas of the adjoining desert. His maddened search went on for several hundred feet before he crossed the road. From that point, he continued his method of search, moving eastward along the road frontage of the RV park. While passing the length of the park, he was able to view deep into the campgrounds. The grounds were nearly full, and several people were moving toward the roadside to see what the excitement was all about. They, too, would soon join in the search.

He continued running and searching until he was able to view the streets and sidewalks of the city. There was no child. Calvin panicked and sweat began to bead on his forehead. Turning, he ran back to the service station where he saw Antonio merge from one side of the building and the father from the other. The children and the mother were searching deep into the sage-covered area that marked the beginning of the desert to the south of the parking lot. Their search was in vain, and they returned to the car. They all stood looking at Antonio. The mother's sobbing had not abated, and she appeared to be going into shock.

Antonio grabbed Calvin's arm again and pulled him to the side. The preacher noticed that the manager and a couple of other customers had joined in the search. They all stood looking at him.

Antonio spun Calvin around, and his short stubby finger resumed its earlier point of fixation as he gave instructions. "Preacher, run quickly and get Gionni. He can help. Don't mention our secret, not even to him. Go! Go quickly!"

There was no need to say more. Calvin did not interject with his thought of "I was about to suggest the same thing;" instead he took off running as fast as his legs would carry him eastward toward the casino of Alexander. Adrenaline rushed through his body like air escaping from a balloon punctured by a sharp pin. The lights from the shops and the street blended together and were only a blur to his tear-stained eyes. He darted and dashed through people on the busy sidewalk; all were frozen in their tracks like dummies standing in store windows. Their statue-like poses were a result of both his erratic running and the loud screams escaping from his lips. Calvin was aware of the crowded sidewalks, but he was unaware that he was screaming for help.

At dusk, the main doors into Gionni's casino were closed. The preacher was surprised to find the inner doors to the conference room also closed. He was unaware the heavy doors were bolted from within to mask the activities that were unfolding. Calvin rushed through the main entry while whispering a prayer of thanks that no one was blocking the interior doors. He rushed to shove them open, as he had the first two, but his body crumpled upon contact with the secured doors. He recoiled and fell to the floor. Energized with the adrenalin that still coursed his body, Calvin effortlessly jumped to his feet. For a brief second, he focused on the sign that was posted on the doors:

PRIVATE MEETING
DO NOT DISTURB
ALEXANDER GIONNI

Calvin was not thwarted by the warning. He tightened his open hands into tightly clutched fists and began to bang on the huge doors.

"Alexander!" he yelled. "Help! We need your help! Alexander! Please open the doors!"

Calvin realized this was the second time in a very short while in which he had called upon the Nephilim for assistance.

He repeated the aggressive banging, completely ignoring the bright colors of the posted warning.

"Alexander!" he yelled, and repeated the knocking series; this time much more loudly and much longer. "Alexander, we need your help. You must come quickly. Do you hear me, Alexander?"

The sound of a large brass bolt sliding in the latch on the other side brought relief to the doors and to the reddened skin of his fists. His roars for help did not subside.

"Alexander! Help! Come quickly. We need your help!"

LeBazeja slightly opened the door, sticking her head through the crevice she had created. Her plans to question the preacher never materialized. The tiny slit of an opening was all Calvin needed to split the doors open with one shove. He rushed into the room where a large feast was taking place. There was not an empty seat to be found. Calvin recognized the faces of many as members of his church. He did not acknowledge any of them. At this time, nothing was of importance beyond his concern for the child.

His eyes were quickly set at the head table where he saw Alexander making his way to him. To Calvin it seemed as if he arose from the chair and was immediately standing over him. There was no recollection of his walking to the preacher. Calvin discerned disappointment in the glare of the Nephilim and assumes it was caused by his uninvited presence. Little did he know that the discontentment was rendered from the Nephilim's inability to read the thoughts of the preacher.

"Alexander! A small five-year-old girl is missing at the convenience store. Come quickly. Please."

From the corner of his eye, he saw Philip rise from the head of one of the tables. In the same timeless and phantomlike movement, he stood with Alexander.

"Okay, preacher. Don't call the police ... yet! It will take hours to get a car down here. Besides, they will only tell us to wait to see if she shows up. Get back up there, John Calvin, and wait. Philip and I will join you shortly."

With those words, he and LeBazeja pushed Calvin through the doors. The doors slammed shut, and he heard the large bolt slide into the lock position. Calvin stepped outside the main doors to the sidewalk. For a moment he wondered if he should stop to tell Rosie about the little girl's disappearance or just return to the store. His mental debate was interrupted by a familiar roar of an engine accompanied with the squealing of rubber tires. The crowd turned with him to see the lights of the Ferrari flick from dim to bright several times in quick succession. The purpose was served; Kara had gotten the attention of the town's preacher. She slid to a stop inches from the "No Parking" area in front of the casino's main entry, inches from Calvin.

"Need a ride, preacher?" Her question was more of a command as she swung open the passenger door and instructed Calvin to get in. With no further thought, he jumped into the passenger's seat; he did need a ride that night. The faster he can got back, the better. He'd have to wait to tell Rosie. There was simply no time.

"I need to get to the gas station quickly," he commanded. "Hurry up; let's go!"

Kara needed no further instructions; she slammed her foot on the accelerator, and the car leapt free from the smoke of the squealing tires. Calvin did not know she was aware of the situation; nor did he know his wife was leaning over the rail of the veranda watching him and Kara speed up the street. Within seconds, the sports car slid sideways, coming to a screaming halt in the parking lot of the convenience store.

Bracing with his left hand on the dash, Calvin grabbed the support bar over his head. Kara accelerated down Main Street and slowed only to turn into the gas station. Calvin was amazed at her driving skills. She sat relaxed in the leather seat, easily steering the car with her left hand. Her right hand worked the gear shift with a fluid motion that was in perfect synchronization with her legs. The up-and-down motion of her legs as they depressed and pressed the pedals on the firewall were accentuated by the miniskirt she was wearing. As the preacher sat in awe admiring her driving skills, he noticed her lacy white panties were exposed as the skirt gave way to the wild action of her legs. He turned quickly to watch her slide sideways to a stop.

Kara glanced at Calvin as he grabbed the door release to get out, and she laughed and asked, "Like what you saw, preacher?"

Calvin turned to her, and their eyes embraced for a split second. In that flash of time, an ageless and voiceless yearning was shared by both. He was mesmerized by the brightness of her blue eyes. He was unable to escape her hypnotic stare and felt that it was her eyes that were illuminating the light of the parking lot. The preacher stared deeper and knew that she also knew the depths of their lust.

"Kara," he started, "there are more important things happening tonight. Let's be serious. Shall we?"

He did not give her time to speak, for he realized he had to let go of those eyes. Calvin got out of the car and made his way to Antonio. Behind the family's car lay the beginning of the vast high sierra desert region. As he looked into the blackness of that region beyond, Alexander and Philip entered the light of the parking lot from the same darkness at which he glared. All three of them joined Antonio and the family he was with. Kara stepped in front of the men and began talking to Antonio in a fluid Hispanic dialogue. Good, thought the preacher, that will help keep our secret. Somewhere in the back of his mind, he filed away the fact that Kara could speak Spanish. She might prove to be helpful in the future.

"Dad," she began, "Antonio says they have searched the area all around the store and could not find the little girl. He says your cashier noticed an old, faded gray truck parked around back tonight with a weird looking driver. He walked around in the desert near the pumps watching the store and campgrounds across the street. After it was dark, he noticed the truck had left. The family wants to call the police."

Alexander tilted his head back and breathed in deeply. It seemed in those brief moments he had devised a plan of search and rescue. He looked at his daughter and Antonio before he spoke.

"Tell them it will take the police nearly an hour to get here, if they come at all. They usually want to wait a few hours to see if we can find the child. Ask them if they have a piece of clothing, or something personal, which belongs to their daughter."

Kara turned to the mother and explained what her father had instructed. The mother rushed to the backseat of the car. There she bent down, picked up a gray sock monkey, and hurried back. A slight look of hope was beginning to form on her face. She placed the monkey in Alexander's large hand and backed away nodding her head repeatedly looking for approval.

An arm slid around Calvin's waist. He knew who it belonged to, and without looking, he lifted his left arm to allow Rosie to slide under his embrace. She said nothing and leaned her head against her husband's chest. Kara ignored the presence of the preacher's wife, but Alexander smiled at her as he turned to Kara.

"Keep everyone here together and make sure no one calls the police. I don't think we'll need them. As quickly as you verify that, call me. Understand?"

"Yes, Dad, I'll take care of it."

Looking at the preacher he said, "Preacher, come with us for a second. Rosie, stay here with Kara and the family. She can help you and John Calvin communicate with the family when he gets back."

As the Nephilim leader turned to walk back into the darkness of the desert, he motioned for Calvin to follow him and Philip. He did not stop when his daughter shouted to him, "Dad, they say she is wearing blue jeans and a pink T-shirt."

His daughter heard, "Thanks Kara," but only the preacher heard him whisper, "We have all we need."

Hidden by the blackness of night, their journey into the desert was short. They only needed to escape the vision of humans.

Alexander and Philip stopped and turned to speak with Calvin. As the chairman of the council, Alexander would be the one to explain their plan to him.

"Well, preacher, you have called on me again for help. What would you have me do?"

"Alexander, cut to the chase would you? You know what has to be done here, and time is of the essence."

"Maybe, preacher, we could have a prayer session here in the desert and trust in your God to come to your aid."

"It is a dangerous thing, Mr. Gionni, to tempt the Lord God. Even you know you are not exempt from that."

"But now you need us. You know, this is two consecutive weekends you have called on me for help. Are you saying you can work with a Nephilim?"

"We can all work together. Do you choose to help or must I call the police?" Calvin pulled out his cell phone and flipped it open. The light of his phone shone like a beacon in the blackness of night and revealed he had a full charge. He held it up to light his vision of Alexander.

"You cannot threaten us, preacher! We have fearlessly faced greater than you since the beginning of time. But since it is a child, we will help."

Alexander turned away from Calvin and spoke with Philip in a language he had never heard. The Nephilim looked over their shoulders from time to time to observe the preacher. Again, it was Alexander that finally turned to speak with Calvin.

"By the way, preacher, that phone won't work out here!"

Calvin laughed in mockery and held the phone up again to show Alexander he had service. Before he could articulate his boastful reply, the phone's bars faded away. The low battery signal chimed only once, and his phone was dead.

The Nephilim laughed in unison and moved several feet from Calvin. Placing the little sock monkey slowly to his face, Alexander breathed noticeably deep and slow with his head tilting backward. During the process, his form changed to that of the Nephilim which now loomed high above the preacher. He shifted to the side and handed the little monkey to his comrade. Philip tenderly rolled the monkey in his hands, hands which were in the process of converting to Nephilim. He breathed deep, and the nature of his being emerged alongside Alexander.

"Got it," he said, and he tossed the sock to Calvin.

"Let's go brother," was Alexander's reply, and the two Nephilim began to hum and move in a circle. Their feet did not move, and to Calvin it looked as if they were standing on a merry-go-round. Gradually they begin to rise upward in the same slow and spiraling motion Calvin observed in the garden last week. They rose several feet above Calvin but not completely out of sight. He watched as Alexander pointed outward to the northern part of the desert. They both vanished before his eyes.

Calvin could see the bright lights of the service station and carefully worked his way back. Rosie had watched diligently for him since his departure. It was she that saw him first and ran to greet him. She wrapped her arms around him, and the two of them walked arm in arm back to the family.

Kara exited the convenience store and walked over to join them. As she approached them, she carefully placed one foot in front of the other, as if she was on a runway modeling her new mini. Calvin felt the arms of his wife squeezing him tighter. Looking down at her, he found her glaring at Kara with a "not so Christian" look of contempt. Kara stopped abruptly as if she forgot something and placed her index fingers to her temples. She closed her eyes and leaned her head back to exclaim to the night air. "No one has contacted the police. We are all waiting directions from the chairman of the council," she mentally told her father.

Silvery duct tape was proportionally too wide to cover the little girl's lips. As a result, the tall, lanky man had folded it beneath her chin and placed a second strip in a horseshoe shape down one cheek, under the chin, and up the other. Her little eyes were nearly swollen shut from weeping, and her tiny body convulsed as she attempted repeatedly to scream through the tape for her mommy and her daddy. Her little arms were taped together in front of her body with the same silvery tape. Her abductor wanted her to see his every move, and she was too tiny and weak to resist his assault. He tossed his old, dirty, white straw hat into his gray primed truck; a truck he had primed with no intentions of ever painting. It nearly matched the faded gray color of its original paint. Besides, he learned long ago that the monthly disability check he drew had to be carefully budgeted to allow him to travel around the country. His addiction was not to drugs, but he was no less driven by its insatiable desires. That night he would appease the burning desire within his twisted soul.

He drove the long-handled spade deep into the loose soil of the sandy shallow grave he had dug in the desert. Unzipping his pants, he urinated in the grave. He did not bother to refasten his pants; it would be a waste of time. His excitement and anticipation was soaring, and he could barely wait. He could play with this one for hours before he buried her alive in the pit and spread his sleeping bag over the fresh dirt where he would sleep until morning. It had been months since his last adventure.

He daringly stepped over the grave and worked his way toward the little girl. Her eyes were wide, and she shook her head. Again and again she frantically pleaded for mercy. He laughed aloud. At times her tiny brown face showed only her fear; then her face changed from a look of fear to a look of begging to be freed. Sadness in both, but neither were effective to him. His sickening laugh vibrated the stillness of the night again and again.

Yellow, rotted teeth smiled at her as he squatted down beside her. He wiped his dark greasy hair back out of his face with one hand, while the other retrieved a large pair of scissors tucked into his back pocket. He roughly grabbed her miniature hands with one of his and slammed her little body to the ground. Her body was pierced with cacti and rocks from beneath her, and when she wiggled, the man lifted her by her arms and slammed her back into the soil again. Her childish frame quivered, and her breath violently ripped from her lungs. She lay still, and her mind drifted into unconsciousness as she fainted. The vagabond waited for her to awaken. He was determined she would witness all that unfolded. Her eyes would be opened wide when he was finished with her and he shoveled the sandy soil on her face.

Her eyes moved rapidly beneath her eye lids before she opened them again. As she stared at him, she did not understand or perceive the intentions of this adult stranger. Her young mind was innocent. This time the tear-stained eyes are mixed with the grinding sands of the desert. He moved slower now, for this one was a fainter. He preferred the fighters over the fainters, but he had developed his art to perfection with the ending the same.

He snipped the large shears in his hand, scaring the child more than imaginable. He laughed again and snipped the scissors louder and more frequently. Lifting one of her pink T-shirt sleeves, he carefully snipped up the sleeve, through the seam of the shoulder, and toward the neck. He spun her around and cut the other sleeve in a like manner. Grabbing it with his free hand, he yanked the shirt free from her body. This would be the only item he kept. It was his trophy and would be displayed on his basement wall with the others.

He stood and walked to the truck, folded the shirt neatly, and placed it on the front seat. Turning back to face his victim, he laughed and watched the tiny child wiggle futilely on the ground. She tried to get to her feet, only to fall again. Her upper body now had no shielding and the briars and brambles had no mercy.

"So, my little precious, you now decide to fight? I think you will be one of my favorites."

He snipped the shears again and again, laughing continuously. Dropping to the ground on his knees, he grabbed the little girl by her feet and yanked her roughly to him. He snatched the tennis shoes off one by one and tossed them toward the grave. The baby girl's eyes grew wider than ever. She no longer peered into the eyes of her assailant, but glared intently over his shoulder into the dark night.

Alexander and Philip soared into the air. The scent of the little girl was strong, and they knew she was near. The desert air held her body odor and offered it up to the Nephilim gladly. Alexander pinpointed her location, and Philip nodded in acknowledgement. The two spread their massive arms in front of them, and the spiny bones of their wings prickle like the hair on humans when they are startled. Flying side by side through the night air, the three miles was covered in seconds. Once they located the old gray truck, they circled it like vultures on a kill. They did not fear the unknown that lurked below, for they had already discussed the outcome of this adventure.

The two of them hovered above the old gray truck, slightly behind the tramp. Kara sent a message to her father that the police had not been called. The town was waiting for his decision. He told her they would return shortly with the little girl. She was alive, and she would be well.

The Nephilim watched as the pedophile returned from the truck and dropped to his knees. Unhurried, they quietly dropped to the ground, standing behind him. It was the tiny child that saw them first. Her memory of the night's horror, and all other visions, would be erased, and she would live. The perverted visions of the tramp would fade away only when his life departed from his body. Alexander decided his death will be a slow one.

The greasy-haired man followed the child's eyes and saw both Nephilim standing tall behind him. He shuttered and nearly fainted. His wobbling body would have fallen on the child if Alexander had not grabbed him by his shirt. The Nephilim lifted him high off the ground to stare deep into his eyes. Alexander passed him to Philip as easily as he had passed the sock monkey to the preacher.

Dropping to one knee, Alexander covered the child's face with his large hand and he hummed. Sleep embraced her, and the memories of the evening were erased from her mind. His large black cape was folded to provide a blanket for the sleeping child, and he moved to the truck to retrieve her shirt. Alexander moved carefully and slid the small shirt over the child's body. The Nephilim rubbed the slit fabrics of the shirt, and they were restored with no blemish. His hands continued to remove the tape from her mouth and hands. He healed the cuts, scars, and bruises on her body. She was healed from all her pain and heartache. Philip watched and held the vagabond by his neck making him watch every move.

"Philip, take the child back. Tell the parents we found her in the desert, and they are not to be angry with her. I'll stay here and take care of this perverted dog. I'll rejoin you later at the feast."

"Maybe I'll return to join you?"

"No. I'll take care of it. You report back to the council and ask them and their families to enjoy the remainder of the night. We'll get Michael over here when I am finished to tow the truck to the pit. You can mention to Antonio that he'll be needed early tomorrow morning."

Philip needed no more instructions, for long ago he came to understand and accept the fact that a decision made by Alexander was not to be disputed. He picked up the little girl and disappeared into the night.

"Now it is my turn to play!" Alexander said as he picked up his prisoner. "Let us see which one of your senses will be deprived first. I can assure you of one thing, your eyes will be the last to go."

Alexander lifted his prisoner by the nape of his neck and shook him violently. The man kicked and struggled to no avail. Alexander toyed with him like a cat with a mouse and tossed him to the ground near the truck. The breath left his lungs, and he begged for mercy. The Nephilim took the man's large shears and clicked them together in rapid succession; a sharp "snip, snip, snip" sound issued forth from the gigantic scissors and echoed through the still desert air.

"Your sight will be the last to go, for I want you to watch every detail. I want you to experience the same fear and hopelessness that you inflicted into the souls of all those little children you abused." Snip! Snip! Snip! The shears echoed again. "The eyes will be the last, but I know what deserves the title of first! Let us remove any signs by which you are classified as man." The shears cut, and a bloodcurdling scream is heard only by the Nephilim leader.

Rosie sat on the hood of the Hispanic family's car. Her husband's back was to her, as he stood close by. She embraced him from behind and laid her head on his shoulder to wait patiently for Alexander and Philip's return. Calvin related to her the evening's saga. From time to time, she glared at Alexander's daughter and wondered, who would wear such a revealing and seductive outfit in this small town? The two women locked eyes occasionally, and their gaze reveals there was no love loss between the two of them. Yet, she admired Kara's ability to speak another language and appreciated her and Antonio's efforts to comfort the family. The father leaned back against the car with his wife clinging to him. Her weeping had not subsided, and the other children clung to the legs of their parents.

Calvin stood motionless in front of his wife, his eyes glued to the dark desert area into which the Nephilim departed. A thousand questions of uncertainty clouded his ability to think clearly. He glanced sideways to observe the family and noticed Kara lifting her head toward the desert. She rose up on her toes, and her nose tilted toward the darkness beyond the small group gathered around the car. He detected the hint of a smile which wiped away any doubt of the outcome. Calvin turned to see only the blackness he saw earlier. The shifting of shadows quivered like a mirage, and then a material form emerged from the desert. It was the form of Philip, who was walking toward the car with a black robe folded in his arms. It appeared to Calvin that he was carrying a baby in the cradle of his arms. His heart sagged, for he had expected to see the child on Philip's hip if she were still alive. Kara, however, knew the child was alive and excitedly gave the good news to the family in a language Rosie and Calvin did not understand. The mother was the first to run and meet Philip. Her husband followed with the children still clinging to his legs and arms.

Kara looked at the preacher and his wife and explains, "Dad and Philip found her roaming in the desert. She got lost, but she's okay. Just scared to death, I suppose. So, it all turned out better than expected."

Calvin turned and wrapped his arms around his wife. They embraced each other and, the preacher whispered a prayer of thanks that only his wife heard.

The laugh of Philip assured them that all was okay. He gathered them around, and with the help of Kara, he explained she had ventured off in the desert looking for her parents. His proclamation that she was not to be punished was uttered with an overture of commandment rather than suggestion.

"You must take more care from this point on in watching your children." Both parents promised faithfully they would, and together with Antonio, they prayed a prayer of thanks.

After interpreting all the information to the parents for Philip, Kara walked over to join Calvin and his wife. Her seductive walk was a little slower and a lot more exaggerated than before. As she approached, she smiled and glared at Calvin. Rosie thought she detected a slight wink at her husband.

"Do you two need a ride back?" Kara asked.

With no hesitation, it was Rosie that answered her. "No thanks, we'll enjoy the walk back *together!*"

"I'll take a ride. I have some things I need to take care of for your dad," said Philip.

"Hop in!" she answered. They wasted no time in their departure.

Calvin hugged Rosie tighter and kissed her on the forehead. Mentally he gave thanks to God for the deliverance of the child, and then frowned with the thought of Alexander thinking he was indebted to the Nephilim. He was not.

Chapter 23

THE STRUGGLING OF TWO NATURES

For the good that I would I do not: but the evil which I would not, that I do. Now if I do that I would not, it is no more I that do it, but sin that dwelleth in me. I find then a law, that, when I would do good, evil is present with me. For I delight in the law of God after the inward man: But I see another law in my members, warring against the law of my mind, and bringing me into captivity to the law of sin which is in my members. O wretched man that I am!

ROMANS 7:19–24

A few women worked feverously in the church kitchen to clean up from the weekly potluck. Calvin was deep in debate with one of the women in his church who did not agree with the topic of his sermon. At least, he thought, she was paying attention. His brief loss of attention was not caused by lack of interest of the theological discussion, but rather he longed to catch sight of Rosie. As if she could read his mind, she emerged from the dining room with a dust pan and broom. The contents of the pan give testimony that she had finished cleaning the dining room.

She smiled at her husband; a smile that displayed beautiful white teeth sparkling in contrast to her dark skin. Her grin provided the encouragement of perseverance he needed; she understood more than anyone the nature of these conversations. Calvin's heart leapt with joy for a second, feeling the love that she had for him. The sparkling eyes masked the odor of fried chicken, and he returned her greeting with a smile of his own. His thoughts returned as he looked down at the little lady: Now I'll be able to concentrate on what you are saying. But no sooner had he pledged his undivided attention, and he was interrupted by the church treasurer.

"Pastor, can I speak with you for a minute in your office?"

"Sure, Charlie, I'll be with you in just a moment."

Calvin was relieved by the intrusion. The elderly lady before him was more interested in an argument than further explanation of biblical truths. He knew nothing he had to say would convince her to believe differently than that which she had preconceived. The preacher politely ended their conversation with his interjection of, "Sister, excuse me, please. We'll have to pick up on this again, okay?"

She replied with a nod of her head. Yet, Calvin understood that she had stated her point from the view of no compromise; there would be no need for further discourse.

A slight eagerness could be detected by Calvin's footsteps as he followed Charlie into his office. He closed the door in the hopes that they would not be disturbed and listened intently as the treasurer spoke.

"Pastor, you've been here only three weeks, but today we have broken the attendance and tithing records. Today it was over four thousand dollars. It's usually around four hundred dollars, so it looks like we are off to a great start under your leadership."

"Thanks, Charlie, but let me assure you it's not me but the Lord's work."

His words were sincere, however, a trickle of pride was observed by Charlie.

"I believe God does provide the increase, preacher, but he has called us to be good stewards. And we must accept responsibility to serve in the capacity we are called. Don't you agree, pastor?"

Calvin was in awe. He wondered if the old man standing before was a Nephilim, or was he a man? Could he be a child of one of the Clan's Nephilim?

After they discussed a few other financial issues, Calvin left the office and fervently rushed to Rosie. He found her in the kitchen with another woman storing the silverware and dishes into the cabinets. They were the only ones left to the clean up. Calvin recognized the back of the other woman's hair and knew it to be Kara Gionni. Their conversation was whispered, and he could not hear what they were saying as he approached. They both laughed aloud, and Rosie patted Kara on her shoulder. She turned and noticed that her husband had entered. She flashed a smile that had already been formed on her face; it was that one that melted his heart.

Today was the first time Calvin had seen Kara in church. The biggest surprise for him was that she accompanied her father. Charlie told him it was the first time in years either of them had been in attendance. He did not know that both had attended for similar reasons, none of which were righteous. He did not get a chance to talk to Alexander, for he and Philip left immediately after service to prepare for a business trip to New York City. They would be gone until the latter part of the week. He had enjoyed having them in church and made a mental note to let them both know before the week was out. Kara was really a pleasure. She listened intently and took notes. When he looked at her, she smiled and nodded her head in agreement seeming to enjoy his message. At times, he noticed as nonverbal amen were formed by her lips; lips, he noticed, that were painted with glossy red lipstick that glistened with a hint of glitter. Rosie did not seem to be overly excited with the assistance she was getting, however, the two of them had found a common area of conversation.

"Ready to go, babe?" Calvin said.

"No. Kara has offered to take me for a little ride out on Highway 50. Would you like to go along with us?"

"Rosie, her car is a small coupe; there's no room for a third person."

It was Kara who answered. "Sure there is, preacher. We can squeeze you in the middle between us girls. You're not saying we are too big are you?"

"I'll take a look first to see if you ladies have room for me."

Calvin turned off the lights, and as they left, he locked the doors behind him. Turning, he watched Kara and Rosie make their way to the only vehicle in the parking lot: a Ferrari F430 Spider. The top was down, and the car was ready for the road. Kara wasted no time getting in and starting the engine. Rosie opened the passenger door and motioned for her husband to get in.

"Rosie, you ladies go ahead and have a good time. I'll wait on you."

"Come on, preacher." Kara spoke up immediately as she pulled her red leather driving gloves from the compartment located to the rear and center of the seats. She pulled out a red leather jacket, folded it, and placed it neatly on the console. She patted it softly as an invitation for Calvin to sit.

"Please, John Calvin," Rosie said. "I'd like for you to go. We won't be gone long. Right, Kara?"

"Right, just out to the top of the first mountain range and straight back. I might even let you drive us back, pastor!"

Calvin submitted and crawled into the car. His shoulders overlapped both the driver and passenger seats and their occupants. Rosie shifted her body toward the door which allowed Calvin to place his right leg in the floor space with hers. He tucked his left leg with his foot under him. It pushed into Rosie's thigh. With his best efforts, he could not contort his body to prevent his left knee from thrusting sharply against Kara's thigh.

"Don't worry, preacher," she said. "I'll use it as an armrest."

Kara extended her right arm over his inner thigh and brought it down to rest while shifting into first gear. The car turned left onto Second Street headed toward Main. Calvin noticed the smoke that had bellowed from the Rock before church had faded to a wisp. He made a move to wave at Antonio standing outside but was rocked off his perch and into Rosie's lap from the rapid acceleration and fishtailing of the Ferrari. They all laughed while he reseated himself, only to be dislodged again as they entered Main Street headed west on Highway 50. This time, he landed in Kara's lap; it was only her laughter that filled the car.

Calvin whispered a prayer of thanks prior to church when he saw Kara enter with her father wearing a dress. Although it was a sleeveless color-block dress in green, white, and blue with a surplice-style top, it at least covered her knees. But now the dress had slid above her knees exposing most of her thighs and the legs that pumped up and down on the pedals.

At the end of the city limits, the speed limit increased to seventy-five miles per hour. The speedometer of Kara's car jumped from fifty-five to eighty in a matter of seconds. With this increase of speed came a forceful wind that spilled over the windshield and lifted Kara's dress. Calvin noticed the pink flowery panties. She slowed the car by gearing down and looked at Calvin.

"Take the wheel, preacher," she said, letting go of it before he had time to grasp it.

Reaching for the steering wheel with his right hand required the preacher to turn his body toward the driver. As he did so, Kara lifted her body and grabbed her dress with both hands. With the lift, she turned to face the preacher. Their eyes fastened, and their lips were only inches apart. Kara tucked the dress tightly beneath her legs and lowered her body slowly, never breaking their fastened eyes. As she turned to face the road, she placed her hand atop Calvin's on the wheel and laughed.

"Okay, preacher. You can let go now!"

Calvin wiggled to turn toward his wife. As he shifted his weight toward his wife, he glanced over his left shoulder to read the speedometer. It was well beyond120 miles per hour.

"Hey," he pleaded, "slow down. I don't want a red Ferrari as my casket when it's my time to go."

She slowed to eighty with a smile. A thought entered her mind, I kind of like a man telling me what to do … sometimes!

A helicopter flew low over the open car and zoomed ahead. As it moves ahead, it wagged from side to side and circled once more to do the same.

The second time, Kara waved and yelled what Calvin and Rosie thought to be an unheard, "Bye, Daddy! Have a great trip."

It did not take long to reach the first mountain range where they stopped at a viewing area. All three enjoyed the mountain scenery. In the desert, the sage was blooming. The sweet odor floated on the thermal currents and spilled into the overlook area. There it buried the burning smell of hot tar lifting from the pavement. Looking out over the vast desert, Calvin could see the mountain range they had left behind to the east. Although he could not see it, he knew that somewhere at the foothills was Copper Town. He hugged Rosie tightly and suggested to Kara that it was time to return home.

Kara offered to let Calvin drive back. He declined, but Rosie did not. Pulling onto Highway 50, she discovered the clutch caught quickly. Flying gravel that turned into squealing rubber as the tires met the asphalt was evidence that her discovery was too late. Once on the road, she set the cruise control to seventy-five and let the car glide across the desert floor until they reached the city limits of Copper Town.

The ride back was more uncomfortable for the preacher than the ride out. Kara refused to crowd to the door to allow Calvin the room Rosie did. She seemed to do the opposite by pushing her body toward the console. She turned slightly toward Calvin and stretched her left arm behind him. Her constant leaning toward Rosie to observe the speedometer caused her breasts to mash tightly against the preacher's arm. With each observation of the speed, she laughed and searched for Calvin's eyes. He did not allow her to secure them again, partly in fear of the temptation and partly in fear of detection by his wife.

While his wife was intensely observing the road, Kara's hand could find no other rest area than Calvin's thigh. He soon stopped squirming and wiggling, for those actions seemed to encourage the exploration of hands by the owner of the car.

After returning to the parsonage, Calvin and Rosie both retired to the balcony with a tall glass of sweet iced tea. A squeaky objection was voiced by Calvin's old wooden chair as he pulled it close to the rail and leaned back on the rear legs. He propped both feet on the rail of the balcony and sighed aloud. Pleasure became evident by his facial expressions as Rosie took a perch on the rail and began to massage his bare feet. After a second long sip of tea, he set the glass on the table next to his chair and leaned back with his eyes closed deep in thought. Without warning, Rosie sprung from the rail, landed beside her husband, and kicked the rear legs of his chair. He heard her laughter before he heard the thud of his body crashing to the floor, still seated in his chair. His head bounced like a basketball, while his arms flailed in both directions knocking over the table and spilling his tea on his chest.

"What in the world are you doing?" he yelled at his wife. The thought to join her in laughter has not registered yet.

"You know what I'm doing, preacher!" she said, using the same accent that Kara used. "I saw you looking at her legs and her panties. Don't say you didn't! And I sure didn't hear you object to those wondering hands of hers, preacher!"

"Rosie, you're right. I was afraid you would get mad if I said something to her. But, really, I couldn't help but see the panties. I did not gawk, and I looked away quickly! Honest! By the way, whose idea was it to go for a ride, and who was it that insisted I go?"

Calvin saw the smile on her face and decided to tease her a little. "What did you think of those flowery panties?"

His intentions to laugh were drained away as her ice cold tea emptied in a steady stream down his face. His attempt to escape was fruitless; the steady stream of sticky fluid followed him. As the last drops splattered on his head, he grabbed her legs, and she tumbled down on her wet husband. He held her tight, and they rolled along the floor. Their laughter was silenced when their lips meet. The kiss was long and as tender as their first. Although she would reflect often on that day's drive, she vowed she would never again share her jealousy and frustration with anyone, including her husband.

More as an effort to stop the loud noise that had awakened him than as a response to answer the ringing telephone, John Calvin grabbed the large black receiver and managed a, "Good morning, this is Pastor McGarney."

The person on the other end began immediately. "Hey, preacher! This is Michael. We've got a change in plans today. I'll pick you up in fifteen minutes. Be ready, ya hear?"

A sharp click in his ear informed the preacher that the caller hung up. My goodness, pondered Calvin, I thought I'd have a little while longer to sleep in this morning. The Lord knows I need it. His thoughts went back to the unproductive talk he and Rosie had until late last night. Try as he might to convince her they needed to leave the place, and leave soon, she was persuaded that God had brought them there, and she was not leaving. Rosie had fallen in love with the climate and the community upon arrival, and there was no swaying her to leave, even though her husband alluded to some of the supernatural threats that he felt loomed over them. At least she listened to him a little closer and didn't accuse him of being crazy. Perhaps, in time, he would be able to divulge all to her.

The sound of running water in the shower accompanied by the hot steam floating over the stall doors were signs he would have no shower this morning. Long ago, Calvin had vowed to never start his day without a shower when water was available. Today there was no time. He leapt from bed and dressed in dark jeans, a black cotton short-sleeve shirt, and his lightweight jungle boots given to him by his son. Standing in front of the mirror, he pulled on a black Ranger's hat. He turned at various angles and approved his selection of clothing. The shower was still running; Rosie loved long, hot showers. Her husband often watched her stand in the shower stall for long periods of time in which she would drain the hot water. Usually, she would tilt her head back and stand there with the water flowing over her face until she felt the warm water fading. Only then would she exchange the shower for her oversized towels. Many times, he had to follow her with only a supply of cold water.

Calvin glanced at his watch as he moved into the kitchen. With a knife, he slapped peanut butter and jam on two pieces of bread and capped them with two other pieces. With a tall glass of milk, he gulped down the sandwiches. The sound of the running water in the shower caused him to chuckle. He visualized his naked wife standing in the shower warming her body with the last drops of hot water.

Moving into the washroom, he retrieved the three vials of nectar and shoved them into his front pocket. A soft rap on the entry door alerted him to Michael's arrival. He moved to the door and opened it to permit Michael's entry.

"I don't have time to come in, preacher. We need to roll!"

"Let me tell Rosie I'm going Michael. She's in the shower and does not know I am up yet."

"Okay, but hurry up. Time is of the essence."

Calvin rushed through the bedroom and into the bathroom. With the water running, he opened the door; an action she detested. He watched as the white suds flowed softly down her perfect and flawless ebony skin. He wished he had more time.

"Hey, babe, Michael called while you were in the shower and told me we need to start earlier today … with whatever venture he has planned for us. He's in the foyer waiting, so I'm out of here. You and Beth have a good time today in Carson City and try not to wear the plastic out, okay?"

"Sure. Now close the door so I can rinse this soap off and get dressed." As a result of the intrusion into her privacy, she offered no farewell kiss.

The preacher followed Michael out of the parsonage, closing the door behind him. He remembered to secure the lock from the inside and heard it click upon latching. Calvin and his new friend make their descent in large leaps and crawled into the black Chevy Silverado. The engine fired, and they pull from the parking lot headed north to the South Loop Road. After they turned, Michael broke the silence.

"Do you have the vials? We're a little short on supply."

"Yes, I have them." Calvin answered, patting his pants pocket to reveal their location. "Where are we going?" he asked.

"Gotta run up to Gionni's and pick up Kara."

"Kara? What's she got to do with this?"

"You'll find out in a few minutes, preacher. We'll wait until the last minute to give you all the details. The less you know the better for all of us. It's been hard enough for us to hide our plans under the scrutiny of the old ones around here."

Calvin wanted to ask more but knew by Michael's tone it would be in vain. The truck turned into the opened gates of the Gionni estate. Calvin looked back and saw them closing. Two large Mastiffs trotted behind the truck. Michael stopped in the circle drive outside the main entry and turned the truck off. He got out of the truck without speaking and motioned for Calvin to follow him. As they approached the main entry, the door opened. Only Kara's head was visible as she peeked around the door and allowed them to enter. She closed the door behind them and swirled around to face them. They both glared into the bright eyes of the Banah, the daughter of Alexander Gionni. She quickly joined them in the center of the foyer.

"Good morning, men. Have you two had breakfast?" she asked, striking a seductive pose in her long, black satin housecoat.

It was Michael who answered, and who was obviously in charge of the morning expedition.

"It's too late for that. If either of you have not eaten, you'll have to grab something for the road. You're part of the game plan, Kara. Are you sure you want to go through with this? Are you ready?"

She nodded yes and instructed the two men to follow her.

The men followed her down a wide hallway to the left of the foyer. As she moved in front of them, her hips swayed causing the gown to move erratically. Calvin inspected the wooden beams more carefully today. His observation revealed that the exterior and interior walls were constructed with solid eight-by-eight inch walnut beams. Larger beams spanned the main entry creating an open cathedral design. All the trim along the stairs and walls were also of walnut. He could not imagine what it must have cost Alexander to build this home. From where did all this walnut come? he wondered.

Kara opened a large, thick walnut door to her left and entered. Calvin and Michael followed her into a bedroom that was larger than most of the homes in Copper Town. A large desk sitting along the right wall was covered with books and other instruments. It was Kara's destination. She stopped there and turned slowly to face Calvin. The preacher followed and stopped within arm's length of Kara; he looked down at the objects of her attention on the desk. Behind him, the door slammed. Calvin turned to find that Michael had not followed them into the bedroom. He was aware that he was alone with the daughter of Alexander Gionni.

"Where's Michael?" he asked.

"He's got an errand to run, but he'll be back in a moment."

"What is it you want to show me?"

If Calvin had lived as a worldly man, he would have been more selective in his questioning. Kara made no comment; she did not have to. The smile on her face and her glistening blue eyes sent a rush of blood to Calvin's face; it flushed red.

"Look at these syringes, preacher. They are filled with pure nectar from the blossoms of Aspen trees. Michael and I have worked hard through the night to gather it. I filled these up while he ran to fetch you." She continued without hesitation, pointing to a neat stack of slender tapered stakes. "Although they are dried now, the wooden daggers are covered with sap. But if they come in contact with water, or blood, the sap will become soluble. My favorites are these." She bent over the desk and pointed to a box of .357 pistol shells. "Have you ever seen anything like this, preacher?"

He bent down to look more closely at the shells. Upon close observation, he replied, "I've seen pistol shells before. To be honest with you, I don't see anything that special about these." He turned to observe her reaction. She was within inches now, and he saw the loosely tied belt slip away. Beneath, her supple breasts sprung forth with a bounce that freed them from the bondage of the robe. They were now on display for the preacher's inspection. Calvin let his eyes slowly sweep downward to inspect the soft lace of her panties. He glanced back at the pistol shells and fumbled for words.

"Eh, what are they?" he asked.

Kara laughed softly and posed the question again. "Have you ever seen anything like them?"

"They look like snake shot."

His face blushed again as he thought that she must have taken his comment for the blue plastic bullets as a description for her breasts.

She did not attempt to refasten her robe as she moved closer to the preacher. Her bosom was separated from him now only by the width of his heavy breathing.

"Yeah, preacher! It's the same thing, but we replaced the shot with sap. You will have to be at pointblank range for them to be effective. The sap must penetrate the body of a Nephilim to be lethal. If you splatter his skin, you'll have one ticked off monster on your hands."

Kara reached out and takes the preacher's hand. Straightening up, she pulled him in the direction of her bed. "Come, Calvin. Let me show you something else," she said. Her robe flowed underneath her arms revealing her body. Calvin lowered his eyes slowly; as he did so, he drank in the perfection of her creation. He was determined to take only one brief look at her lacy panties, and then he would put a stop to this.

Perhaps his plan would have worked, but she wore nothing but the robe. Calvin's blood boiled with passion. He could hardly breathe, and the swelling in his face throbbed in unison with other parts of his body. He followed the Banah, being pulled as a puppet by its master.

As they neared the giant bed, he pulled back slightly to resist the force by which he was being towed. As if in scripted reply, Kara let go of his hand and turned to face him. Resist as he may, Calvin could not take his eyes from the smooth, tanned skin of Kara. She knew his eyes were locked on her nakedness, and she spared not the preacher. With a soft and seductive shrug of her shoulders, the robe slid down her body and gently crumpled in a pile at her feet.

Calvin was not thinking of temptation or how he might flee. He was paralyzed with the beauty of this woman's body. Other than his wife, he had never seen a naked woman, not even in a magazine or movie. Before he could gather himself to escape the temptation, Kara stepped into his arms. They embrace tenderly; his head swam, and he felt as if he would faint. Blood continued to gush through his veins like water rushing over a broken dam. He could barely wait for the anticipated kiss that followed. Their lips touched softly like rose petals, and Calvin's heart pounded hard and strong. The kiss was long, and he did not remember when they separated. He remembered nothing but the kiss. With his eyes closed, he relived the kiss in his mind, and his hands explored the softness and warmth of her body.

Kara tenderly gripped his lower lip with her teeth. With her arms wrapped around his waist, she pulled him toward her as she backed toward the bed. Calvin opened his eyes and finally realized the white skin of this woman was not his wife. He searched his spinning head for something to grasp to help him out of this mess before it was too late.

The story of Joseph and Potipher's wife rose to mind, but he wondered what Joseph would have done if the wife had been as beautiful as Kara. Although Joseph's cloak had been torn off, Calvin's temptation stood before him in naked splendor. He thought of David and Bathsheba and confessed that Kara would be his Bathsheba. Nevertheless, the pain and agony David brought upon himself, his family, and his people warned Calvin to run, but he allowed himself to be pulled closer to the bed. Kara's blue eyes sparkled like diamonds in front of his, and he felt he would faint at any moment. Reaching deep into the depths of his soul, the preacher found a solid rock of meditation upon which he could have solid footing as he traveled along the slippery path he was upon. He braced his feet and declared he would stand against the wiles of the devil. He stopped abruptly. The stop jolted Kara, and she lost her grip on his lip. A small trickle of blood seeped down from it.

A thought streamed through his mind: If I can get my breath under control, maybe I can think clearly. Then maybe I can put a stop to this.

Yet, truthfully, he did not want to stop. He took his eyes away from hers and her grip loosened. His mind raced again with prayer: Stronger is he that is in me than he that is in the world. The preacher whispered a barely audible, "No, we cannot do this."

His resistance seemed to excite Kara, and she pulled his hands upward to her breasts and whispers, "Come on, preacher. There was only one perfect man who ever walked on this earth. Everybody sins."

Again he thought, Lord! You said you'd never give us any temptation too strong for us to endure, and that you would always prepare a door for our escape. Forgive me, Father, for my failures, but I did not enter into this room for the purpose of sin. Tricked, yes, but where is the door?

"Come on, John Calvin. I'll make it worth your time. It will be something you'll never forget."

Only Rosie used the name John Calvin in the way Kara uttered it, and perhaps that was all it took to jar Calvin back to his senses. After all, he was the preacher, and his conduct had to be worthy of his calling. He stepped away from the beautiful and naked daughter of the Nephilim, Alexander Gionni. Doing so he thought, We wrestle not against flesh and blood, but against principalities, against powers, against the rulers of the darkness of this world, against spiritual wickedness in high places. He realized it was not the Banah he was fighting; a higher force was seeking to devour him.

"Kara, I can't do this! It's a wrong to you, to my wife, to me, and especially to my God. It has nothing to do with you being undesirable, for I do want to bring this sin to fruition, but there is a Spirit of a Holy nature that dwells within me that cannot partake of ungodliness. I apologize for my moments of weakness, but I just cannot do this."

Calvin turned to leave and saw the door open before him. Michael burst into the room and covered his back with a deluge of slaps.

"Congratulations, preacher. You passed the test. Kara told me the only way she would join in on this adventure was if you were real and sincere."

The preacher turned and saw Kara walking to the bed. She picked up a stack of clothes and began dressing as she faced the two men; she was not modest and grinned at them.

When she was finished dressing, she posed for them. She was wearing blue jeans, a tight-fitting, heavyweight red shirt, and hiking boots.

"I'm ready. Let's make this happen!"

Racing to the desk, she grabbed a leather bag and carefully stuffed it full of her weaponry. She turned and motioned for the men to follow her as she headed into the hallway toward the foyer. Down the hall they went like three kids racing for the door to play outside after heavy rains had left them housebound for days. Entering the foyer, Kara skipped across the large room and opened the door to Alexander's study.

"Come," she said, "I thought the preacher man would be mine today, but I made plans just in case."

Calvin looked at Michael and asked, "What does she mean by *hers*?"

"Preacher, if you had given in to her, your life as a preacher would be over. Your marriage would be over, and your life here in Copper Town would be on the dark side. Calvin, you and Kara would have been mated by the Council. If you refused to be her mate and tried to return to Rosie, she would have driven a dagger through your heart. Then you would have been burned and your ashes scattered in the desert."

"I halfway believe that!" Calvin chuckled.

Michael did not laugh and replied, "Believe me, preacher, when I say it's the truth!"

"Michael, I noticed Kara had a small circular scar on her stomach. Who's mark?"

"It was Slim; he forced the mark of the Yada on her when she was younger. Alexander is not very happy about it?"

"How does Kara feel about that?" Calvin asked.

"Well, preacher, she says it will never happen, and that's why she is joining us today."

The two men followed Kara into Alexander's study. She moved to his large desk and pulled three identical, heavy nylon web pistol holsters from the bottom drawer. Each holster housed three matching, chrome-plated pistols. Unknown to Calvin, they were old Smith and Wesson Model 19s with four-inch barrels. Kara's hands moved swiftly from one pistol to the other. She pushed the cylinder release on each and loaded it with the plastic-covered loads she had in her bedroom. After she dropped six rounds into each cylinder, she swung the pistols clockwise in her right hand. The centrifugal force closed the cylinders, and with her left hand, she spun the cylinder by holding the trigger at half cock. She then carefully lowered the hammer and shoved each pistol back into the holsters.

Within seconds, Kara had all three pistols loaded and secured inside the web holstering. She tossed one to Michael and one to Calvin. She and Michael were synchronized with their actions. Both grabbed the holster by the handle of the pistol and dropped it down to their thigh, where it naturally lined up with their extended arms. From that point, they fastened two Velcro straps securely around their thighs, stretched the long Velcro straps from the top of the holsters through their belts, and fastened them to the other side of the strap. The preacher followed their examples.

"You'll need to make contact with the muzzle for these to work, preacher. They are close-range weapons, so don't waste them on distance. If you get a chance to shoot, keep shooting."

Kara turned and leapt effortlessly to the top of the high wall and retrieved the Sword of the Maseth. Like a cat she landed within arm's distance of Calvin and handed him the sword. He recognized it from his earlier encounter with Alexander and took it. The sword glowed red as it did earlier in his hands. Kara and Michael exchanged glances, and both shared a smile of confidence with this new discovery.

"Strap it to your side, preacher," Kara instructed and tosses him the sheath she also retrieved from the wall beneath the sword.

"I don't know how to use one of these," was his reply.

It was Michael who answered him. "Preacher, if a gang of men were attacking your wife, and there was a metal baseball bat lying nearby, would you use it to help defend her, or would you just use your fist?"

"I'd pick up the bat, of course."

"And what in the world would you do with it?"

"I'd swing it hard to keep them out of arm's reach, and besides, it would do more damage than my fist."

"Now you've got it. Use the sword in that manner. It will do more damage than a baseball bat. Besides, you are defending your wife, believe it or not."

Calvin strapped the sheath around his waist, letting it dangle on his left hip, and slid the sword into it. As he lets go of the handle, the fiery glow faded.

"For over a hundred years, the people in this town dug all over this area looking for that sword. Many thought they were mining for precious ore, but when Alexander decided to permanently settled the clan here, he knew a Sword of the Maseth was already prepared and waiting for a Bachar. Of course, the clan made millions of dollars with the ore they dug up. Alexander could never rest until the sword was found. They dug it up years ago, at nearly six hundred feet below the surface. It's his most precious acquisition."

Michael looked at Kara and said, "I'll take the Medieval Broad Sword."

Kara removed the sword with its sheath from high on the wall with the same easy leaping movement she used before and handed it to Michael. He pulled the sword out to show it to Calvin. The blade was nearly thirty-three inches long and shined like polished silver. It glistened as it reflected the light in the hollow of the heavy blood groove that ran the length of the blade. Including its curving cross guard, heavy pommel and black grip, it was over forty inches in length.

Kara had already retrieved the sword of her choice and strapped it to her waist. She pulled the sword out and laid it on Alexander's desk. The preacher would never know it is one of a kind. It was the victorious sword of King Arthur: the Excalibur. To Calvin, it was a thirty-one-inch silvery sword, polished to the point that it appeared to be made of mirrors rather than metal. The historical etchings, which Calvin could not discern, were numerous on the blade, hilt, and pommel. The sword was over forty and a half inches long. It was a large and cumbersome weapon in the hands of a woman, but Kara yielded it with both precision and ease. She was not an ordinary woman; she was a Banah, the daughter of a clan leader.

Michael looked at her and laughed. "Boy, if we only had time to tell the story behind that blade and the role your dad played as Merlin!"

She laughed, too, and replied, "If we live another day, maybe we can fill the preacher in, eh? But for now I'll take King Arthur's Templar as a backup."

"The one he used to swear in his first knight?"

"That's it," she said, and laid a short fourteen-and-one-half inch mirror finished sword on the desk. It had similar markings as the Excalibur and measured nearly twenty-two inches in total length.

"Now, would you and the preacher like a back up?"

"Give us the matching Spartan Laconia Short swords."

Kara retrieved two ancient Greek swords and laid them on the desk. They were made of forged steel, leaf shacked, and double edged. They were nearly twenty inches long with tangs of flat cross sections. The hilts were bound on both sides by bone and covered with thin sheets of metal. Although original, they were in mint condition. Alexander had kept them in the family since his acquisition several hundred years before.

Kara retrieved three shoulder harnesses made out of the same black, heavy nylon and laid them on the desk with the swords. On the front of each strap were two long, slender wooden spikes that looked like long tapered candles. The spikes were freshly carved from green saplings. Calvin noticed sap seeping from the freshly peeled bark. Each had been shoved into small fasteners that would ordinarily hold large-caliber rifle cartridges.

After Kara distributed them to the men, the three of them slipped them on and fastened the latches on the front. Kara retrieved a rifle from a shelf behind the desk and tossed it to Michael.

"A contribution from Luther," she said. "Of course he must stay out of this."

"Of course," confirmed Michael. "You have only one dart?"

"No, I have two others," she said and laid them on the desk.

Michael unloaded the dart in the chamber of the tranquilizer gun, on loan from the local veterinarian, and laid the dart on the table. "Now, preacher, I need the vials I gave you."

Calvin pulled them from his pocket and placed them in the outstretched hand of Michael. The Banah, son of the Nephilim Philip, poured the fluid from the vials directly on the blades of the swords and handed them to Kara. She in turn, used a small brush to spread the liquid along the surface of the blades. Trying to be helpful, Calvin pulled the Maseth Sword out and laid it on the desk. His efforts were not performed without the sword flaming.

"You won't need it with that sword, preacher," Kara stated. "If you do, we may all be in trouble."

He retrieved the sword, which flamed again, and returned it to the sheath. Michael took the last vial and filled the three darts. He chambered it with one of the darts and swung the rifle over his head by placing one arm through the swing. It lay flat on his back and was barely visible from the front. When they left that day, their weapons would be placed in the back of the truck, but upon arrival, they would gird themselves again in like fashion. The other two darts he capped and shoved into the cargo pocket on his left thigh.

Kara gave the last instructions. "Go ahead and sheath the swords and buckle up. The sap is nearly dry, but the inside of the sheaths will help preserve the fluid. They'll only come out once from this time on, make 'em count."

All three of them were dressed completely in minutes, and they stood to observe one another. The trio resembled a conglomeration of a SWAT team and a group of medieval knights.

Michael broke the silence. "Preacher, perhaps it would benefit you to pray for our adventure? And, who knows, we also could be beneficiaries of them."

Calvin nodded in agreement and prayed. He prayed for victory of good over evil; he magnified a sovereign God who was in control even when the world perceived Him as dead. He gave thanks for the many blessings he had experienced throughout his life, and finally, he asked for protection for the three of them as they traveled into unknown waters. Conclusively, he stated, "Amen!"

Michael smiled at him and said, "So be it!"

Kara echoed with, "Let it be so!"

The three of them made their departure in full regalia.

Chapter 24

CHAINED UNDER DARKNESS

These are spots in your feasts of charity, when they feast with you, feeding themselves without fear: clouds they are without water, carried about of winds; trees whose fruit withereth, without fruit, twice dead, plucked up by the roots; Raging waves of the sea, foaming out their own shame; wandering stars, to whom is reserved the blackness of darkness for ever.

JUDE 13–14

Thousands of questions raced through the mind of the preacher, yet he dared not ask. Although he did not know the specifics of their plan, he was aware that all was centered on a common thread they all shared: marks of the Yada. Each one of them was willing to risk life or limb in an effort to exonerate the dreaded Nephilim responsible for the marks: Pavel "Slim" Swarkovi. Calvin resolved to sit quietly by the window of the bench-style seat in Michael's truck as it churned down the drive of the Gionni estate and headed west on the South Loop Road.

Kara, too, sat motionless between the two men. Earlier all three of them had been filled with enthusiasm and were eager to set the day's activities into motion. Now their eagerness had turned to a sullen realization that they were about to embark in mortal combat with a creature that had been honed by millions of years of conflict. He would show neither fear nor mercy if they failed in their quest. Each of them weighed the possible outcomes and decided to push forward; there would be no turning back now!

It took only a few minutes for the truck to circle the Loop to the north side of town. To the occupants of the truck, the trip seemed an eternity. Kara and Calvin began to adjust their weapons as the truck turned right onto Second Street and rolled into the parking lot behind the parsonage. Although it was barely audible, the soft crunch of gravel sounded like thunder as the truck came to a stop near the stairs leading upward into the parsonage. The silence of the engine provided some relief to the trio as they exited and silently pushed the doors closed. They returned the silent wave of greetings from Antonio as he ceased work in his garden, leaned on his rake, and watched the three prepare their weaponry. There was no look of surprise on the Mexican's face. Instead, he gave them a look of perception coupled with frustration; a frustration that appeared to come from the fact that he had not been invited to join the quest.

Michael gave the command with a motion of his hand to ascend the steps of the parsonage. His light footsteps brought him speedily to the top, where he turned to watch the others follow. Kara motioned for Calvin to follow Michael, and she followed on his heels. Her nearness revealed a new relationship she had developed for the preacher; she would now serve him as his guardian. This new relationship was based upon her respect and admiration for a man who lived what he preached. Sure, he had a little slip for a moment, and the two of them had kissed, but she had never known a man that could turn back after he had gone that far with her. With this newfound admiration, she had vowed to give her life for him if it was needed. Besides, she mused, *if he was the called Bachah, my chances of survival are best invested in his hands.*

After they joined Michael on the landing, he motioned to the roof with his thumb and turned to face the wall. With an effortless leap, he disappeared over the twelve-foot wall. Calvin stood looking upward, his mouth agape at the ease of the feat. In his upward gaze, he saw Michael's head appear over the edge, and he motioned for them to follow.

Kara leaned against the wall with her back, bent her knees, and cupped her hands together, forming a stirrup for Calvin. She nodded her head and whispered, "Up you go! Give me your foot!"

"I still can't reach the top, Kara," Calvin whispered. His lips brushed the sides of her ear, and his breath was hot on her skin.

Kara whipped her long, blonde hair, which she had gathered into a ponytail, and turned slightly, placing her lips close to the preacher's ear as she commanded, "Give me your foot and jump!"

The authoritativeness of her voice startled Calvin. Before he realized what he is doing, he placed his right boot in Kara's hands, squatted, and jumped. He was immediately conscious that his leap, or rather Kara's toss, was going to put him too high over the wall. He would land near the center of the building. He grimaced and stiffened his body for an inevitable crash, but just as he cleared the top, Michael grabbed him. The Banah placed him silently down on the flat roof beside him. As his feet touched the tarry turf of the roof, he observed Kara's nimble landing beside them. With the open arms of gesture from Michael to huddle, the three of them pushed their foreheads together.

"Where's the portal?" asked Kara.

"I don't know, but the preacher does. Calvin," he continued, "you are the only one that has been through the Garden's upper portal. That entitled you to go through it. Once it is opened, as your guest, we can enter through it. Do you remember where it is?"

Calvin looked around and remembered the view he had over the roof of the store. He moved only a few feet to his left and lined up the store across the street with Gionni's home. Slowly, he inched to the center of the roof and whispered to Michael, "It's somewhere here, but I don't see it."

"You won't be able to see it until it opens. All you have to do, Calvin, is want it to be opened. Think about it; you must will it to be so."

Calvin's mind shifted from the fear that prevented him from opening the portal to the thought of Rosie and the mark of the Yada she bore upon her body. He silently swore an oath he will enter the Garden and face the Nephilim for Rosie's sake. As he walked in a calculated straight line toward Main Street, he saw a circling distortion of tar on the roof. It turned bright red with fiery yellow streaks and materialized like lava flowing from a volcano. Swirling rapidly, it grew wider until it was near six feet in diameter. The blazed action of its spin faded into a dark discus that developed as a black circle embedded in the roof. He stepped upon the circle and turned to look at his companions. Michael and Kara watched attentively as the preacher lined up the landmarks and moved across the rooftop in search of the portal. Both had unsheathed their swords and followed after him.

The preacher watched them approach him and gestured downward to his feet. He followed with a shrug of his shoulders as if to ask, "What now?" Without warning, the support of the portal was gone, and Calvin crashed through several feet of air. His fall took him through the rock formation of the bower, where he crumpled with a crash on the rocky floor of the Nephilim Garden. As a result of the brutal landing, he slipped into unconsciousness. His limp body rolled sideways across the rocky terrain.

"He'll crash through like a rock when he finds it," Michael whispered. "It's the only way."

Kara nodded. "He may drop sixteen to twenty feet into the garden, Michael. It has to be at least that high. Have you heard any descriptions of the garden?"

"No, I have not. They keep it pretty much to themselves. As far as I know, Calvin and Rosie have been the first humans to walk inside the area of the Temple Garden."

"How far do you think Slim is in his healing process from the human blood?"

"I don't know, Kara. He's been in there for a week, and it usually takes one to three weeks for recovery. I'd say the transformation is near complete now. It won't be long, and he'll be right back in there. I know one thing for sure: he knows we are here."

"Oh no!" interrupted Kara as Calvin dropped through the portal disc and disappeared from their view. The daughter of Alexander rushed forward and dropped through the portal behind the preacher. Her sword was held high by the handle with both hands. The point was angled downward in anticipation of spearing the hideous creature she knew was waiting below. Her long ponytail waved high above her head, like a banner before it vanishes, through the garden portal. Michael's boots brushed the tip of her hair on an angle of descent that would place him near Kara's landing. His broad sword was also held high above his head with both hands. He was ready to swing it forward upon landing.

Calvin was unconscious for only a fraction of a second. He felt as if a ton of bricks had been placed on his chest, for he could not breathe. He blinked his eyes in rapid succession to focus upon the gruesome creature standing over him. His left foot pinned Calvin to the rocky floor in the center of the bower. This Nephilim had no resemblance of his human form. He was much larger and grotesque than the preacher remembered from the night he so viciously slew the outlaw bikers. Mammoth-sized muscles rippled and twitched beneath his dark cobalt skin.

Pavel opened his arms wide as Calvin watched helplessly. His wings spread wide, making the Nephilim look like a prehistoric bat. His ears were alert and erect; much higher on his head and a lot more pointed than Calvin remembered. His hair bristled on his head like an angry attack dog as he moved the foot from the preacher's chest. He stooped and lowered his head toward him. With eyes glowing bright red as fire, he displayed his long caninelike fangs.

Calvin felt the hot breath of the Nephilim inches from his face, as he hissed, "You dare to enter our temple, preacher man? Today, you will die."

The Nephilim stood erect, and again placed his foot on the chest of the preacher, but no pressure was applied. Kara fell crashing through the portal with her knees flexed. Her feet landed astraddle the preacher's head. She reversed the grip and twirled the sword high over her head. Unprompted, she flexed her elbows and slashed downward and to her left at Slim. Her swing came to a halt with the sword parallel to the floor. She twisted her hands ninety degrees and sprung upward with a backslash across the creature's neck. She missed the second strike, but the first left a deep gash in the side of her foe's left shin. His blood splattered the preacher and spewed onto the surrounding stones of the columns and floor.

The Nephilim disappeared with a leap before the first drop of blood fell. He vanished into the thick green vegetation of the garden, as Calvin quickly rolled to safety. He climbed to his knees, and after air returned to his lungs, he stood.

During Calvin's roll to safety, Michael arrived through the portal. He swung his sword high in a ready position as Kara had, and the two of them circled the preacher slowly while he regained his breath and his composure.

"We can follow the blood trail!" Kara quipped. Her voice indicated she was ready for action.

"No!" warned Michael. "It's what he wants. Besides, the trail won't go far. He's already healing. We'll stay till preacher is ready."

"I don't think he'll wait, Michael!"

"No! He'll charge us. Be ready. He'll pick one of us and put every ounce of power he has into killing that one. He'll try to take us out one at a time. Hurry, preacher! Get up and get your sword ready."

Calvin raised the Sword of the Maseth high, mimicking the stances of his hybrid companions. The sword transformed into a burning torch sending an orange flickering light throughout the perimeter of the bower.

Smash! The startling noise sounded like a long rod slapped sharply across the top of a canvas tent. All three of them jumped with a startle, and Calvin curled his body into a tight wad. Realizing the source of the crash was above them, they shifted their gaze overhead to the tall walls of the bower. There they saw the Nephilim: however, their observation was not in time to prevent him from leaping to the floor and grabbing Calvin. He lifted him high above the floor and struck at his neck with his exposed incisors. The fangs fell in a stabbing motion toward the juggler vein of the one he had decided to destroy first: the preacher.

Michael hurdled upward off the floor. With both hands, he swung his broad sword with so much force toward the Nephilim's neck that his near miss sent him spinning through the air like a ragdoll. He crashed into the green foliage and rolled to his feet instantly, facing the creature. The precision of his swing required Pavel to shift his head sideways to avoid the deadly strike. In so doing, his fangs missed the neck of Calvin and sunk deep into the muscular portion of his shoulder. The pressure of the bite exceeded that of a grizzly bear. As a result, the preacher screamed out with pain. Before a second bite could be inflicted, Kara flew through the air like an acrobat. Her legs were spread, and she straddled the back of the Nephilim. Both of her arms were raised high above her head, but the sword was missing. In its place were two of the long, wooden spikes saturated with the deadly fluid. She plunged the two darts deep into the base of the Nephilim's neck. Both slice downward at angles that brought the tips together deep within the Nephilim's flesh.

A bloody screech gurgled from the throat of Pavel as he realized the source of the deadly venom. In one fluid motion, he dropped Calvin and swung Kara from his back. Like an enraged bull at a rodeo, he reached back with both hands and yanked the pegs out of his back. He spun and watched Kara smash into a stone pillar, where she slid down atop one of the golden boxes. Throwing both of his arms backward and over his head, and with a dart in each, he sent them like arrows toward Kara. She ducked and leapt to her feet as the wooden pegs struck the golden box where they shattered into several splintered pieces. As the fragments fell to the rocky floor, the Nephilim disappeared again into the foliage.

Kara rejoined the group and they once more begin to circle.

"He's after the preacher," said Kara.

Michael nodded and added, "Yeah, I noticed. Preacher," he continued, "I know you're in a lot of pain, but you must hang on to that sword and swing it. He'll make a loud noise or scream on every attack. It's meant to startle you. Predators do that. It causes their prey to freeze for a second. I'll tell you what, you watch the top of the walls, and Kara and I will watch the sides."

"Good job with the spikes, Kara! How much damage do you think they inflicted?" Michael asked.

"Some, but I fear it wasn't as much as we would have liked. He got them out pretty quickly. The next time I'll squeeze off a round or two from the pistol. We'll see how quickly he gets them out."

Crash! A large object slammed through the vegetation behind them striking into the stones of the floor. As Kara and Michael spun in the direction of the noise, Calvin readied his burning sword. This time he did not flinch. He stood with his sword burning brighter than before, ready to do battle with the ancient being. Kara turned to face the opposite direction. She would not fall for the distractive noise of the large stone thrown over their heads by Pavel. She stood ready unaware that Slim had singled her out for his attack. Her stance was unwavering as the Nephilim charged. His large right hand struck outward and across her body as he retreated again into the garden. He decided to deploy a strike-and-run strategy. His retreat was not before Kara placed the muzzle of her pistol against his body and pulled the trigger. The loud blast of the gun applauded her marksmanship. She had just sent a plastic bubbled bullet loaded with the deadly fluid deep into the monster's massive intestines. Kara reeled clockwise from the blow he delivered and dropped to her hands and knees. Blood spilled from her body.

"Kara, are you okay?"

Looking at the blood, Michael knew the answer to his own question. Frustration stirred his inner thoughts and was displayed on his face. How could I have fallen so easy for that old trick? he thought.

Kara collapsed with a soft thud into a puddle of her own blood on the stony surface of the garden. She rolled over in the ever-increasing crimson pool and stared up at the preacher and the Banah. Both of her breasts have been ripped open with two deep gashes that penetrated to the depths of her ribs. Another long gash from the talons of the slash of the Nephilim barely missed her throat. A fourth one ripped open her stomach. She gritted her teeth and tried to force a smile that never materialized, yet she managed to report the effects of her shot.

"Gut shot!" she said. "I got him! But it was a gut shot."

"It'll work, but it will just take a little more time," Michael acknowledges. "Sorry I fell for that distraction maneuver. I should have known better."

"Will it kill him?" asked Calvin.

"No, it's just going to weaken him and give us a fighting chance. We still have to take his head. That's where you come in, preacher, with the sword."

"Give me your shirt, Michael," Kara instructed her companion.

Michael yanked the shirt off, popping all the buttons and ripping it down the back. He spreads the two pieces, still connected by the collar, into one long bandage and wrapped it tightly around Kara.

"You'll have to hold it together tightly in the front to keep pressure," he said. "We'll have to get in touch with Alexander."

Michael reached over his shoulder and removed the dart rifle. He held it ready, muzzle facing outward as if he was a member of a SWAT team.

"Are you ready, preacher?"

Calvin answered, "Yeah."

Kara wrapped the shirt tightly around her upper body and across her stomach to apply direct pressure and to absorb some of the bleeding. Her head grew faint, and she collapsed to the floor on her back. Her exhausted efforts were rewarded with the vision of Pavel's stealthy landing atop the stone bower.

"He's coming from above!" screamed Kara.

This time it is Michael who was singled out for the attack. The blast of the rifle sent a dart deep into the chest of the Nephilim as he fell on Michael. His heavy body pinned the Banah to the ground where they both lay motionless. To Calvin it appeared as if the fight was over, but he sprung forward and sank the burning sword deep into the back of the Nephilim. Pavel cursed the preacher as he vanished again into the Garden.

"Preacher," Kara faintly cried, "you must aim for the neck! You had him. Don't stop swinging the blade until you have his head, understand?"

"Don't you get it, Calvin?" Michael added with a voice filled with excruciating pain. "It looks like it is up to you now."

Calvin looked at Michael who was still sprawled on the floor. His right leg was bent under his body, twisted and broken. The jagged ends of a broken femur protruded through his thigh.

Michael acknowledged Calvin's evaluation of his leg, evidenced by his facial expression. He said, "It's busted up worse that it looks, and my rib cage is crushed. It looks like Slim has decided to take me and Kara out in order to get to you, preacher."

"He looks pretty weak now," Kara whispered. "I think his strength has been rendered to that of a human. It will take him a while to recover from the venom."

"Yes, but he's still crafty. Looks like you'll have to go after him alone, Calvin."

"He shifted to human form as he left," added Kara.

"That means he was healed from the curse of human blood. If he grows weak in the human form it'll be easier, Calvin."

Kara pressed the blood-soaked shirt tighter and managed to sit up and look at Calvin. "Just be careful. He has the power to transform. What you know as Slim is his chosen form, but he can appear as others. Don't be deceived."

"Oh, Kara!" The words slithered from the garden and reached the ears of the three within the bower. They all know it as the voice of Slim. Although sinister, it carried the tone of a young child as it repeated the words.

"Oh Kara! Oh, my sweet, little Kara! So, you don't want the mark of Yada from old Slim, eh? Tell me, my little queen, is it gone now? Perhaps with other parts of your beautiful body it's gone!" The child's voice was more hideous than before. He cried out again from the depths of the garden. "You're not parading that little body around now, are you?"

"Go, John Calvin." She pointed in the direction of the Nephilim.

Calvin moved slowly into the lush, thick vegetation of the garden. His sword burned bright and lit the ground for his footsteps of the path he had chosen. The preacher prayed, and scripture verses flowed from his lips. Normally, fear would cause caution, but now he was determined to end the life of Slim.

There was a rustle in the vines ahead, and he raises his sword high, prepared to strike. The sword's elevated position cast a brilliant light into the leafy flora. He was not prepared for what he saw and gasped, nearly dropping his sword. It was Rosie. She stood before him completely nude; her shining blackness reflected the brilliance of the sword's radiance.

"Rosie!" he yelled.

Another voice pierced the eerie light of the scene from behind him. It was Kara's. Desperation strained her voice. "It is not Rosie, John Calvin. It's Slim."

"No, it's me, John Calvin," declared Rosie.

"What are you doing here?" asked the preacher, ready at any moment to drop his sword and run to embrace his wife.

"Slim came through the door of the parsonage this morning before Beth arrived. He brought me in here as a hostage. He knew you were coming. He told me all about the night in the RV camp. Help me, Calvin! Please, I'm so scared!"

The preacher lowered his sword with his right hand and closed the short distance between them. She stepped toward him with arms open to embrace him about his lower back. Calvin's heart anticipated the sweetness of his beloved wife's embrace.

"It's entirely my fault for bringing you here," he said, watching as Rosie slipped form the green foliage and starts toward him with open arms. Behind her there was another sparkle of light in the undergrowth. He stared intently and discovered it to be a refection of light from the short Templar's blade held high in Kara's hand. "Kara, no!" he yelled.

Rosie looked over her shoulder in the directions of Calvin's view and saw Kara, but it was too late. The slender blade thrust through her upper body from the rear and protruded several inches beyond her bare breasts. Blood seeped instantly down her stomach, yet with outstretched arms she lunged forward to feel the arms of her husband for one last time. She grabbed her husband by his shoulders and looked down at the tip of the Templar. Lining the tip up with Calvin's heart, she peered into his eyes and moved toward him. Kara removed her sword from Rosie's back just as their bodies collided. She gripped Rosie's hair with one hand, yanked her body backward, and sunk the Templar again into her chest.

Rosie sunk to one knee and looked up at her husband. "Help me, Calvin! What have you let her do to me?"

Anger overcame Calvin, and without hesitation, he swung his sword high over his head grasping it with both hands to end the life of this blonde-haired half-breed. In mid stride, the blade of his sword turned to crystal, and he was unable to move. From his grip upon the sword flowed an energy that jolted every ounce of his body. Like an electrical charge, it rendered him helpless, and he released the sword. Only then was he able to step backward in amazement, for the sword remained motionless and suspended in midair. He and Kara both watched as it turns to its shiny metallic form and dropped toward the pebbled floor of the garden. Before it could strike the turf, Kara caught it with her right hand. She gripped the handle tight with both hands and spun her body in a complete circle. The momentum she generated with the spin sent the sword on an orbital path that did not cease until it passed through the neck of the kneeling Rosie. It was a brutal action, and Calvin's heart filled with grief and hatred as he saw his wife's head fall to the ground.

Pulling his short sword form his belt, he leapt forward and stabbed

Kara. She grabbed his hand, holding the blade tight, and pulled him close. She grabbed the back of his head with her other hand kissed his cheek. "Look!" she whispered, pointing to Rosie's lifeless body.

Calvin's tear-streaked face painfully turned to look at the mutilated body of his beautiful wife. He blinked away tears that enable him to see the lifeless body of his wife slowly turning into the body of Slim. With a sizzling sound, Slim was transformed into the Nephilim, Pavel. As they watch, a loud blast echoed throughout the garden, and with a puff of smoke, the Nephilim was gone.

The preacher realized his mistake and looked back at Kara. She smiled, still holding his head, and said, "It's alright. I understand. You missed the vital organs. I think I'll be okay. If Dad makes it back tonight, I know I will."

"'Alexander is not scheduled to be back until Thursday. We need to get out of here and get you to a hospital!"

"No! No! If I don't make it until Dad gets back, that's just the way it is! Now, help me back to the portal."

Calvin placed his arm around Kara's waist and helped her back to the center of the garden. Her left hand rested on his shoulder as she limped. Calvin was in awe when he noticed the blood had ceased from flowing from her wounds. Her limp was not as noticeable as earlier, and her strength seemed to be returning.

"You seem to be a little stronger, Kara!"

"Yes, children of the Nephilim heal quicker than humans," Kara assured Calvin.

"You'll have some pretty nasty scars."

"Only until Dad gets home."

"Oh, yeah, I forgot."

Just as the two of them stumbled into the center of the bower, the light pouring down through the portal was blocked with darkness. It was followed with a flicker, and then resumed as before. The shifting light was caused by Luther entering the Temple Garden. He landed in front of Kara and Calvin as soundless as a cat. He crouched like a tiger ready for battle. A red backpack was slung over his shoulder, which he removed as he dropped to the ground in front of Kara and Calvin.

"Dad, eh," Luther's stare was fixed on Calvin as if he needed to be selective in which words he would choose to use. He continued. "Dad telephoned and said you needed help. I brought medical supplies."

His gaze was fixed on Kara's bloody torso, and he instructed her, "Take the shirt off and sit down." He began unzipping the pack and laying out antiseptic cream and a large, sterile gauze to bandage Kara's wounds. The bloody remnants of her clothes were tucked back inside his pack. Luther made quick work of attending to Kara's wounds and was constantly looking about into the depths of the garden. He instructed Kara to hold the large, sterile gauze to her breasts as he wrapped her torso tightly. Luther slipped his polo shirt over his head and handed it to his sister. Subtle moans slipped from her mouth, as she cautiously put the shirt over her head and settled it on her bandaged body.

Luther stood and looked around. His survey complete, he began to work on Calvin's shoulder.

"I guess I'll need a tetanus shot for the bite?" Calvin asks. He watched as Luther cleaned and dressed the bite on his shoulder.

"No, Nephilim are not affected by germs that are dangerous to humans, nor do they carry infectious diseases. This is to protect you from other infections until Dad arrives tonight. "

"You need to take care of Michael. He seems to have suffered some serious injuries."

"It's too late, preacher. Michael is dead."

Calvin stepped back aghast and looked at Kara. She nodded and said," He knew it, preacher. He didn't want you to be distracted."

"What about Alexander?"

"He has the gift of healing, preacher, as long as there is life. You should know there is only one resurrection."

"Yes, I know. I was growing fond of Michael."

"He's like Dad," Kara added, allowing tears to roll down her checks, mix with her blood, and splash crimson on the floor. "I wish he knew about Slim's death. That's all he cared about, freeing Kristen from Slim. At least now, she and I are both free."

She looked at Luther and climbed to her feet with no assistance from him. Luther grasped the broad sword by its blade and freed it from Michael's lifeless grip. He flipped it into the air a hundred and eighty degrees, and the handle came to rest in his hand. He crouched and surveyed the ceiling area. Calvin was amazed at the muscular structure of Alexander's son. He looks like Conan! he thought to himself.

"What are you doing?" Kara asked. "It's time we got out of here. I'll leap through the portal first, and you can toss Calvin through. I'll catch him."

"Not so fast, little sister. Dad said there was a Seraph with Slim. He will not let us leave alive. Can the preacher turn the sword?"

"No, I don't think he can. In the hands of the Bachar, it guards the user. He struggles."

"I guess Dad sent him here for nothing."

Kara looked at Calvin and back to her brother. "He has the power of the Maseth and a fearless drive. He may be our only chance against the Seraph."

"Okay, grab the Excalibur and stand ready. You lie here and help us watch for his attacks."

Before Kara could assure her brother she would contribute to the cause, he sailed into the uppermost part of the bower. His knees were flexed to absorb his landing on the stony bower. He slashed across the top of the formation from right to left and sprung back to the center of the rocky floor of the bower. His moves seemed to Calvin as being precise and well determined, yet he seemed to slash at nothing but the air. Kara heard the crinkling noise of broken glass before she saw what Luther saw earlier. He was her older, Banah brother, and had lived many years prior to her birth. He had learned much from his Nephilim father and remembered all of what he learned of the Seraph. A large, star-shaped specter standing on the rocky rim shattered into hundreds of pieces as a result of the blow by Luther.

Like heavy raindrops rushing down a steep roof to gather as one in the flowing gutter, the gemstone pieces rushed to the center of the room and became one. As they spring upward into the glassy physical form the Seraph chose for its manifestation, they took on an oval shape with hundreds of sparkling barbs jutting outward. The retransforming has been awkwardly slow, yet deliberate. It reminded Calvin of ants crawling toward one common burrow.

The Seraph's alteration continued until it had taken on Nephilim-like characteristics. Its head, arms, and body were all covered with the transparent barbs. Although his stance had divided them, they all saw his face. If several people circled the being, they would all see its beastlike face, for it appeared to look in all directions. At times it reminded the preacher of a bear, then a lion, and then an eagle. His mind could not keep up with the spontaneous shifting. It served its purpose to distract.

Luther froze from the hypnotic glare of the beast. To him its face was shifting not as animals, but as humans. Thousands of faces of people he had known for years rolled before him, as if on a cylinder. Each one tempted him to reflect upon the relationship and adventures he had with it. The rolling screen ceased and became a flashing imagine of portraits flashing one after another until he stared into the mirrored surface and saw himself.

This was the conversion the Seraph had planned from the beginning. All the moving images were only foreplay in which the spirit would challenge Luther to face himself. Kara's brother relaxed his grip on the broad sword for only a second. It was the opening the Seraph needed. Instantaneously, the beast's structure changed in flight into a glass spear. The Banah's sidestep prevented the spear form piercing his vital organs. Unfortunately, the shimmering javelin penetrated the muscular part of his torso beneath his ribs. Luther grabbed the tail of the spear before it passed completely through him. His body remained in its previous frozen stance.

From the stone floor behind her brother, Kara struck upward with the Excalibur at the lance's point and severed the spike into two pieces. The larger section dropped to the stones. Luther withdrew the frontal section and shattered it against the pillars in front of him. The tinkling sound was heard again, and the long section next to Kara flowed like water to the shattered pieces, where it became whole again.

Assuming the shape it had before, Luther found himself looking into the mirror once more. He sprung forth to thrust the crystal phantom as it started the spinning faces anew. Luther's sword disappeared into a cloud of quartz fragments into which the beast has transformed. Each slither was razor sharp, and in unison they jetted toward the Banah. Instead of a defensive move, it countered as an inundation of deadly missiles, which exploded to impale Luther. He could not avoid all the fiery darts. His clothing, boots, and body were ripped to shreds from the attack. The Banah warrior staggered and managed to draw the courage and strength to turn and face the creature again. His body seeped life-sustaining fluids soaking his clothing of rags to crimson.

Calvin rushed in with his sword which blazed as a midnight torch. The creature emitted a high-frequency screech that was intermingled with the tinkling of glass. His form shifted to that of the preacher as he leapt to the top of the bower. The startled look on Calvin's face gave testimony to the accomplished purpose of the change. The beast had changed to the glass spear and propelled itself toward the preacher. No one had time to react to the speed of this charge. Luther was the sharp spear's target, and he was too weak to avoid the assault. In the form of the javelin, the Seraph entered the heart of Kara's brother. The Banah's death would not be in vain; he grabbed it for the second time and held it firmly.

Kara bound from the floor behind her brother, and with an upward motion, she snipped the spear. Her blade sliced some of the shredded clothing on Luther's back. Her action was nonstop, and her foot work was swift as she stepped through with her right foot behind Luther, aside his left shoulder. The blade was now raised high as she swept her left foot forward and around her brother's shoulder and dropped it in front of him. She assumed a horse stance as the blade traveled down Luther's chest and sliced through the spear again, inches from her brother's hand. Luther drew the crystal sliver from the center of his chest and fell to the ground, grasping it in with his fist.

"The sword," Kara yelled to Calvin. "We need the light beam. Touch the sword to the pieces."

Calvin unsuccessfully tried to will the sword form the burning torch to the shimmering beam of light, but it only flamed brighter and hotter. He realized it was his emotions that controlled the sword, and at present, it was anger that controlled his emotions. Soft puffs of air escaped from his lips as he slowed his breathing and regained his composure. The preacher shifted his emotions from anger to serenity. The sword changed in unison with him. In his hands, the torch became a beam of light shining brighter than the midday sun.

"Touch the pieces!" shouted Kara, as she feverishly slashed at the crystal pieces seeking to flow toward the one in Luther's hand. "Don't let them come together. Hurry, preacher!"

Calvin touched the piece nearest to him with the brilliant tip of the sword. Upon contact, its movement stopped, and it changed from transparent to opal and cast multiple tiny rainbows across the garden greenery. With the fading of the rainbows, the opal turned to a diamond lump and ceased all forms of life. Surprisingly, before his eyes, the solid chunk of diamond crumbles into a pile of small diamonds.

The preacher wasted no time in stabbing the other two pieces with the tip of his sword and stood with Kara to watch the repetitive process.

"You did it," she shouted, slapping the preacher on the back.

Her attention turned quickly to her brother, who was sitting on the stones with his arms spread open as if seeking one last hug from his sister. She dropped to face him, and the two clutched each other for the last time.

"Get the preacher and yourself out of here and away from this place quickly, while you can," he whispered. It was a whisper only audible to his sister, and with it, he smiled and died in her arms.

Kara tenderly laid her brother on his side and rolled him to his back. While on her knees, she swooped up a handful of diamonds and stuffed them into the pocket of Calvin's cargo pants. Thrusting the tip of her sword into the stone floor, she leaned heavily upon it and rose to her feet.

"Come," she said, "it is time to leave. Our work here is finished."

The two of them sheathed their swords and moved to the center of the bower. Kara fashioned her hands into a familiar stirrup and looked intently at Calvin. "You will have to help more this time, preacher. Jump hard when you leap, and be ready to help me if I don't make it all the way out."

"Okay," answered Calvin. He placed his right boot into her cupped hand and bent much lower on his right knee than earlier. From this deeper crouch, he was able to flex his muscles more as he sprung upward. Although badly injured, Kara's strength was greater than either of them expected, for the preacher sailed through the portal and crashed on the flat roof of the casino. He rolled to his feet and stood near the portal.

Below, Kara winced from the pain caused by the exertion of propelling the preacher through the portal. She breathed quickly two or three times, and then bent her knees to make her own jump to safety. Grasping her sides with her hands, she leapt through the portal.

Calvin was waiting with both arms open in preparation to grab his new friend if her leap was short. Kara's jump brought her to the rim of the portal, where she landed on one knee with the other leg dangling through the opening. For a second, she was perfectly balanced and seemed ready to climb out. Exhausted, she teetered on to the roof and slipped backward toward the opening that was now beginning to swirl with orange and red light. She knew if she slipped back through there would be no strength for another attempt. To compound her problem, the portal was closing with Calvin's departure. If she was caught in the Garden, she would be slain. Alexander's daughter or not, Dormin would allow no departure through his door. Not even her father could save her.   She had to exit with the one she entered since she had not been invited by a Nephilim. She could never return on her own.

There was no need to worry. Just as she teetered on the edge of the portal, Calvin leapt across the opening and grabbed her with both arms like a linebacker tackling a quarterback. The momentum carried both of them onto the roof with a crash. It was Calvin who took the force of the fall as he landed on his back. Kara lay on top of him still held tightly in his arms. Eventually, he loosened his hold and Kara slid off his chest and lay beside him. With her eyes closed and her head resting on his chest, she felt the preacher gently push her long, blonde hair back from her face. The band that held it together in one long strand had broken, and her hair flowed like honey over her shoulders. His fingers continued to glide over her eyes and mouth in an effort to wipe away the dried blood that had been awakened by her sweat. The preacher tenderly rubbed and patted her shoulder, as if she was a small child. She, in return, cuddled her head on his chest beneath his chin, and her hand slid to his chest. Kara raised her head and kissed Calvin on the neck. It was a gesture of thanks, but she confirmed it with her words.

"Calvin, you saved my life. Now it's time for me to return the deed."

"You don't owe me anything. It was a group effort. We both need to be thankful that God has brought us through safely."

"Listen to me carefully, my friend. You must leave Copper Town before my father returns, or you will die."

"I can't leave without Rosie. The Lord knows I have tried to get her to leave, but she won't. She already thinks I'm crazy, and she'll never believe what has just happened."

"Calvin, where do you think Rosie is?"

"She went shopping with Beth Rogers. They'll be back this evening."

"No, Calvin, she didn't go shopping. When we get down from here, check her closet and drawers. She packed her suitcases and left you this morning."

"Rosie would never do that! Our love for each other has lasted for nearly forty years, and there is nothing that would cause her to leave."

Calvin was frustrated and angry with Kara's report. He removed his arm from beneath her head and sat up to face her. She continued.

"It is her love for you that convinced her to leave. She is protecting you Calvin, and besides, she knows more about this place than you might realize."

"But how would she know? And where would she go?"

"Beth filled her in with a lot of details. She was part of our plan from the beginning. Beth dearly loved her son Michael and despised what Slim did to Kristen. As for where they went, I don't know. All I know about Rosie is that Beth is dropping her off at the airport today. She would not tell any of us where she was going. She said she might go to your son's home at Fort Bragg. She also mentioned her family in southern Mississippi and even Riley. I just don't know, but you must leave here quickly and find her. She is in danger."

"Come on. I have to see this for myself."

Calvin stood and pulled Kara to her feet. The two of them worked their way to the eave of the roof above the parsonage entry, where they stopped to survey the area. Across the street, Antonio waved to them and raced across the street to join them.

The preacher began the descent first by sliding his body over the edge of the roof, and he struggled to ease his body downward. Hanging by his hands, he was fully extended and still several feet to the landing. He slipped and fell to the top of the stairs. What should have been a bone-jarring crash was softened by the assistance of Antonio who caught him and broke his fall.

Calvin looks at Antonio and said, "Thanks, my friend. Now help me with Kara."

Kara swung out gently on her right hand, with her left hand still clutching the deep gash in her abdomen. With her strength depleted, her exhausted body slipped much in the same manner as Calvin's. However, there were two men to break her fall. Thus, her landing was much softer than the preacher's, but no less graceful.

"Sit here," Calvin instructed Kara, as he helped her slide her back down the wall until she was sitting on the porch. "Antonio, stay here and take care of her until I get back."

The little Mexican answered, "*Sí*," and squatted beside her to nurse her wounds.

Calvin opened the parsonage door and raced to the bedroom closet. He grabbed the bifold doors to Rosie's closet with both hands and yanked them open. Dumbfounded, he stared at the empty closet. Overwhelmed with grief, he slouched backward on the bed and hung his head. The cold hard truth of Kara's words sunk deep into his soul. He was rendered speechless and unable to respond to Kara's prompting from the door to his bedroom.

Sympathetically, she said, "Come, Calvin! It's time to go!"

The preacher watched as Kara makes her way slowly to him with the assistance of Antonio. Both extended their hands to Calvin, who wiped the tears from his eyes, and then dried them with the sheet from the unmade bed. He grasped their extended hands and stood; the tracks of new tears were clearly visible. As they turned to leave, Kara slipped her arm around his waist and whispered with encouragement, "I have a plan, Calvin. Antonio will help us; won't you, Antonio?"

"Yes, I will," he answered.

Chapter 25
LAST RIDE

And, behold, I come quickly; and my reward is with me, to give every man according as his work shall be.

REVELATION 22:12

It was a quiet and slow journey from the parsonage to the Gionni estate. Michael's Silverado traversed the distance as if absorbing the pain and sadness of its three passengers. As the sun cleared the mountain peaks at the head of Golden Canyon, Calvin glanced at his watch in amazement. Only forty-five minutes had passed since he checked his watch on the way down from picking up Kara, yet it seemed as if their time in the garden had lasted for hours.

Kara lifted her head from Calvin's shoulder as he turned Michael's truck onto South Loop. Her breathing was faint, yet she gave a light chuckle and whispered to Calvin, "Time is not always relevant; nor is it what it seems."

The preacher nodded in agreement and looked at Antonio who was holding Kara's right hand. His small and stubby hand held Kara's hand, and he alternated from pats of consolation to soft and affectionate rubbings of concern. Kara's wounds appeared to be healing, but Calvin knew she was extremely weak from the excessive amounts of blood she had lost.

"Here is the plan, Calvin," she began. "You take my car to the Harley dealership in Reno. When you get there, go around back to the service department and ask for J. R. He's the head mechanic and an old friend of mine. Tell him I sent you for the Harley, and I will pick my car up tomorrow. I've already written a letter for you to give him."

"Already, how did you know what was going to happen?"

"I didn't. Our activities today were much broader and complicated than you will ever know. You might say that we had everything covered."

"Oh, I see, or I think I do."

"Calvin, after you drop me off and get the letter, go back to the parsonage and gather only what you can haul on your Harley. You must take your sword with you, too."

"How am I going to tote that on my cycle? Maybe you can tell me what's wrong with the Honda?"

"The Honda will never run again without some major engine work. So just listen, will you?"

"Go on," Calvin declared, for he realized he has no options.

"Alright, when you get the Harley, take the back roads to wherever it is you will flee. Everyone knows you will be heading east, so be careful. Trust no one, preacher; not even your old friends or family. The Nephilim tentacles reach deep into every community on the face of this planet. When Dad arrives in Reno on his private jet, he'll fly directly here in his helicopter, and the first thing on his agenda will be to find you."

"You will not be able to hide your involvement in this battle," Calvin warned.

"I won't have to hide at all. I can't lie to Dad anyway. But if I don't know where you're going, he won't be able to read my mind to find you. So, don't tell me where you're going or what route you will travel. Be smart and let patience be the determining factor of your travels."

Antonio grunted in acknowledgment as the truck turned into the Gionni driveway. The sensor in Michael's truck activated the electronic locks, and the gates swung open. Pulling up beside Rosie's car parked in front of the main entry, Calvin stopped and turned off the ignition. After he exited the driver's door, Kara slid to him, and he helped her from the truck. As her boots touched the asphalt drive, her knees buckled, and she began to tumble to the ground. Calvin swept her up in his arms and started for the double doors of the Gionni home. Upon his approach of the doors, he heard the growls of Alexander's pet Mastiffs which sat one to each side of the door. They remained motionless after Kara spoke to them in a language Calvin, nor Antonio, understood. Then she added in English, "Hey, boys! It's okay. Everything's alright!"

Antonio threw both doors open wide permitting Calvin easy entry into the main foyer. He followed closely as Calvin put Kara gently down on the leather sofa. The softness of the large couch welcomed her with its embrace of lushness, and she sank deep into the billows of its arms. Looking up at the preacher, she pointed to her father's study.

"In the middle drawer on the right hand side, you will find two brown envelopes. Fetch them for me, please."

Calvin quickly retrieved the envelopes. One was thin, and although sealed, appeared to be empty. The other was stuffed full and several inches thick. When he returned to the foyer, he discovered that Antonio had positioned himself on the sofa with Kara's head in his lap; he was busy rubbing hair from her eyes and massaging her temples. Calvin walked to them, and dropping to his knees, he handed the envelopes to Kara.

"The large one," she began, "is for you. It contains several thousands of dollars. So, preacher, be careful that you don't lose it. The small one is for J. R. at Reno. With this, he'll have you on the road in a few minutes. He won't ask any questions, and don't make any comments to him. Just take the bike and go. Do you understand all this, preacher man?"

"Yeah, but what's the money for?"

"Consider it payment for your time and trouble here in Copper Town, or consider it your severance pay. It's a gift from me, and it's yours!"

"Thanks," Calvin murmured and dropped his head.

"One more thing, preacher, tradition says the Sword of Maseth will control the Bachar. It seems you are trying to control it. The events of today should have turned out differently if you were truly the Bachar. But nonetheless, practice with the sword and protect it. The entire Shachar clan will be after you. After the events of today, they will not fear you, nor will they rest until they have your head. They will now have doubts that you are the Bachar of the Shachar Clan. Now, go, Calvin. Go quickly, and don't look back!"

Calvin took the other brown envelope from her, and placing it with his, he stuffed it under his T-shirt and tucked it back into his pants. Bending slightly forward, he placed a moist kiss on the top of Kara's forehead and turned to leave. Antonio tagged along on his heels. His short legs nearly ran to keep up with the brisk pace of the preacher. Calvin knew the sooner he made his departure from Copper Town, the sooner he could begin his quest to locate his beloved Rosie.

Kara's Ferrari made the return trip to the parsonage in record time. Although in a hurry to get started, the realization of his circumstances warned Calvin to exercise caution. It was a caution that carried a warning to draw no attention to himself, especially by speeding. After parking the Ferrari at the foot of the parsonage steps, Calvin rushed up the steps with Antonio still dogging his footsteps. Under Kara's instructions, he would not leave preacher's side until he departed from Copper Town.

Calvin's modus operandi unfolded in his mind. As a result, every move he made was decisive and punctual. First, he grabbed a small duffle from the laundry room and stuffed it with his leather riding gear and helmet. He shoved in the warmer clothes and sat on the bed to replace his combat boots with his riding boots.

Next, he toted the half-filled duffle into his bedroom, where he crammed in several pairs of jeans, shirts, and under clothing. From the bathroom, he retrieved his private toilet articles and headed back to the living room where he retrieved his Bible and two small, framed photos. One photo was of him and Rosie, and the other pictures were of the two of them with their son. He stuffs them in the duffle carefully between two shirts.

Calvin swiftly changed out of his blood-splattered pants into a pair of jeans he left on the sofa the previous night. With one hand, he grabbed the bloody trousers, and with the other, he turned the pockets inside out allowing the contents of diamonds to spill into the duffle. Antonio's eyes open wide. Their enlarged whiteness was comical to Calvin, and he laughed while patting his friend on the back. He offered him one of the diamonds, but Antonio shook his head and refused the gift. The keeper of the Rock knew it would be discovered. He would invite no suspicious inquiries from the Nephilim. Finally, he retrieved the extra set of cycle keys from a small kitchen drawer and turned to face his shadow.

"Well, my friend, I guess this is where we say good-bye."

"Kara says you will need to fill up the car at the gas station. I'll ride with you there."

Antonio grabbed the duffle from Calvin's hands. This would be his last opportunity to be of assistance to the preacher. He beat Calvin to the door, and the two of them raced down the steps to the Ferrari.

Knowing the car was well known by the inhabitants of Copper Town, Calvin pulled from the drive slowly and deliberately, as not to draw attention. Perhaps the people gathering on the sidewalks would pay less attention if the tires were squealing.

Upon arrival at the gas station, they found a large delivery truck parked near the farthest set of pumps. Calvin pulled into the outermost lane, which placed the truck between him and the store. The bright, little car was hidden from view of the store manager. Antonio, who was holding the duffle, exited. He placed the bag onto the passenger seat determined to reach the pumps ahead of Calvin to pump the gas for him. Calvin tucked the sword behind the seat. There it would be secure and out of sight for his trip to Reno. He followed Antonio to the pump and handed him his credit card. Looking cautiously around, he surveyed the area, while his friend returned his card and began filling the car with gas. It would be the last time he used it. Cash would be exchanged for services from this point on. When he was finished filling the car, Antonio walked with Calvin to the rear of the car. They both glanced up and down the streets of the town. It was Calvin's last view of Copper Town. However, he was jarred from his thoughts by a strange voice.

"Where do you think you're going?"

The voice was deep and threatening. It belonged to the store manager, who was moving from behind the truck toward Calvin. He covered the distance in lightening quick pace and grabbed the preacher by his jacket collar with his left hand. In the process of his actions, his head tilted backward with a slow rhythmic fashion. The slow intake of air into his lungs was audible to the preacher. He resembled a large wolf with a rabbit in his paws, enjoying his supremacy before devouring his meal. The magnitude of the store manager seemed to change enormously as he stood looking down at Calvin with his back to Antonio. The manager was so intently concentrating upon the preacher that he did not notice the little Mexican as he stepped to the side of the car and withdrew Calvin's sword.

The manager snapped his head forward into Calvin's face and snorted, "Alexander says you are not to leave, preacher! Thus, it looks like you will stay with me until he arrives."

The manager leaned ever closer, laughed, and threw his head back, once again emitting a shrill and menacing laugh. It chilled Calvin's blood, and all he could do was stare up into stone black eyes.

The moment he glared deep into the ghoulish face of the manager, he knows he was Nephilim. There would be no time for fear that day, and no time for dialogue with the hideous creature. As Calvin stared into his eyes, they clouded with gray. His head suddenly rocked slowly from left to right, while blood oozed down the denim company shirt. The preacher stepped sideways, an action that allowed him to escape the loosened grip of the manager and to avoid his head as it left his body and toppled to the pavement with a sickening thud. As his body quivered and began to crumple to the ground, Calvin saw Antonio standing behind him. The

Sword of the Bachar was covered with fresh Nephilim blood. He smiled at the preacher and spit on the fallen body.

He spit again as if dust was trapped in his mouth as he whispered to Calvin, "Vampires! I hate these stupid vampires!"

"They are not really vampires, Antonio,' Calvin tried to explain. "They are … eh … well … they are … it's a long story!"

"Vampires." Antonio spit again on the dead carcass. "They're blood-sucking vampires, preacher. Don't forget it! And I hate 'em all."

Calvin's second attempt to explain the phenomena of the Nephilim was interrupted by a popping noise as the manager exploded into millions of fine, black dust particles. A warm western breeze from the desert rushed in to lift them up and carry them away. The wind scattered them along the sandy area beyond the parking lot. No signs of the manager were left. Antonio rushed to the pumps, grabbed a few paper towels, and turned to wipe the blade free of the Nephilim blood. To his amazement, it too had disappeared from the sword. Regardless, he wiped the blade in rapid succession, as if cleansing it from some unseen horror. He returned it to its sheath behind the seat and smiled at Calvin.

"It's time to go, preacher!" He grins and continued. "Until we meet again."

"What about you, Antonio?"

"I think I will be okay, preacher. I've burned a lot of bodies for these blood suckers, animals and humans alike. Tonight, I'll burn more."

"Will they kill you, Antonio?"

"Don't know, preacher. For some reason, they cannot read my mind. They all think I'm crazy, with the exception of Kara. I like her. She has helped keep some of the pressure off me and my family. If not for my family's safety, I'd take up the fight with you."

"Okay. Till we meet again."

"Preacher?"

"Yes, Antonio?"

"Practice with the sword. Gather some help and return soon. I think this is your fight, and when you come back, you can count on me. I'll be ready."

Calvin saluted the little man, and with no other words left to be spoken, he climbed into the car and headed west on Highway 50 toward Fallon. There he turned north on 50 Alternate to Fernley. He was cautious to observe the speed limit. At Fernley, Calvin merged onto I-80 west. Thirty minutes later, he turned into the Harley Davidson parking lot in

Reno. He drove to the back, parked the car, and went into the service department where he asked to see J. R.

"Tell him Kara Gionni sent me," Calvin stated to the clerk who turned to fetch the mechanic. The comment was made in hopes of expediting the summons, but little did he know that nothing rushed J. R. After what seemed like an eternity, a rough-looking character emerged from the shop. He beckoned Calvin to follow as he turned and disappeared back through the same door he entered. J. R. was perhaps a few years older than Calvin, but years of late-night activities left the mechanic looking much older. His long, curly red hair, streaked with strands of gray, was pulled together in the back with a black leather cord. A black and red Harley Davidson bandana kept the sides tucked in, and his face was covered with the same kind of reddish gray hair. A pair of John Lennon-type glasses with thick lenses balanced on the tip of his nose. He's a scary character, Calvin thought. I wouldn't want to run into him in a dark alley.

J. R. extended his hand in a shake, which he followed with a bump into Calvin's chest with his right shoulder. He stepped back with a serious look as his glasses nearly slid off his nose and asked, "What's up with Kara? I saw you pull up in her car."

Calvin pulled the thin brown envelope from his pocket and handed it to J. R. "She said to give this to you."

"Am I to read it now or later?"

"Now," Calvin answered, "I am to wait for your reply."

J. R. reached into his pocket and retrieved a lock-blade knife. A loud click echoed throughout the mechanics work area as he flipped the knife open with a quick flick of his hand. It was so quick that Calvin imagined it to be a switchblade knife. With precision, J. R. slid the blade under the flap and opened the envelope. He removed the letter from Kara and read it.

"Come," he said. "But first, give me the keys to that four-wheeled ride of hers." Calvin tossed the keys to him and watched as he turned and took a set of keys from the pegs on his wall. He looked at Calvin and commented. "Come, I was told not to work on this bike till I heard from Kara. She owns the store. It was a gift from her dad. She told me what's wrong with your bike." He laughed and continued. "She and I had good times before she moved to Copper Town. Don't see her much anymore, but I see she is still up to some of her old tricks."

He grabbed a set of pliers, and they walked outside to a storage building containing several bikes stored for repairs. The preacher noticed each one had a small yellow tag containing owner information and a scheduled date for repair. Calvin's bike had no tag. J. R. kneeled down beside the bike and grasped the main fuel line with his hand. In seconds, he loosened the clamp and pulled the line free to visibly inspect the line. Laughter rolled across his bushy beard as he took the pliers and removed a small wooden pin from the bowels of the fuel line. Tossing it aside, he reattached the line and fastened the clamp.

J. R. stood, placed the key into the ignition, and flipped it clockwise to the start position. He worked the throttle vigorously to prime the dry carburetor and touched the ignition button on the right handle bar. The unmistakable sound of a Harley Davidson twin bore roared in the shop.

"There you go, brother. It might have taken me some time, but I would have found the problem. Kara says to tell you there's no charge, and she hopes you can take a joke. She also tells me you are rushed for time, and that I need to get you out of here quick. There's a bonus in this for me. So man, get out of here and ride safe."

The mechanic slipped a few hundred bills from the envelope, folded them in half, and shoved them deep into his front pocket. After helping Calvin push the bike outside, he closed and locked the door. J. R. waved good-bye and vanished into the shop.

Calvin rushed to the Ferrari and grabbed his duffle bag and sword. He planned to stop at nightfall to dress warmer. For now, it would be jeans and a T-shirt. He would ride long and hard before he would again be at peace. The contents of the duffle were quickly emptied and stored in the saddlebags. He distributed more weight into the left bag, for he would counter balance the loaded bike on the right side with the sword. Running the sheathed sword along the top of the muffler baffles beneath the saddlebag, he secured it with small bungee cords and stepped back to observe his work. Although the sword slightly extruded beyond the rear tire, it appeared to be part of a custom exhaust system. He smiled.

The preacher slid his helmet over his head and fastened the strap securely. Placing his hand near the motor shroud, Calvin felt the heat. He pulled on his gloves, kicked the shifter down to first gear, and idled from the parking lot. He turned left on 395 headed south. The people at the Harley dealership would later report he headed south. After a few miles of riding, Calvin turned north on Virginia Avenue to Interstate 80 and east to 395 again, where he headed north. All would know he was headed east, but none would suspect him of traveling north on 395 through California into Oregon.

Calvin rehearsed his route in his mind: I'm going to listen to Kara and patiently work my way back to Riley. They will all think that I have chosen a more direct route to the south, but I'll travel north for a day or so, and then travel east along the Canadian border. I'll ride this afternoon and all night tonight. After that, I'll ride only at night and stay on secondary roads. It'll be a little cooler, but I think that's the best route. If all goes well, I should be in Washington State by daybreak.

Chapter 26
THE SMOKING FLAX

A bruised reed shall he not break, and smoking flax shall he not quench, till he send forth judgment unto victory.
MATTHEW 12:20

"Job well done, Hunter," would never be uttered in my ears again. But that's exactly what Harley would say if he were here to see the completion of his story. The large stack of handwritten manuscript was neatly stacked on the table beneath my backyard gazebo. It replaced the crumpled sheets from my initial attempts that I tossed haphazardly about my kitchen. A large chunk of coal with its lustrous blackness served as a paperweight to prevent the light breeze of the morning air from scattering the pages about.

Yes, I have finally completed John Calvin's story. I'll wrap the pages neatly and drop them off at the post office after lunch. Meanwhile, I am near completion of another laborious task assigned to me. Perhaps it has not consumed as much of my time, but nonetheless it has been physically strenuous. Since it was my first endeavor of this nature, it has emotionally drained me as well.

I have already swept most of the pasty white debris, along with several large fragments, into a five-gallon bucket. Sweeping the bottom of the oven with a small wire brush, I must inspect the debris for any metallic pieces that may have been neglected in my late-night labors. A shining metal zipper in the oven reminds me of the neglect from my haste. It is

259

removed and cast aside temporarily. I will return it to the bag of ashes upon completion of the final stage of my preparations. I observed my dad perform this job when I was younger, but I never thought it would be assigned to me. I was eager to please Dad, however, a tiny ounce of remorse pricks my subconscious mind due to the magnitude of the task.

Switching the electric motor to the "on" position, it churned immediately in anticipation of the lumpy material I will pour from the bucket into the intake flume attached on top. As I pour the material into the flume and it drops into the grinding teeth, the motor barely slows from its high-speed rpm's, even when the larger chunks drop into the grinding metal cogs. At the output flume, I have tied a large canvas bag by its drawstrings, and I watch the contents of my bucket as they are sifted into smaller fragments as they pass through the grinder and into the bag.

Flicking the electric switch to the "off" position, I stand for a few seconds and listen to the motor's hum fade away as it comes to a halt. Untying the strings, I inspect the finished product. In my hands I have a bag weighing nearly five pounds. The contents are still pasty white but there are no signs of the large fragments. The contents are consistent in size and resemble coarse sand, thus I return to the burner and sweep in the metal zipper. Tying the bag off, I drop it to the stone rocks beside the oven.

I will leave Riley after dropping the manuscript off at the post office. On my way out of town afterward, I'll scatter the ashes into the Big South Fork River from the old downtown bridge. It won't take long for the muddy waters of the river to carry them away.

It has been a hot and demanding job, but the heat is not near as bad when one works through the chilly night air. The old crematory has not been used in years. Prior to using it, I had to do some repairs and clean it up. Afterwards, it took me nearly six hours to get the furnace over 1,800 degrees Fahrenheit. An experienced operator with a modern chamber needs only a couple of hours to get the furnace that hot and to maintain it throughout the procedure. Fighting to maintain that temperature required another six hours for me to accomplish my obligation.

From frustration more than exhaustion, I collapse beside the manuscript. The white towel that kept me company throughout the night once again fills my hands and absorbs the moisture from my dampened forehead. I cannot help but reflect upon my past. My father moved from Nevada years ago to farm the fertile grounds of the river bottoms. The farm was just a hobby, for his mission was to oversee the excavation of this area for ore. He was very thorough and punctual, and he completed his duties with perfection.

I was relieved when my tour in the military was over. It was difficult hiding my physical and mental superiority from those around me, but I had learned to do that while attending high school. I am amazed to this day how people never notice others around them. My aging process was slow, and I looked the same at graduation as I did when I was a freshman. The military career allowed me to hide from any eyes that might have been suspicious of me until my services were needed here. Putting in for one transfer after another prevented any lasting friendships in the military, for I rarely kept acquaintances longer than three or four years. Now the townsfolk laugh and contribute my youthful appearance to the long athletic training I had in the service.

I remember, too, John Calvin wanting my promise to write his story. Since I had a lot of time on my hands, he felt I could get it done. Little did he know I had more time on my hands than he could imagine. Several times during his story, I laughed inwardly knowing he was giving me all the information I had been told to gather from him. So, the writing task was not so unbearable. I had more than all the information I needed to complete my assignment. Laughter rolls from my lips again, as I drop the manuscript into the overnight box and tape it closed. Soon, I will mail the box at the post office. Fixing the address label to it, I rise and look down to inspect the completion of the second assignment. The label reads:

To: Alexander Gionni
South Loop Road
Copper town, NV 89547

A gray and cobalt Harley sits in my barn, and soon I will depart for Copper Town on the bike. It'll be fun enjoying the wind in my face, feeling my hair blow across my back from beneath the helmet, and sensing the vibrations of the engine between my legs. Soon I will join my father and his clan in Copper Town. The tenth sword was found here last week, and my father returned with it. I have signed the farm over to my mother's nephew since I no longer need it. The sword I took from John Calvin is tied to the Harley just like he had it. It'll ride well there.

Before I took John Calvin's life and burned his body, I did have my way with him. Perhaps it was because I owed him. After all, he took Rosie from me. I loved her long before he did. I wonder from time to time what type of relationship we might have had if John Calvin had not come into the picture. Maybe I cannot help but hope that once in Copper Town we will become more than friends. I have been informed that Alexander has claimed her for himself and that she bore his mark of the Yada. I certainly don't plan to challenge a Nephilim clan leader for a woman, but one never knows what the future holds for us that are Banah, nor for those that are Nephilim. Yes, I was the first to love the beautiful Rosie.

My clothes are packed on the Harley, but I have one last thing I must do. This old house has been our home for years, while my father searched for the sword. Knowing it was here also alerted the clan that a Bachah would come forth from this land. It was not by chance we observed John Calvin as he grew up and followed the way of the Maseth. Alexander followed him for years until the time was right to bring him to Copper Town, yet he dared not take his life. I suppose I knew years ago that the task would be relegated to me someday.

I light the torch in my hand and toss it through the back door of the old farm house. Standing outside until the flames burn high and the house is consumed with fire, I know I no longer have to hide away. In a few days, I will join my kind in Copper Town, and for the first time in my life, I will live. Yes, I realize it has been hard, but the sacrifices of those years of human servitude were made for the survival of the clan; a small price for me to pay in return for all that my father has done for me. Yes, today I feel alive and ready to face whatever tomorrow may bring my way; for I am Hunter, the daughter of a Nephilim.

Glossary

Bachar - A warrior called from the Maseth to bear one of the ten Swords of the Maseth. One sword was formed by the song of the Son of the Ancient of Days and assigned to each of the Nephilim clans for their destruction by a Bachar if they took innocent blood or continued to violate their Book of Kimriyr. The swords are physical, with supernatural powers hidden in the earth from the Nephilim. The Bachar are referred to as Torch Bearers.

Book of Kimriyr - A book of laws and guidelines the Nephilim use. Gross violations of this book can result in the Ancient of Days sending forth a Bachar to destroy that Nephilim clan.

Book of Maseth - A guideline for the chosen of the Ancient of Days. To avoid coming under the seductive power of the Nephilim, the Maseth must abide by the ways of the Ancient of Days.

Edum - Eden.

Erets - The planet Earth.

Maseth - Humans chosen by the Ancient of Days. Once chosen, they bear the sign, or aura, of the Ancient of Days. If a Nephilim reveals himself to a human, and they accept the ways of the Nephilim, they become slaves to the Nephilim. These humans and any who are not the chosen are called non-Maseth. An assault on a Maseth can be life ending for the Nephilim. If the Maseth does not follow the Book of the Maseth, he may be turned over to the Nephilim by the Ancient of Days.

Prison of Dead - Referred to by the Maseth as Hell.

Raphah - A Nephilim who has retained the gift of healing by touch. All Nephilim in prehistoric days had this gift in their unfallen nature. At present, only three Nephilim remain with this gift. A Raphah cannot heal himself.

Shachar - Alexander's Clan; it means black and beautifully shiny. The change in coloration from the original gold to black was a result of rebellion against the Ancient of Days in prehistoric days.

Sign of the Yada - A small circular scar about a half centimeter in diameter. The scar is located on the center of the woman's torso anywhere between the shoulder and the navel. The mark is usually received by consent after a Nephilim has seduced the woman, and she has consented to breeding. The revealing of the Nephilim to the woman must be done prior to the Yiqqaha. Only the Nephilim making the mark can release the woman from her obligation. The scar is made when the Nephilim spittle is placed on the woman.

Time of the Final Order - End of life as all know it now, and the beginning of a new earth and heaven by the Ancient of Days.

Yada - A Nephilim who chooses to sire hybrids at the time of the Yiqqaha. They may also mate only for breeding a hybrid. Infidelity is frowned on by the Nephilim clans. During the mating time, they will also teach the human women the ways of the Nephilim.

Yiqqaha - A fifty-year gathering which is known as the Feast of the Nephilim. It lasts for ten days. At that time there is a, or can be, consummation of the Yada. The human women who have accepted the sign of the Yada will spend the whole ten days with that Nephilim for breeding reasons. At this time, Nephilim can chose to take a mate. In so doing, it will be for the life of the human. The feast is held in the fall during the new moon of the harvest season.

About the Author

The author is a retired public school teacher and administrator. He has served as a bi-vocational pastor and worked extensively as an evangelist/missionary in Cape Town, South Africa. There his work has been under the supervision of the Executive Director of Cape Missions International. At the time of this publication, he is working at planting a "home-based" church in rural Tennessee. He has been married to Paula Davidson since 1969 and the two of them have two children and three grandchildren.

The author has a B.S. degree in secondary math education from Tennessee Tech and a M.A. degree in the same area from Cumberland College, KY. He has an Ed.S. in educational supervision from Tennessee Tech and a Ph.D. in Pastoral Ministry from Newburgh Theological Seminary in Indiana.